"Men are no~~t~~ ~~...~~ ~~...~~

"Why not?"

"They're not … necessary."

"Every community needs some men."

She broke his hold on her and stepped back. "Ours does not."

He scoffed. "How do you build your houses?" He gestured toward the cabin. "Didn't Frederic build this one?"

"He helped, but we know how to do it without a man. We built our own homes."

"What about protection? A man can pro—"

"We can protect ourselves."

Not against an army. But Zoltan didn't want to remind her of the recent death of her sister. It would be too cruel. "Men have a lot of uses."

She gave him a dubious look. "Really?"

"Of course. A man can … build a fire."

She shrugged. "I can do that."

"A man can provide food for his family."

"I am an excellent hunter."

"A man can till the soil and plow the field."

"We have a donkey."

By Kerrelyn Sparks

How to Seduce a Vampire
(Without Really Trying)
The Vampire With the Dragon Tattoo
Wild About You
Wanted: Undead or Alive
Sexiest Vampire Alive
Vampire Mine
Eat Prey Love
The Vampire and the Virgin
Forbidden Nights With a Vampire
Secret Life of a Vampire
All I Want for Christmas Is a Vampire
The Undead Next Door
Be Still My Vampire Heart
Vamps and the City
How to Marry a Millionaire Vampire

Also Available
Less Than a Gentleman
The Forbidden Lady

KERRELYN SPARKS

HOW TO SEDUCE A VAMPIRE
(WITHOUT REALLY TRYING)

AVON

An Imprint of HarperCollins*Publishers*

This is a work of fiction. Names, characters, places, and incidents are products of the author's imagination or are used fictitiously and are not to be construed as real. Any resemblance to actual events, locales, organizations, or persons, living or dead, is entirely coincidental.

AVON BOOKS
An Imprint of HarperCollins*Publishers*
10 East 53rd Street
New York, New York 10022-5299

Copyright © 2014 by Kerrelyn Sparks
ISBN 978-0-06-210776-3
www.avonromance.com

First Avon Books mass market printing: May 2014

Avon Trademark Reg. U.S. Pat. Off. and in Other Countries, Marca Registrada, Hecho en U.S.A.
HarperCollins® is a registered trademark of HarperCollins Publishers.

Printed in the U.S.A.

10 9 8 7 6 5 4 3 2 1

To all the Love at Stake readers,
you amaze me!
You have kept the Undead alive
for fifteen books!

Acknowledgments

As you can see in the dedication, my characters and I owe so much to our readers. Thank you for all the fantastic support and encouragement you've given me over the years! I'd also like to thank the booksellers and librarians who have promoted my series and the romance genre in general.

Many thanks also to the professionals at Harper-Collins, who make me look smarter and cooler than I could ever hope to accomplish on my own: my editor, Erika Tsang, and her assistant, Chelsey; Tom of the Art Department, who continues to gift me with the most amazing cover art; Pamela and Jessie of the Publicity Department; and many more who work behind the scenes. A big thank you to Michelle Grajkowski of Three Seas Literary Agency, my number one cheerleader. And my thanks also to Shelley and Peggy of Webcrafters, who built and maintain my website and design the artwork for my ads and swag.

On the personal side, I am blessed with ongoing

support and love. My dear friends and critique partners, Sandy, M.J., and Vicky, are the best! And my husband and children inspire me, make me laugh, and keep me strong. You have my undying love and gratitude!

Chapter One

*W*hen Zoltan Czakvar entered the armory of his Transylvanian castle, his gaze automatically shifted to the arrow that had killed his father. Barely visible where it was mounted on the far wall, the arrow still made him stop in his tracks. Still made his nerves tense. Dammit. He should rip the bloody thing down, toss it into a fire, and be done with it.

Since he was a man who prided himself on never quitting until a job was done, the arrow served as a painful reminder of his one major failure. He'd never found those responsible for murdering his father and destroying his village. Unfortunately, those events had transpired in 1241, so any chance at success seemed long gone.

He had tried. God, how he had tried. Starting at the age of fourteen, he'd traveled with that damned arrow for years, desperately searching for anyone who might know where it had originated. A curious design was carved into the wooden shaft of the arrow, making it unique. But no one ever recognized it. It remained a mystery to this day, mocking him and reminding him of all he had lost.

With a sigh, he set down the ice chest he had carried down the dimly lit spiral staircase. When this part of the castle had been completed in the fifteenth century, this cavernous room in the cellar had become the armory. The medieval pikes and battle-axes were gone, but an assortment of swords and crossbows remained, along with a modern array of firearms and ammunition.

Like most of the castle, the cellar was now wired for electricity. He switched on the lights. Although the far corners of the room remained dark, the nearby walls gleamed with an impressive display of swords that reflected the light and eased his sour mood. Like loyal friends, they had served him well over the centuries. A good sword was still the weapon of choice for him and his older undead companions. His modern friends were different.

He glanced at his watch. Ten minutes until the appointed meeting time.

The supplies he'd brought down the night before were neatly arranged on the long wooden table. A few knives. A box of cartridges for an automatic handgun. Another box filled with some shotgun shells and hand grenades. And a long box containing modern arrows. He moved the ice chest to the end of the table. The dry ice inside would keep the bottles of synthetic blood cold for days.

"Hey, Zoltan," a voice emanated from the spiral staircase. "Are you down there?"

Damn. It was Howard, his new security guy. Zoltan turned to face the huge were-bear as he bent over to keep from clonking his head on the low entrance into the room. "No need to check up on me. I'm fine. I thought you were taking your wife out to eat."

"I am. She wanted to clean up first." Howard's sharp gaze wandered about the room, then lingered on the supplies on the table. "So this is the armory."

"Yes." A week ago, Zoltan had hired Howard's wife, Elsa, and her team of renovation experts to do some work on the crumbling east wing and tower. They'd jumped at the chance to feature a real Transylvanian castle on their home improvement television show. Meanwhile, Howard had barely seen his wife for the past six months, since he'd been stationed in Japan. His boss, Angus MacKay of MacKay Security and Investigation, had asked Zoltan to accept the were-bear as his new head of security so the couple could enjoy some time together.

Zoltan knew that was only an excuse. For the last three centuries, he had served as Coven Master for Eastern Europe. One of his duties was protecting his constituents from the evil vampires known as Malcontents, so he'd pissed off his share of enemies over the years. More recently, he'd broken up a band of Malcontent human traffickers. Angus was worried they would seek revenge, so he expected Howard to do a complete overhaul of the security measures at both the castle and Zoltan's townhouse in Budapest.

Zoltan had reluctantly agreed. How could he decline, when Elsa had begged him to agree with such a hopeful expression? She'd been excited all day, waiting impatiently for her husband, who had arrived about an hour ago. Bad timing, as far as Zoltan was concerned, since he had a secret meeting scheduled to begin in eight minutes.

"I'm sure you're eager to be with your wife," he told the were-bear, "so I'll give you a tour of the castle tomorrow evening. Or, if you like, my assistant, Milan, can give you a tour in the morning."

Howard nodded. "I just met him upstairs. He . . . talks a lot."

Zoltan winced inwardly. No doubt Milan had been trying his best to keep Howard from coming downstairs. "Why don't you take one of my cars into the village? Milan can show you where the garage is."

"He already offered to do that." Howard frowned. "You know, as your new head of security, I have to tell you I'm shocked by the lack of it around here. I've spotted only one surveillance camera, outside by that iron gate—"

"The portcullis, yes."

"And it's not working."

"I see, well . . ." Zoltan walked toward him, motioning toward the staircase. "We can discuss it tomorrow. Enjoy your evening."

Howard didn't budge. "As far as I can tell, everyone in the castle knows you're a vampire."

"Yes."

"And that restaurant you recommended—I called to get directions, and the guy asked if I was staying at the castle with the local Vamp."

"There was no need to call. There are only two streets in the village and one restaurant. You can hardly miss it."

"That's not the point! Zoltan, how many people know you're undead?"

He shrugged. "Quite a few, I suppose. This is Transylvania, after all."

"It's too big of a risk. You should do some of that mind control stuff and erase their memories."

With a sigh, Zoltan glanced at his watch. He only had six minutes. "It's their memories that provide my security. The people in this area know that they and their ancestors have been safe for generations because of me. I've protected them from Mongols, Ottoman Turks, Hungarians, Prussians, Germans, Russians, and countless gangs of thieves and brigands. The villagers would never let anyone harm me. You might call them my first line of defense."

Howard tilted his head, regarding him curiously. "So that's why the mortals I talked to claim you're a hero? Even so, I have to object—"

"So do I. If I'm such a bloody hero, why am I alone?"

Howard scoffed. "How would I know? I'm worried about your lack of security, not your lack of nookie."

"Eloquently put." Zoltan motioned toward the staircase. "And on that note, you shouldn't leave your wife waiting."

"I'm serious about this, Zoltan. It doesn't matter how many loyal friends you have. It takes only one enemy to kill you."

"Indeed." Zoltan gestured again toward the stairs. "We can discuss my imminent demise tomorrow. Have a good evening."

"Why do I get the feeling you don't want me down here?" Howard asked.

"He doesn't want you to see me," a voice said from a dark corner.

With a groan, Zoltan turned toward the Vamp who had just teleported in. "You're early."

"I'm starving." He stepped into the light, dropped an empty ice chest on the table, and retrieved a bottle of synthetic blood from the full ice chest.

Howard stiffened. "Russell."

The ex-Marine gave him a wry look as he wrenched the top off the bottle. "Howard." He took a long drink.

Howard's gaze narrowed on the items on the table,

then switched to Zoltan. "How long have you been supplying him?"

Zoltan shrugged. "About two years."

Frowning, Howard crossed his arms. "You mean since the time he went AWOL?"

"Thereabouts. Would you rather he starve to death? Or be forced to bite people?"

"We'd rather he report in every now and then," Howard growled.

Russell paused with the nearly empty bottle an inch from his mouth. "Don't mind me. Just keep talking about me like I'm not here."

Howard shot him an annoyed look. "You think we don't worry about you? Angus keeps sending J.L. and Rajiv to China to search for you."

"I know." Russell finished the bottle and wiped his mouth with the back of his hand. "I've had to bail them out of trouble a few times."

Howard snorted. "They wouldn't have been in trouble if they hadn't been looking for you."

"I didn't ask anyone to look for me." Russell snapped a new clip into his handgun, then wedged it under his belt. "I suppose you're going to tell Angus I was here."

Howard glanced at Zoltan. "You never told Angus about this?"

Zoltan shook his head. "I don't work for Angus."

"He's your friend. And he's Russell's sire." Howard turned to the ex-Marine. "Aren't you supposed to have some loyalty toward him?"

"He didn't change me." Russell stuffed the pockets of his old coat with more cartridges for his handgun. "Master Han did. Angus just finished the job. It was Zoltan who took me in and helped me adjust."

"We would all help you," Howard insisted. "Do

you think we wouldn't feed you? Or give you supplies?"

Russell dropped the shotgun shells into a worn canvas bag. "You would, but there would be a price. You would expect me to answer your questions."

"It's called cooperation. We're on the same side, you know. We all want to see Master Han dead."

Russell's eyes flashed with anger. "He's *mine.* Your kind of help just gets in the way. You're too damned busy trying to save his soldiers—"

"They're mortal," Howard argued.

"They agreed to join him in exchange for their superpowers." Russell slid a new knife into each of his boots. "They made their choice. It's not my problem if they have to pay for it."

"Their superpowers came from a demon, so when you kill them, they go to hell."

"Like I said. Not my problem." Russell hooked the hand grenades onto his belt.

Howard sighed. "Will you at least go to Japan to see what's happening? I've spent the last six months there with our team of doctors and scientists. They've turned more than a hundred of Master Han's soldiers back to normal."

Russell scoffed. "Brilliant. Now they have only nine hundred to go."

"Howard?" Elsa's voice called down the stairs. "Are you there?"

"Just a minute!" Howard paused at the entrance to the stairwell. "Come back tomorrow night, Russell, so we can talk."

"No thanks." Russell opened the box of arrows.

Howard frowned at Zoltan. "I'll talk to you when I get back from dinner."

"No hurry. Enjoy your evening." Zoltan watched as

the huge were-bear wound his way up the narrow stone staircase. "The minute he's out the door, he'll call Angus."

"If he waits that long." Russell swung the quiver off his back and set it on the table next to the box of arrows. "I'll just fill this up and be on my way." He glanced at Zoltan. "Are you going to be in trouble now?"

Zoltan snorted. "What can Angus do to me? If he's in Japan, it might already be daylight there. He'll call me when he wakes up so he can grouse at me, but in the end, he'll thank me for taking care of you. He's not a bad guy, you know."

Russell gathered a handful of arrows from the box. "We have different priorities."

Zoltan nodded. Angus and his employees, like Howard, wanted to protect mortals from bad vampires, but Russell simply wanted Master Han dead. The evil warlord had attacked Russell during the Vietnam War, leaving him in a vampire coma for forty years. When Russell had been discovered in a cave in Thailand, Angus had completed the transformation process so Russell could wake up and join the ranks of the Undead. For the last two years, Russell had been searching Master Han's massive territory, waiting for his chance to kill the evil vampire.

Russell shoved an old arrow aside to make room in the quiver for the new arrows. Zoltan blinked, hardly believing his eyes.

"Wait!" He lunged toward the quiver. The feathers of the old arrow looked familiar.

He pulled it out, his heart racing at the sight of carvings on the staff. Had he found a duplicate after eight hundred years? He zoomed over to the arrow mounted on the wall so he could compare the two.

The arrowhead on the new arrow was modern, but otherwise, the two were exactly the same.

He turned to Russell. "Where did you find this?"

A wary look crossed Russell's face before he turned away to finish stuffing the quiver with new arrows. "I wouldn't know. I teleport all over southern China, northern Myanmar, and Tibet. And I scavenge along the way. I could have picked it up anywhere."

"You have to remember." Zoltan approached him. "It's important."

Russell swung the quiver onto his back. "I have no idea."

"You're not trying." Zoltan gritted his teeth. "I have to know—"

"I can't tell you."

Zoltan's heart stilled. Russell was purposely keeping his face blank. "You mean you *won't* tell me."

"I have to go." Russell grabbed the ice chest. "Thanks for the supplies."

"Wait!" Zoltan leaped forward and latched onto Russell's arm just as he began to teleport.

As soon as they materialized, Russell shoved him away. "What the hell are you doing?"

Zoltan quickly regained his balance and looked around. Countryside. Treeless, rolling hills. Yellowish grass nearly to his knees. A half moon and countless stars gleaming in a clear sky. "Where are we?"

"You shouldn't have come. Go back home."

Zoltan showed him the arrow, still grasped in his right hand. "This is the only clue I've found in almost eight hundred years. Tell me where it came from."

"I can't."

A streak of anger sizzled through Zoltan. "I've been helping you for two years, so you will tell me—"

"I can't!"

"Dammit, Russell!" Zoltan clutched the arrow tightly. "It's because of an arrow like this that I became a vampire. I couldn't stand the thought of dying without knowing what happened. I had to stay young and healthy to keep searching for the truth. I gave up my mortality for this, so tell me where you found the damned arrow!"

A pained look crossed Russell's face. "Fine. Two weeks ago, I was following Lord Liao and a troop of soldiers when they were attacked by a smaller force. I figured the enemy of my enemy is my friend, and they were taking some heavy casualties, so I helped them. We killed most of Lord Liao's soldiers, but of course, he teleported away. I was wounded and fell unconscious. I would have died when the sun came up, but they saved me."

"Who are they?"

Russell groaned. "The only thing they asked for in return was that I not tell anyone who they are and where they live. I'm sorry. I really do appreciate all you've done, but I can't say anything more."

"Very well. Keep your mouth shut and point in the right direction."

Russell snorted. "Why is this so important to you?"

Zoltan lifted the arrow. Moonlight gleamed off the steel tip. "An arrow much like this one killed my father."

"You want revenge then?"

Zoltan shook his head. "I'm sure the culprit is long dead. I want answers."

Russell shifted his weight. "Sometimes there aren't any. Just go back home. They want to be left alone."

"Who are they?"

"Go home." Russell teleported away.

Zoltan lunged toward him, but he was gone.

"Dammit." It was just as well. Russell wasn't going to give him any more information.

Pivoting in a circle, Zoltan took in his bearings. The middle of nowhere. No weapons on him, other than the arrow. He took out his cell phone and checked his location on the GPS. *Tibet*.

He considered returning to the castle to grab more weapons and a coat. Even though it was the middle of May, spring was late here. A cold wind was blowing from the north, ruffling the grass that had yet to turn green.

On his phone, he spotted the nearest village, over a hundred miles to the southwest. Why waste time going home? He could be at this village in half an hour, asking questions.

He set off at a brisk pace, excitement building inside him. This was a lot more interesting than what he normally did every evening. Work in his office in Budapest. He was dressed for work—white dress shirt, red tie, an expensive Italian suit and loafers. Not at all suitable for an adventure in Tibet, but if he got into any sort of trouble, he could simply teleport back home.

Tibet. Did the people who had killed his father travel all the way from Tibet? When he'd searched for them centuries ago, he'd covered Eastern Europe, western Russia, and the Middle East. Finally, in the northwestern part of India, he'd given up, unable to believe that anyone would travel that far to kill someone in Transylvania.

Was his father's murder somehow connected to his mother's mysterious background? She'd been from the east, but no one knew where exactly. His father, a merchant who traveled the Silk Road, had fallen in love with her and brought her home.

Could she have been from Tibet? Zoltan's pulse quickened. After almost eight hundred years, he might finally get some answers.

He teleported as far as he could see, then repeated the process until he was close to the village. The landscape gradually changed, growing more hilly and forested. He teleported to a high branch of a pine tree so he could survey the village. It was nestled in a valley along the sides of a stream. No electricity. A few lanterns were lit along the one main street. He checked his cell phone. Out of range. If he returned, he'd need to bring a satellite phone.

He dropped to the ground, adjusted his suit and tie, then sauntered casually into the village. An old woman was hunched over a homemade broom, sweeping her front porch.

When Zoltan greeted her, she straightened, eyeing him with suspicion.

He greeted her again, using English and giving her a smile. Then he showed her the arrow. "Do you know where—"

She launched into a tirade of angry words, shook her broom at him, then rushed into her ramshackle house, slamming the door behind her.

Zoltan sighed. He should have realized there would be a language barrier. Over the centuries, he'd learned nine languages, but the Tibetan spoken in this village was not one of them.

He spotted a man sitting on another porch, drinking from a leather pouch. "Good evening." He lifted the arrow. "Do you know where—"

The man stumbled to his feet, muttering under his breath. Then he waved his arms as if trying to chase Zoltan away. When that didn't work, he spit in the dirt, then rushed into his house and slammed the door.

Silly human is trying to get himself killed.

Zoltan turned toward the voice but saw only a dog resting on a porch a few houses down the road. Of course. Since early childhood, Zoltan had possessed the strange ability to communicate with animals. They were often his best source of information, since the conversations were purely mental and devoid of any language barriers.

He walked slowly toward the dog, sending him a message. *Why would my questions get me killed?*

The dog jerked to a sitting position. *What was that?*

It's me. Zoltan stopped in the street, ready to teleport away if necessary. It was always hard to predict how an animal would react. Most dogs were friendly, but every now and then, one would feel threatened and attack.

What? The dog tilted his head to the side and quirked his ears. *Are you talking to me?*

Yes. I have the ability to communicate with animals.

Are you kidding me? The little spotted dog leaped off the porch and scampered toward him. *Can you really talk to me? Can you hear my thoughts?*

Yes. And you can hear mine.

Holy dog poop! The dog pranced around him in a circle. *This is so awesome! I didn't know humans had thoughts. Some of them don't seem very bright, you know, so I wondered. Have you always been able to do this? Could you do it when you were a puppy? You must be a weird human. I think you smell a little weird. Do you like to eat? I like rabbit. Would you like to be my friend?*

Sure, Zoltan replied as the dog circled him for the fifth time. This was obviously one of the friendly dogs. *Can you relax a little bit?*

Why? Are you having trouble keeping up? I've always suspected humans are slow. You don't smell like the other humans I know. I could pee on you so you'd smell better.

No thank you.

The dog suddenly jumped and looked to the side. *What was that?*

I'm not sure.

I think it was a rabbit. I like rabbit the best. Are you hungry? I am. If you throw your stick, I'll bring it back to you.

Zoltan showed the arrow to the dog. *I'd like to know more about this stick and the people who made it.*

The dog sat in front of him and tilted its head. *Do you have any food with you?*

No. But I could pat you on the head.

The dog's tongue lolled out while it considered. *Okay.*

Zoltan patted its head. *Good dog. So what do you know about the makers of this arrow?*

The dog's tail thumped on the ground. *They're hunters. Fierce warriors. The humans here are afraid of them. You should stay away from them.*

Zoltan rubbed the dog's ears, and its tail wagged so hard that its rear end wiggled. *Why should I stay away?*

Because they'll kill you.

Zoltan paused. *Where are they?*

You stopped petting me. And I shouldn't tell you, cause you'll get yourself killed. I've always suspected humans aren't very bright.

Zoltan patted its head. *What a smart dog you are. Where are they?*

In the mountains to the south. Do you want to play with me now?

I have to go. Thank you for your help.

You're leaving? But we just met. And you're my friend now.

You're a good dog. Zoltan gave it another pat, then zoomed out of the village.

Wow! The dog's voice grew dimmer. *You're really fast for a human. I bet you could catch a rabbit. Just don't get yourself killed, okay?*

Neona pressed a hand into the round earthen mound where her twin sister, Minerva, was buried. Two weeks had passed. Two weeks since half her soul had been wrenched from her. Tears sprang to her eyes, and the same litany of questions ran through her mind.

How can I live without you? How will I face each day? Her hand fisted around a handful of dirt, squeezing it into a hard ball as a jolt of anger ripped into her grief. *Why didn't you fight harder?*

A tear rolled down her cheek, and Neona dropped the clod of dirt. She knew the answer. Seven years earlier, her sister had given birth to a son. Male children were not allowed in Beyul-La, so Minerva had been forced to give the little boy to the Buddhist monastery thirty miles away. Her broken heart had never quite mended.

At first, Neona had tried her best to alleviate her sister's pain by putting up a cheerful front. But as Minerva's despair had grown more entrenched, frustration and regret had seeped into Neona's heart. She and her sister should have defied the queen and kept the baby boy.

With a sigh, Neona lay back on the grassy hillside and gazed up at the stars. How could they have defied the queen, when she was their mother? They could have ended up banished from Beyul-La. How could they have left their home and everything it meant to them?

Neona loved Beyul-La. It was the most beautiful valley in the Himalayas. In all the world, she suspected. It gave them life and purpose, while the outside world seemed to promise only hardship and death. But there had been times when they'd lounged on the grass, stargazing, that Minerva had claimed they were prisoners.

"Look how vast the sky is," Minerva had said. "The world around us must be just as wide. Do you not yearn to see it?"

Neona had attempted to soothe her sister's unhappiness by repeating the words they'd heard since childhood, the mantra that had comforted them for years, making them feel special and important. "We are the chosen guardians of this sacred valley and its secrets. Our mission is noble and necessary."

"What is noble about being forced to give away my baby?" Minerva had muttered bitterly.

With a sigh, Neona wiped the tears from her face. The mantra no longer provided comfort. And her sister had escaped the only way she knew how. In death. The battle two weeks ago had claimed her and four others.

"Neona!" a sharp voice reprimanded her. "You shouldn't spend your life here among the dead."

Neona sat up to see Lydia approaching her. For a few seconds she considered reminding her old friend that she had some of her family members buried here among the dead. A line of five new earthen mounds now marred the hillside, alongside one older mound covered with grass. But the haggard look on Lydia's face stopped Neona from speaking. Lydia was suffering in silence.

All the warrior women of Beyul-La were suffering. The battle two weeks ago had been devastating. In a matter of minutes, their number had gone from eleven to six.

Lydia stopped halfway up the hillside. "The queen has sounded the alarm. An intruder has crossed into our territory."

Neona leaped to her feet and rushed down the hillside. "Only one?"

"It appears that way." Lydia accompanied her to the small village of a half dozen stone buildings with thatched roofs.

The other women were there, lighting a few torches before the main campfire was extinguished to leave the valley in darkness. Then the five women hurried to the cave where Neona's mother, Queen Nima, was waiting.

The torches were slid into brackets on the stone walls, and the large room brightened. Pink- and cream-colored stalactites glistened with moisture high overhead, and sparkling water fell from a fissure in the stone wall, splashing into the pool below. Behind the pool, a narrow corridor wound deep into the inner recesses of the sacred mountain. In front of the pool, there was a wide stone floor, worn smooth over the centuries.

Queen Nima paced across the floor and motioned to the owl perched on the back of her throne. "He has spotted one male intruder, invading our territory from the north."

Lydia's niece, Winifred, muttered a curse. "Do you think it could be Lord Liao?"

"Possibly," Nima replied. "Or one of Master Han's soldiers."

"They've never gotten this close before," Neona

said. The battle two weeks ago had occurred forty miles from their border. The women warriors of Beyul-La had borrowed horses from the nearby village to travel that far to fight the enemy, for it was imperative to keep the sacred valley a secret.

"No man can be allowed to see Beyul-La," Nima warned them once again. "Freya, take the eastern territory. Winifred, the west. Neona, the north. And Tashi, the south. Find him. If he's a lost villager, show him the direction home. Threaten him with death if he returns. If he's one of Master Han's men, kill him without hesitation."

The four women bowed their heads to acknowledge the acceptance of their orders.

Neona rushed to the area where they kept their armor and weapons. She always wore the breastplate and helmet left by her father, a warrior from Greece.

"There are only six of us now," Winifred said as she slipped on a metal-studded leather breastplate.

"We know that," Lydia muttered, watching her one remaining daughter, Tashi, put on armor.

"I think we should each consider having a daughter," Winifred continued.

"Perhaps," Queen Nima replied. "We will discuss it later. First we must deal with this invasion."

"Oh, I see what Freddie means," Freya said, coming to her sister's defense. "The intruder might have potential."

"Exactly!" Winifred nodded. "He could be fair of face, strong, and fleet of foot."

Lydia snorted. "More likely, he's a stumbling fool who has lost his way and doesn't have the sense to get home."

"But if he's a good specimen," Winifred argued, "we should consider taking his seed."

Freya sheathed her sword. "I hope I find him."

Winifred scoffed. "It was my idea. I should be the one to find him."

With a laugh, Tashi handed them each a coil of rope. "Here. In case you need to tie him up."

Neona frowned. Freddie and Freya seemed awfully eager to have a child. Didn't they care that they would have to give the baby away if it was male? Neona had tried only once to get pregnant, but when the seed had failed to take root, she'd secretly rejoiced. After seeing the pain her sister had gone through, she was afraid of falling into that same trap of despair.

"Very well," Queen Nima conceded. "You will take the man's seed, but only if he is exceptional. Our daughters must be warriors, superior in mind and body. And don't forget the main purpose of this mission."

Neona nodded, while the other women murmured, "Yes, your majesty."

With a growing sense of unease, Neona slid on her father's helmet. It was brass with a black plume and decorated cheek guards. She'd always wondered what had happened to the brave Greek soldier who had journeyed so far from home and become the father to her and Minerva.

When she was young, she'd asked her mother, and Nima had said he'd gone back to Greece. Then she'd warned Neona never to speak of him again. Over the years, Neona had come to suspect that her mother had not told the truth.

"Stay true to our noble cause," Queen Nima reminded them. "Once you are done with the man, kill him."

Chapter Two

$\mathcal{F}$rom his perch high on top of a craggy peak, Zoltan surveyed the countryside around him. The landscape had become increasingly mountainous as he'd traveled south. Up here, he could see farther, but the cold wind was slicing through his suit. As a Vamp, he could endure it better than most humans, and since he'd always prided himself on never quitting till a task was done, he decided to press on.

A large bird flew by, a hawk, Zoltan thought. It was a shame he'd never been able to communicate with birds like his mother could. If so, he could have asked the hawk the location of the fierce warriors that the dog had warned him about. Or perhaps the bird would know something about the feathers on the end of the new arrow he still held in his hand.

A few years ago, he'd taken the old arrow from his castle to some scientists in Budapest so they could examine it using modern technology. The results had surprised everyone. The arrowhead was ancient, similar to those used by the army of Alexander the Great. The carvings were unknown. The feathers were from a golden eagle, and the wood had come from a king cypress tree, which grew in parts of China and Tibet. The scientists had concluded that the arrow had been crafted in ancient Greece, using wood that had been imported from the east. They'd urged him to donate it to a museum, but he'd declined.

Now he had to wonder if the scientists had gotten it backward. What if the arrow had been crafted here in Tibet, using an ancient Greek arrowhead? Did that mean the so-called fierce warriors had traveled all the way from Tibet to Transylvania to kill his father?

Zoltan had always wondered if his father's murder had been an act of revenge after the death of his mother, but it didn't seem likely. It would have taken months to travel such a long distance in 1241. And his father had been murdered only a few hours after his mother.

Unless . . . could the murderer have been a vampire? A Vamp could have teleported to Transylvania. Or maybe the fanciful tale told by a few surviving villagers had been true. They'd given him a horrifying account of monsters and warriors so fierce that no living person could have ever defeated them. Zoltan had always suspected their elaborate story was nothing more than a pitiful piece of fiction to justify their failure to save their village and loved ones. If only he could remember more of that fateful day . . . but he'd spent most of it unconscious. He'd awakened the next day, miles from the village with no idea how he'd arrived there.

He took a deep breath. That was 1241. Those warriors, even if they had been fierce and monstrous, were now dead. Unless they were vampires . . . But if they were bad vampires, why did they fight Lord Liao two weeks ago? Why did they save Russell?

Zoltan levitated higher in the air, gritting his teeth against the cold wind. Higher and higher so he could see over the mountaintops. There, to the south, were those lights?

He focused on them so he could teleport there, but then with a flash, they disappeared. Damn.

How could he give up now? He teleported across the valley to the top of the next mountain, then continued to teleport, zeroing in, as best as he could surmise, on the area that had been lit. After ten minutes of traveling, he landed on a sloping hillside, surrounded by forest. He had to be close now.

Dead leaves and needles cushioned the ground, softening his steps as he moved downhill. Every now and then, the forest cleared for an outcropping of large boulders that gleamed silver in the moonlight.

With his superior hearing, he caught the sound of a trickling stream far to his right. It was running down the hill to the valley below. And behind him, the tiny snap of a twig.

Animal or warrior? He paused to listen more closely. A whooshing sound. He dove behind some bushes just as an arrow missed him and thudded into a tree.

He glanced up at the arrow. The same carved design on the staff. The feathers of a golden eagle. He'd found them!

Or rather, they'd found him. He teleported to a nearby outcropping and crouched on the rocks, scanning the forest.

There. A glimpse of brass glinting in the moonlight. One warrior. He was stealthy, Zoltan had to give him credit for that. The warrior had managed to sneak up on him, and that rarely happened.

Other than that, the warrior didn't appear that impressive. Slim build. A little below the average height for a man. The brass breastplate wasn't a good idea, since it reflected the moonlight and gave away his position. The helmet had a black horsehair plume running down the center and cheek and nose guards that covered most of the warrior's face. He was equipped with bow and arrow, sword, and at least one knife that Zoltan could spot. The warrior looked fierce enough, but archaic, as if he should be sacking Troy, not wandering about Tibet.

The old arrowhead that had killed his father had come from ancient Greece.

Zoltan called out in Greek, "I come in—" He flattened himself on the rock a second before an arrow whooshed over his head. "Peace," he whispered. The warrior wasn't big, but he was quick and had excellent aim in the dark.

"Are you a vampire?" Zoltan yelled in Russian, then, leaving his arrow on the rock so his hands would be free, he teleported behind the warrior. Meanwhile, his foe answered his question by firing another arrow over the pile of boulders.

Zoltan breathed deeply, taking in the man's scent. Rich with blood. AB negative. Human.

The warrior drew his sword, advancing slowly on the rocky outcropping.

Zoltan teleported behind the boulders and waited. "I come in peace," he said in Hungarian as the warrior came into view. "*Pax*?" He jumped back to avoid a jab from the man's sword. Dodging behind a tree, he tried Romanian and Serbian. Wood chips flew as the warrior's sword struck the tree.

"*Français? Deutsch*?" He lunged to the ground and rolled as the sword made another swipe at him. "Dammit, I just want to talk!"

The warrior hesitated, his sword raised overhead.

Zoltan eased to his feet. "You understand English?" The sword sliced down with a swoosh, and he leaped to the side. To hell with this. Zoltan lunged forward, seizing the warrior's sword arm, then lifting it up and squeezing till the man gasped and dropped the weapon.

The warrior retaliated, using his left hand to grasp Zoltan around the throat. Strong fingers dug into his neck.

Zoltan grabbed the warrior's wrist and wrenched his hand away. "You understand English, don't you? Stop your attack."

The warrior made a sound of frustration as he tried to free his hands from Zoltan's grasp. He fell backward, taking Zoltan with him, then planted his feet in Zoltan's stomach and shoved hard, flipping him over.

With a thud, Zoltan landed on his back. He rolled over and made a grab at his opponent. Unfortunately, his hands only caught hold of the man's bow and quiver of arrows, and he ended up pulling them off the warrior's back as the man jumped to his feet.

When the warrior made a dive for his sword, Zoltan leaped on the man's back, smashing him into the ground. With a cry, the man reared back, clonking Zoltan in the head with the brass helmet.

"Ow!" Zoltan was stunned for only a second, but that was enough time for the warrior to wriggle free and make another lunge for the sword.

A trickle ran down Zoltan's temple, and the smell of blood made him hiss. This had gone on long enough. With a roar, he jumped to his feet. Then using his vampire strength, he swung the warrior around and shoved him against a tree.

The brass helmet hit the tree hard, causing another gasp to escape the warrior. Zoltan pinned the man's arms overhead and leaned close.

"Now cease your—" Zoltan stopped, taken aback

by the eyes that glared at him. They were the bluest he'd ever seen. An improbable royal blue.

He moved to the side, just barely missing the man's attempt to knee him in the groin. Still, the blow struck his hip hard, making him grunt in pain. Damn, what kind of warrior would go for a man's groin?

He narrowed his eyes. The noises coming from the warrior had been a little high pitched. Could he be . . . ?

Zoltan released the man's wrists and ripped the helmet off. Long black hair cascaded, falling past the warrior's shoulders and framing a face that was delicate and feminine. An expression as stunned as his own. The helmet slipped from his hands, thudding on the ground at his feet, as he stood there, transfixed. She was exquisite. The most beautiful woman he'd—

"Aagh!" Her knee hit home, and Zoltan fell to his knees, doubling over.

She lunged to the ground to reclaim her sword.

"Dammit," Zoltan growled as he seized one of her ankles and jerked her feet out from under her. She fell onto her side and rolled, lifting her sword overhead.

"Enough!" Gritting his teeth against the pain, Zoltan jumped on top of her, grasped her sword arm, and slammed it to the ground.

She went for his throat again with her left hand, but he grabbed her wrist and pinned it down. She wriggled beneath him, but he pressed his weight on top of her.

"Enough," he whispered.

Her eyes widened, and she grew very still as she studied him.

He had a strange feeling she was assessing him. "How do you do? My name is Zoltan. And you are . . . ?"

She continued to stare at him.

"I'm afraid we got off to a bad start, but I assure you

I mean you no harm." He gently pried the sword from her hand and tossed it to the side. She didn't object when he took hold of her wrist again. "Now that's better. You were about to tell me your name . . . ?"

"You are extremely strong and fleet of foot," she said softly, as if she was thinking out loud.

"So you do speak English."

She frowned. "You are fair of face and seemingly intelligent."

He winced. "Seemingly?"

"It is unclear."

"Then allow me to clear it up for you. My intelligence is fine."

She gave him a look that seemed to indicate he'd just proven his lack thereof. "It was not wise of you to come here."

He snorted. At least she thought he was fair of face. "Actually, I thought it was very clever of me to find you." Even if it had taken him eight hundred years. "I have some questions, you see, regarding an arrow—" He glanced toward the rocky outcropping where he'd left the arrow and froze.

A snow leopard crouched on the rocks, ready to pounce.

Slowly, never taking his eyes off the wildcat, Zoltan eased off the young woman and reached for her sword. "When I stand, back away. Then run home as fast as you can."

"You intend to protect me?" she asked. "Why? I was trying to kill you."

"Yes, but you failed." He glanced at her, giving her a wry smile. "Don't worry. I won't hold it against you."

Her eyes widened and she lay very still, staring at him.

Maybe he'd shoved her around too hard. She seemed

stunned. He gave her a little shake. "You should go home now, okay? I'll take care of this." He'd protected people for almost eight hundred years, so it wasn't something he questioned anymore. He simply did it.

He straightened, facing the pile of boulders with the sword clenched in his hands.

The snow leopard hissed.

"You're very brave," the woman said behind him.

"Seemingly," he muttered, lifting the sword. "Now back away slowly."

Pain exploded in his head as something slammed into the back of his skull. He fell forward, dropping the sword. *Why?* The word skittered around his aching brain just before everything went black.

"**G**ood kitty." Neona rubbed the young snow leopard's ears. "Although I should fuss at you for breaking that twig. You ruined my surprise attack."

The eight-month-old leopard butted its head against her leg.

"Well, you did make up for it, so you're forgiven. That was very clever of you, pretending you were going to pounce on us." She smoothed a hand down Zhan's spotted back.

The snow leopard had become her companion after she'd found him seven months earlier while on guard duty. She'd taken the kitten home, where two of the women had been able to communicate with him. Zhan's mother and littermates had been killed by a pack of wolves, and he had managed to survive by crawling into a rabbit hole.

Even though Neona didn't possess the gift of communicating with animals, Zhan clearly preferred her to the other women. Probably because she was the one who had rescued him and nurtured him back to health. She suspected the cat still had enough wildness to dislike the other women's ability to read his mind.

Right now, she wouldn't object to having someone to communicate with. She had to decide what to do with the man who called himself Zoltan.

He was still lying on his stomach, unconscious. She winced at the size of the goose egg on the back of his head. She'd hit him hard with the blunt end of her knife, suspecting he possessed an extrahard head.

Her gaze drifted past his broad shoulders, down his back and legs. He had a powerful build, yet he was nimble on his feet. The way he had evaded her attack was amazing. He was an excellent specimen, as Winifred would put it.

Gently Neona turned the man over, and her heart squeezed in her chest. She'd called him fair of face, but that had been a huge understatement. She'd never seen such a handsome man in her life. Nor a man this fast and strong. The men who lived near their territory were either poor farmers or Buddhist monks, not the type of man who could sire a daughter who needed to be a warrior. And since the area was remote and snowed in half the year, outsiders were rare. A man like this Zoltan was extremely rare. Strong, fleet of foot, and incredibly handsome. When he had smiled at her earlier, she'd forgotten how to breathe.

What a beautiful daughter she could have. If only she dared. The daughter could inherit this man's courage, too.

Kneeling beside him, she placed a hand on his broad chest. "He wanted to protect me even though I attacked him. He has a noble heart."

The snow leopard butted her hand away with his head, and she smiled.

"Are you jealous? Don't worry. Once I'm done with him, I'll have to kill—" Her breath caught. How could she do that? It was one thing to kill a man in the heat of battle, but to lie with him and then kill him? That had to be wrong. Her mother, the queen, would disagree. She always said that nothing was more important than preserving the secrets of Beyul-La.

Neona closed her eyes as a wave of grief crashed over her. Her sister was more important than anything, but now she was gone. Minerva never would have taken a man's seed and then killed him.

Drawing in a shaky breath, Neona made her decision. She would convince this man to leave and never come back. He might be hard to convince, given his questionable intelligence, so she would have to be firm. Threaten to kill him if she ever saw him again.

In order to succeed, she needed to remain in charge of this situation. After all, she was a warrior woman, so she could never submit to a man. Once he agreed, she would take what she needed, then send him on his way. She pulled a length of coiled rope from a drawstring pouch on her sword belt, then proceeded to tie the man's hands together. Then she dragged him close to a tree and tied the end of the rope around the trunk.

He moaned.

Was he coming to? Her heart pounded in her chest as she knelt beside him. Was she really going to do this? *Coward*, her inner voice chided her. If one of the other women had found him, they would be finished by now.

Should she undress him? It wasn't strictly necessary, but she suspected he was a glorious sight to see.

She lifted the slim piece of red silk that was knotted around his neck. "He dresses strangely." She gave it a tug, but it only tightened around his neck.

"Sorry." She slipped her fingers above the knot and managed to loosen it. As she pulled her hand back, she grazed his chin and felt the prickle of whiskers.

Curious, she touched his cheek. How odd a man's whiskers were. How strangely . . . appealing. Her stomach fluttered with a peculiar sensation, and she quickly withdrew her hand. The man was far too handsome. Even with the trail of blood that oozed from his temple. His hair was shoulder length, the color the deep, earthy brown of freshly tilled soil. His eyes were closed now, but she recalled their color—a golden brown like burnished amber. His nose was straight and strong. His brow wide and intelligent.

Seemingly intelligent, she smiled to herself, remembering how indignant he had looked. Apparently it mattered to him what she thought of him. Even that appealed to her.

She leaned close to look at the cut on his temple. It would be a shame if she left the poor man with a scar. Especially as handsome as he was.

He moaned again and she sat back, waiting to see if he'd open his eyes.

When he didn't, her gaze wandered down his body. Was he still in pain where she'd kneed him? It was a regrettable move on her part, especially now when she needed his groin to be fully functional.

All the women of Beyul-La possessed a gift, and hers was the ability to heal. Unfortunately, in order to take away the pain, she had to take it briefly within herself.

She extended her hand a few inches above his pants. Was she really going to do this? She bit her lip. What choice did she have? The man was as close to perfection as she would ever find. When would a chance like this ever happen again? An image formed in her mind of a little girl with long dark hair and amber eyes. A brave, noble heart and dazzling smile.

Neona's eyes filled with tears. She'd lost her sister, but she could have a daughter. A daughter to love.

Or a son to break her heart.

A tear rolled down her cheek. "Please, God, let me have a girl."

She lay her hand on his groin, closed her eyes, and soon, a low, throbbing ache vibrated into her hand. The man would be all right. The worst of the pain had already subsided. She drew the remaining pain out of him, and it rushed up her arm.

"What the—?"

Neona gasped, opening her eyes. Her hand flinched, tightening its grip on his manhood.

He gave her a wry look. "What are you doing?"

She jerked her hand away and winced as his pain spread through her body before dissipating. "I-I was—"

"What the hell are you doing?" he demanded, apparently just realizing that his hands were tied together and the rope was attached to a tree.

"I can explain—"

"Dammit!" He tugged at the ropes. "The leopard is right there! Release me so I can protect you."

"The cat is with me."

"What?"

Stay in charge, she reminded herself. She lifted her chin and looked him in the eye. "Remain calm. This will not take long."

"*What?*"

"I plan to take your seed."

Chapter Three

At first, Zoltan wasn't sure he'd heard her right. Maybe she'd clonked him so hard he was hallucinating. But what a hell of a dream! This beautiful woman wanted to jump his bones? Just the thought made his groin tighten.

But in what world was this normal? She'd come out of nowhere, attacking him, knocking him unconscious, and now she wanted his *seed*? If he had any sense, he would teleport away from her and her pet . . . leopard? Or at least teleport out of the ropes she'd bound around his hands.

But the second he teleported he would be letting her know he was a vampire. It was a trump card that he'd rather hold onto until necessary. Besides, if he teleported home, he might never see her again. How could he leave without learning more about her? She was the most intriguing woman he'd ever met.

So he would stay for a while longer, but on his terms. Which meant he had to take charge of the situation. Step one, remove the most immediate threat.

He eyed the snow leopard and sent it a mental message. *Are you really her pet or just pretending?*

The leopard sniffed and looked away.

I know you can hear me, cat. Harm either of us, and I'll skin you alive.

The leopard turned back, its golden eyes narrowing into slits. *Big words from a guy who's tied to a tree. Oh, I'm so afraid.*

You should be. You'd make a nice pair of slippers.

It arched its back and hissed at him.

"Zhan." The woman shook her head at the leopard. "Behave."

The cat edged over to her, giving her a wide-eyed, innocent look.

"That's a good kitty." She rubbed its ears, and it purred. "Now run along and play for a little while."

Did you hear that, cat? Zoltan told the leopard. *She wants you to go away.*

It glared at him. *I'm her favorite. Not you.* The leopard stalked across the clearing to a tree, made a show of sharpening its claws, then slinked into the woods.

Step two, Zoltan thought. *Take charge of the conversation.* He eyed the woman. She was sitting quietly beside him, biting her lip. Nervous. That was a good sign. He didn't want to think that she did this sort of thing often. "Did I hear you correctly? You want my *seed*?"

Her cheeks flushed slightly, but she looked him in the eye. "Yes."

"Was this your plan all along? Knock me out, tie me up, and rape me?"

She winced. "It's not rape."

"What else would you call it when you forcibly plan to take my seed?"

"I figured you would be willing."

"To be raped?"

She grimaced. "It's not rape as long as you agree."

"What if I don't agree?"

She looked dumbfounded for a moment. "I thought men were always agreeable."

His hands fisted tightly around the rope as an unexpected surge of anger skittered through him. How many *agreeable* men had she found over the years? Probably plenty. What red-blooded male wouldn't agree to letting a beautiful woman ravish him in the woods? *Dammit.*

He took a deep breath. *Stay in control.* "Before I can consider your offer, I have to know exactly what you expect of me."

Her gaze drifted to his groin. "I thought it was obvious."

"On the contrary, there are numerous issues that must be addressed." Thankfully, her gaze returned to his face. He didn't want her to notice the growing bulge in his pants.

She frowned. "Issues?"

"Yes. For instance, how long will I be required to perform? Will I receive compensation for any injuries incurred during the act?"

Her eyes widened. "Injuries?"

"It happens. I've been known to get terribly wild. Fortunately, you appear to be in excellent health, so you should survive the ordeal. Do you mind signing a waiver?" He enjoyed the growing expression of horror on her face. "Which position do you want to use? Or do you prefer multiple positions? How many times do you wish to climax?"

Her mouth dropped open. Then she shook herself and glared at him. "Ten."

He blinked. Was she calling his bluff? "Ten what? Positions or climaxes?"

She hesitated a second, then lifted her chin. "Both."

He stifled a laugh. She wasn't letting him get the better of her.

Jerk, the leopard grumbled. *Stop playing cat and mouse with her.*

Zoltan glanced up and spotted the cat lounging on the branch of a nearby oak tree. *You were supposed to leave.*

It thumped its tail on the branch. *I'll leave when I feel like it.*

Does she jump men like this every night? Zoltan asked.

What do you think? The leopard narrowed its eyes. *Look who's jealous now.*

I'm not— Was he? Zoltan pushed that thought aside and turned back to the woman. "Are you sure you can handle ten climaxes?"

She shrugged. "Are you sure you can deliver?"

He smiled, enjoying the way she stood up to him. "I'll do my best. But it might take an hour or so, depending on—"

"Oh, no! We must be quicker than that. No more than five minutes at the most. In fact, we had better start right away before Freddie and the others find us."

Another jab of anger shot through him. "Freddy? Who the hell is he?"

"Freddie's not—"

"Not tied to a tree, is he? Was he last night's five-minute conquest?"

Her mouth dropped open.

How jealous can you get? The leopard eyed him with disdain.

I'm not! Shit. He was. Jealous of the unknown lovers of a woman he'd barely met. He must be going insane.

The woman's blue eyes flashed with anger. "You think I do this every night?"

"How would I know how many men you've tied up and ravished?"

"I haven't ravished you!" With a huff, she rose to her feet. "I don't think I want to anymore."

She was going to leave? "I apologize."

She gave him a dubious look.

Beg for mercy, the cat snarled.

Sod off, he replied, then looked at the woman. "I insulted you. I'm sorry." When she still looked unconvinced, he sighed. If he wanted her to stay, he'd have to be honest. "I don't like the thought of being another nameless guy in a long line of—" He stopped himself from saying "*lovers.*"

Her eyes softened. "I wouldn't like that, either. If it makes you feel any better, I have only tried this once before, and it did not result in the desired outcome." She frowned. "I am not sure this would work, either. Offhand, I can think of several legitimate reasons why we shouldn't mate."

"Like insanity?"

She looked alarmed. "Are you?"

He winced, then said, "No."

Liar, the cat snickered.

Go chase your tail, he replied.

The woman gave him a wary glance. "I would not wish to cause anyone to break a sacred vow. An exceptional man like you is probably married."

Exceptional? That made his heart leap. "I'm single." When she looked relieved, his heart did another leap.

"You might prefer men."

"No."

"You might have a disease you do not wish to—"

"No!"

"Or you might be unable to do the—"

"Hell, no!"

Her mouth twitched. "Then all that false bravado about multiple positions and—"

"Not false."

She gave him a pointed look. "I know you were trying to frighten me into changing my mind. So there's only one reason left that I can think of." Her shoulders slumped as her gaze fell to the ground. "You find me undesirable—"

"I'll do it." What the hell was he saying?

Her gaze jerked up to meet his. "You agree?"

"Yes, but with . . . three conditions."

Her eyes narrowed with suspicion. "What are they?"

How the hell would he know? He was making this shit up as he went. "Number one. I need to know your name."

"Oh. That's easy enough." She sat beside him, crossing her legs. "I am Neona."

Neona. He repeated her name in his head. He liked the sound of it. "Greek for 'new moon'?"

She ignored his question. "What is your second condition?"

"You have to untie me."

She winced. "I don't believe that is wise."

"How do you expect me to give you ten climaxes if I can't use my hands?"

She scoffed. "You were in jest."

"You think so? Untie me and find out."

She bit her lip, considering, then pulled out the knife sheathed to her calf. "I will not hesitate to use this if you hurt me."

"I would never harm you."

She gave him a doubtful look, then sawed through the ropes that bound his wrists.

Once released, Zoltan sat up and, rubbing his sore wrists, watched her slip her wickedly sharp knife into the sheath strapped to her leg. Her linen trousers looked worn and ragged along the hem. Homemade, he thought, just like the leather moccasinlike slippers on her feet.

Where did this woman live? Why had she attacked him? "The third condition is that we get to know each other."

A wary look crossed her face. "I don't see why that is necessary."

"It is. I find you very . . . interesting." Not to mention beautiful, brave, and fascinating.

She shook her head. "I don't think you need to know me in order to—"

"On the contrary. I need to be in the mood to have sex. And my mood will improve the better I get to know you."

"There is not much I can tell you."

"Do you have secrets?" He leaned toward her. "Now you're even more intriguing."

She winced. "Can we please get on with it? I'm running short on time."

"Because Freddy will show up? Who is he?"

"A friend. Winifred." After a pause, she added, "So she's female."

"I gathered that," he muttered. "And how did you learn English?"

She hesitated, her gaze shifting to the woods as she considered her response. "From an Englishman."

Zoltan's mouth twitched. She was as clever as she was beautiful. "And where is this Englishman? Is he tied to a tree somewhere?"

She scoffed. "Of course not. He went home." She glanced at Zoltan and added, "To England."

He gritted his teeth. Apparently, she still doubted his intelligence.

"Do you know enough now?" She unfastened the ties on her breastplate. "Shall we begin?"

He swallowed hard when she pulled off her armor. The breastplate must have been hot, for her thin linen top was damp with sweat and molded to breasts that were sweetly rounded and firm. "I . . . I'm not in the mood yet." Hopefully, she wouldn't notice the ever-growing bulge in his pants.

She frowned at him. "Is it normal to be this slow?"

He groaned inwardly at the sight of her nipples hardening in the cool air.

You might as well enjoy yourself while you can, the leopard grumbled. *Since you don't have long to live.*

Zoltan glanced up at the cat. *What do you mean?*

She's going to kill you when she's done.

He flinched. *You're lying!*

She told me herself. The leopard licked a paw. *Once she's done with you, you're out with the garbage.*

A chill ran down Zoltan's spine. Could this be true? Was Neona intending to kill him? His mind tensed, rejecting the thought. He couldn't believe it. He wouldn't.

And yet hadn't she tried to kill him from the start? Was she so heartless that she could have sex with a man and then execute him? If he had sex with her, could he impress her enough to change her mind?

He winced. Performance anxiety had just taken on a new meaning. He'd be a fool to risk it.

"We're running out of time," she reminded him. "This mood that you require—is there something I can do to help you achieve it?"

"Yes." He studied her carefully. Somehow, she didn't seem like a cold-blooded murderer. "I'll need a kiss."

Her brows lifted. "I don't see how that can help, but

very well." She leaned closer and gave him a peck on the cheek.

"I mean a real kiss." Her confused look twisted his insides. Dammit. Was she an innocent or a killer? "Didn't you say you've done this before?"

"Yes, once. But he did not require any kissing beforehand." She slanted an impatient look at Zoltan. "He wasn't slow. I found him remarkably quick and efficient."

Zoltan winced. And that was her first time? The asshole must have hurt her. If she'd killed him, the jerk had probably deserved it. "Not all men are alike. Close your eyes and keep them closed till I tell you to open them."

She frowned. "What are you going to do?"

"Kiss you." He took hold of her shoulders. "Now close your eyes."

Her eyelids flickered shut, and he eased closer till his breath feathered her cheek. She trembled slightly. He ran the tip of his nose along her cheek, headed toward her mouth. Glancing down, he noted her breasts moving as she breathed faster. She was reacting.

He glanced at her eyes. Still shut. He slid his hands up her neck to cup the back of her head. Lightly, he brushed his lips against hers. Another tremble.

He kissed her, moving his lips slowly and gently. When she moaned, he glanced up and found her eyes wide open with a stunned look. "It's all right," he whispered.

She shook her head. "I feel strange. My stomach is . . . quivering."

Was she truly that innocent, or was she luring him in for the kill? "Close your eyes and kiss me back." When she hesitated, he took her hands and placed them on his shoulders. "Neona."

Her eyes searched his.

"Kiss me." He pulled her close, and this time, when his lips molded to her mouth, she responded. Tentatively at first, but then with growing boldness. He deepened the kiss, invading her mouth with his tongue. She flinched, then stroked his tongue with her own.

With a groan, he covered her breast with his hand. She gasped against his mouth.

"Neona," he whispered, glancing up to make sure her eyes were still shut. He flicked a thumb over her hardened nipple, and she moaned. "Remember me."

He teleported to the top of a nearby tree.

She sat there a moment, her eyes still closed, her lips pink and swollen. He winced at the uncomfortable bulge in his pants. Even with the threat of imminent death, he'd still found himself growing hard. He wanted her. He wanted to believe she was sweet and innocent, not a cold-blooded seducer and killer of men.

She opened her eyes, and with a gasp, she looked around. "Where did you go?" She scrambled to her feet. "How did you leave? I didn't hear you."

She spun about, surveying the woods. "Zoltan? Where are you?"

A noise to her left made her jump to face it. The leopard paced into the clearing, and she sighed. "Oh, it's you." She turned, scanning the woods once again. "Why did he leave?"

She crossed her arms as if suddenly cold. "I thought he liked me." She regarded the spot on the ground where they had sat and kissed, then her shoulders slumped. "I should have known that men cannot be trusted."

She put her breastplate back on, and the leopard nudged her leg with its head.

"I'll be all right." She patted the leopard's head. "After all, men have no place in our lives." With a sigh, she sheathed her sword.

I know you're there. The leopard glanced up at him. *You're not a normal human, are you?*

Was she really going to kill me?

The leopard stretched, arching its back. *I guess we'll never know, since you chickened out and ran away.*

I didn't run. Zoltan winced. But he had chickened out. In the throes of lovemaking, she might have been able to catch him off guard. And if she had stabbed him in the heart with that knife, he would be dust.

She located her bow and quiver, swung them onto her back, then picked up her helmet. Headed downhill, she moved at a quick pace, the cat trotting alongside her.

Zoltan teleported from tree to tree, following her.

Jerk, the leopard called up to him.

He groaned inwardly. He felt like a jerk, spying on her, but how else was he going to find out who she was? And where she lived? She'd made it clear that she didn't want to tell him anything.

"Neona!" a female voice called from the bottom of the hill. Three women, all dressed in armor, were waiting by a small stream.

Neona greeted them in a language he didn't understand—Tibetan, most likely— and they talked for a moment before traversing the valley. Who were these women, Zoltan wondered. All four of them had quivers on their backs filled with arrows that looked like the one that had killed his father.

What did they say? he asked the leopard.

Why should I tell you? the cat sneered back.

You're a male. I'm a male. We should be on the same side. Unless you're just a big momma's boy.

The leopard stopped, its fur ruffling. *She lied. She told them she didn't see anyone.*

His heart leaped. Was she trying to protect him? Or forget him?

The four women approached the other side of the valley where a rock wall extended high overhead. There was a hole in the wall about shoulder high where water gushed out into the valley to join the stream. Above the hole, there was a ledge. The leopard jumped onto the ledge, then scampered from ledge to ledge till it reached the top of the wall.

Apparently someone was waiting there, for a rope ladder was tossed down. One by one, the women climbed up the ladder and disappeared over the top of the wall.

Where are they going? Zoltan asked the leopard.

Home, the leopard called back. *Don't even think about coming here. They'll kill you. Men are not allowed in Beyul-La.*

Zoltan waited ten minutes, then teleported to the top of the rock wall. His breath caught. Before him lay a beautiful valley, completely hemmed in by mountains. He spotted five women walking toward a village of a half dozen stone houses built in a circle. In the center of the circle, another woman lit a fire.

The six women stood next to the fire, talking, while the cat lounged on the grass.

So this was Neona's home. *Beyul-La*. Where men were not allowed. Zoltan snorted. They couldn't stop him from coming back. He still had questions he needed answered. And he needed to see Neona again. One kiss was not enough.

Chapter Four

"*Y*ou didn't see anyone?" Queen Nima asked as she heated up a skillet over the central fire.

"No, your majesty." Winifred used her knife to gut the six fish she'd trapped earlier in the stream that traversed their valley.

"Not a soul," Freya added, taking the fish from her sister to scale them.

Neona cast a nervous glance toward Zhan. He was lounging on the grass, his nose twitching at the smell of dinner. Tashi and her mother, Lydia, could both communicate with animals, but since they'd said nothing, it appeared that the leopard was keeping quiet about Zoltan.

"The owl said the invader came from the north." Nima looked at Neona. "You didn't see him?"

Neona shook her head, then pretended to be entirely focused on stirring the pot of rice. What on earth was she doing? She'd never lied to her mother before. Or her friends. At first, she'd told herself she was simply avoiding unnecessary embarrassment. Who, among the female warriors, would want to admit that she'd captured a prisoner, tied him up, and then managed to lose him?

It *was* embarrassing, but now Neona ackowledged there was more to it than that. Meeting Zoltan had been special, and not simply because of his extraordinary strength and handsome appearance. She'd never seen an unarmed man survive one of her attacks before. He'd also proven a worthy opponent during their verbal sparring.

A challenge, that was what he was. A challenge physically, intellectually, and even emotionally. She'd lived long enough to know such an occurrence was extremely rare. Precious, even. So it was something she wanted to keep to herself, hoarding it like a treasure.

But at the same time, she felt some anger with him and herself. He'd agreed to mate with her, but then he'd run away. Why should she protect a man who couldn't honor his agreement? How could he kiss her like that, then leave?

Just thinking about the kiss made her stomach flutter. *Remember me*, he'd whispered. As if she could forget a man like Zoltan. So strong and handsome. Fearless and noble . . .

She winced. How could she be so attracted to a man she hardly knew? Maybe it was a good thing that he'd run away. She couldn't allow herself to develop feelings for him. The women of Beyul-La could not have relationships with men. It had happened a few times before, and the results were always bad. Disastrous, even.

"I wouldn't worry about it, your majesty," Lydia said as she prepared the dough for their flatbread. "It was probably a drunken villager who scurried back home once he realized he'd ventured into our territory."

Nima sighed. "Probably so." She dropped the fish into the hot skillet.

"If you like," Tashi said, "the next time I'm in the village, I could remind them that invading our territory means death."

Nima nodded. "Do that."

"Yes, your majesty." Tashi ducked her head and smiled.

Neona exchanged a look with Winifred. Freddie suspected that Tashi had taken a lover in the village, and that was why she volunteered to go there once a month to barter for rice, flour, and the occasional bolt of fabric.

For weeks, Neona had refused to believe that Tashi would bed a villager. The men there were farmers, not warriors. Their seed would not produce the exceptional daughters who were needed to protect this sacred valley. Besides, developing a relationship with a man was dangerous. They could never be trusted with the secrets of Beyul-La. That was why they were not allowed here. And it made no sense for the women of Beyul-La to leave the valley to live with a man. Neona had seen numerous villages in Tibet and Nepal, and in each place, the women lived poor, subservient lives. It was not a life a warrior woman could ever accept.

But something new had happened to make Neona reconsider her disbelief of Tashi's alleged affair. Zoltan's kiss. Even now, her lips tingled at the thought of his mouth on hers. If that was the sort of excitement Tashi was enjoying, then Neona could understand the desire to take a lover. She hadn't wanted Zoltan to stop. The movements of his lips and hands had awakened a yearning deep inside her. She closed her eyes, remembering the touch of his hand on her breast.

"The bread is ready," Lydia announced, jerking Neona back to reality. Lydia stacked hot loaves of flatbread into a basket and passed it around.

Neona spooned rice into six bowls, then passed them around till everyone had one. Another wave of grief swept over her. It was hard, at moments like this, not to recall that only two weeks ago, there had been eleven of them sitting around the fire. Now there was an empty space next to her where her sister, Minerva, had sat.

Minerva had been able to make delicious salads from the vegetables grown in the garden and from the many wild plants and berries that flourished in the valley. Neona hadn't attempted to duplicate her sister's recipe yet. Just the thought of it brought tears to her eyes.

"Here." Nima chopped off the fish heads and scooped them into a wooden bowl. "Give this to your cat, Neona."

"Thank you." Neona took the bowl over to Zhan. Luckily, the queen had accepted her pet. The leopard had earned everyone's respect by killing any mice that tried to get into their storeroom.

Neona placed the bowl in front of him and rubbed his ears to thank him for keeping her secret.

"The cat's complaining again," Lydia muttered as she took a portion of fish onto her plate.

Tashi nodded. "He says he's tired of fish and wants rabbit instead."

Neona gave her pet a pointed look. The rascal. Was he letting her know that his continued silence came at a price? "I'll go hunting for rabbit tomorrow, okay?"

The leopard butted his head against her hand and purred.

Neona returned to her seat close to the fire and

picked at her dinner. Maybe she should hunt tomorrow evening in the same area where she'd met Zoltan. Maybe she'd see him again.

Maybe she was losing her mind. She ripped her piece of bread in two. Relationships with men always ended the same way. With disaster. If she had any sense, she'd hope never to see him again. She would forget all about him. And his last words, which kept echoing through her head.

Remember me.

Having worked up an appetite from his unexpected adventure, Zoltan teleported straight to the kitchen in the basement of his castle. From the fridge, he selected a bottle of AB negative, since it reminded him of Neona, then he popped it into the microwave, noting the time on the clock. Almost midnight. He'd been gone three and a half hours.

When his cell phone started dinging over and over, he checked it. Over thirty missed calls and texts? He'd deal with it later. For now, he needed food, a shower, and a change of clothes.

He guzzled down half of the warmed-up bottle, then proceeded up the backstairs to the Great Hall. To his surprise, Elsa was pacing back and forth by the front door. Shouldn't she be upstairs with her husband?

He took another sip of blood. "Is there something wrong?"

With a gasp, she spun to face him. "Zoltan! You're all right!"

"Yes, of cour—"

"We were worried sick!" She strode toward him.

"He's back?" Howard's voice boomed from the stairway leading to the armory. No doubt his superior hearing had caught the sound of his wife's shout. The were-bear burst from the stairwell into the Great Hall.

"Good evening." Zoltan took another sip from his bottle. "Did you enjoy your—"

"Where the hell have you been?" Howard stalked toward him, scowling. "We came back from dinner, and you were gone! Milan was frantic because he couldn't find you anywhere, and you were missing some important meetings in Budapest."

"Oh, right." Zoltan winced. He'd completely forgotten about the closing on his latest real estate venture. And then there was the other meeting with the Society for Architectural Preservation. "Not to worry. It can all be rescheduled."

"That's not the point!" Howard gritted his teeth. "This was my first night here as head of security, and I lost my client!"

"I wasn't lost. I knew exactly where I was."

"*I* didn't know." Howard gave him an exasperated look. "We tried calling you, but you didn't answer the damned phone. Do you know how embarrassing it was to tell Angus you were missing?"

Zoltan groaned inwardly. "You called Angus?"

"Yes. He was in Tiger Town in China, so he was still awake. He came right away and brought Mikhail with him. Angus and I have been searching the castle and the grounds. Mikhail and Milan are in Budapest, searching for you there. Oh, I need to let them know you're okay." Howard whipped out his cell phone and started texting.

"Oh, my gosh!" Elsa eased closer to Zoltan. "Is that dried blood on your forehead?"

Howard glanced up. "You were attacked? I'll need a full report." He sent his texts and pocketed his cell phone.

Zoltan took a deep breath. "I understand you're accustomed to protecting children like Tino and Sofia, but let me explain something. I'm on my third term as Coven Master of Eastern Europe. I'm CEO of one of the largest businesses in Hungary and Romania. And I'm almost eight hundred years old. I don't *report* to anyone."

Howard stared at him, unfazed. "You do now."

Zoltan frowned. He should have never agreed to this. Howard and his wife were acting like nursemaids. Even now, Elsa was circling him and shaking her head like he'd been caught with his hand in a cookie jar.

"Look at your clothes!" Elsa fussed. "Your jacket is torn, and you're covered with dirt and leaves."

"Milan can take the suit to the cleaners." Zoltan moved toward the grand staircase. "Now, if you'll excuse me, I'd like to—"

"I'm not done." Howard stepped in front of Zoltan to block him. "Where did you go?"

"It's Friday night. You're not the only one who had a date."

Howard scoffed. "You said earlier you didn't have a girlfriend. And what kind of date leaves you with a bloody wound on your head? If you have an enemy stalking you, I need to know about it. Where the hell were you?"

Zoltan tamped down on his growing frustration. These people weren't going to leave him alone till he answered. "Fine. I was . . . fighting an Amazon warrior in Tibet."

Elsa's eyes widened.

Howard stared at him blankly for a few seconds, then snorted. "No, really. Where were you?"

"Is he all right?" Angus called out as he zoomed through the front door at vampire speed.

"I'm perfectly fine," Zoltan announced. "There was no need to make such a fuss—"

"Ye were missing for over three hours." Angus's kilt swished as he came to an abrupt stop in front of Zoltan. "And ye have enemies. We had every right to be concerned." His green eyes narrowed. "Ye took a blow to the head?"

Zoltan waved a dismissive hand. "It'll heal during my death-sleep."

"Why did ye no' answer yer phone?" Angus asked.

"I was out of range. If I go back, I'll take a sat phone with me."

Angus nodded. "If ye go back where?"

Zoltan frowned. For some reason, he was reluctant to let anyone else know. Neona was keeping him secret, and he wanted to do the same for her.

"He said Tibet earlier," Howard muttered. "But I don't know if he was kidding."

"Tibet?" Angus arched an eyebrow. "Does this have anything to do with Master Han? Or Russell? I heard ye've been supplying him."

"It's not related to either of them. It's personal. Now if you'll excuse me . . ." Zoltan reached for the banister and started up the grand staircase. If he could just get away from all these people, he would enjoy some time alone to think about Neona. And strategize his next move.

"Is he all right?" Mikhail asked.

Here we go again. Zoltan turned and saw that Mikhail had just teleported into the Great Hall with Milan.

"Sir!" Milan rushed toward him. "We've been looking all over Budapest. We were worried about you."

"I am perfectly fine, as you can see." Zoltan cast an annoyed look at Angus. "I didn't realize I would need anyone's permission to leave my own house."

Mikhail snorted. "Yeah, he's fine. If you don't mind, I'll get back to Moscow. Pam's working tonight, and I don't like to leave her alone."

Zoltan lifted a hand. "Good night, old friend."

Mikhail smirked. "I hope she was worth it." He teleported away.

"She?" Milan repeated.

Zoltan shrugged. "Mikhail was making an assumption."

Angus eyed the wound on Zoltan's temple. "If ye were seeing a lass, she's no' verra happy with you."

"Nothing I can't handle," Zoltan muttered.

Angus grinned. "I'll be going, then. Emma's waiting for me in London. I havena seen the lass in three weeks." He teleported away to be with his wife.

"So is the Amazon warrior real?" Howard asked. "Is she the one who attacked you?"

Zoltan ignored the questions. "Milan, I'll be ready to go to Budapest in thirty minutes. See if you can reschedule the meetings I missed. And call the tour agency."

"Yes, sir." Milan whipped out a small pad and pencil from his jacket and took notes. "Is there a problem with the tour?"

"Tour?" Howard asked. "What tour?"

"There are tours in the castle every Tuesday and Thursday afternoon," Elsa explained.

Howard grimaced. "A bunch of strangers roaming about the castle?"

"It's a guided tour," Zoltan muttered. "They never leave the guide."

"How can you be sure?" Howard demanded. "Is the guide trained for crowd management? Is he armed?"

Zoltan snorted. "That wouldn't seem very welcoming, would it? We have two elderly women from the village who earn extra money by conducting the tours."

"It's very popular with the tourists," Milan added, smiling. "They all want to see a real vampire castle."

"*What*?" Howard stiffened. "You publicize this place as a *vampire* castle? Holy shit. This is a security nightmare!"

Zoltan waved a dismissive hand. "It's all in fun. The tourists don't really believe it."

Howard gave him an incredulous look. "It only takes one wacko, armed with a wooden stake, and determined to scour the castle till he finds you. And you'll be completely defenseless in your death-sleep—"

"In my house in Budapest," Zoltan interrupted him. "I don't sleep here on the days of the tour, Howard. I didn't get to be this old by being an idiot."

Howard's eyes narrowed. "What kind of security do you have in Budapest?"

Zoltan groaned. "I didn't know you would be so relentless."

"I didn't know you would be so lax when it comes to your own safety." Howard crossed his arms. "But don't worry. I'll fix everything."

Zoltan wondered what it would take to send the were-bear into hibernation. "Milan, tell the guides that the east wing and tower will be off the tour while renovations are being done. Construction will begin on Monday, so this will affect the next tour on Tuesday."

"Will do." Milan made a note, then adjusted his glasses. "If I might say so, the tourists will be very disappointed to miss the main attraction in the tower."

"Oh, that reminds me." Elsa turned to Zoltan. "Alastair is worried that the wooden box we built around the mummy won't be enough protection if a stone wall collapses. He thinks we should move it to a safer location like the chapel. Then it can remain on the tour."

Zoltan nodded. "All right, but be careful—"

"Wait a minute." Howard lifted a hand to stop him. With a stunned look, he looked at his wife and then Zoltan. "There's a mummy?"

"Oh yes." Milan nodded as he made notes. "A very old mummy. Very popular with the tourists."

Howard ran a hand through his hair. "This place is crazy."

Zoltan gave him a wry smile. "Welcome to Transylvania." He zoomed up the stairs, leaving the werebear behind, finally speechless.

Chapter Five

The boy was near death, his body bleeding and bruised, an angry red burn seared across his back. Neona moved her hands over the gashes and bruises, taking in as much of his pain as she could endure. In the distance, where the village and castle were located, smoke billowed into the sky. The stench of burning bodies made her choke. Gathering up her courage, she placed a hand on the boy's burned back. Fire sizzled up her arm.

With a cry, Neona sat up in bed. Gasping for air, she looked around her dark one-room house. She was home in Beyul-La. Far, far away from that terrible memory. She hadn't dreamed about it in many years.

Moonlight filtered through an open window, lending just enough light to make out the shape of two chairs and a small table in front of the hearth. A trunk containing her clothes rested at the foot of her bed. Another trunk sat at the foot of Minerva's bed across the room. Her empty bed.

Neona's heart stilled as another wave of grief swept over her, leaving her cold and numb.

"Minerva," she whispered. "Who will listen to me

now in the still of the night? Whom can I trust with my secrets?"

Sleep had been difficult since the battle two weeks ago. When Neona would finally fall asleep, she dreamed of her twin sister. Memories of growing up in the valley, running through the green pastures, laughing, playing in the stream. But the dream would always take a sinister turn, and she would see Lord Liao's sword plunging through her sister's chest, see her sister falling to the ground. Then Neona would wake up with tears streaming down her cheeks and her heart aching so much that she thought it would burst.

But tonight had been different. Why, after all these years, would she dream about that boy? It had been a horrendous day, full of death and destruction, a day she'd tried hard to forget.

"Why did I have that dream?" She glanced at Minerva's bed, imagining what her sister would say.

Did something different happen to you today?

"Yes," Neona whispered. "I met a man. A man so special I couldn't tell anyone. But I would have told you."

Silence.

Tears filled her eyes. "It must have been a warning to shield my heart. So I would remember what happens if any of us chooses a man over our sacred duty."

Steeling her nerves, she wiped her cheeks. It was a good thing Zoltan had disappeared. She was too vulnerable right now, too easily swayed by a false sense of affection. She would have to be strong. The price of losing one's heart to a man was always the same. Death and destruction.

Innocent or killer? The question reverberated in Zoltan's mind. It was the following evening, and he was in his office in Budapest, reading a report. But the words on the page kept blurring before his eyes as his brain replayed last night's meeting over and over.

The memory always started with the best part of their meeting. The kiss. He would recall how sweet Neona had tasted, how strong yet delicate she had felt in his arms. She was the most fascinating combination of toughness and tenderness. Her words had been bold, but her body had trembled at his touch. *Innocent*.

But then the leopard's warning would slice through his memory like a knife, ripping it to shreds. Then he would recall how she'd attacked him at first. He'd been unarmed, but she'd shown no mercy. No hesitation. *A killer*.

With a groan, he tossed the report on his desk. Innocent or killer? Which was she? Who were the women of Beyul-La? Was it a convent? But he'd never heard of nuns who went around ravishing and killing men. Maybe they were a man-hating cult? Why did they have arrows similar to the one that had killed his father? Were they descendants of the ones who had murdered him and destroyed the village? It seemed crazy, but he might have discovered a centuries-old cult of female assassins living in a place called Beyul-La.

Had Neona attacked him because he'd ventured too close to their home? The leopard had said men weren't allowed there. They would kill him if they found him there.

He did a search on his computer for Beyul-La, but

just as he expected, nothing came up. The word *beyul* existed, though, and it meant "hidden valley in the Himalayas." The example cited was called Barun Valley, and the photo looked similar to the valley he'd seen. Green and lush, surrounded by snow-peaked mountains. The local people, the Sherpa, called such a place sacred. Paradise on earth. Fantasies were told of hidden valleys like Shangri-La, where the people never aged and lived forever in peace and harmony.

Zoltan snorted. There was nothing peaceful or harmonious about Neona. He'd turned his back on her once, trying to protect her, and she'd clobbered him. At least all the injuries he'd incurred had completely healed during his death-sleep.

Should he see her again? God, he wanted to. He'd enjoyed talking to her. He'd really enjoyed kissing her. But would she be glad to see him or try to kill him?

He'd never know if he stayed here in Budapest. Unfortunately, he had a full schedule of meetings until midnight, and then he had to return to his townhouse, where the ballroom was used twice a month for Coven Court.

As Coven Master of Eastern Europe, he had to preside over the proceedings, pass judgments, and generally keep the peace among his constituents. Occasionally, some Malcontents would get out of hand and he'd have to borrow some employees from Angus to go after them. For centuries, he'd been keeping law and order. And building a successful business. He owned the old castle and surrounding area in Transylvania and a great deal of real estate in Budapest, Hungary, and Sofia, Romania.

Business was good. Work kept him busy. So busy that he could usually forget that he was alone. He solved other people's problems, protected them from Malcontents, Communists, Nazis, Ottoman Turks, Mongols. On and on, for centuries.

He leaned back, closing his eyes. He was tired. Tired of the same activities stretching on into eternity. It was times like this when he sorely missed his old friend Istvan.

As the local vampire, Istvan was already old and wise when Zoltan had met him as a child. And when Zoltan had suddenly become the new Count of Czakvar at the age of fourteen, Istvan had lent him advice and wealth in order to rebuild the castle and village. At the age of twenty-nine, Zoltan had despaired that he would grow old and die without discovering the truth surrounding the deaths of his parents, and he'd begged Istvan to change him. Since Istvan had been a friend of his father's and was also keen to solve the mystery, he'd agreed to become Zoltan's sire.

Over the years, Istvan became a second father to Zoltan. The old vampire warned him that acquiring wealth was important, even necessary, for a Vamp. It meant security and freedom. So Zoltan had amassed a small fortune. He felt secure enough these days, in spite of Howard's fussing, but he didn't feel free. He just felt . . . tired.

Istvan had died in the Great Vampire War of 1710, killed by the evil Casimir. Zoltan had tried his best to step into the shoes of his mentor, volunteering to take over Istvan's job as Coven Master of Eastern Europe. Zoltan had been reelected in 1750, then again in 1850 and 1950. Apparently, no one else wanted the responsibility.

Istvan had also taught Zoltan that time spent protecting mortals would give his life meaning. Zoltan had accepted that as his noble purpose. But the longer he lived, the more mortals he saw grow old and die. He couldn't really protect them from death. Was his noble purpose nothing more than vanity to make himself feel better?

With a sigh, he opened his eyes, and his gaze fell on the computer screen and the photo of Barun Valley. Paradise on earth. Similar to Beyul-La, but the ridges around Beyul-La had seemed impenetrable, so that the valley was completely cut off from the rest of the world. Beautiful, but so isolated. What would cause a handful of women to live alone in such a place? Why were they willing to kill to keep it secret?

Zoltan sat up. This was what he needed. A new quest. He would discover the secrets of Beyul-La and win the heart of Neona. If she didn't kill him first. And he might also solve the mystery of his first quest and find out what had happened that fateful day in 1241. Because of the arrow, he had a strong feeling it was all connected.

A knock sounded on the door, and Milan peeked in. "Sir, I'm sorry to say this, but your meeting in five minutes has to be postponed. They just called, and they're running late. They don't expect to be here for thirty minutes—"

"That's fine." Zoltan's heart started pounding. In thirty minutes he could teleport to Tibet and back. "Oh, Milan," he said when his assistant started to shut the door.

"Yes, sir?" Milan looked back in.

"Clear my schedule for tomorrow. In fact, clear it for a week."

Milan's mouth dropped open. "You're taking a vacation?"

"Yes." Zoltan grabbed a pen and some paper.

"But you never take a vacation. Not in the five years that I've worked for you."

"You've been with me five years?"

"Yes, sir." Milan blushed slightly and adjusted his glasses. "You hired me after I graduated from college."

"Oh." Zoltan thought back. Milan's grandfather had been the steward at his castle for years. And Milan's father, the head gardener, had turned the gardens into one of the highlights of the castle tour. They were always there, every night, just like Milan. "I don't recall you ever taking a vacation."

Milan's blush deepened. "You-you never gave me one. Not that I'm complaining. You've taken care of my family for more generations than we can remember. It is an honor to be working for you."

Zoltan groaned inwardly. He'd been so obsessed with work that he hadn't noticed what was happening to the mortals around him. And he prided himself as their protector? "Good God, Milan, you should have told me what a terrible boss I am."

"That's not usually wise for an employee, sir."

"You're taking a vacation. Now."

"I am? But should we both be gone at the same time, sir?"

"Oh, right. You have to stay."

Milan's shoulders drooped. "Yes, sir."

"But you're promoted. You know everything that's going on, right? You know all the building managers and business contacts?" When Milan nodded, Zoltan made a decision. "Very well. You're in charge now. Double, no, triple your salary. And when I get back, you go on vacation. Okay?"

Milan stared at him, his blue eyes wide.

All of a sudden, Zoltan felt fifty pounds lighter.

And much more energetic. *Free.* "I'll see you in thirty minutes, Vice President."

Milan nodded. "Yes, sir." He closed the door.

With Zoltan's superior hearing, he heard a victorious whoop on the other side of the door. Smiling, he wrote a note in English.

Dear Neona,

I'd like to see you again. Please meet me here at midnight.

Zoltan

He grabbed the note and teleported back to the clearing where he'd fought and kissed Neona the night before. From the top of the rocky outcropping, he retrieved the arrow he'd taken from Russell. Then, using his vampire strength, he rammed the arrow into an oak tree, pinning the note.

But what if one of the other women saw it? Would Neona be in trouble? He pulled the arrow out, then levitated up to the branch where the leopard had lounged the night before. He pinned the note there. It was too high to be noticeable by most, but hopefully, the leopard would find it and tear the note off to give it to Neona. It was a long shot, but what else could he do? He couldn't waltz into Beyul-La, where he was forbidden. Unless he managed to remain hidden.

He wandered down to the stream, watching and listening, but no one was around. He eyed the rock wall where water gushed out. That water had to be coming from Beyul-La. He teleported to the top of the ridge, then across the top branches of trees till he had a good view of the village.

Only glowing embers remained in the central fire pit. The houses were dark. The women had probably retired for the night. He spotted the leopard trotting up a hillside toward a series of mounds. Burial mounds? There were five of them. No, six. The sixth one was grown over with grass and harder to see in the dark. The other five were brown with newly piled dirt, topped with large rocks that gleamed silver in the moonlight.

Something moved next to a mound. One of the women? He teleported closer. Yes, a woman, dressed in green and brown linen that blended into the hillside so well she was scarcely visible.

He teleported to a tree close to her. Was it Neona? It was hard to tell when all the women had long black hair and slim bodies.

She sat very still, her hand resting on a dirt mound, her head bowed. With her other hand, she wiped her cheeks. She was crying.

Zoltan winced. Five of the graves were new. As far as he knew, only six women remained. Russell had said they'd been taking heavy losses when he'd joined the battle. Why was Lord Liao fighting these women?

The leopard approached her, bumping his head against her leg. She gave him a pat, then lay back on the grass, staring up at the sky. *Neona.*

Whom was she crying for in the middle of the night? A family member or close friend? His heart squeezed as he watched her. He knew how it felt to lose all his family and his closest friend.

He would have to be careful with her heart. It was already raw with pain. And he'd have to make sure Lord Liao didn't kill any more of these women. An inner voice warned him that once again he was taking on the responsibility of protecting mortals, but he ignored it. Neona was special. He couldn't let anyone harm her.

The next time Russell came for supplies, he'd have to answer some questions. Who were the women of Beyul-La? And why was Lord Liao and Master Han's soldiers attacking them?

Cat, he mentally nudged the leopard.

Zhan looked around, its golden eyes gleaming, till it spotted him in the tree. *You fool. If they catch you here, they will kill you.*

I left a note on the tree branch where you sat while Neona and I were talking.

You did more than talk. The cat glared at him. *Hurt her and I'll gnaw your foot off.*

Zoltan ignored the threat. *Help her find the note tomorrow. I want to see her again.*

The cat thumped its tail on the ground. *Why should I help you?*

Because she's sad. And I want her to be happy.

The cat blinked slowly. *Maybe I'll help. Maybe I won't.*

Fair enough, Zoltan conceded. *Watch over her, okay?*

Zhan didn't respond, but rested a paw on Neona's leg.

Zoltan took one last look at her, then teleported back to his office. Three minutes till the meeting. He smiled to himself, straightening his tie. If all went well, he'd be with Neona tomorrow night.

Chapter Six

"*Y*ou smell rabbits around here?" Neona asked her pet leopard. "I haven't seen any tracks."

Zhan trotted ahead of her, presumably following the scent of some sort of prey. According to Tashi, who could communicate with him, the cat wanted his favorite meal again. So Neona had taken him hunting at dawn.

She stopped, recognizing the clearing they were in. This was where she'd met Zoltan. The rising sun shot fractured rays through the trees, causing the morning dew to sparkle on the grass. It was a beautiful place, the perfect setting for a memory that continued to haunt her. Who would have known a man could be that strong, yet kiss that sweetly?

A deep sense of longing enveloped her heart. God help her, she wanted to be special to someone. She was surrounded by friends in Beyul-La, but with her sister gone, she felt so alone. There was no one to open her heart to, no one to hold her when she ached inside. Of course, as a warrior woman, she wasn't supposed to need comforting. She certainly wasn't supposed to seek comfort from a man. Even an exceptional man like Zoltan.

Where did he come from? He didn't look like any villager she'd ever seen. Had he truly wanted to kiss her? Or had he merely tricked her into closing her eyes so he could escape? Why did he run away? Did he not enjoy the kiss? Maybe he didn't like her.

She shook her head. Why would he like her when she'd clobbered him? She exhaled slowly, reminding herself once again that his disappearance was for the best. She couldn't fall for a man and shirk her sacred duty. Especially now, when they were at the beginning of a new cycle.

But why did she have to keep reminding herself? Even now she found herself peering carefully into the forest, hoping for a glimpse of him.

The leopard drew her attention when he suddenly scrambled up a tree.

"What are you doing? You won't find a rabbit up there." Her breath caught when she noticed a piece of paper stuck to the branch with an arrow. "What is that?"

Zhan ripped at the paper with his claws.

"Don't destroy it!" Could it be a note from Zoltan?

A piece of the paper floated down, and she grabbed it.

Dear Neona,

I'd like to see you again. Please meet me here at midnight.

Zoltan

Her heart leaped into her throat. "He wants to see me!"

Zhan made an annoyed huffing noise and jumped down to the ground.

"How clever of you to find the note." She hugged the leopard, then rubbed his ears. "You must have recognized his scent."

Zhan butted his head against her.

"Good kitty." Her heart thudded as she folded the letter and slipped it into her tunic pocket. Did she dare meet Zoltan? And the even bigger question, did she dare take his seed?

She swallowed hard. Why not? He had agreed to mate with her. It would be cowardly to run away from such a golden opportunity. Still, she needed to think this through. "Let's find something for dinner." She could make her plans while they hunted.

She strode down the hill toward the stream. It was easier to spot tracks in the muddy areas there. Her heart pounded with each step. She could see Zoltan tonight! An inner voice warned her that it might be unwise, but she shoved it aside. She wasn't shirking her duty. If she had a daughter, she would be fulfilling it.

Should she take him to Frederic's old cabin? It wasn't far from here. The women had used the cabin two weeks ago to house the vampire, Russell, when he was injured. They had felt honor-bound to take care of him after he'd saved Queen Nima's life during battle.

Neona figured the cabin was a more suitable place for mating than the woods. She would have to take fresh sheets and some supplies from Beyul-La without anyone noticing. And she would need to bathe and wash her hair.

She pressed a hand against her chest, where her

heart continued to pound. This was exciting! *Be careful,* an inner voice warned her. *You could lose your heart to him.* She pushed those thoughts away. She'd lived with gloom and despair for two weeks. It was time to think more positively. This had to be for the best. Because for the first time since losing her sister, she felt alive.

After waking from his death-sleep in the bedroom of his castle, Zoltan's thoughts immediately turned to Neona. Would she be waiting for him at their meeting place? Had the leopard helped her find the note?

His excitement grew as he showered and dressed. This time he wore more suitable clothes—jeans, brown T-shirt, hiking boots, and a green hooded jacket with zippered compartments. He teleported down to the kitchen for a quick meal.

"There you are," Howard said as he materialized.

"Good evening." Zoltan nodded at the were-bear and his wife, who were seated at the kitchen table, sharing a bowl of ice cream.

"We thought we'd find you here after sunset," Howard said, his gaze drifting down to Zoltan's hiking boots. "Going somewhere?"

Ignoring him, Zoltan took a bottle of AB negative out of the fridge, twisted off the top, and set it in the microwave.

"We heard you were taking a vacation," Elsa said.

"Yes." Zoltan rummaged through the fridge till he found some bagged blood. He zipped it into one of the large pockets on his jacket. Emergency rations, just in case.

"Milan is in shock," Elsa continued. "He said you haven't taken a night off in five years."

"Guess I'm overdue." The microwave dinged, so Zoltan removed the bottle and poured the warmed-up blood into a glass.

Howard spooned some ice cream into his mouth. "Let's get to the point, okay? I need to know where you're going."

Zoltan gave him an annoyed look. "I'll take a sat phone with me this time."

"So you're going back to Tibet?" Howard set down his spoon. "You're going to see the Amazon warrior again?"

"Maybe." Zoltan upended his glass, guzzling down the blood.

"Why do you want to see a woman who beat the crap out of you?"

Zoltan swallowed so hard that his eyes watered. "She didn't beat the— Look. Whomever I choose to see is none of your business."

"It is my business when it affects security," Howard argued. "From what I can tell, you have no regard whatsoever for your personal safety. There are no guards here. No working surveillance cameras. You let strangers roam about the castle that you publicize as a *vampire* castle, and you let everyone in the vicinity know you're a Vamp."

Zoltan shrugged and drank more blood.

Howard sat back, folding his arms across his chest. "I've been giving it a lot of thought, and I think I know what's going on here."

"Really?" Elsa's eyes widened as she ate more ice cream. "What?"

Howard leaned toward her and lowered his voice. "Gregori explained it to me. When a Vamp reaches his five hundredth birthday, he normally falls into a state of deep depression."

"Oh no." Elsa gave Zoltan a worried look.

He snorted and drank more blood.

"And Zoltan here is about eight hundred years old," Howard continued. "So he could be *seriously* depressed."

Elsa winced. "The poor man."

Zoltan gritted his teeth. "I'm not so old that my hearing is gone."

Howard leaned closer to his wife. "It explains everything. Why he's so careless about his own safety. Why he's no longer interested in his job. Why he insists on seeing a woman who beat the crap out—"

"She didn't beat the crap—" Zoltan took a deep breath. "This is ridiculous. I'm not depressed."

Elsa gave him a sympathetic look. "You won't be able to get better until you admit the problem."

"I'm *fine*!" Zoltan tossed the empty bottle in the recycle bin so hard that it shattered. He winced. Sometimes he forgot how strong he was.

Howard and Elsa exchanged a knowing look.

Zoltan groaned. "I'm not depressed. I'm just . . . tired." *And lonely.* "I'm going now."

"Wait!" Howard jumped to his feet. "You can't leave without a sat phone. And you shouldn't face the Amazon warrior without some weapons. You'll need a knife, a sword, and a handgun."

"I can't go on a date fully armed!"

Elsa's eyes lit up. "This is a date?"

Zoltan winced. Now he'd said more than he had intended to. "Maybe."

Elsa looked at her husband. "This is a good sign. If he's dating, maybe he's not so depressed after all."

"But if he were thinking clearly," Howard whispered back, "he wouldn't date a woman who beat the crap out—"

"She didn't beat me!" Zoltan strode toward the door. "I'm getting the sat phone, then leaving."

"Wait!" Elsa rushed toward him. "You shouldn't go on a date empty-handed. Do you have flowers or something?"

Zoltan paused. Elsa might have a point. "What should I bring?"

Elsa frowned, considering, then her face brightened. "I have a box of chocolates I haven't opened."

Howard stiffened. "That was my gift for you."

"You can get me some more." Elsa squeezed her husband's arm. "This is an emergency. Zoltan needs something now."

Zoltan nodded. "Chocolate might be good. I doubt she gets much of it."

"Maybe it'll keep her from beating the crap—" Howard stopped when Zoltan glared at him.

"The box is in our bedroom." Elsa started out the door. "I'll be right back."

"We'll be in the armory," Howard called after her.

Zoltan made his way quickly to the armory with Howard right behind him, asking questions along the way.

"What's her name? Where does she live? Does she look like Xena, the warrior princess? Why did you beat you up?"

Zoltan ignored him and selected a sat phone off a shelf in the armory.

"Let me see that." Howard grabbed it and started pushing buttons. "Okay. It's charged up and working well. I'm putting in my number and Angus's and

Mikhail's. If anything goes wrong, I want you to call. Either Angus or Mikhail should be able to teleport to you right away."

"I understand." Zoltan reached for the phone, but Howard kept pushing buttons.

When Howard's cell phone went off, he smiled. "Okay, now I have your number." He handed the sat phone to Zoltan. "I recommend you take at least one knife."

"I'll be fine." Zoltan dropped the sat phone into a pants pocket. "If I'm really in trouble, I'll just teleport back here."

"Does she know you're a Vamp?"

Zoltan shook his head. "I don't think so." Although her cat knew he wasn't normal. Fortunately, she wasn't able to communicate with her pet.

"Does she know about Vamps?"

"Probably. They were fighting Lord Liao and some of Master Han's army two weeks ago."

Howard's eyes narrowed. "What does Lord Liao have against them?"

"I don't know." Zoltan shrugged. "There's a lot I don't know. That's one reason I want to go back."

Howard nodded. "They might turn out to be good allies against Master Han."

"Hello?" Elsa's voice carried down the spiral staircase, then she appeared in the entrance to the armory. With a smile, she handed a gold foil box to Zoltan. "Here you go."

"Thank you." The box was too large for any of his pockets, so he zipped up his jacket and slid it inside.

"Good luck! Oh—" Elsa raised a hand to stop him. "I wanted to let you know. We'll be moving the mummy Tuesday morning, so it will be in the chapel for the tour that afternoon."

"All right." Zoltan nodded. "Good evening." His heart started pounding. Would Neona be waiting for him? He didn't want to materialize in front of her, so he would teleport a short distance away and walk to the clearing.

Neona smoothed the clean sheets on the bed, then took one final look around the cabin. A fire was burning in the hearth. The kettle was full of water and ready to heat up over the flames. The old English tea set had been washed and placed on the table, along with a bowl of fresh berries she'd picked earlier in the day.

She adjusted the sash around her tunic. These were her finest clothes, an embroidered silk tunic and pants. She'd told the other women that she was hunting tonight with Zhan, so she'd left wearing her usual green and brown linen, with her good clothes, a towel, and some soap stashed in the bag she wore on her back.

She'd washed up in her favorite place, where the stream from Beyul-La jetted out into the neighboring valley. Then she'd dressed in Frederic's cabin and readied it for Zoltan's visit. The cat kept getting underfoot, as if he didn't think he was getting enough attention.

She patted Zhan's head. "I know I cannot continue to see him. But if I could just have a daughter . . ." She tensed as the fear of having a son crept into her thoughts. No, she would have to think positively. She would have a daughter, a beautiful daughter with Zoltan's hair and eyes. Then she would have someone to love. And she wouldn't have to spend the rest of her life with a broken heart.

Zhan curled up in front of the hearth to take a nap. She took a deep breath, then started for the clearing. With each step, her heart pounded louder in her ears. *Remember to stay in charge*, she warned herself. *Take his seed if he is willing, then send him on his way. Do not become attached to him.*

She stopped, her breath catching when she saw him. He was contemplating the night sky, his head tilted back and the moonlight illuminating his profile. The sharply defined line of his jaw, the shape of his cheekbones and nose, the strong length of his neck. How could he be even more handsome than she'd remembered? His shoulder-length brown hair was brushed back from a wide brow. The wound on his temple was completely healed.

He turned toward her, and she froze under the intensity of his stare. It had been a mistake to ever question this man's intelligence. His sharp eyes cut through her as if he wanted to peel back her skin to examine her soul. His gaze lowered to her clothes, then returned to her face. "I'm glad you came."

She drew in a deep breath, steeling her nerves. "Zhan found your note."

He stepped toward her. "You look beautiful tonight." He smiled. "But then you would look beautiful every night."

Her heart skipped a beat at the sight of his smile. Who was this man, that he could affect her so easily? "Where do you come from? Are you staying at the nearby village?"

After a pause, he replied, "I have passed through there." He removed a box from his jacket. "I have a gift for you."

She blinked in surprise. First he'd used flattery, and now he had a gift? Hadn't she made it clear that she

wanted to mate with him? There was no need for him
to act so gallantly. As if he were . . . *courting* her.

Her nerves tensed. Why would he court her unless
he wanted to win her affections? She couldn't allow
that to happen. After tonight, she'd refuse to see him
again.

She glanced at the shiny gold box. "That was not
necessary, but thank you."

"Do you not like chocolate?"

She searched her memory of all the books she'd
read from Frederic's small library. "Hot chocolate?"

"Not the drink." Zoltan gave her a curious look.
"Have you never eaten chocolate?"

She felt heat warming her cheeks. When Frederic
had returned to England, they'd lost their only contact with the outside world, and now she felt woefully
ignorant. "Come with me, and we shall have some
tea." She turned and headed down the hill.

Zoltan walked beside her. "Are you taking me to
your home?"

"No." She shook her head. "That is not allowed. I
am taking you to Frederic's cabin."

"Is he a friend of yours?"

"He's Freddie's and Freya's father. He taught us
English."

"He's the one who went back to England?"

Neona nodded, remembering how distraught Freddie and Freya had been. And their mother, Calliope,
had been devastated. Queen Nima had declared
that it was just further proof that men could not be
trusted. They always betrayed you in the end.

She wouldn't let that happen. Zoltan couldn't hurt
her if she refused to let him into her heart.

"The cabin is this way." She pointed to a clearing
downstream where the stone house was situated.

He followed her inside and looked around. "Is your home similar to this one? No running water or electricity?"

She wasn't sure what electricity was. "There is running water in the stream outside." She hesitated, wondering if she should suggest he lie down on the bed. Perhaps she should give him time to get comfortable. He'd said the other night that he needed to be in the mood.

She set the kettle over the fire. "It will take a moment for the water to boil."

"That's fine." He placed the gold box on the table in front of the hearth.

Zhan looked up from his nap and hissed.

"Ssh." She hushed the cat. "Why don't you go outside? You can warn me if someone comes."

Zhan stalked toward the door, snarling at her guest. Zoltan followed the cat, chuckling as the cat gave him one last hiss.

"So long, cat." He shut the door, then strolled around the perimeter of the room. "This is nice." He stopped to admire a white silk banner embroidered with red and pink blossoms.

"Frederic's wife made it."

"Does she live here?"

"She . . . passed away."

Zoltan turned to face her. "I'm sorry. Were you close to her?"

Neona tossed a few more sticks onto the fire to increase the heat. "There is no need to discuss anything personal. Once we have had our tea, we can . . . proceed." She motioned toward the bed.

He glanced at the bed, then back at her, his eyes narrowing as he looked her over. "What you're wearing is very pretty. Did you make it?"

"Yes." She adjusted the sash. Why did she feel like he was imagining her without her clothes? "We do quite a bit of sewing in the winter. We can be snowed in for months."

"You don't get lonesome?"

She swallowed hard. The next winter would seem endless without her sister. "We keep busy. We make our clothes and shoes. A new supply of arrows. I make ointments and medicine. Some of the women make pottery. And of course, we practice our fighting skills every day."

His mouth twitched. "I'm sure you do. I've been told more than once that you beat the crap out of me."

She lifted her chin. "You were told correctly." His answering smile caused an odd fluttering sensation in her stomach. He didn't seem intimidated or angered by her show of strength. On the contrary, he acted like he enjoyed it. And that only served to make him more appealing.

Don't fall for him, she reminded herself. She straightened the teacups and saucers on the table.

He wandered over to a wooden chest that was topped with a stack of books. "These are in English."

She sighed. He seemed determined to pry into her personal life. "Those belonged to Frederic."

Zoltan rummaged through them. "A world atlas. A Bible. Some novels—*Ivanhoe* and *A Tale of Two Cities*."

"Those were his favorites."

"They all look well read. This one is falling apart." He picked up a book and studied the faded lettering on the spine. "*Pride and Prejudice*."

She selected a plump wild berry from the bowl on the table. "That one is my favorite. I read it every winter."

"Interesting." He set it down carefully, then looked

at her, the corner of his mouth curling up. "So your favorite is about a man and woman falling in love."

Warmth invaded her cheeks, but she ignored it and slipped the berry into her mouth. Juice spurted from the fruit as she bit down, and she quickly pressed a hand to her mouth. She swallowed and licked her lips, painfully aware that he was watching her intently, his gaze riveted on her mouth.

More heat flooded her face. Was he remembering their kiss? She turned to look at the fireplace. It was taking an eternity for the water to boil. But the way he was looking at her might indicate that he was now in the correct mood.

Steeling her nerves, she faced him and motioned toward the bed. "Please make yourself comfortable."

He surprised her by sitting at the table in front of the hearth. "Would you like to try one?" He opened the gold box.

She moved close to the table and studied the chocolates. They came in different shades of brown and three different shapes—round, square, and rectangular. Finally, she selected a round one and bit into it.

Instantly her mouth was filled with the richest, creamiest, sweetest sensation she'd ever tasted. "Oh my!" She licked her lips to keep drool from trickling out.

He smiled. "I guess you like it."

She nodded and put the rest of the piece in her mouth. It was truly heavenly. What other wondrous things from the outside world was she missing? She put the lid on the box, then turned back to the hearth to check on the water.

"So Frederic lived here?" Zoltan asked.

She nodded. "Frederic Chesterton."

"And his wife and daughters lived here, too?"

"No, the women live in . . . another valley."

"Why didn't he live with them?"

"It is one of our rules. No man is allowed in—" Neona glanced back with an apologetic look. "I guess our ways must seem strange to you."

"What about *your* family?"

Neona sighed, wishing the water would hurry up and boil. "I'd rather not talk about myself."

"It was my third condition, remember? We have to get to know each other."

She glanced back at him. Would he really refuse to bed her if she didn't tell him more about herself? Maybe a little information would be all right as long as she didn't disclose any secrets.

She wandered back to the table and opened the tin that contained tea leaves. "I never knew my father. He went back to Greece." Or did he? She spooned some tea leaves into the pot. "My mother is our leader. Queen Nima."

Zoltan's eyes widened, then he grinned. "So you really are a warrior princess?"

She scoffed. "No. I'm not in line for the throne."

"Why not?"

The kettle whistled, finally, and she hurried to the hearth, relieved for the brief respite from his questions. She wrapped a towel around her hand, then carried the hot kettle back to the table.

"Why can't you be queen?"

She poured steaming water into the teapot. "It's . . . complicated."

"Then explain. I have nowhere else to go." He gave her a wry smile. "And I'm seemingly intelligent."

Neona smiled in spite of herself. "Yes, you are." She set the lid on the pot to let the tea steep. "We all have special gifts, and I have the wrong one."

"How can a gift be wrong?"

Would the man never stop with the questions? She motioned toward the bed. "It's late. Perhaps we should . . . rest for a while?"

His eyes glimmered like glowing amber. "You keep trying to seduce me."

She swallowed hard. The way he was looking at her made her stomach quiver. "Don't you want to be seduced?"

His mouth curled up slowly. "I'm not in the mood yet." He patted the chair next to him. "Talk to me. I want to know what kind of gift you have and why it's wrong."

She eased into the chair, all too aware that his arm was now resting on the back of it. "I'm a healer. When I touch an injury, I can take away the pain and help it heal."

"That's an excellent gift."

"Not really. I have to feel the pain, too."

"Oh. That's bad." He sat up suddenly. "Is that why you had your hand on my pants? You were healing me?"

She nodded. "I needed you to be functioning properly."

"I see." His mouth twitched, then he gave her a wide-eyed, innocent look. "I'm afraid I'm still suffering from residual pain."

"From two nights ago?"

"You kneed me really hard. I could use your healing touch."

She narrowed her eyes. "I think you're lying."

"You're right." He grinned. "But it was worth a shot."

She smiled back.

"You have a pretty smile."

Her heart squeezed in her chest. *Don't fall for him. Just get this over with.* "So you're functioning properly now?"

"I'll be fine once I get in the mood."

How could such a strong, virile man be so slow? "Maybe I should touch you after all. To help you get in the mood." She reached for his groin, but he grabbed her hand.

"What kind of gift do you need to be queen?" he asked, encasing her hand in both of his.

She groaned silently with frustration. "Why do you need to know? You cannot be queen. You are a man." She pulled her hand from his grip and eyed his groin with suspicion. "That is, if you can ever get in the mood."

His jaw shifted. "I'm getting there. Just a few more questions. What kind of gift does the queen need?"

"She must be able to communicate with . . . winged creatures." Neona winced. Now she'd said too much.

Zoltan inhaled sharply. "You mean birds? Your mother can talk to birds?"

"Yes." She gave him a wary look. "That probably sounds strange."

"No. It doesn't." He gazed into the fire for a moment. "Are there other women in your group who have had that gift?"

"My twin sister, Minerva, did, but—" Neona tensed, afraid a wave of grief would sweep over her. She steeled her nerves and continued, "Winifred has the gift, so she will be the next queen."

Zoltan turned toward her. "You had a twin sister?"

"Let me see if the tea is ready." Neona jumped to her feet and grabbed the teapot. Her hands trembled, and some tea splashed onto the table.

"That's all right." Zoltan took the teapot from her and set it down. "I don't really need any tea."

She sat back down and clenched her hands together in her lap. "I think we've talked enough."

"You lost your sister?"

She nodded. "Two weeks ago."

"I'm so sorry." He reached over and took hold of her hands. "I've lost my loved ones, too."

She glanced at him and saw the pain shimmering in his golden amber eyes. "I'm sorry."

He squeezed her hands. "What happens if you get injured? Are you able to heal yourself?"

She shook her head. "There was another healer. Frederic's wife, Calliope. But she died about six years ago. I couldn't save her."

"And now you're on your own? You relieve everyone's pain, but there is no one to help you?"

Tears filled her eyes. "The pain I have cannot be healed."

"I know." He reached up and brushed her hair back from her brow. "But I would give you comfort if I can."

He was so tempting. *Oh, God, don't fall for him.* Her heart yearned for someone to hold her and care for her. But it couldn't be Zoltan. She had to have a daughter. She could hold and cherish a daughter.

But what if she had a son? Would Zoltan react like Frederic had when Calliope had given birth to a son? Frederic had waited till the boy was old enough for school, and then he'd taken him to England. He'd left his mate and daughters behind. Abandoned.

A tear rolled down her cheek. What if she fell in love with Zoltan? How could she bear to lose him? Good God, she could lose him and a son. The pain she was feeling now could triple. "I cannot do this." She jumped to her feet and ran for the door.

"Neona!"

She dashed outside, headed for the stream.

"Neona." Zoltan grabbed her arm to stop her. "What happened? Did I say something wrong?"

She shook her head. "You're not wrong. You're too right! I could fall for you."

"Would that be so bad?"

She broke away from his grip. "I don't want your heart. The only thing I wanted from you is a daughter!"

He stiffened. "What?"

"I told you. Men are not allowed here." Tears streamed down her cheeks as she backed away. "I wanted a daughter, but I changed my mind. It's too big of a risk. I can never see you again. Good-bye."

Chapter Seven

$\mathcal{S}$tunned, Zoltan watched her run along the stream with her pet leopard trotting behind her. All she had wanted from him was a daughter? Had she planned to bed him, then never see him again? Was he nothing more than a damned sperm bank?

A blast of anger surged through him. She was rejecting him without giving him a decent chance. Even more infuriating was the thought that she would have dismissed him from the start if she'd known the truth. She would have considered him entirely useless. Hell, she probably would have killed him. For the truth was his sperm was dead.

Dammit. He could give her jewels and gowns. Mansions and castles. He could give her pleasure. In time, he could have given her love. As a Vamp, he could even give her immortality. But she wanted the one thing he couldn't give. A child.

Rejected again. For the same damned reason. Over the centuries, he'd fallen for a few women. The affairs would last for a year or two, but they always ended the same way. The lure of immortality would fade, and then they always left him for a man who could give them children and grow old with them.

A few years back, something had happened that had given Zoltan hope that he could break the cycle of rejection. A brilliant Vamp scientist, Roman Draganesti, had figured out a way to insert their Vamp DNA into live human sperm. Now the Vamps with mortal wives were having kids like crazy. Technically, he could give Neona children, but it would require a trip to Romatech in New York, where Roman worked.

Zoltan wasn't sure she would ever agree to go there for the artificial insemination process. Roman could probably guarantee her a daughter if that was what she really wanted. But would she expect Zoltan to drop her and his daughter off in Tibet, never to see them again? He would not abandon her or his child, dammit!

And why the hell couldn't a woman want him for himself? Was he so damned unlovable that a woman could only want him for the children he might provide? He'd been rejected in the past for that, but he would not sit by and let it happen again. Not with Neona. She was different. Somehow, her fate was linked to his. They were connected. He wasn't sure how, but he knew in his gut that she belonged with him.

He charged toward Neona, using vampire speed to catch up with her. Six feet behind her, he slowed to a rapid walk.

The cat looked at him and snarled. *Get lost.*

No. He glared at Neona's back. "So that's it? You're giving up?"

The cat huffed. *Great idea, yelling at her. That will make her like you.*

Shut up, cat. "Talk to me, Neona. Why did you change your mind all of a sudden?"

She kept walking. "I decided it was unwise."

"Bullshit. You're afraid. What kind of warrior are you? I thought you were tougher than that."

She whirled to face him, her clenched hands raised and ready to punch him. "I beat you once. I can do it again."

"Then do it!" He spread his hands in surrender. "Tie me up and ravish me."

"I don't want to anymore!"

"Why not?" He stepped toward her. "Are you afraid you might develop feelings for me? God forbid you might feel close to me while I'm inside you."

She swung a fist at him, but he jumped back.

Oh, you're making fine progress, the cat sneered.

Sod off! "You know what really pisses me off?" He stepped closer. "That you see me as a damned sperm bank. There is more to me than my ability to father children. And there is a hell of a lot more to you than your ability to bear a child!"

She blinked, staring at him.

The cat hissed. *Stop yelling at her, or I'll claw your foot off.*

Not before I stuff it down your throat. Zoltan gave the cat an annoyed look, then lowered his voice and motioned back to the cabin. "Why don't we go back in and talk? I thought we were getting along very well."

She slowly lowered her fists. "I cannot be a . . . friend to you."

"Why not? I like you. I thought you liked me. We were getting to know each other. That's what couples do—"

"We cannot be a couple!"

"We can!" He grabbed her by the shoulders. "I'm not giving up on you."

A pained look crossed her face. "You have to. There is no future for us. Men are not allowed here."

"Why not?"

"They're not . . . necessary."

"Bullshit. Every community needs some men."

She broke his hold on her and stepped back. "Ours does not."

He scoffed. "How do you build your houses?" He gestured toward the cabin. "Didn't Frederic build this one?"

"He helped, but we know how to do it without a man. We built our own homes."

"What about protection? A man can pro—"

"We can protect ourselves."

Not against an army. But Zoltan didn't want to remind her of the recent death of her sister. It would be too cruel. "Men have a lot of uses."

She gave him a dubious look. "Really?"

"Of course. A man can . . . build a fire."

She shrugged. "I can do that."

"A man can provide food for his family."

"I am an excellent hunter."

"A man can till the soil and plow the field."

"We have a donkey."

He snorted. "You can't replace a man with a donkey. They are stubborn creatures who won't do as they're told."

Her brow arched. "And there's a difference?"

He gritted his teeth.

The cat yawned. *You stepped right into that one, moron. Go chew on your fleas.* Zoltan planted his hands on his hips. "A donkey doesn't have hands. He can't do repairs around the house. Or cook. Or clean."

"I can do those things myself."

"What about those ten climaxes you wanted? Are you going to do that yourself, too?"

She lifted her chin. "What makes you think I haven't?"

Dammit. Zoltan searched his brain. "I know! What if you can't open a jar? You'll need a man for that!"

Pathetic, the cat muttered.

She shrugged. "Our jars do not have lids. We tie a piece of fabric around—"

"What if you need a hug? And don't you dare mention that damned donkey!"

She laughed.

"There! You see. You need me around to make you laugh."

"Actually, the donkey has made me laugh a few times."

He scowled at her. "I refuse to compete with a donkey."

"You don't have to compete at all." Her face grew sad. "I shouldn't see you again."

"I'm not giving up on you." He stepped closer. "Who will listen to you in the middle of the night? Who will you share your secrets with?"

She gasped, her eyes widening. "Did you hear me?" She shook her head. "You couldn't have. I was alone."

"Hear what?"

"Nothing." Her eyes filled with tears.

"You're grieving for your sister, I understand that."

She closed her eyes briefly. "You don't understand how long we were together, or how long we will be apart."

The first part of her sentence struck him as odd, since he assumed she'd been with her twin for only about twenty-two years. But facing the rest of her life alone was clearly causing her pain.

When a tear rolled down her cheek, he smoothed it away with his thumb. "I could be with you for a very long time. Trust me." He kissed her cheek.

She trembled. "Men cannot be trusted."

"I would never hurt you. Trust me." He kissed her other cheek.

"Men cannot—"

He stopped her by planting his mouth on hers. She tensed at first, her hands splayed against his chest. But as he moved his lips gently and insistently, her fingers slowly dug into his jacket. He deepened the kiss, and with a moan, her mouth opened.

Yes. He explored her mouth, claiming it as his own. She would belong to him. This was no mistake. The arrow that had haunted him for almost eight hundred years had led him to her. She knew the answers he'd sought for so long. She'd touched his heart that had been cold for so long. Their fates were entwined, he could feel it in his bones. This was the woman he'd waited centuries for.

He scattered kisses across her face and down her neck. Her breaths grew quick and agitated. Her hands slipped up around his neck.

His groin hardened, and he debated how far he should go tonight. As much as he wanted to bed her, it didn't seem fair to take her when she believed the act would result in pregnancy.

But he could pleasure her. Give her one of those climaxes she wanted. He slipped his hand to the front of her tunic and palmed a breast. The silk was so thin that he could feel her nipple hardening.

"Neona," he whispered in her ear. "Let's go back to the cabin."

She leaned back, giving him a nervous look. "You're in the mood now?"

"Yes." He grasped her hips and pulled her tight against his erection.

She gasped. "You . . . you're vibrating."

"I am?" He glanced down, then realized the sat phone was buzzing in his pants pocket. *Dammit.* If he didn't answer, would Howard send Mikhail looking for him?

"Just a minute." He stepped back and retrieved the phone from the pocket. "Why the hell are you calling, Howard?"

"Good evening to you, too," Howard grumbled. "Russell showed up here out of the blue and insists you talk to him. I tried to get him to tell me what the problem is, but he said it had to be you. Something about an arrow."

Zoltan winced. He would have to go. "I'll be there in a few minutes." He hung up.

Neona eyed the phone curiously. "You were able to talk to someone far away?"

Had she never seen a phone? "Yes." He dropped the phone into his pocket. "I'm afraid I have to go."

She nodded and stepped back. "It's for the best. I shouldn't see—"

"Don't say that." He touched her shoulder. "I will return tomorrow night. Meet me at the cabin at midnight."

She regarded him sadly. "Good-bye, Zoltan." She turned and walked along the stream.

So long, loser. The cat trotted after her.

I will win her, cat. You can count on it. Zoltan watched her for a minute, then stepped behind some trees to teleport home.

Neona returned to the rock wall where the stream from Beyul-La jetted out in a waterfall. The rope ladder was there, but she realized she couldn't go home, not when she was still dressed in her finest clothes. With a sigh, she started back to Frederic's cabin, where she'd left her hunting clothes.

As she walked, she scanned the forest. Where had Zoltan gone to? The village? It was about fifteen miles away, with nothing but a footpath to show the way. Did he have a horse tethered in the next valley?

She shook her head. There was no point in thinking about him so much. Even if she did enjoy being in his arms. When he kissed her, she forgot all reason. Her heart swelled with such yearning that she could not hold him long enough. With an ache in her heart, she realized it had happened. She was falling for him. She wanted him.

But how could she ever have him?

She entered the cabin and let her gaze wander about the room. There was the embroidered banner he'd admired, the books he'd looked over, the gold box of chocolates he'd brought.

The tea had steeped too long, but she needed a strong drink. She drank as she tidied up the cabin, putting out the fire and hiding the gold box under some blankets in the wooden chest. She rinsed out the teapot and cup in the stream outside, then back in the cabin, she changed into her brown and green linen tunic and pants. She stashed her good clothes in her bag and swung it onto her back along with her quiver of arrows.

She grabbed her bow and headed back to the rock wall. Zhan joined her on the way.

She patted his head. "Zoltan had to leave. It's for the

best, I suppose. I should be grateful it didn't go any further." She could have loved him and lost him. She could have lost a son. Breaking off the relationship now was the only way to save herself from heartache. Then why did she feel so miserably sad and lonely?

While Zhan scampered up the rock wall, jumping from one ledge to another, she climbed the rope ladder. At the top of the wall, she pulled the ladder up. And the tears began. With each tug, she was sentencing herself to a long life of loneliness. There was no place for a man in her life. Zoltan might come tomorrow night, but she would not be there. Better to live lonely than risk shattering her heart.

She dropped the end of the ladder on the ground. It was done.

"How was the hunting?" a voice asked behind her.

The queen. Neona quickly wiped her face. "No luck tonight. I'll try again at dawn." She took a deep breath and faced her mother. "You're welcome to join us if you like."

"I'll be busy in the cave tomorrow." Queen Nima tilted her head, studying Neona. "Did you see anyone in our territory?"

Her stomach clenched. "No."

Nima gazed out into the neighboring valley. "The owl landed on my windowsill and told me there was an intruder."

Neona swallowed hard. Had her mother seen her walking about in her finest clothes?

"We must be extra vigilant," Nima continued, "especially now that we're in the beginning of a new cycle."

"I understand," Neona murmured.

"I fear Lord Liao will continue to search for our valley. He may have sent spies." Nima turned to look at her daughter. "If any man discovers our valley or our secrets, he must be executed."

Neona nodded. "Yes."

Her mother arched a brow. "The correct response is 'yes, your majesty.' Did you think I wouldn't notice that you have neglected to use my title for the past two weeks?"

Neona tamped down on a sudden surge of anger. "I have had other things on my mind."

"The death of your sister." Nima nodded. "I understand that you're hurting. That is why I have not reprimanded you for the lack of respect."

Neona scoffed. "And you are not hurting? Minerva was stabbed to death right in front of us!"

"We all risk death when we engage in battle. You know that. Now let us return to our homes." Nima started down the path to the base of the valley.

Neona's hands fisted. How dare her mother dismiss Minerva's death that easily. "We shouldn't have given away her baby!"

Nima halted and looked back, her eyes narrowing into slits. "That was seven years ago. What is done is done."

"It was never done for Minerva." Neona walked toward her mother. "She never recovered. If we had kept her baby, she would have fought harder. She would still be alive!"

Nima's eyes flashed with anger. "Do not make such ridiculous claims. Besides, there was no way her son could remain. Men are not allowed here."

"He was a baby! What harm could he have done?"

"He would still grow to be a man."

Neona motioned toward the neighboring valley. "You let Frederic live close by."

"And he was never allowed into this valley." Nima

made a sound of disgust. "He had two daughters with Calliope and still abandoned her. I should have killed him when I had the chance."

"That would have gone over well with his wife and daughters."

"Drop the sarcasm," Nima hissed. "We all know the rules and why we have them. Your insolence is appalling, but I will tolerate it this one time since you are in mourning."

How good of you, Neona bit back the words. Her anger grew as she watched her mother turn her back and walk away. "What happened to my father?"

Nima halted, her spine stiffening. "You go too far. I told you never to speak of him."

Neona approached her. "Did you kill him?"

Her mother turned to face her. "Hypocrisy does not suit you. We are warriors." She stepped closer. "How many men have you killed, Neona?"

"In the heat of battle, it is self-defense. We must kill in order to survive."

Nima's mouth twisted with a wry smile. "And what makes you think your father didn't fight back?"

Neona's gut churned. Killing men in battle was one thing, but killing a man after mating with him?

The queen patted Neona on the cheek. "Pull yourself together. Nothing matters except fulfilling our sacred duty."

"Minerva mattered."

Nima closed her eyes briefly with a pained look. "In the end, she was weak. Don't let that happen to you." She turned and walked down the path into the valley.

Neona remained behind with tears stinging her eyes. Zhan butted his head against her leg, and she crouched down beside him.

"Sacred duty," she muttered. All her life, she'd heard that nothing mattered except keeping the valley and its secrets safe. "Minerva mattered. Her son mattered."

And Zoltan mattered. Even though it hurt like hell, she could not see him again. He was venturing far too close to Beyul-La. Not only was her heart at risk. His life would be over if he was caught.

She hugged Zhan. "Love matters."

Chapter Eight

*W*hen Zoltan teleported into the kitchen, he found Russell seated at the table with Howard. There was a tense silence between the ex-Marine and werebear. A large box of donuts rested on the table, and Howard was working his way through them. In front of Russell, there was an open bottle of Blissky, a mixture of synthetic blood and whisky.

"Oh, there you are. I hope you don't mind, but I helped myself." Russell filled his glass and poured another one for Zoltan.

"What's going on?" Zoltan sat across from Russell.

"Do you want him to hear this?" Russell tilted his head toward Howard.

"I'm not leaving." Howard reached for a donut.

"Hear what?" Zoltan asked. "I was in the middle of something, so this had better—"

"It's important," Russell said. "Howard told me you were meeting an Amazon warrior tonight. So you found the women who made the arrow you took from me?"

"Yes." Zoltan leaned forward, his elbows on the table. "What can you tell me about them?"

"Not much. They're a secretive bunch." Russell downed his glass of Blissky. "They're in danger from Master Han."

"Why?" Zoltan and Howard asked at the same time.

"I don't know." Russell poured himself another glass. "I've been spying on Lord Liao for a while now. I can learn more from his camp because he and his soldiers complain to each other. At Master Han's camp, I can't get near him. He's too heavily guarded, and no one says anything there for fear that Han will kill them."

"Great guy," Howard muttered.

Russell nodded. "I overheard Lord Liao talking to his minions, and he's getting frantic. Apparently, Master Han said he doesn't miss the two vampire lords who were killed. And he bragged that he doesn't need the demon Darafer in order to take over the world. He says he can do it all by himself. So Liao is worried that his days are numbered if he can't prove his worth to Master Han."

"And he can prove his worth by attacking the women of Beyul-La?" Zoltan asked.

Russell's eyes widened. "Is that who they are? They wouldn't even tell me that much."

"Beyul-La?" Howard asked as he retrieved a cell phone from his pocket. "How do you spell it?"

"You won't find it online," Zoltan told him. "I already looked. It's a hidden valley in the Himalayas. I don't know why, but no men are allowed there. When I first approached the place, one of the women tried to kill me."

"Sheesh," Howard breathed. "What are they hiding there?"

Zoltan shrugged. "I don't know."

"Whatever it is," Russell said, "Master Han wants it. And Liao is determined to get it for him."

Zoltan winced. "There are only six of them now. They can't fight off an army of supersoldiers."

Russell nodded. "That's why I'm here. To see what we can do." He gave Howard an annoyed look. "I guess you'd better let Angus know about it."

"We could send a group to make first contact with them," Howard suggested. "Angus would go with—"

"They'll try to kill any man who approaches," Zoltan interrupted. "They don't believe men can be trusted."

Howard sat back, frowning. "But you've been meeting one of them?"

Zoltan nodded. "Neona."

"The healer?" Russell asked.

A spurt of anger jabbed at Zoltan, surprising him with its intensity. *Damn.* He was jealous that Russell had met her first. "How do you know her?"

"I hardly know her at all, so you can relax." Russell gave him a wry look.

Was he that obvious? Zoltan sat back, affecting a nonchalant look. "How did you meet her?"

"I spent a few months following Lord Liao around Tibet. He was asking villagers where he could find the hidden valley of warrior women. I guess the news got back to the women, because they attacked. They were outnumbered but were fighting so fiercely that I joined in to help." Russell downed his glass of Blissky and slammed it on the table. "I was so close to killing Liao, but the bastard teleported away. Then the rest of his army fled. I was wounded and lost consciousness. When I woke up, I was in a cabin. Frederic's cabin, they called it."

Zoltan nodded. "I know the place."

"I found out later that I had saved their queen's life, so they felt honor-bound to nurse me back to health," Russell continued. "They had borrowed some horses from a nearby village, and they used them to carry me and their dead back. I was unconscious in the cabin when the sun rose, so I started sizzling. They realized I was a vampire and shuttered all the windows."

Zoltan winced. "How did they feel about you being a Vamp?"

"When I woke up, they were staring at me like I was some kind of monster. Then they gave me a bowl of blood to drink." Russell grimaced. "It tasted awful. They'd gotten it from a donkey."

Howard chuckled.

Zoltan smiled to himself. The damned donkey was good for something.

Russell poured himself another glass. "They were amazed that my body had healed itself. The wounds from the battle and the burns from the sunlight had all disappeared, and their healer hadn't needed to do anything."

Zoltan nodded, relieved that Neona hadn't been forced to feel Russell's pain.

"They were shocked that I had taken their side in the battle." Russell swallowed some Blissky. "They know about vampires, but they thought we were all evil. I tried to explain that there's a group of good Vamps in the world who make it their goal to protect mortals. And I told them I was determined to kill Master Han myself. They liked that idea and thought I would be better suited for the task than them, since I'm also undead. So after I promised not to tell anyone about them, they let me go. I would have kept my word, but I'm worried about them being in danger."

"You did right by telling us," Zoltan assured him. "I'm worried about them, too."

"That arrow you wanted to know about—" Russell poured the last of the Blissky into his glass. "The healer gave it to me. Lord Liao killed her sister, so she asked me to use her arrow to kill him." He sipped from his glass. "If you still have the arrow, I'd like it back."

"I'll get it for you." As far as Zoltan knew, it was still stuck in the tree branch where he'd pinned the note.

Howard reached for a donut. "I think the warrior women will make good allies against Master Han."

Zoltan nodded. "I'll keep seeing Neona so I can gain her trust. And I'll convince the women that we're on their side. They're so outnumbered that they're going to need our help to defeat Lord Liao and Master Han."

"Sounds good." Howard bit into his donut. "And Russell needs to find out more information. We've got to know what Han and Liao want from these women."

"Will do." Russell finished his drink.

"Take a sat phone so we can call you," Howard added.

Russell scoffed. "No, thanks." He vanished.

"Dammit," Howard muttered and stuffed the rest of the donut in his mouth.

Zoltan pushed back his chair and stood. "I'll be going, too."

Howard jumped to his feet. "Where?"

"Upstairs to the library. Do I need permission?"

"No. But I want to talk to you about the tours. They're a huge security risk, so I'm wondering why you allow it to go on. From what I can tell, you don't need the money."

"I don't." Zoltan carried the empty glasses to the sink. "But the villagers do. The restaurant, hotel, and shops stay in business because of the tourists. And the ladies giving the tour make a nice salary. The guy who drives the bus makes a living for his family. The women who make the shawls and jewelry that are sold in the shops—"

"Okay, I get it." Howard raised his hands in surrender. "And you trust all those people to keep you safe?"

Zoltan tossed the empty Blissky bottle into the recycle bin. "It's worked for centuries. I keep them safe, and they return the favor."

"It only takes one unhappy villager to offer your story to the media for a tidy sum of money."

"And the other villagers will tell the media that he's crazy." Zoltan sighed. "Look. There will always be folktales about vampires, especially in this part of the world. If you tried to hush it up completely, it would only look suspicious. It's better to play along with it, like a joke no one really believes."

"I guess so." With a frown, Howard closed the box of donuts. "But it's still my job to keep you safe. How is your security in Budapest? Do you have bodyguards?"

"I have a butler and housekeeper who live there. They're husband and wife, and they're the only ones who know where the secret door to my bedroom is hidden. I keep the door locked and barred from the inside, so no one can enter unless I teleport inside and open the door."

"Another vampire could teleport inside."

Zoltan snorted. "They would have to know where the room is. And they're not going to teleport during the day because they're as dead as I am. Trust me,

Howard. My security system isn't high tech, but it works."

"I'll want to check it out personally."

Zoltan waved a hand dismissively. "Not tonight. Go see your poor neglected wife."

"She's not neglected!"

"Good night, Howard." Zoltan strode upstairs to the library off the Great Hall. He gave the bellpull a tug to let his steward, Milan's grandfather, know he was back in the castle. Then he paced about the room, thinking about everything Neona had told him.

Her mother, the queen, could communicate with birds. Neona's deceased sister had been able to, also, and another woman, Winifred, could. It seemed too big a coincidence that his own mother had possessed the same gift as three other women in Beyul-La. His mother had come from the East, so he suspected she had lived in Beyul-La. If so, how had his father managed to find her? How had he convinced her to come to Transylvania?

And then Neona had wanted Lord Liao killed with her arrow. Did the women have a long history of seeking revenge against those who had killed one of them? According to the few survivors in 1241, a group of fierce warriors and monsters had killed his father and most of the villagers before setting the buildings ablaze. Had those warriors been the women of Beyul-La? Were they the monsters, or had there been something else with them? How had they traveled such a long distance? How had they disappeared afterward with no trace other than the one arrow embedded in his father's chest?

"My lord." Domokos knocked on the door.

"Come." Zoltan had tried years ago to convince Milan's grandfather not to address him so formally. But as far as Domokos was concerned, Zoltan was a count from an ancient line of counts, so all the servants had to give him the respect he was due.

Domokos entered with a tray laden with a warm bottle of blood and a wineglass, which he set on the table in front of the hearth. "Would you like a fire, my lord?"

"No. I'm fine, thank you."

Domokos opened the bottle and poured until the wineglass was half full. When his hand shook, Zoltan moved forward to help him.

"Allow me, my lord." Domokos set the bottle down and regarded Zoltan with tear-filled eyes. "May I say how honored we are over Milan's promotion. His success wouldn't have been possible if you hadn't paid for his education and taken him under your wing. He will do his best to make you proud."

"I'm sure he will. Thank you, Domokos. That will be all for this evening."

"Yes, my lord." Domokos bowed his head and hobbled to the door.

When had he started to walk like that? And when had his hair turned silver? "Domokos."

"Yes, my lord?"

Zoltan hesitated. How long had Domokos been his steward? Thirty or forty years? "Are you watching out for your health? You can retire whenever you like at full pay. Just let me know."

He smiled. "I know, my lord. There are enough servants here that all I really do is supervise. I choose to do this one chore every evening, since it is my pleasure to serve you in person."

Even after eight hundred years, Zoltan could get caught off guard by the loyalty of those mortals who surrounded him. True, he took care of them the best he could, but they seemed more of a blessing to him than he deserved. "I am the grateful one, Domokos. You've taken care of me for . . . years."

Domokos's eyes twinkled with amusement. "Sixty years, my lord."

Zoltan blinked. "That long?"

Domokos grinned. "Yes, my lord. Good night."

"Good night, Domokos." Zoltan watched him close the door. Sixty years? How did time pass by so quickly? Working five years with Milan had felt like five months. Apparently he'd become such a workaholic that years were zooming by him unnoticed.

Something nagged in the back of his mind. The six women of Beyul-La. He'd seen them from a distance while they'd sat around the fire, eating. They had all appeared young, most probably in their twenties, but that couldn't be right. One of them was the queen and Neona's mother.

He strode to his desk and turned on the computer. He needed more information. Something concrete that he could investigate. Maybe Frederic?

He sat down and typed Frederic Chesterton in the search box. To his surprise, there were several articles. Frederic Chesterton had been one of the members of a doomed British expedition to the Himalayas. They'd planned to map a northern approach to Mount Everest, but the team had gotten lost in a sudden snowstorm in Tibet. In 1922.

Zoltan's mouth dropped open. This couldn't be right. He kept reading. A surprising development had occurred in 1933 when a man calling himself Frederic Chesterton arrived in England with a six-year-old boy. His surviving family accepted him back, claiming he truly was Frederic Chesterton. He'd aged eleven years but had no memory of that time. When newspaper reporters tried to interview him, he told them he had suffered from amnesia and couldn't tell anyone where he had been or who had given birth to his son.

Zoltan swallowed hard. According to Neona, Frederic had fathered two daughters with Calliope. But if the two girls were born in the 1920s, they would be elderly by now. And all the women of Beyul-La looked young.

A chill ran down his back. Was the myth of Shangri-La based on fact? Was Beyul-La a valley where no one grew old?

He recalled the words Neona had said about her sister. The sentence had seemed odd at the time, but he'd figured it was her grief that had been coloring her words. Now he wondered if her grief had actually caused her to be honest.

You don't understand how long we were together, how long we will be apart. Was Neona facing an eternity without her twin? Was that why she sat crying by her sister's grave in the middle of the night? And how long had they been together before her sister's death?

A memory flashed through his mind of his first sighting of Neona. She'd been dressed in armor, looking like an ancient Greek soldier sacking Troy.

"Good God," he whispered. How old was Neona?

Chapter Nine

$\mathcal{T}$ he next evening after sunset, Zoltan quickly showered and dressed. He was eager to see Neona but nervous about asking her about her age. Normally that would be considered rude, but in this case, it might be cause for murder.

She'd tried to kill him the first time they'd met, and she'd mentioned several times that men were not allowed there. So he assumed the women were guarding a secret they couldn't trust with anyone else. Eternal life would fit the bill.

Was that what Master Han and Lord Liao were looking for? As vampires they already enjoyed the possibility of eternal life, but maybe they thought the women's secret would enable them to live during the day. That would give them a huge advantage over the Vamps who were dead and vulnerable during the day. If Master Han possessed the secret, he could rule the vampire world.

It would also give him a tremendous amount of power over mortals, since he could decide who received the gift of eternal life and who didn't. He would be a god among mortal men.

Zoltan walked into the kitchen for a quick meal and found Howard seated at the kitchen table, polishing off his box of donuts.

"You're going back to see your girl, right?" Howard pushed a sat phone and a knife across the table. "Neona was her name?"

"Yes." Zoltan dropped the sat phone into his pocket but ignored the knife. How could he win her trust if he arrived with a weapon?

"I e-mailed a report to Angus. He agrees with us."

Zoltan finished his glass of blood. "Where is Angus now?"

"Still in London with Emma."

Zoltan walked over to the fridge while he considered. "Can you ask Angus to check on something for me?"

"Sure. What is it?"

"I want to know what happened to a guy named Frederic Chesterton. He may be dead by now, but his son might be alive and remember something."

"Remember what?" Howard asked.

"Something from the first six years of his life."

Howard frowned. "Does this Frederic own the cabin Russell mentioned?"

"He lived there for eleven years." Zoltan slipped a plastic bag of blood into one of his jacket pockets and zipped it shut. "I should be going now."

Before Howard could object, Zoltan teleported back to the clearing where he'd first met Neona. She was almost four hours ahead of him, so midnight would come soon. He levitated up to the tree branch to retrieve the arrow Russell wanted back, then hurried down the mountainside to Frederic's cabin in the valley.

It was an idyllic place. Green meadows, forested

hillsides, a gurgling mountain stream, and the waterfall shooting out of Beyul-La. He could see why Frederic Chesterton had stayed for eleven years. Especially if he'd been in love with one of the women.

As Zoltan approached the cabin, his heart beat faster. No woman had ever intrigued him as much as Neona did. She was such a fascinating mixture—tough but innocent, fierce yet tender. Beautiful, but totally unaware of it. He'd never met someone who needed love as much as she did. She was a lonely soul like him and, he suspected, an old soul as well.

Somehow their paths were connected. He'd felt that from the beginning. She held the answers to the mysteries from his past. And he was becoming more and more certain that she was his future. He just needed to convince her.

He would hold her in his arms and woo her with kisses. He would gain her trust. And her love. The prospect made his heart pound with anticipation.

He strode into the cabin. "Neona?"

His heart sank. The cabin was empty.

Was he waiting for her? Neona glanced up at the moon, which was three-quarters full in the clear starry sky. Zoltan had said he'd meet her at midnight, but she didn't have a way to know the exact time. Her contact with the outside world was so limited that she'd never needed to keep track of time.

She'd seen a clock before. Frederic had owned a pocket watch that he'd given to Calliope before leaving. Freddie was the proud owner now, even though the watch had broken years ago.

Neona wandered over to the grassy mound where

Calliope was buried. Moonlight glistened on the long grass, lending it a silvery hue. A breeze blew down the mountainside, rustling the trees that flourished higher up the hill.

"I miss you," Neona whispered to the other healer.

Calliope had died six years ago when the new cycle had started. Her death had devastated her three daughters. The oldest daughter, Farah, fathered by a Persian long before Frederic's arrival, now lay buried next to Calliope. Farah had died two weeks ago in the battle that had claimed five of the women of Beyul-La. Only Winifred and Freya remained from Calliope's line.

Neona paused in front of Farah's grave, bowing to pay her respects before moving on to the mound where her sister was buried.

"Minerva." She sat next to the mound. "I had the dream again last night." It seemed like the memory should have faded with time, but she could still see the injured boy so clearly in her mind. He'd remained unconscious the entire time she'd treated him. He'd taken some harsh blows to the head, some gashes to his shoulders, and a nasty burn down his back. "Why do I keep dreaming about him? And that terrible day?"

No answer.

Neona sighed. "It must be a reminder of what happens when one of us shirks our sacred duty to follow a man."

She gazed up at the stars. As much as she wanted Zoltan to be different, she couldn't allow herself to trust him. If she continued to see him, she would be putting the secrets of Beyul-La at risk. She could end up destroying everything if she wasn't careful.

"I know I mustn't go to him." But what if Zoltan was waiting for her?

She imagined him pacing in front of Frederic's cabin. Would he become angry, like he had last night? Would he feel betrayed when she didn't come?

The thought made her heart ache. She didn't want to cause him pain. By nature, she was a healer. She took pain away; she didn't cause it. But because she was one of the guardians of this valley and its secrets, she'd also been trained to be fierce in battle. She knew how to be ruthless when her own life was hanging in the balance.

Now it was her heart that was at stake, so she had to be ruthless where Zoltan was concerned. And she had to be honest with herself. She was hopelessly attracted to the man. It would be far too easy to fall in love with him.

"Why am I so drawn to him? I hardly know anything about him. Where does he come from? Why is he so curious about me?" She mentally ticked off what she did know about him. Handsome, brave, quick, strong, intelligent, honorable, charming, sweet.

She winced. How could she not fall for such a man? He'd tried to save her life when he'd thought she was in danger from Zhan. Noble and protective, she added those to her list. Then she smiled, remembering how offended he'd been when she'd told him men were unnecessary. There was a vulnerability to him in spite of his strength. He seemed to need love as much as she did.

"Did I tell you that he kissed me again?" Neona whispered, then closed her eyes, letting the memory of last night's kiss flood over her. He'd been so sweet, so tender, and incredibly exciting because beneath it all she had sensed a fiery passion ready to burst into flames and consume her. He'd pulled her tight against him, and she'd felt his swollen manhood, large and straining against the confines of his pants.

If she went to him tonight, she might end up in bed with him. Skin touching. Arms embracing. Legs entwined. The images racing through her mind made her heart pound, made her yearn to give in to desire.

But it was too dangerous. She knew deep inside that bedding Zoltan would change her irreparably. He would take her heart along with her body.

She couldn't let that happen. For both their sakes. How could she live with herself if she encouraged his affections and he was killed because of it? Each time he invaded their territory, his life was in danger.

"I mustn't go to him." She pulled her knees up and hugged them. It was the right decision. The wise decision. So why did she feel like screaming in frustration?

A twig snapped behind her, and she instantly pulled the knife from the sheath strapped to her calf, then turned to look.

It was Zhan, emerging from the forest.

"Oh, it's you." She slipped the knife back into its sheath. "I was wondering where you'd gone off to."

The snow leopard drew closer, moving from the shadows into the moonlight.

She sat up, noticing the arrow gripped in Zhan's mouth. It looked like the arrow that had pinned Zoltan's note to the tree branch.

Her eyes narrowed on the folded piece of paper stuck on the arrowhead. "Did you just come from Zoltan?"

Zhan dropped the arrow at her feet, and she huffed in indignation. "You rascal. Whose side are you on?"

Zhan sat, curling his tail around his front paws as he gazed intently at her.

She nudged the arrow away with her leather slipper. "I don't want this. And I can't believe you went to see him."

Zhan continued to stare at her.

Her gaze drifted to the note. Blast that man. He knew her curiosity would get the better of her.

"Fine. I'll read it." She pulled the note off. "But that doesn't mean I'll go see him. My mind is already made up. He can beg all night, and it won't affect me in the least."

Zhan blinked at her slowly.

"Traitor," she muttered and opened the note.

Neona,

I have taken over this valley and the cabin. This territory is now mine.

"What?" She read the first two sentences again to make sure she hadn't imagined it. "He can't take over our territory!"

No women are allowed here. If you attempt to invade my territory, I will attack. I advise you to stay away.

Zoltan

Neona scoffed. The gall of the man! "He advises *me* to stay away? From my own land!"

She jumped to her feet, wadding the note up in her fist. "How dare he! I'll show—" She stopped with a sudden thought, then gave Zhan an incredulous look. "He's doing this on purpose, isn't he? He knows this will make me come to him."

She jammed his note into the drawstring pouch

that dangled from the sash tied around her waist. "The fool. He thinks to manipulate me? This ridiculous game will get him killed! If any of the other women catch him in the neighboring valley, they will execute him on the spot."

Leaving the arrow behind, she stalked toward the ridge where the rope ladder lay in waiting. And to think that just moments ago, she'd been listing his finer points. Ha! She would add stubborn, manipulative, and sneaky to the list.

"I will not fall for this outrageous ploy of his. I will force him to leave, even if I have to tie him up and haul him like unwanted baggage to the nearest village."

She dropped the rope ladder over the ridge.

Zhan scampered down the rock wall, then ran toward the cabin.

As she started down the ladder, her heart pounded so loudly that it thundered in her ears. It was only anger, she told herself. She was not excited about seeing him again. The tightness in her chest was annoyance, not yearning.

When the cabin came into view, she stopped, her heart lurching at the sight of smoke curling from the chimney. He had made himself at home. As if he belonged here. With her.

Tears blurred her vision, and she quickly blinked them away. She mustn't let him know how badly he tempted her. If he knew, he would never leave. And he had to leave before he was captured and killed.

Did you bring the food? the young snow leopard asked as it darted into the cabin.

Yes. Zoltan set the plastic container on the floor.

Smells good. The cat started eating. *Mmmm.*

Is she coming? Zoltan asked as he peered through the open door. The cat made a noise he interpreted as affirmative.

After pacing about an empty cabin for thirty minutes, Zoltan had finally acknowledged that Neona wasn't coming. Luckily, he'd heard her pet lurking nearby, so he'd made a deal with it. Deliver a note to Neona, and he would supply the cat with a delicious meal. When Zhan had scampered off with the arrow and note, Zoltan had teleported home and raided the kitchen pantry for several cans of tuna. He'd tossed the tuna into a plastic container and teleported back.

Anger battled with apprehension as he waited for Neona. Part of him was afraid of losing her. Another part was furious that she'd refused to see him. Was he that damned easy to reject?

He spotted her in the moonlight, moving quickly along the stream, determination in every stride.

He stepped just outside the door and glanced at his watch. "You're forty-seven minutes late."

She halted a distance away from him, eyeing him with a wary look. "I have no way of telling time."

Of course. He should have realized that. "I'll bring you a watch tomorrow."

She scoffed. "I don't intend to see you tomorrow. I wasn't going to see you tonight. I only came because of that stupid note—"

"I'll bring you a watch tomorrow," he repeated. "Is there anything else you would like? Some books, perhaps?"

A pained look flitted across her face before she shuttered her expression, but it was long enough to verify that he'd made a good guess at something she secretly yearned for.

She shook her head. "I cannot accept presents from you. How would I explain it to the other women?"

"Don't explain it. Hide them under your bed. You're good at keeping secrets, aren't you?"

Her eyes narrowed. "So are you. I have no idea where you come from." She walked toward him. "You're not Chinese or Tibet—"

"Don't come any closer." He held up a hand to stop her. "This is my cabin now, and women are not allowed."

"That is ridiculous! *Men* are not allowed, and that includes you. Do you really think you can steal our cabin by simply saying it is yours?"

"Isn't that what you've done? Can you prove this land is yours? Just because your people have lived here for a long time doesn't make it yours. Do you have a deed?"

Her eyes widened with a look of alarm. He made a mental note to check the legal ownership of this land. If the women didn't own it, he would make sure they did. It would be a good way to earn their trust.

She lifted her chin. "I did not come here to argue with you. I want you to leave. Immediately."

He leaned against the doorjamb and crossed his arms. "No."

She made a sound of frustration. "If any of the other women see you, they will not hesitate to kill you. You must leave tonight and never come back."

"Are you trying to protect me?" He straightened. "Is that why you're rejecting me?"

"I'm rejecting you because you're insufferable!" She leaned down to whip the knife from the sheath strapped to her leg, then pointed it at him. "Leave now."

"Make me."

She glowered at him. "Fine." She threw the knife, and it spun through the air before lodging with a thunk in the door frame beside him. "Take that as a warning. Next time I aim for your chest."

He glanced at the knife. She'd missed his shoulder by less than a foot. After a few seconds of alarm, he'd realized her trajectory was off, so he'd stood his ground.

He gave her a wry look. "Now you see why I can't allow women here. One small disagreement, and you become violent. Obviously women can't be trusted."

She huffed. "It is men who cannot be trusted."

"You let Frederic live here for eleven years. I try to stay one measly night and you throw a knife at me?"

"I'm trying to save your life, you fool!"

"Now you're calling me names." Zoltan heaved a sigh. "Poor Frederic. Did he suffer abuse like this?"

She gritted her teeth. "Men cannot be trusted. We thought Frederic was different, but even he betrayed us in the end."

"He didn't betray you."

"He did! He broke Calliope's heart when he left."

"He never betrayed you. He told everyone he had no memory of where he had been or who had given birth to his son."

Neona's eyes widened. "How do you know about his son?"

"That's the reason he left, isn't it? He didn't want his son forced to live here as a prisoner to your damned secrets."

"We-we're not prisoners," she whispered, then shook herself visibly. "How do you know all this? Do you know Frederic?"

"I saw it on the Internet."

She frowned. "What is that?"

"Information. What I really found interesting was that Frederic returned in 1933. About eighty years ago. And yet you claim he taught you English."

Neona stiffened, her face turning white.

"How do you do it? Is it a special plant that grows only in your valley? Is it in your food? Your water?"

"*Stop!*" She ran toward him and placed her hand over his mouth. "Don't say the words. Please." Tears glistened in her eyes.

He took her hand in his. "Neona."

A tear slipped down her face. "Don't say the secret out loud. If you do, I'll be honor bound to . . ."

"To what?" He searched her eyes. "Do you really think you can kill me?"

She pulled her hand from his and yanked the knife from the door frame. "Don't push me. You already know too much." She pointed the knife at his chest. "Leave. Now. *Please.*"

Damn if she didn't have the tip right over his heart. He tensed, ready to grab her with vampire speed. "No."

She pressed enough to cut a hole in his jacket but not enough to draw blood. "Leave."

"No."

Another tear fell down her cheek. "I don't want you here."

"Liar."

She skimmed the tip of the blade down his shirt, past his belt to his jeans. "Leave." The tip scraped against the metal zipper.

He winced. "What happened to the daughter you wanted? And those ten climaxes?"

"I told you. I changed my mind."

"Then I'll change it back." When she glanced up at him, he made his move, wrenching the knife from her hand and spinning her around so that he held her with one arm locked around her middle, the other around her shoulders with the knife pressed to her neck.

She gasped. "How did you move so fast?"

He nestled his cheek against hers and whispered in her ear, "Do you know why I keep refusing to leave?"

"Because you're a stubborn fool?"

"That may be true, but should you say that when I have a knife to your throat?"

"I don't think you'll hurt me."

"Ah. Maybe you trust me after all."

"No." She trembled when he nuzzled her ear.

"The reason I refuse to leave"— he planted kisses along her cheek—"is that I want you. I want to be your mate and cherish you forever."

"It's not possible," she whispered.

"We'll make it possible." He slid the flat edge of the knife down her crossover tunic and sliced through the ribbon that tied it shut at her breasts. "Don't you feel it, Neona? I was meant to find you. To court you. To love you."

She shuddered. "Please . . ."

"And you were meant to be mine." He nudged the knife under her sash and sliced right through it. She gasped as her tunic fell open.

"Neona." He tossed the knife aside and slipped his hand inside her tunic, splaying his hand against her bare skin. Her rib cage heaved with each breath.

He kissed a trail down her neck. "Spend the night with me. Spend every night with me."

A moan escaped her. "Don't you understand why I want you to leave?"

"You're worried one of your friends will kill me."

"Yes! They already suspect me. An owl reports to

my mother every time you come here. I cannot allow you to risk your life just to see me."

"You care about me, don't you?"

She shook her head. "We cannot be together."

"We can. Let me love you." He slid his hand up to cup her breast.

She gasped. "How can I trust you? I know so little about you."

"You know you want me." He gently kneaded her breast, then ran his tongue along the curve of her ear. "Let your desire be greater than your fear."

With a cry, she turned to face him and grabbed his jacket with her fists. "If you break my heart, I will kill you myself."

"You have a deal." He swung her up in his arms and strode inside the cabin.

Stand guard for us, he ordered the cat, then kicked the door shut after the leopard ran outside.

Chapter Ten

She was still afraid, Neona acknowledged as Zoltan stretched out on the bed beside her, but her desire had overpowered her fear. She needed to feel loved in a way that only Zoltan could give her. The way he touched her as if she was a rare treasure, the way he looked at her like he hungered for her soul, the way he kissed her as if they could melt together and become one.

He was kissing her now. Touching her. Making her stomach quiver and her heart race. She wrapped her arms around him, wanting more. More. Why was she so desperate? Was she falling in love? Or so starved for affection that she was fooling herself?

She shivered as he nibbled down her neck. "Zoltan."

"Mmm?"

"This is happening so quickly. Is that . . . normal?"

He propped himself up on an elbow and looked at her. For a second, his eyes appeared red and glowing, and she tensed. But after he blinked, they resumed their usual amber color. It must have been a reflection from the fire blazing in the hearth.

"I'll go as slowly as you want." He brushed her hair back from her brow. "I know it's hard for you to trust me."

"I'm not sure I can trust myself. I'm hurting so much from losing my sister, I may be desperate to feel love."

He frowned. "If that were the case, then you could go to the nearest village and pick any—"

"No, I couldn't." She'd seen many male villagers over the course of her life, and none of them had attracted her like Zoltan. She touched his cheek. "They're not you."

He turned his head to kiss her palm. "If your sister were still alive, would you feel differently about me?"

She grazed her fingertips along his whiskers. "No. I would feel the same." So her fear was groundless. She would have known that earlier if she could have talked it through with her sister.

Her heart squeezed in her chest. From now on, it would be Zoltan whom she entrusted with her innermost thoughts and feelings. "No man has ever affected me the way you do."

A corner of his mouth curled up. "That's good. 'Cause I'm crazy for you."

"Crazy?"

"I'll try to explain myself better." He skimmed a finger down her nose. "I think about you all the time. You're the most beautiful, brave, and intriguing woman I've ever met." He ran his finger over her lips. "I want to bring joy back into your life. Whenever I feel that your heart is aching, my heart aches with you."

She sucked in a breath. How could she have questioned her feelings for this man? "I want you so much, I feel like my heart will burst. How can you be so perfect?"

He winced. "I'm not. There are things about me . . . you may not like."

"I know. You're a little slow to get in the mood." She raked her fingers through his long, soft hair. "But we can work on that."

His jaw shifted.

She wound a strand of his hair around her finger. "You're also incredibly stubborn, but I like that, because it made you refuse to give up on me."

"That is true. I will not give up on you. I will not betray you, nor abandon you."

God, how she wanted to trust him. Was it as simple as this? A leap of faith? She wrapped her arms around his neck. "Then take me, Zoltan. Make love to me." She glanced down at his pants. "When you're ready, that is."

With a growl, he pressed himself against her.

"Oh." Her breath caught. He was definitely ready.

He peeled her tunic open and gazed at her breasts. She shivered under the heated look. Were his eyes turning red again? Before she could get a closer look, he leaned over her and teased a nipple with his tongue.

She gasped. "Oh! I didn't realize—" She cried out when he sucked her nipple into his mouth.

"Zoltan." She dug her fingers into his scalp.

He continued to suckle her, then grazed his whiskers across her chest to the other nipple.

Her thighs squeezed together as a deep yearning settled between her legs. Heat sizzled along her veins, making her want to throw off her clothes. She pulled at his jacket—

He sat up suddenly, his head turned toward the door.

She scrambled onto her knees and tugged at his jacket. "Take it off."

"Wait." He ran to the door as a flurry of scratching noises sounded outside. "They're coming."

"What?"

He opened the door and her cat raced inside, hissing.

"They're coming!" He stepped outside to grab her sash and knife.

"Zoltan!" She leaped out of bed. "You must leave!"

He slammed the door shut, bolted it, and handed her the knife. While she slipped it back into the sheath attached to her leg, he quickly knotted her sash together. "Put this back on and tie it over the other knot so it won't show."

She grabbed the sash. "Stop worrying about me. Get out of here now."

He looked about the room. "I don't want you to be in trouble."

"Zoltan, they'll kill you if they find you here." She quickly tied the sash. "Go out the back window now!"

He grabbed one of Frederic's books off the wooden chest and handed it to her. "Tell them you couldn't sleep and came here for a book. You were reading in bed."

Voices shouted outside, followed by the screeching sound of swords being pulled from their sheaths.

Panic seized Neona, and she shoved Zoltan toward the back window.

"I'll be fine," he whispered, pausing to grab the plastic container of food off the floor.

A fist pounded on the door.

"Neona!" the queen shouted. "Open this door!"

"Just a minute." Neona made sure Zoltan was at the back window before she slid the bolt. She cracked open the door. "Is there a problem?"

Queen Nima flung open the door, and Neona

jumped back. She glanced over her shoulder, but Zoltan was gone.

"Who was here?" the queen demanded as she circled the room, her sword drawn and ready.

Neona lifted the book in her hands. "I was just—"

"No one outside." Winifred paused in the doorway.

"Did you check this window?" Nima pointed her sword at the back window.

"I did." Freya stepped into view outside and peered at them through the open window. "I was here waiting, but no one came out."

Nima frowned at her daughter. "What are you doing here? Why does the owl keep telling me there's an invader?"

Neona swallowed hard. "I've been having trouble sleeping." At least that much was true. "I shared my house with Minerva for so long, and now she's not there. So I came here, thinking a book might help."

Her mother's eyes narrowed with suspicion.

Freya gave her a sympathetic look. "I'm sure it's hard on you. I don't know what I'd do if I lost Freddie."

Winifred nodded. "It was bad enough to lose our mother and Farah."

Queen Nima surveyed the room, then sighed. "We had the cabin surrounded. We would have seen someone leaving." She shook her head. "I don't know what's wrong with that owl lately. Freddie, put the fire out, then you and Freya take a quick look through the woods."

"Yes, your majesty," the two women murmured.

"Neona, take the book home with you. No more leaving the valley in the middle of the night."

Neona followed her mother out the door, with Zhan trotting alongside her. She glanced toward the woods, wondering if Zoltan was running to the nearest village. He had a good head start, so he should be able to arrive without Freddie or Freya catching him.

But they had surrounded the cabin. She glanced back at the house. How had Zoltan managed to escape?

Zoltan watched from the top of a tree as Neona accompanied her mother back to the rope ladder. Two of the warrior women were below, searching the hillside.

A sour taste of self-disgust lodged in his throat. He felt like a damned coward, leaving Neona alone to handle the fallout. But she would have been in a lot more trouble if he had stayed. Not to mention the fact that they had looked ready to skewer him first and talk later. These women took their no-men-allowed rule seriously. Before he made himself known to them, he would need to prove that he was on their side.

He teleported straight to the library in his castle, then called Milan to have him investigate the area in Tibet where the women of Beyul-La lived.

"We need to safeguard the area for them, make it off limits to any outside development," he told Milan as he e-mailed the coordinates from the GPS tracker on his cell phone. "Get as much surrounding territory as you can."

"I understand," Milan answered. "You realize this could cost in the millions?"

"Yes, I know. Keep me apprised." Zoltan hung up and called Angus. "Were you able to track down Frederic Chesterton?"

"Aye," Angus replied. "He died here in London during a bombing raid in the second human world war. I've located his son, Franklin, and he's agreed to meet me tomorrow. I was going to call to see what ye wanted me to ask him."

"You'll have to be careful. Franklin may not remember anything from the first six years of his life. If he's who I think he is, his mother was one of the warrior women of Beyul-La. Calliope. She died six years ago. He has sisters, Winifred and Freya, who are still alive. If he remembers them, he might enjoy hearing about them."

"Verra well. I'll use some mind control first to see what he remembers before proceeding." Angus paused. "Howard told me what he knows, that these warrior women are hiding something that Master Han and Lord Liao want. Any idea what it could be?"

Zoltan paused, not ready to divulge his suspicion that the women had some sort of fountain of youth. Neona's strong reaction had seemed to confirm it. "I'm working on it. And working on gaining Neona's trust. I was wondering if Emma would be—"

Angus chuckled. "We were thinking the same thing. Since they doona trust men, we could send our own warrior woman. Emma's ready to go."

"Good. I'll let you know when." Zoltan hung up, then paced about the library. He gave the bellpull a tug so Domokos could bring his late-night bottle of warmed-up blood.

As he wandered about the room, he wondered how to go about making a good first impression on the women of Beyul-La. Gifts, perhaps? But what would they like? He thought back to what Neona had said about the long winters. They made their clothes. Should he give them some bolts of silk? Some embroidery thread? They also practiced their fighting skills every day.

Of course! Weapons. He had some new hunting knives in the armory they might like. And perhaps a supply of arrows? Some new swords?

What else? His gaze drifted across the bookshelves in his library. The books in Frederic's cabin were practically falling apart from heavy use.

He sat at his desk, and on the computer, he located an online bookseller. But what to buy? Apparently, the women had enjoyed *Ivanhoe* and *A Tale of Two Cities*, so he ordered a few books by Sir Walter Scott and Charles Dickens. And Neona had said *Pride and Prejudice* was her favorite, so he bought some other works by Jane Austen.

Domokos shuffled inside and set his tray on the table by the hearth. "Is there anything else I can do for you, my lord?"

"No, I'm fine. There should be a package arriving tomorrow. Books."

"Yes, my lord." Domokos filled a wineglass with synthetic blood.

"Do you know of any authors similar to Jane Austen?"

"Excuse me?"

"I need some books like *Pride and Prejudice*."

"Ah." Domokos gave him a curious look. "Have you taken a sudden interest in Regency England?"

"I'm buying some gifts," Zoltan muttered. "I need to make friends with a group of women."

"Women?"

"You heard me." Zoltan gave his steward an annoyed look as the old man brought the wineglass to him. "Any ideas?"

"My wife likes to read historical romance novels."

Domokos handed him the wineglass. "I believe they are quite similar."

"All right. I'll get some of those." He took a long drink.

"My wife is also particularly fond of vampire romance."

Zoltan swallowed so hard that his eyes watered. "Are you serious? Do people really write those? And read them?"

"I'm afraid so, my lord. They appear to be quite popular."

"Why?" Zoltan set the glass down. "We're dead half the time. And until recently, we couldn't father children."

Domokos's mouth twitched. "I believe the writers are focusing on your other attributes, my lord."

Zoltan gazed at him blankly.

Domokos cleared his throat. "Your prowess in the bedchamber, my lord."

His eyes widened. "How would they know what I'm doing in bed?"

"They don't, my lord. It's fiction."

"Oh. Right."

"Although they do seem to make the heroes all extremely gifted and well endowed. With skills that are quite legendary." Domokos shrugged. "Like I said, it's fiction."

Zoltan's jaw shifted. "Right."

Domokos's eyes twinkled with amusement. "Is there anything else I can do for you, my lord?"

"No." Zoltan gave him a wry look. "You've helped enough."

"Then I'll wish you a good evening, my lord." Domokos bowed and hobbled toward the door.

"Fiction," Zoltan muttered as he searched through the top-selling books in historical romance. He added a few more books to the shopping cart, then paid extra for one-day delivery.

Books and weapons. What else could he bring as a peace offering? It felt like he was forgetting something. Given the fact that Lord Liao was searching for them, he was tempted to equip them with short-range missiles.

He finished his bottle of blood, then took it and the wineglass to the kitchen. There, he left a note for Howard on top of his donut box.

Castle tour this afternoon, so I'm sleeping in Budapest. Will return after sunset.

Sheesh, the damned bear was training him to report in. He went to the armory and selected half a dozen hunting knives and swords, plus a box of arrows. He left them on the table, then teleported to the library in his townhouse. There he paced about restlessly, wishing he were still with Neona. *Make love to me,* she'd urged him. Would she still be that eager when she learned he was a vampire?

He pushed that thought aside and focused instead on how wonderful she'd felt in his arms. Firm, muscular, sweetly rounded. Whatever her age was, she looked like she couldn't be more than twenty-five.

Her armor had made her appear like an ancient Greek soldier. Had the armor come from her father? When had a Greek army traveled that far east?

He turned on his computer and did a search. Alexander the Great had reached as far as India before his army had rebelled, demanding to return home.

Had one of the soldiers deserted, fleeing north into the mountains? He winced at the date: 326 BC. Could Neona be over two thousand years old?

"Damn," he whispered. He was used to always being the older one, but this made his eight hundred years seem puny.

Two thousand years, living in Beyul-La, protecting . . . what? The fact that they were old? What was the point in living that long if you lived in a prison? Unless there was something else they were protecting.

Like what? It couldn't be gold or jewels, not when they lived so simply, with their homemade clothes and shoes. He racked his brain but couldn't come up with anything else.

A sudden thought caused a chill to run down his spine. Neona might have been alive in 1241. She might have been one of the fierce warriors who had avenged his mother's death. She might have even shot the arrow that had killed his father.

"Shit." Was he falling in love with his father's killer?

Chapter Eleven

$\mathcal{T}$ he next evening after sunset, Zoltan jerked awake in his hidden bedroom at the townhouse. With a burst of energy, he showered, dressed, and teleported to the kitchen of his castle for breakfast. One good thing about being a Vamp, he thought as he waited for his bottle to heat up in the microwave, was that no matter how troubled he was, he always slept like the dead. Literally.

Now he was alive again, and the worries were back. Had Neona taken part in the murder of his father and the deaths of so many villagers back in 1241? How could he ask her such a question?

Innocent or killer? It kept going back to the same question. He wanted to believe in her innocence, but reality kept showing him something else—Neona shooting arrows at him that first night. Swinging a sword at him. Hell, she'd raked a knife down his body last night. But that was to convince him to leave. She wasn't trying to kill him anymore. She wanted to protect him.

Would that change when she found out he was a vampire?

The microwave beeped and he removed his bottle,

glancing at the time. Would she meet him at the cabin again at midnight?

"Shit!" He slammed the bottle down. *The watch!* He'd promised her a watch!

"Dammit." He knew he'd forgotten something.

"There you are." Howard entered the kitchen, carrying a new sat phone. "I brought this for you."

Zoltan ignored him and guzzled down his bottle of blood. He'd teleport into town. There was a jewelry store on Main Street that catered to tourists. Old man Janos would have some nice watches.

Howard set the sat phone on the counter next to him. "Some packages arrived for you today. Two boxes of books. But before you leave—"

"I have to go somewhere first."

"What? Where?"

"Town." Zoltan tossed the empty bottle into the recycle bin. "I need to buy a watch."

"You have a watch."

Zoltan gritted his teeth. "Are bears always so damned nosy?"

"Ah. It's for your girlfriend."

"Do me a favor and put all the books in a duffel bag. And there are some weapons on the table in the armory. Pack them up for me, too. I'll be right back."

"You'd better come back," Howard said quickly before he could teleport away. "We moved the mummy this morning, and Elsa wants to make sure you're happy with it."

"Fine." Zoltan teleported to a dark alley close to the village square where the two streets intersected. Main Street and High Street.

Some villagers were seated outside the pub, drinking, while some others sat in front of the restaurant, eating. A few waved and called out greetings as he strode toward the jewelry store. He waved back, then pulled on the door handle. Locked. *Damn.* Janos was closed for the day?

He teleported inside. "Janos!" The old man lived in the back, so he should hear him. "Janos?"

"Coming!"

Zoltan wandered toward the first glass case, looking for a woman's watch. Necklaces, rings . . . a set of wedding rings caught his eye. Simple, but elegant.

"My lord?" Janos limped slowly into the room. He'd suffered an injury back in the second human world war. "I was just about to have supper."

"My apologies for disturbing you. I won't take much of your time. I need a watch."

Janos's gaze shifted to Zoltan's wrist. "You have a watch."

"I need a woman's watch."

Janos gasped.

Was it that shocking? "I've bought jewelry for women before," Zoltan growled.

"Not in my lifetime." Janos stepped closer, his eyes sparkling with excitement. "Are you serious about her, my lord? Will there be a countess soon at the castle?"

Zoltan grimaced. It was a bloody shame he didn't have time to buy the damned watch online. Now Janos was going to spread the word, and before the night was over, the whole village would be planning his wedding.

"I have some lovely engagement rings over here." Janos scurried behind the first glass case, moving exceptionally well for a man with a limp.

"I want a watch," Zoltan muttered. "And no publicity regarding the matter."

"Oh." Janos's shoulders slumped. "Very well." He

hobbled over to another case as if he were suddenly in pain again. "I'm afraid we're running low. The tour bus this afternoon was filled with newlyweds, and they bought the best ones."

"What?" A frisson of horror skittered through Zoltan when he realized the watch case was practically empty. "I only need one. A pretty one."

"I ordered some more after the tour bus left. They'll be here in a few days."

"I need something tonight!"

Janos winced. "Well, as you can see, we have a few men's watches. And then there's this one." He retrieved a watch from the case and set it on a square of black velvet. "These are very popular, especially among the younger women. I suppose your lady friend is on the young side?"

Zoltan gritted his teeth. She might be over two thousand years old. He eyed the watch with its hot pink band and sparkly decoration. "What is that? A cat?"

"Hello Kitty," Janos murmured. "I can give you an excellent price for it."

Zoltan grabbed the watch and studied it closely.

"Is she fond of cats, my lord?"

He snorted. "I suppose so. Box it up. And when your new ones come in, save the most expensive one for me."

"Yes, my lord. Of course. We'll let this one be on the house, shall we?"

"Thank you, Janos." Zoltan shoved the small gift box into his jacket and teleported back to the castle. He found Howard in the armory stuffing the box of arrows into a huge duffel bag.

"Good, you're back." Howard set the last of the books into the overloaded bag and struggled to zip it shut. "I promised Elsa you would drop by the chapel. I helped Alastair move the mummy this morning before the tour, and Domokos followed us the entire time, warning us that you would throw a fit if anything happened to it."

Zoltan snorted. "I don't throw fits."

Howard gave him a curious look. "Domokos said it was special to you, but he wouldn't explain why."

"I'll go there now."

Howard straightened. "Wait. You need your—"

Zoltan teleported to the courtyard and looked around in the moonlight. The main keep where he and his servants lived was in excellent shape since he'd renovated it about twenty years earlier, but the east wing and tower were in bad shape. They were now sectioned off with yellow tape.

He zoomed over to the chapel. Built five hundred years ago, it still boasted the original stone walls, but he'd had to replace the roof and stained glass windows two hundred years ago.

Inside, he found Elsa equipped with a spray bottle of glass cleaner and a roll of paper towels, busily polishing up the glass case that housed the mummy. The wooden chairs had been removed to make room for the glass case, which was now resting on several wooden crates so it was waist high.

"Good evening," Zoltan said.

Elsa jumped, turning to face him. "Oh, you came." She set down the Windex bottle and paper towels on a windowsill. "The glass got all smudged with fingerprints from the tourists. I wanted to make sure you were happy with the mummy's new home."

Zoltan walked around the glass case, studying the familiar form inside. "She looks fine."

Elsa approached. "I thought it might be a woman, but I wasn't sure. Did you know her?"

Zoltan nodded, his mouth quirking with a wry

smile. "She would probably find it amusing to be housed in a chapel."

"Why? Was she very religious?"

Before Zoltan could answer, Howard rushed inside the chapel and screeched to a halt.

He glowered at Zoltan. "You had to teleport here? Don't you know exercise is good for you?"

Zoltan snorted. "Would I live longer? What took you so long?"

"You left your sat phone in the kitchen." Howard handed it to Zoltan.

"Guess what?" Elsa grabbed her husband and pulled him over to the glass case. "Zoltan just told me the mummy is a she. I already suspected that, though. See the long hair? And she's a little short, just around five feet, although I suppose men were shorter, too, at one time."

Howard leaned over the case and grimaced. "All I see is a shriveled-up, horrid thing. Why would anyone want to keep something so creepy?"

Zoltan winced as he pocketed the phone.

"Oh no!" Elsa fussed at her husband. "She's very interesting. If you look closely, you can see all kinds of detail. Like the gown. Another reason why I thought it was a woman, although I think men used to wear long robes, too. But look at her sleeves and the hem of her skirt. See the embroidery? It's deteriorated over time, but I bet it was beautiful when it was new."

"But look at that." Howard pointed at the mummy's right hand. It reached out, the blackened fingers outstretched like the talons of a bird. "It looks like she's trying to grab hold of you. How creepy is that?"

"It does look kinda scary," Elsa conceded, then glanced at Zoltan. "Do you know why her hand is like that?"

He nodded. "She was buried with a Bible under her hand to keep her soul from roaming the Earth and seeking vengeance. Over the centuries, the Bible deteriorated but left her hand frozen in that position."

"Creepy," Howard repeated, and Zoltan shot him an annoyed look.

"Why did they think she would seek revenge?" Elsa asked.

Zoltan stepped closer to the case. "She was murdered by the villagers."

Elsa gasped. "Why?"

"It's a long story." Zoltan placed his hand on the glass, where it rested over the outstretched hand of the mummy. "They thought she was a witch."

"Oh." Elsa's eyes widened. "So that's why you said she'd think it was funny to be here in the chapel."

"She was executed for being a witch?" Howard asked.

Zoltan sighed. Both Howard and Elsa looked fascinated, so it was obvious they would hound him with questions if he didn't tell them more. "The villagers couldn't decide whether to stone her or burn her, so they did both. And then they couldn't bury her in holy ground in the churchyard, so they stuck her in a cave and sealed it. Years later, there was a rock slide down the mountain that opened up the cave, and the villagers discovered that her body had mummified."

Howard made a face. "So they brought her out and put her in a glass case? Why would they want to look at something this creepy?"

Zoltan gritted his teeth. "They thought it was the best way to keep an eye on her. So they could make sure she stayed dead."

"But you knew her, right?" Elsa asked. "Was she really a witch?"

"No. I've always believed she was innocent. The

count at the time was a merchant who traveled the Silk Road to China. He'd lost his first wife when she gave birth to his son, so I suppose he was lonely. He came back from one of his journeys with a new wife from the East. The villagers didn't know what to make of her. She didn't speak Romanian, she wasn't Christian, and she looked a little different. She converted and took the name Donna Maria, but people still suspected her. When the Mongols invaded and killed most of the villagers, the survivors pointed their fingers at her. She was from the East, so she must have caused the Mongols to invade."

"She became a scapegoat," Howard concluded.

"Exactly," Zoltan agreed. "Everyone had lost most of their families, so they were eager to blame someone. They tied Donna Maria to a post in the village square and decided to execute her."

"But she was married to the count," Elsa protested. "Surely he stood up for his wife."

Zoltan shook his head. "The count's eldest son was killed by the Mongols. He was so devastated that the poisonous gossip from the village took hold of him. He started to believe that he'd brought home a witch. The thought that his son's death and all the other deaths were ultimately his fault made him fall into a deep despair. So he did nothing to save his wife."

Elsa winced. "The poor woman. She must have felt so betrayed."

"I'm sure she did." Zoltan regarded her sadly. "But at the same time, I can see why people thought she was a witch. She could communicate with animals and birds."

Elsa stiffened. "I can communicate with animals. And my aunt can communicate with birds. Thank God we live now and don't have to worry about being stoned to death."

"Wait a minute." Howard lifted his hand and gave Zoltan a pointed look. "Aren't you able to communicate with animals?"

"What?" Elsa's eyes widened. "Can you really?"

Zoltan nodded. "Something I inherited." He touched the glass above the mummy's face. "Along with the almond-shaped eyes."

Elsa gasped. "Oh, my God."

Howard stiffened. "You mean . . . ?"

Zoltan nodded. "That's why the steward said she's special to me."

Howard blinked, then snorted with laughter. "Your momma's a mummy?"

Elsa swatted his arm and whispered, "Don't make fun." She turned to Zoltan. "I'm so sorry your mother suffered like that. I'm sure she was a lovely woman."

"Yeah." Howard shifted his weight, wincing. "Sorry about calling her creepy."

"Repeatedly." Zoltan gave him a wry look. "I should be going now."

Howard nodded. "I brought the duffel bag. It's just outside the door."

"Thanks." Zoltan glanced one more time at his mother. He was ninety-nine percent sure that she had come from Beyul-La. It would explain her odd gift. And her secrecy about her past.

Had Neona come with the other women to avenge his mother's death? Did the arrow on the wall in the armory belong to Neona? Innocent or killer?

He swallowed hard. For the first time in centuries he was falling for a woman. He needed to gain her trust, but she was convinced that men couldn't be trusted. Was she basing that assumption on what had happened to his mother? For there was no doubt in his mind that his father had betrayed his mother in the cruelest way.

When she'd needed her husband the most, he'd turned his back on her. Abandoned her to a horrific death.

That was the main reason why Zoltan had never wanted to avenge his father's death. He'd always figured the count had gotten what he deserved. But still, he wanted answers.

What had happened that day in 1241? He'd tried to protect his mother, standing in front of her and taking some of the stones meant for her, even some of the flames. But somehow he'd awakened the next day a few miles away from the burned village with no memory of how he'd gotten there. Would Neona know?

But how could he ask her without revealing who he was? Would she ever trust him if she knew he was the son of the betrayer? And a vampire, too.

For the first time, he realized that his courtship of Neona was not going to be easy. It wasn't a simple matter of seducing her with kisses and chocolate. To choose him, she would have to overcome a mind-set that had been firmly etched in stone for centuries.

With a troubled heart, he picked up the duffel bag and teleported close to Frederic's cabin.

She was nowhere in sight. Zoltan set the heavy duffel bag on the floor of the cabin and wondered what to do. The strategy he'd used the night before wouldn't work again.

The worried feeling in his heart grew heavier. What if she was in trouble? How far would the queen go to make sure Neona didn't leave Beyul-La? He gritted his teeth. He would not give up on her. Once he set his mind on a task, he never quit.

A sound outside drew his attention. Was the

cabin being watched? He teleported out and took cover behind some trees. Soon he realized what was making the noise. The snow leopard was wallowing in a pile of fallen leaves.

Cat! he called. *Where's Neona?*

Leave me alone. Zhan rolled onto his back. *It's the end of the world.*

What? Zoltan ran toward him. *Is Neona in trouble?*

Doomed. I'm doomed. You might never see me again.

Why? Has something happened to Neona?

They won't let her leave the valley. So she didn't hunt today. The cat flopped over and let out a howl of despair. *My food bowl is empty!*

Zoltan scoffed. *That's what you're worried about? You're a leopard, you big wuss. Go kill your own rabbit.*

Zhan shuddered, his fur bristling. *It might fight back and bite me.*

You big baby. Zoltan planted his hands on his hips. *Don't you know you're supposed to be a mighty hunter?*

I am? Zhan gave him a wide-eyed look. *Will you show me how?*

Not now. I'm worried about Neona. Do you know where she is?

The cat huffed. *How can I answer when I'm starving to death?*

I'll bring you some food.

Zhan sat up. *Really?*

Zoltan teleported back to the kitchen and emptied three cans of tuna into a plastic bowl. Since he might have to search for Neona, he stuffed some plastic containers of blood into a jacket pocket, then teleported back.

Wow! The leopard jumped back a foot. *How did you do that? Did you bring the food?*

Here. Zoltan set the bowl in front of the leopard,

and it immediately started eating. *Is Neona all right?*

Zhan looked up between bites. *The last time I saw her she was by the burial mounds.*

I know where that is.

Don't go up the rope ladder. Or near the waterfall. There's a guard at the top of the wall. She'll see you and shoot you full of arrows.

I'll be fine. An idea sprang into Zoltan's mind as he watched the leopard eat. He pulled out his sat phone and called Milan. "Any news about the land in Tibet?"

"I'm afraid it's bad news, sir," Milan answered. "The land belongs to the Chinese government, and they refuse to sell to a foreigner."

"I understand. Let's try this approach. We set the land apart as a wildlife sanctuary for snow leopards. Call Howard Barr at the castle."

"The were-bear? What can he do?"

"He can put you in touch with Rajiv in Tiger Town. Rajiv's the head tiger there, and he has Chinese citizenship. If he'll agree to be our front man, we can channel the money through him."

There was a pause, then Milan said, "So I call the bear to contact a tiger to save some fictional leopards?"

Zoltan snorted. "The leopard is real."

"Is he a shifter, too?"

"No, thank God. Let me know how it goes." Zoltan pocketed the sat phone and patted the jacket pocket containing the watch. *Cat, I'm going now. Hide the bowl when you're done.*

Okay. Zhan looked up at him. *She cried last night.*

Zoltan dragged in a hissing breath.

Don't get caught.

I don't plan to. He teleported close to the burial mounds.

Chapter Twelve

*W*as he waiting for her again at the cabin? With a sigh, Neona settled on the grass next to her sister's grave. It was impossible to see him tonight. Her mother suspected her, so she had ordered the other women to take turns guarding the rock wall where they kept the rope ladder stashed.

Neona had sent her pet leopard to the cabin with instructions not to let Zoltan approach the rock wall where he might be seen, but she couldn't be sure Zhan had understood. Even so, he had scampered off in the right direction. She hadn't dared attach a note to him, since whoever was standing guard might spot it and it would serve as proof that she was indeed meeting someone secretly.

The night before she'd had to endure yet another lecture from her mother on the unworthiness of men. They could never be trusted. They wanted only sex and power. And they could get both from the women of Beyul-La.

The pool of Living Water in the cave's throne room had enabled the women to fulfill their sacred duty over the course of many centuries. Men would never accept their dedication to duty. All they would see was a way to live forever as the richest and most powerful men in the world. So any man who learned their secret had to be executed. It was harsh, the queen admitted, but it worked. The secret had remained intact.

Over the centuries there'd been only one exception to the rule. Frederic. He'd been near death when Calliope had found him in the mountains. She'd erected a makeshift shelter for them, and in the days it had taken her to heal him, they'd fallen in love. She'd begged Nima to allow him to live in the neighboring valley, and Frederic had managed to convince them that he could help them. The outside world was changing quickly, he'd said, and they would be helpless to deal with it if caught unprepared.

Nima had been doubtful at first, but after Winifred was born and exhibited the gift of communicating with winged creatures, the queen had changed her mind. Freya was born a year later, and she possessed another useful gift—the ability to make crops flourish. Meanwhile, Frederic taught them English and all he could about the outside world. His love for his wife and daughters was so great that he'd been happy to accept his exile from his homeland. But that had changed after the birth of his son. The prison he'd accepted for himself, he could not accept for the boy. When Franklin had turned six, old enough to start school, his father had taken him back to England.

Nima had taken his desertion as proof that all men were alike. Ultimately, they could not be trusted.

But Zoltan insisted that Frederic had kept their secret. He'd remained faithful. Neona wanted to believe that some men could be trusted, for she hoped Zoltan was one of them. He knew too much. She could only pray that he would remain trustworthy and silent.

As much as she wanted to be with him, she knew the best way to keep him alive was to break off with him completely. For how many years would she think of him, dream of him? He would be out there somewhere roaming the earth, while she remained here, forever shackled to their sacred duty.

"I'm not allowed to leave the valley now," Neona whispered to her sister. Had she become the prisoner that Minerva had warned her about? Could she live the rest of her long life without love? Without Zoltan?

She rested her hand on the dirt of her sister's grave. "He attracts me like no other man. He excites me. Surprises me. Makes me laugh. Makes me burn." Her fingers dug into the dirt. "He makes me long for the impossible."

But there was something about him that was niggling at the back of her mind. Last night, he'd taken her knife and spun her around to grab her at a speed that had been incredibly fast. There had also been something odd about his eyes. She was no longer sure it had been a reflection from the fire. And then somehow he had managed to escape the cabin without being seen.

A mystery man. Even that made him appealing to her. He excited her mind as much as her body.

She released the clod of dirt and brushed her hands together. There was no point in speculating about who he was or where he'd come from. She could never see him again. Tears filled her eyes, and she blinked them away. *Think about something else.*

By the light of the three-quarter moon, she spotted the arrow Zoltan had used last night to have Zhan carry a note. It lay close by on the ground. He must have found it in the woods where she'd shot at him a few times that first night. She should go back to collect the fallen arrows, but she couldn't leave the valley. Couldn't ever see him again.

The tears spilled over.

"Neona," a voice whispered behind her.

A male voice. With a gasp, she turned around.

He was uphill at the edge of the forest. He stepped toward her, his form still partially hidden in shadow.

"No!" she whispered, jumping to her feet. She looked around nervously, then dashed toward him. "Zoltan." She shoved him into the cover of the forest.

He caught her by the arms. "Are you all right?"

"No! You're scaring me. If anyone catches you here, they'll kill you!"

"I had to make sure you're all right."

"I'm fine. Please, go!"

"You've been crying." He wiped her cheek with his thumb.

The simple gesture made more tears flow, and she clung to him as he held her tight. *Just a few minutes*, she thought as she wrapped her arms around his neck. After a few minutes, she would let go of him forever.

"I was worried about you," he whispered, his hand rubbing her back. "Did you get in trouble?"

She shook her head. "Just the standard speech about how men cannot be trusted."

"You can trust me." He released her and pulled a box from his jacket. "I told you I would bring you a watch tonight, and I did."

She took the box from him and pivoted, scanning their surroundings.

"There's no one around," he assured her. "I already checked."

"But how did you get here? There is only one way into this valley, and it's being guarded." She looked around again. "They must have seen you."

"No one saw me." He motioned toward the box. "I changed the time for you."

How had he managed to get here? Neona glanced uphill. The mountains surrounding Beyul-La were high and treacherous. It would take several days to enter the valley that way. The only group to ever attempt it had been the expedition Frederic had been on, and everyone had died but him.

"It's all right, Neona," Zoltan said softly.

She shook her head. "You're not safe here. You shouldn't have come."

"I promised you a watch, so nothing was going to stop me."

Her heart squeezed in her chest. He was a man of his word. She opened the box and stared. This wasn't anything like the pocket watch Frederic had owned.

"It's not that great, I know," Zoltan mumbled. "I have a better one on order—"

"It's beautiful," she whispered, touching the sparkly kitten. "It's too pretty to hide in a pocket."

"It goes on your wrist. Here, I'll show you." He took the watch out and fastened the band around her wrist.

"The color is so bright." She felt the band and gasped. "It's so strong, yet it bends. What is this wondrous material?"

"Plastic," he muttered.

"It's amazing!"

He winced. "I'll get something in gold and diamonds—"

"No! I love this." She smiled at the sparkly kitten. "Zhan will love it, too."

"I saw him down at the cabin."

"Oh, good." She turned her wrist, admiring the way the watch sparkled in the moonlight. "I sent him to keep you away from the rock wall so you wouldn't be seen." With a sigh, she unfastened the watch. "I cannot let this be seen, either."

"Hide it if you must, but please accept it."

She glanced up at him.

"Accept me."

Her heart stilled. "I-it is not possible. You must know they will kill you if they find you here."

"I'll stay in Frederic's cabin."

"I fear even that is not safe." She slipped the watch into the linen pouch that dangled from the sash tied around her waist. "You know too much."

"Frederic must have known. He was allowed to live here."

"He was the only one." Neona glanced downhill at the burial mounds. "Calliope begged for him on her knees."

"How did she meet him?"

"It's a long story."

"We have all night." Zoltan sat on the ground and patted the spot next to him.

She glanced around one more time. Perhaps it was safe here. The others would never believe that he'd managed to sneak past the guard. She sat next to him, her legs crossed, while he stretched his long legs out in front of him and rested back on his elbows. The ground was soft with a thick cushion of dried pine and fir needles.

She told the story of Calliope and Frederic, carefully avoiding any references to the women's sacred duty.

"I'm sorry I never got to meet her," Zoltan said. "She sounds very brave."

"She was." Neona pointed at the burial mound on the far right. "That is Calliope's grave there."

He sat up so he could see the mounds. "Which one belongs to your sister?"

Neona swallowed hard. "Third from the right."

"I wish I could have met her, too. Who are the others?"

She gave him a dubious look. "You really want to know?"

"Yes. This is your life, and I want to share it with you."

Her eyes misted with tears. "The other mounds belong to those who died in battle two weeks ago. Actually, almost three weeks now. It's been five days since we met."

He nodded. "Five glorious days."

She gave him a wistful smile, then gestured toward the burial mounds. "Next to Calliope is her oldest daughter, Farah. Farah's father was a Persian soldier. She was . . . a bit older than Winifred and Freya."

"A few centuries older?"

After a pause, Neona nodded. He already knew, so there was hardly any point in lying. "Next to Farah is my sister, Minerva. The next two are Lydia's daughters. Pema's father was Tibetan, and Mahima's father was Indian. The last grave is Lydia's mother, Anjali."

Zoltan grimaced. "Lydia must be heartbroken."

"Yes." A tear rolled down Neona's cheek. "She has one daughter left, Tashi."

"What happens if one of you gives birth to a son?"

Neona sighed. "It happened to Calliope, and once to my sister."

Zoltan turned to face her. "Then you have a nephew? Where is he?"

"The queen took him to the Buddhist monastery

about thirty miles from here. He should be about seven years old now."

Zoltan gave her an incredulous look. "The queen is his grandmother. How could she give him away? What harm could a child possibly bring to you here?"

Neona winced. Zoltan's objections sounded much like her own. "I know our ways don't make any sense to you."

"No, they don't. You complain about men not being trustworthy and abandoning you, but you abandoned a baby boy."

"I know! It nearly killed my sister. She cried for weeks. And then she was never quite the same. I don't think she fought very hard at the last battle."

"Damn," he whispered, then took Neona's hand. "I'm sorry."

"It was wrong. I realize that now." She gazed sadly at her sister's grave, her vision blurred with tears. "I should have fought for her. I should have fought to keep the baby."

"Don't blame yourself. You've always said that men are not allowed here. It has to be hard to defy centuries of tradition."

"I do blame myself." She pulled her hand free as a tear fell down her cheek. "I am ashamed. I had to lose my sister before I started to question things."

"Can you tell me what is going on here? What could be so important that your sister had to endure so much pain?"

Neona sniffed. "We have a . . . a sacred duty. I cannot explain more. This is the way it has always been."

"But sometimes things can change over time."

She shook her head. "The pact we made is binding forever."

"A pact with whom?"

She winced. She was telling too much. Inhaling slowly, she attempted to steady her nerves.

"How did all this get started?" Zoltan asked. "Why are you so convinced men are the enemy?"

She wiped her cheeks. "It's a long story."

"I'm not going anywhere."

She studied him, wondering how much she should tell, how much she should trust him. "It began before I was born."

"And that was when?"

She bit her lip, wondering how he would react. "Frederic estimated my age at over two thousand years."

Zoltan sucked in a breath. "Okay. That's about what I figured."

"You did? How?"

His mouth curled up on one side. "I'm seemingly intelligent. And may I say you're looking quite well for your age."

"Does it disturb you?"

He snorted. "I'm the last person on earth who thought he would fall for an older woman." He stiffened suddenly with an alarmed look. "If you leave here, will you turn into a two-thousand-year-old corpse?"

"No. I would start to age naturally."

He exhaled a gust of air. "That's a relief. Then you could leave with me."

"No!"

He grabbed her hands. "Why not? You know we belong together."

"I told you. We have a sacred pact. I must remain here to fulfill my duty."

"Which is?"

She winced. "I cannot say."

With a groan, he released her hands and fell back onto the ground.

She looked around to make sure no one was in sight.

"Fine," he mumbled. "Then I'll stay here with you."

She twisted to face him. "You cannot. It's not safe—"

"Dammit." He glared at her. "You make it really hard to court you." When she smiled, his eyebrows rose. "Is that amusing?"

Her smile widened. "I cannot help it. I like the way you refuse to give up on me."

His eyes twinkled with humor. "Then you're in luck, for you won't find a more stubborn man than me. I never give up."

"I see you are modest, too."

"Damned straight." He stretched and placed his hands behind his head. "Tell me how it started."

"What started?"

"How you all became a cult of man-hating warrior women in the middle of nowhere."

"I don't hate you."

"You tried to kill me a few times."

"That was unfortunate."

"Why?" His mouth twitched. "Because you failed?"

She shrugged. "The night is still young."

"You little—" He pulled her down onto her back and leaned over her. When she smiled up at him, he smiled back. "You're *my* man-hating warrior woman, and don't forget it."

She touched his cheek. "I won't."

"Good." He kissed her nose, then lay beside her, gathering her up into his arms. "So tell me the story."

"All right." She turned to gaze up at the stars.

"Many centuries ago men began making swords of iron and killing each other to gain land and power. There was a maharaja in what is now northern India. His army took over great portions of India, Pakistan, and Nepal, killing and destroying, showing no mercy. The more land and power he acquired, the more ruthless he became. People in the surrounding territories quaked in fear that his army would turn on them next. Villages sought to appease him by sending their most beautiful maidens to him to be his concubines."

"Did it work?"

Neona shrugged. "If the concubine pleased him, he would allow her family to live. Three young maidens were sent to him. One from India, one from Nepal, and one from Tibet. In their fear and despair, they turned to each other and became friends. After the maharaja raped them, they were distraught and failed to fawn over him. He killed their families and let them be used by his guards."

Zoltan grimaced. "What an ass."

"It became even worse. The maharaja died in battle, and his son and heir decided some of his father's concubines should be executed at the funeral as a human tribute. The three maidens were among those who were chosen."

"Shit." Zoltan sat up. "What happened to them?"

She sat up, too. "They escaped."

"Yes!" He punched the air.

She smiled, enjoying how engrossed he was in the story. "They went north into the mountains, hoping to lose the soldiers who were tracking them. The one from Nepal knew how to cross the mountains, and then the one from Tibet took over. They found this valley of Beyul-La and swore never to trust men again."

"Are they still alive?"

Neona sighed. "Only one. My mother, Queen Nima. She was the one from Tibet who found this hidden valley. Eventually, she mated with a Greek soldier and gave birth to Minerva and me, but it was done out of necessity. I don't think she ever recovered from the abuse she suffered at the hands of the maharaja."

"Who were the others?"

Neona pointed to the last burial mound on the left. "Anjali was the maiden from northern India. She mated with a Greek soldier to have Calliope, then a Roman soldier to have Lydia. Tashi, Winifred, and Freya are her granddaughters."

"And the third one? The one from Nepal?"

Neona pulled her knees up and hugged them. "We don't like to talk about her."

"Why not?"

"She fell in love and left us. The queen warned her that men cannot be trusted, that her lover would betray her. And he did. He let her die a terrible death."

Zoltan sucked in a long breath. "What was her name?"

"Dohna."

"Donna Maria," he whispered.

Neona looked at him. He seemed awfully pale. "Are you all right?"

He nodded. "I think I was meant to come here. All those years of searching, and I'm finally here. With you." He turned to her and took her gently by the shoulders. "You are the one I've been waiting for. I'm falling in love with you."

Her breath caught. "Zoltan—"

"Neona." He cradled her face in his hands. "Do you love me?"

Her eyes filled with tears. "It's impossi—"

"If you love me, then nothing will be impossible."

"I . . . I want to believe you."

"Then do." He kissed her brow. "Believe me." He kissed her nose. "Trust me." He kissed her mouth. "Love me."

With a cry she threw her arms around his neck.

"Neona." He hugged her tight, then nuzzled her face, trailing kisses along her cheek till he reached her mouth.

She opened for him, welcoming him, stroking his invading tongue. How could she ever give him up? He was all her heart had ever longed for, all her mind had ever dreamed of, all her body had ever ached for.

"Unhand her! Now."

Neona jolted at the sound of her mother's voice.

"You're surrounded." Nima stood behind them in the woods, her sword drawn.

Neona looked around frantically. Winifred was to one side, Freya to the other, and both had arrows cocked and aimed at Zoltan. Lydia was downhill, between them and the burial mounds, her bow and arrow ready. At this short distance, none of them would miss.

Panic seized Neona. "*No!*"

Zoltan squeezed her shoulders. "Stay calm."

"Release her and move away!" Nima yelled. When he lifted his hands and scooted back, she motioned to Lydia. "Kill him."

"No!" Neona threw herself in front of him just as the arrow was released. Zoltan grabbed her and twisted, putting his back to Lydia.

His body stiffened as the arrow struck. He fell forward on top of Neona, a hissing sound escaping from his mouth. He grimaced, and for a flash of a second, fangs sprang out before he clamped his mouth shut.

Neona gasped. Had she really seen that? She searched his face but only saw pain in his eyes.

He grunted with more pain as Freddie and Freya yanked him to his feet. Freddie tied his wrists together while Freya looped a rope around his neck. They pulled him back into the moonlit clearing, closer to the burial mounds.

Neona gasped at the sight of the arrow protruding from his back and the dark stain of blood spreading down his jacket. Lydia cocked another arrow, aimed at his chest. Nima walked toward him, her sword pointed at him.

Neona scrambled to her feet. She had to stop them somehow. But did he really have fangs? Was he some kind of monster?

"How do you do? I am Zoltan—"

"Did I say you could talk?" Nima poked him with her sword.

"Don't hurt him!" Neona ran toward them. Maybe she'd imagined the fangs. It had happened so fast. And it was dark.

Nima scoffed. "Have you lost your senses? This man has seen our valley. He will die tonight."

Chapter Thirteen

Zoltan gritted his teeth as the rope bit into his neck. They were leading him about like a damned dog on a leash. The arrow in his back stung like hell. Fortunately, the queen's jab at him with her sword had missed the bags of blood stashed in his jacket. The stab had barely broken his skin, so it wasn't bleeding nearly as profusely as the wound on his back was.

Still, the scent of so much blood ignited his vampire senses, and it took every ounce of his control not to give in to the rampant power that sizzled through his veins. Given free rein, his undead instincts would have him teleport free, steal the queen's sword, and decapitate everyone at vampire speed. They could all be dead in a matter of seconds. Well, everyone but Neona. Over the centuries, he had acquired excellent control.

With a low growl, he acknowledged that beheading Neona's mother and friends was not a likely way to earn her trust. He needed to convince these women he was their ally, so he would have to play nice. No glowing eyes and fangs.

With all the pain he was enduring, he had to wonder if he was a fool. He could have teleported away the instant the arrow was shot. But Neona had leaped in front of him, and his immediate reaction had been to save her. He'd been so shocked that he'd acted without thinking. In almost eight hundred years, he couldn't recall anyone ever trying to save him. He'd always done the rescuing, the protecting.

But Neona had tried to save him. Did that mean she loved him?

He glanced at her as they came to a stop by the fire pit in the center of their small village. Her love might be short-lived. If given another chance to save him, he wasn't sure she would. He'd seen the stunned look of horror flit across her face when his fangs had sprung out.

She doubted him now; he could feel it. There was a distant wariness to her stance, a reluctance to look him in the eye. She said nothing as one of the women looped his leash around a pole and reeled him in till he was only a foot away. He turned to survey their small village, but the arrow in his back knocked against the pole, inciting another burst of pain.

Was this where they planned to execute him? The irony struck him like a punch in the gut. His mother had been tied to a pole in the village square, and his father had done nothing to save her. Now, eight hundred years later, the same tragic scene was being replayed. Would Neona turn her back on him and let him die? Did she think he was an evil creature, just like Father had thought about Mother?

He glanced at Neona, but her head was turned away. She was refusing to look at him.

Just teleport home. Save yourself and forget about her. Tears filled his eyes. He'd thought she was the one. If he left now, he'd be admitting it was over, that she'd given up on him. He clenched his fists. *Bear with it just a few more seconds. Give her a chance.*

The three women with bows aimed their arrows at him, and the queen lifted her arm. Any second now she'd drop her arm and the arrows would fly. He looked at Neona one last time. Tears were running down her cheeks.

"Stop!" she screamed and ran to position herself in front of him.

His heart squeezed in his chest. She still believed in him.

"Move aside!" the queen shouted.

"Don't kill him." Neona fell to her knees and clasped her hands together as if in prayer. "I beg of you, grant us the mercy shown to Calliope. This man is my mate."

Zoltan opened his mouth to agree, but he was interrupted by the queen.

"We cannot take mates! Even Calliope's mate deserted her."

"But we have Freddie and Freya because of him." Neona motioned to two of the women with cocked bows. "I could give us more daughters. We need more women, you know that."

One of the women lowered her bow. "That is true. What is the harm in keeping him alive till he fathers a child?"

"I agree with Freddie." A second woman lowered her bow. "He could live at our father's cabin."

That had to be Freya, Zoltan thought. She was almost identical to her sister, Winifred. The only difference was the golden tint to Winifred's brown eyes, whereas Freya's eyes were hazel green.

"Too dangerous," the third female bowman said. "He could escape and tell others about us."

The queen nodded. "Lydia is right. We cannot allow him to leave this valley alive."

"I'll keep him in my house." Neona rose to her feet. "Please. I want a daughter so badly." She glanced back at Zoltan, avoiding eye contact. "This man is strong and fair of face. I believe he could give me an exceptional daughter."

"He does seem strong," Winifred said. "He must be in pain, but he hasn't even moaned."

"He must be fleet of foot, too," Freya added. "He managed to sneak past Tasha."

The queen scowled at him. "How did you get past our guard?"

"I come in peace—"

"Men are never peaceful," Nima hissed, then looked at her daughter. "You see how he avoids telling us the truth. He cannot be trusted. He's corrupting you, making you forget your sacred duty."

"No!" Neona shook her head. "It is part of our duty to produce daughters for the future. This man can give me one."

Zoltan winced inwardly. Was this her strategy for keeping him alive, or was it how she truly felt? Was he nothing more than a sperm donor?

The queen gave him a disgusted look. "He will bring you nothing but misery. Lydia, bring Tashi here. I want to know how this man sneaked past your daughter."

Lydia turned pale. "Yes, your majesty." She strode from the village.

"Winifred, rip the arrow out of him," the queen ordered. "Let's see if he's as strong as you think."

"Yes, your majesty." Winifred handed her bow and arrow to her sister, then circled behind him.

With a grimace, Neona looked away. Zoltan wasn't

sure how she felt. She was definitely trying to keep him alive, but at the same time, she was refusing to make eye contact with him.

He felt Winifred planting her hand firmly on his back and he gritted his teeth, preparing himself. Any second now. He closed his eyes so no one would see them glow.

A blast of searing pain exploded across his back. He gasped but managed not to moan or reveal his fangs.

"It's out," Winifred announced behind him. "He's losing blood fast."

He dragged in a hissing breath. He needed to feed. Soon.

"I will lay my hands on you to heal you," Neona whispered. "It will stop the bleeding and take away the pain."

He opened his eyes to frown at her. "You will not."

Her gaze lifted till her eyes met his. "There is no need for you to be in pain."

"I will not have you take my pain upon yourself."

"Interesting." Winifred stepped in front of him, regarding him curiously. "I think he likes you, Neona."

"I promised her I would bring her no harm," Zoltan said quietly.

Neona looked away, but her eyes glistened with tears.

"That's so . . . sweet." Winifred exchanged an amused look with her sister.

The queen scoffed. "And so it begins. He will deceive you with his pretense to care, and he'll wheedle his way into your affections with his lies. I should kill him before he corrupts you all."

Zoltan eyed the queen. How had she managed to remain so hateful over the millennia? You would think a person would mellow out after a few thousand years. "You won't have to kill me. I'll bleed to death soon enough."

"I'll fetch some bandages and medicine." Neona ran inside a nearby building.

Winifred crossed her arms, studying him. "So how did you meet Neona?"

"We met five nights ago." He attempted a bow, but the rope around his neck stopped him. "How do you do? My name is Zoltan."

"I'm Freddie, and this is my sis—"

"Hush!" The queen glared at Winifred. "He already knows too much."

"I've been looking forward to meeting you all," Zoltan continued as if this was a social event. "I brought gifts for you. They're in the cabin in the next valley. A set of hunting knives and other weapons. Some books—"

"Weapons?" Winifred asked.

"Books?" Freya's eyes lit up.

"Enough!" Nima glared at the two girls. "Do you not realize what he is doing? Flattery, manipulation, and deception. He seeks to destroy us."

"I want to help you," he insisted. "You're in danger from Master Han and Lord—"

"I knew it!" The queen drew her sword and pointed it at his heart. "You're a spy from Lord Liao."

"No. I'm on your side."

"You lie." She pressed the point of her sword against his jacket.

The queen was going to be hard to convince. Zoltan decided it was time to pull out a trump card. "You can trust me. This place is in my blood. I am Dohna's son."

With a gasp, the queen stumbled back. The sword fell from her hand, hitting the ground with a thud.

Winifred and Freya exchanged shocked looks, then turned back to stare at him.

Meanwhile, the leopard ran into the clearing. *Oh, no! You got caught? I told you not to get caught. Why are you covered with blood?*

Zoltan gritted his teeth. *I got shot.*

What can we do? Zhan ran in a circle around him. *I know! I'll bite the queen on the ankle. Then you make a run for it. Neona can live with us in the forest, and we'll go hunting for rabbit every day! It'll be great!*

Cat, I'm tied to a frickin' pole.

Oh. That's a problem. Zhan attempted to climb the pole, but halfway up, he fell to the ground. *Don't worry! I'll get you loose.* He attacked the pole, clawing furiously.

Zoltan snorted. At this rate, the cat might have him free in twelve hours. He'd have to teleport before then to avoid the sun. And if he didn't eat soon—

"You lie!" Queen Nima emerged from her shock to yell at him.

"It is the truth," Zoltan said. "My father was the Count of Czakvar in Transylvania. He brought home a new wife from the East, and they called her Donna Maria. When the Mongols invaded in 1241, most of the village was slaughtered. Those who survived blamed Donna Maria and declared her a witch. My father had just lost his eldest son in battle, and in his despair—"

"Are you excusing him? That monster?" Nima's face turned red with rage.

Zoltan swallowed hard. He had a sick feeling in his gut that Neona's mother had killed his father. *Dammit.* After eight hundred years of wanting to know the truth, he now found himself reluctant to ask the question.

"Your majesty." Winifred pulled the queen back. "Don't let him upset you. He must be lying."

"Right," Freya agreed. "How could he be alive in 1241?"

The three women huddled together, speaking Tibetan and glancing furtively at him.

Cat, what are they saying? Zoltan asked.

Zhan stopped clawing to listen. *They wonder how you could be centuries old. The queen is very upset. She thinks Dohna may have taken some of the Living Water with her and given it to you. It's not supposed to be given to a male.*

Living Water? So that was their fountain of youth. Zoltan looked around. *Is it the stream that runs through the valley?*

No, it's the pool inside the cave. Never go inside there. If they catch you, they'll kill you for sure.

Neona emerged from the building, her arms full of supplies. "Sorry it took me so long." She hurried toward Zoltan. "I had to make some more bandages. We used up most of them three weeks ago after the battle."

Zhan trotted up to her and rubbed against her legs. "Good kitty," she whispered as she set down a bowl and pitcher of water near Zoltan's feet. Inside a basket, there were torn strips of white linen and a pottery jar. She removed the knife from the sheath on her leg and sawed through the ropes tying his hands together.

"Neona," he whispered. "Thank you."

She ignored him, focusing on his hands.

"What are you doing, Neona?" The queen grabbed the sword she'd dropped earlier.

"I need his hands free so I can take off his jacket."

Neona sheathed her knife, then removed his jacket and tossed it aside. The leopard ran over to sniff at it.

The queen sheathed her sword. "You missed his latest lie. He claims to be the son of Dohna."

Neona gasped and her eyes met his. "How can that be?"

"That's what we're wondering," Nima muttered, glancing back at Winifred and Freya. "How could he have lived so long?"

Neona's face turned pale.

Was she remembering the fangs she'd seen? Zoltan watched her intently, wondering if she was going to tell everyone he was a vampire.

She grabbed her knife, and, with trembling hands, she cut his T-shirt and ripped it open. "We don't know if Dohna had a son."

"So you agree he is lying?" Nima asked.

"I don't know what to think of him," Neona said softly. She poured water into the bowl, then wet a cloth and wiped the blood from the small stab wound on his ribs.

"I am still the same," Zoltan whispered.

She ignored him and opened the pottery jar to smear some salve on the small wound.

"How would he even know about Dohna?" the queen demanded. "Did you tell him about her?"

Neona winced.

The queen scoffed. "You see how he twists your words to deceive us."

Neona didn't answer. She grabbed a strip of linen and wrapped it around his torso to cover up the small wound.

"I am telling the truth," Zoltan said. "How else would I know that my mother could communicate

with both birds and animals? The villagers thought
she was a witch and that she had caused the Mongols
to attack us."

"And then your so-called father let them kill her?"
Nima shouted. "If you are who you claim to be, then
you are the son of the man who betrayed us!"

Neona gave him a wary look as she tied off the bandage.

"I blame my father, too," Zoltan said. "I tried to
save my mother. They were throwing stones at her,
and I blocked them. And when they threw a torch,
I jumped onto the kindling to keep it from catching
fire. It burned my back—"

Neona cried out and stumbled back. "You—oh my
God, you're the boy?"

"You were there?" Zoltan asked. It seemed clear
now that the women of Beyul-La had attacked his
village, but his stomach clenched at the thought of
Neona going on a killing rampage.

"You remember him?" Nima asked her daughter.

"When we arrived, the villagers had just set fire
to the kindling. Dohna was already dead, and there
was a boy on the ground in front of her." Neona's
eyes widened as she turned back to Zoltan. "It's you.
That's why I started having the dream."

She pulled his ripped T-shirt off as she circled
behind him, then used it to wipe the blood off his
back. "Oh God. It's really you."

She stumbled in front of him, and the bloody T-shirt
slipped from her hands to fall to the ground. "I didn't
recognize you. Or maybe I did. I started having the
dream." She studied his face. "Do you remember anything?"

"No." He shook his head. "I woke up the next day a
few miles from the village."

"So he speaks the truth?" Nima asked.

Neona nodded, tears gleaming in her eyes. "I remember the burn mark. And the scars on his back and shoulders. I touched them all and felt the pain."

Zoltan's heart stilled. "You . . . healed me?"

A tear ran down her cheek. "When I first saw you, lying in front of Dohna, I knew you had tried to save her. You were near death, so I took you away to heal you."

"You saved me," he breathed. Neona had been with him, far away from the village. She'd been busy saving his life, not killing the villagers. Innocent or killer? His Neona was innocent.

He glanced at the queen. No doubt she'd taken part in the massacre. And since she was the leader, it seemed highly likely that she was the one who had killed his father.

The queen noted his stare and stiffened. "Why have you come here? Do you seek revenge for your father?"

He groaned inwardly. His theory appeared correct. "I only wanted answers." He took a deep breath. "Right now, I'd like to stop bleeding."

"Oh, of course! I'm sorry." Neona grabbed the wet cloth to clean his back. Then she smeared some salve on him and wrapped a bandage around him. "This medicine will stop the bleeding and keep the wound clean."

Winifred stepped closer. "So you're really Dohna's son?"

He nodded. "I was fourteen when she died."

"How have you lived so long?" Nima demanded.

Neona paused in the middle of tying off the bandage. "He needs rest. It is a wonder he's still standing."

"How did you know Dohna was in trouble?" he asked. "How did you get to Transylvania so quickly?"

The queen's eyes flashed with anger. "You are our prisoner. You do not ask questions."

The leopard hissed at the queen, then ran to hide behind Zoltan.

"I should take him to my cabin so he can rest," Neona suggested.

"Can we go find the presents he left for us?" Winifred asked the queen.

"Tomorrow. Tonight we must take turns guarding Neona's house." Nima regarded Zoltan with suspicious disdain. "Do not be swayed by his false generosity. He wants something from us."

Freya snorted. "He wants Neona in bed."

Blushing, Neona emptied the bowl of bloody water. "He will be too weak."

"You want to bet?" he asked softly. Once he drank the two plastic bags of blood hidden in his jacket, he would be much stronger.

Her blush deepened as she gathered up her supplies. Zhan butted his head against her leg.

"We have returned," Lydia announced as she approached with her daughter.

Tashi frowned at Zoltan, then fell to her knees. "Forgive me, your majesty. I don't know how I missed him. May I kill him for you?"

"I would be honored to assist her," Lydia offered.

Zoltan groaned inwardly. More bloodthirsty women.

"I have decided to keep him alive," Nima announced. "He is Dohna's son."

Lydia gasped, her eyes widening as she looked him over. "How can that be possible?"

"It is true," Neona said. "He is the boy I saved."

Tashi gave him a curious look as she rose to her feet. "He's not a boy now."

"I have a name. Zoltan."

Lydia stepped closer, studying him. "He does look a bit like her. The shape of his eyes . . ."

"You knew my mother?" he asked.

Lydia sighed. "We were all heartbroken when she left with that bastard."

"I am pleased we have this opportunity to bring Dohna's bloodline back where it belongs." Nima waved a hand in his direction. "This man will mate with Neona and give us Dohna's granddaughter."

Lydia's eyes narrowed. "If he is Dohna's son, then he is also the son of that bastard."

"That is true," Nima agreed. "His father betrayed Dohna in the worst way. We dare not trust this man." She drew a knife from her belt and placed it at the base of Zoltan's throat, then sliced through the rope around his neck. "He will remain imprisoned in Neona's house until she becomes pregnant. Then we will kill him."

Chapter Fourteen

Zoltan ripped the cap off the first bag of blood and guzzled it down. He was in Neona's house now, alone at last. He'd managed to grab his jacket before being led here. Lydia was standing guard outside, and she'd closed and barred the window shutters to keep him from escaping. The only light in the house came from a small fire in the hearth.

He squeezed the last drop from the plastic bag, then grabbed the second one. A knock on the door gave him half a second to drop the bags on a bed and throw his jacket on top. The door opened, and Tashi entered with a wooden tray.

"We thought you might be hungry." She set the tray on a round table in front of the fireplace. "The tea is hot." She moved the earthenware teapot to a trivet on the table.

"Thank you." Zoltan inclined his head.

She gave him a curious look. "Are you really Dohna's son?"

"Yes."

Tashi glanced at the door, then stepped toward him

and lowered her voice. "Did your mother give you something . . . special to drink?"

She had to be referring to the Living Water. The women suspected that was why he was still alive. "Where is Neona?"

Tashi snorted. "Eager to get started, are you?" Her gaze drifted down his bare chest to his jeans. "I wouldn't be in such a hurry if I were you. The minute she's pregnant, you're—"

The door opened and Lydia peered inside. "There is no need to talk to him."

"Yes, Mother." Tashi hurried outside.

Lydia gave him a dubious look, then closed the door.

He grabbed the second bag of blood and ripped off the cap. Halfway through it, he was feeling strong enough to slow down. He took sips as he looked around. It was a small house. One room. Years of a wood-burning fire had permeated the walls and furnishings with a rustic scent. There were two beds, across from each other, pushed up against walls that were lined with some sort of woven reed mat. Their form of insulation, he figured. It probably got damned cold here in the winter.

There were a few framed pictures on the walls. Long rectangles of bright silk, embroidered with flowers and butterflies. He smiled, imagining Neona sitting in front of the fireplace on a cold winter evening, creating a work of art with needle and thread.

The bedsheets were unbleached linen, soft from years of use and washing. The pillows and comforters were stuffed with something soft. Lamb's wool, he guessed from the faint scent. A small table sat between the two beds. On top rested a candlestick and the book Neona had taken from Frederic's cabin the night before. At the foot of each bed rested a large wooden trunk.

The fireplace was on the far wall, opposite the two beds. In front of the fireplace, a table and two chairs sat. Two beds, two chests, two chairs. Neona must have shared this house with her twin sister.

He finished the second bag of blood and zipped the two bags into a jacket pocket. Then he wandered over to the hearth to put on another piece of wood. The fire greedily engulfed the new fuel and sent flickering shadows across the room.

He eyed the plate of food on the tray. Some sort of flat bread, jam made from berries, and cheese. He picked up the teapot to look at it. Pottery painted in a simple red and green geometric design. Was this the handwork of one of the women?

The trivet caught his eye. It was black and slick. Slate? He set the pot on the table and picked up the trivet. It was slightly pliable, with smooth edges. Not stone. Or pottery. Leather? It seemed too thick for that. He leaned over the fireplace and held the edge of the trivet over the fire. It didn't catch fire, didn't melt. It barely felt warm. The floor of the fireplace was made entirely of the odd black tiles.

Another knock sounded on the door. He set the trivet down and picked up the teapot as Tashi entered once again. He poured some tea into a small round cup without handles.

"I thought you might want to clean up." Tashi placed a bowl and pitcher next to the tray and frowned at the plate of food. "You didn't eat."

"I was waiting for Neona. When is she coming?"

"Are you in a hurry to die?" Tashi gave him a wry look. "Neona's with Freddie and Freya. They're getting her ready for you. And making a big deal out of it." She rolled her eyes. "They act like this is a wedding."

His heart stilled. Would Neona see it that way? Could she accept a vampire for a husband? His groin tightened at the thought of a wedding night.

"But it is more like your funeral," Tashi continued. "You shouldn't have come here."

"I'm in love with Neona. And I want to help you defeat Lord Liao."

Tashi stiffened. "We don't need your help."

"You do. There are only six of you."

Tashi winced. "You will never convince the queen to trust you."

"I have to try." Zoltan looked around the small house. He might be here several days. He needed to teleport back home and grab a supply of blood. And he needed to make plans with Angus. "How long will it take Neona to get here?"

Tashi shrugged. "I don't know."

"I should rest before she comes. Can you tell her to come in thirty minutes?"

"Do we look like we would own a clock?"

"Neona has a watch. I gave her one."

Tashi's eyes widened. "Really? Is it true what Freya said, that you brought gifts for us all?"

He nodded. "True. I'd like to be accepted here."

"The queen will never accept a male here." With a sigh, Tashi walked toward the door. "Some things never change."

The sad tone of her voice made Zoltan suspect that she might be open to change. "Will you tell Neona?"

Tashi nodded. "Thirty minutes." She left, closing the door behind her.

Zoltan grabbed his jacket and looked around as he prepared to teleport. The trivet. It was bothering him because he couldn't tell what it was. He picked it up, checked the time on his watch, and teleported straight to the kitchen of his castle.

Howard had his wife pressed against the kitchen counter as he slipped a chocolate-covered strawberry into her mouth.

Zoltan dropped his bloody jacket and the black tile on the counter. "Sorry to interrupt."

Howard jumped and turned. "What the—holy crap! What happened to you?"

Elsa choked and swallowed, her eyes watering. "Oh, my God! Do you need a doctor?"

"I'm fine." Zoltan glanced down and winced. His bare chest was smeared with blood, and more blood had seeped through the bandages Neona had tied around him.

Howard gave him an incredulous look. "Why do you keep seeing that woman? She beat the crap out of you again!"

"No, she didn't." Zoltan motioned to the stab wound by his ribs. "Her mother did this. And it was one of her friends who shot me with an arrow."

"And that makes it okay?" Howard scoffed. "I take it back. You're not depressed. You're insane." He whipped out a cell phone. "I'm calling Mikhail. He has some medical supplies."

"I don't need doctoring." Zoltan pulled a bottle of Blissky from the cabinet. "But do call Mikhail and Angus and anyone else who can come for a strategy meeting. We have to come up with a plan to help the women of Beyul-La."

Howard frowned. "The same women who just treated you like a dartboard?"

"They'll come around." Zoltan poured a glass of Blissky and downed it. The blood gave him a jolt of energy, and the whisky took the edge off the pain. He grabbed the black tile. "Get everyone here now. I'll be right back."

"What? Where—"

Zoltan teleported to his office in Budapest. "Milan," he called as he entered his assistant's office.

Milan jumped to his feet. "Oh, my God! What happened to you?"

Zoltan shrugged, then grimaced from the pain of moving his shoulder.

"Sir!" Milan ran toward him. "Shall I call a doctor?"

"No, I'm fine. I'm in a hurry. I need to get back to something."

"A battle?" Milan adjusted his glasses as he eyed the bandages. "Are you sure that's wise, sir? If I might say so, you appear to be losing."

Zoltan smiled. "I'm fine. How's it going with the land deal?"

"Rajiv met with the government officials. He said they wanted an exorbitant amount, about ten million—"

"Send it. I need the deed right away."

Milan gulped. "Yes, sir."

"And see what you can find out about this." Zoltan handed him the black mystery tile.

Milan frowned, turning it over in his hands. "What is it?"

"I don't know. Send it to the lab at the university. The guys who investigated the arrow. And put a rush on it. I want to know by tomorrow night."

"Yes, sir."

"How's business? Do you have everything under control?"

"Yes, sir!" Milan's gaze shifted back to the bloody bandages. "How is your . . . vacation?"

"Great! See you later." Zoltan teleported back to the kitchen.

Mikhail and his wife, Pamela, had arrived and were sitting at the table with Howard and Elsa. J.L. Wang was helping himself to a Bleer from the fridge, and Emma MacKay was pouring herself a glass of Blardonnay.

She gasped. "What happened to you?"

"I met the other warrior women of Beyul-La," Zoltan explained. "Is Angus coming?"

"Yes, as soon as he finishes his interview with Franklin Chesterton." Emma poured a second glass of Blardonnay and offered it to Zoltan. "I went with Angus, since my psychic powers are much stronger than his, probably because I was already telepathic before I was transformed. I was able to see that Franklin has quite a few memories of his childhood. Apparently he and his father discussed Beyul-La often."

"That's good." Zoltan took a long drink of the mixture of synthetic blood and Chardonnay, then headed toward the table. "Shall we get started?"

"I brought a medicine kit," Mikhail said. "Do you want a shot for the pain?"

"I'll be fine." Zoltan sat next to J.L. Wang.

J.L., aka Jin Long, had worked for the FBI before becoming a vampire. As an employee for MacKay S&I, he was in charge of security for the West Coast Coven, situated in his hometown of San Francisco. Recently he'd done some assignments in China, since he knew the language.

"We read Angus's report," J.L. said, "so we're all up to date. Amazon women, hiding in a secret valley. Why? Are they scary looking?"

Zoltan shook his head. "Quite the contrary."

"Did you figure out what Lord Liao wants from

them?" Emma set the bottle of Blardonnay on the table along with her glass and took a seat.

Zoltan refilled his glass. "I believe so. The woman I've been seeing is Neona. She looks like she's twenty-two, but she's over two thousand years old. And her mother, the queen, is even older. I think she dates back to the Iron Age."

A series of gasps went around the table.

"Holy crap," Howard muttered. "And I thought *you* were old."

Zoltan gave him a wry look. "They have a fountain of youth. Living Water, they call it. I haven't seen it yet, but I believe it's a pool in a cave."

"So Lord Liao wants the fountain of youth?" Elsa asked. "But he's a vampire. He's already immortal."

"I think he's trying to prove his worth to Master Han," Zoltan explained. "If they take control of the Living Water, then they could wield a tremendous amount of power over the mortal world."

J.L. nodded. "Han could make mortal governments bend to his will."

"No wonder the women of Beyul-La are so distrusting," Emma said. "Whoever controls the Living Water could potentially control the world."

Mikhail leaned his elbows on the table. "We need to earn their trust. How many are there? Six?"

"Yes." Zoltan took another long drink. "I'm trying to convince them I'm on their side. I have an advantage there, since my mother actually came from Beyul-La."

Elsa gasped. "The mummy was one of the Amazon women?"

"What mummy?" Pamela asked.

"The mummy in the chapel is his mother," Elsa whispered to Pam.

J.L. snorted. "His momma's a mummy?"

Zoltan sighed. "As I was saying, I'm the son of one of the original founders of Beyul-La, so they're reluctant to kill me like they would some other guy. They've existed for centuries with the mind-set that men cannot be trusted."

Emma frowned. "We can't change something that ingrained overnight."

"I know." Zoltan drank some more Blardonnay. "Two of the women would still like to kill me—the queen and Lydia. I think Lydia's daughter, Tashi, could be open to change. And the two younger ones, Winifred and Freya, were born in the 1920s, so they missed the major man-hating events that the older ones went through. And they grew up with a loving father for a while, so we have a good chance of convincing those two that we're good guys."

"They're the daughters of Frederic Chesterton?" Emma asked, and Zoltan nodded.

"That's five of the women." J.L. looked at Zoltan. "What about the sixth?"

Neona. Zoltan wasn't sure how she felt about him. "I think she's on my side."

Howard's eyes narrowed. "You don't seem very confident. Is there a problem?"

Zoltan drank some more Blardonnay. It seemed to be helping with the pain. "They don't trust men. They trust vampires even less."

Pamela winced. "You haven't told them you're a vampire?"

"How did you explain being old enough to be the mummy's son?" J.L. asked.

"They think my mother gave me some of the Living Water to drink." Zoltan took another sip.

"Ah." Pamela nodded. "That would explain it."

Howard swallowed down some beer. "I wonder what would happen if a Vamp drank the Living Water."

Zoltan finished his glass. "I wondered that, too. If it enables a Vamp to stay awake during the day—"

"Master Han would have a huge advantage over us." J.L. grimaced. "He could kill us in our death-sleep."

Pamela gasped. "This is terrible!"

Mikhail patted her shoulder. "Relax. We don't know if the Living Water has any effect on a Vamp at all."

Everyone at the table turned to look at Zoltan.

He swallowed hard. "You want me to try it?"

"We have to know what would happen," Mikhail told him.

Zoltan frowned.

"Cheer up." J.L. gave him a wry smile. "It's not like the water could kill you."

Zoltan shifted in his chair. The women would kill him if they caught him in their cave, drinking their precious water.

What else were they hiding? "I keep feeling like I'm missing something. Shouldn't there be a . . . purpose for their long lives? Why live forever in secret?"

The others at the table were quiet as they pondered his question.

Zoltan thought back to what Neona had said. "She said the pact was binding forever."

"What pact?" Mikhail asked. "With whom?"

Zoltan shook his head. "I don't know."

"Maybe they're protecting someone?" Emma asked. "Or something?"

J.L. hit the table with the palm of his hand. "I know! The abominable snowman!"

Zoltan sat back. "What?"

The women at the table laughed, while Mikhail shook his head.

"I'm serious," J.L. insisted. "It's a Himalayan thing."

"There's no such thing as an abominable snowman," Howard muttered.

"Says the were-bear," J.L. smirked. "You might be related to him."

Howard growled.

"I have to leave soon." Zoltan glanced at his watch. "Emma, be ready to come when I call you. Maybe tomorrow night, or the next."

She nodded. "I'll be ready."

"The neighboring valley has a cabin where Frederic Chesteron lived. I'll try to get the women's permission for us to use it as our headquarters." Zoltan rose to his feet. "I'll be back in a few minutes."

While the others talked, he teleported up to his bedroom, cut the bandages off, and took a quick shower. Then he dressed, threw some clothes into a duffel bag, and teleported back to the kitchen. Everyone was still talking.

He stepped behind the counter and loaded a small ice chest with bottles of blood and ice.

Howard joined him. "What are you doing? You act like you're moving to Beyul-La."

"I have to gain their trust."

Howard scowled at him. "Talk to them all you want, but when the sun rises, come back here. Do not do your death-sleep there."

Zoltan closed the ice chest. "Neona tried hard to keep me alive. I think I can trust her."

"You *think* you can? You're going to risk your life on a hunch?" Howard removed a set of silver handcuffs from his jacket. "Don't make me use these."

Zoltan stepped back. If Howard managed to get a cuff on him, he'd be unable to teleport.

"Do I have to remind you how completely helpless you'll be?" Howard continued. "If you must go, take me with you."

"I can't take you on my wedding night!"

The room hushed. Everyone stared at him.

Zoltan winced.

Emma stood. "Did you get married?"

"Not . . . really. It's a . . . long story." Zoltan remembered the wedding rings he'd admired at the jewelry store. He glanced at his watch. "Howard, tell Domokos to go to the jewelry store tomorrow and pay Janos whatever I owe him."

With a groan, Howard raked a hand through his hair. "I don't know whether to congratulate you or use these damned handcuffs."

"I have to go." Zoltan grabbed his duffel bag and the ice chest.

"If you get the slightest inkling of danger, teleport back here," Howard warned him.

"I will. But if I hope to gain Neona's trust, then I'll have to trust her." As Zoltan teleported, Tashi's words echoed in his head. It was either a wedding or his funeral.

Chapter Fifteen

*H*uman *or monster?* Neona asked herself for the hundredth time. He looked human. He kissed like a human. Bled like a human. Felt pain like a human. And he was the boy she'd healed all those centuries ago. A boy who had almost died trying to protect his mother.

He was the same noble person. He'd grown into the man who had tried to protect her when he'd thought her leopard was going to attack. The man who had taken an arrow in his back to keep her from being harmed. He was the man her heart still yearned for. *Human.*

But as soon as she convinced herself of that, the memory flashed across her mind. Fangs, sharp and lethal, erupting from his mouth. *Monster.*

She shuddered in spite of the hot water she was sitting in. Freddie and Freya had dragged her to their house to prepare her for what they called her wedding night. While filling the tub with hot water and flower petals, they'd teased her with bawdy jests.

Freya had insisted on washing Neona's hair with some soap she'd made from the local wildflowers that bloomed each spring.

"You're so lucky," Freya said as she rinsed Neona's hair. "You've caught such a gorgeous man!"

Man or monster? Neona wondered again with a growing sense of panic. How could she spend the night with him?

"He's very strong and handsome." Freddie dug through the chest at the foot of her bed.

"And so devoted to you." Freya sighed. "When I think about how he risked his life to come here to see you—"

"I know!" Freddie removed a pair of red silk slippers. "And then he refused to let her feel his pain."

Freya sighed again. "What a gorgeous man!"

Or a gorgeous monster. Neona hugged her knees in the small wooden tub.

A knock sounded on the door, and Tashi slipped inside. "He says he needs thirty minutes to rest."

Freya snorted. "I wonder what for."

"He said he gave Neona a watch." Tashi looked around the room.

Neona motioned to her clothes piled on Freya's bed. "In the pouch."

Tashi and Freddie jumped at her clothes and searched through them.

"I found it!" Freddie pulled the watch out. "Good heavens! It's beautiful!"

Tashi touched it reverently. "The cat sparkles."

"There's a cat?" Freya ran to look. "I love cats!" She took the watch from her sister. "I wish a man would give me presents like this."

"There are presents for us, remember?" Freddie sat on the edge of her bed. "At our father's cabin."

"This is so exciting!" Freya admired the watch, then grinned at Neona. "You're so lucky!"

Neona sighed. How could it be lucky to fall in love with a vampire? She hated to admit it, but that was what he had to be. It explained his fangs and his ability to move quickly. The red glowing eyes must have been real. Was that a sign of hunger? When she spent the night with him, would he see her as his bride? Or would she be the wedding feast?

Tashi sat on the bed next to Freddie. "Maybe we should accept Neona's man. After all, he's Dohna's son. And he wants to help us defeat Lord Liao."

Freya set the watch down on the bedside table. "I wonder if he has any friends. It's so hard to find suitable men around here."

Tashi shrugged. "I found one."

Freddie grinned. "We thought you had."

Tashi nodded. "I only get to see him once a month." Her shoulders slumped. "I'm tired of keeping it secret. And I'm so tired of going all the way to the village to see him. I wish I could live there. Or he could live here."

Freddie winced. "The queen would never allow it."

Tashi sighed. "I know."

As Neona dragged a comb through her long, wet hair, she wondered if it was time for some changes in their world. Why did Tashi have to endure such a sad situation? Minerva had been miserable, too. So miserable she'd lost the will to live.

Neona bit her lip, knowing her thoughts were verging on mutiny. "If you love him, you should go live with him. What can the queen do to you? Kick you out? That would be exactly what you want."

The other women gasped.

"But our sacred duty," Freya whispered.

"It would continue. As long as the rest of us are here." Neona gave Tashi a sympathetic look. "I don't want you to be miserable."

Tashi's eyes glimmered with tears. "I thought about running away with him. After all, I had two sisters who could look after my mother and grandmother. But I never expected to lose them in battle. Grandmother, too. My mother is in so much pain. How can I leave her now?"

Neona nodded. It was almost three weeks now since the battle, but the emotional wounds were still raw for those who had survived.

Freya sniffed. "I wish that battle had never happened. How could we lose *five* of us?"

"I know!" Freddie jumped to her feet. "We've never lost anyone before. We've always been victorious!"

Tashi grimaced. "I've fought more battles than I can remember. We never had any trouble defeating the enemy."

"We never fought a vampire before," Freya muttered.

"True. We always fought mortal men." Tashi shuddered. "That damned vampire."

Freddie clenched her fists. "I *hate* vampires!"

Neona winced. How could she ever tell the other women that Zoltan was undead? Her mother was already looking for a reason to kill him. "Maybe some vampires are good. Like that Russell guy. He saved the queen's life."

Tashi tilted her head, considering. "I didn't know what to make of him. It seems strange for a vampire to be good."

Freya nodded. "It's like calling the sky green or the grass blue."

"But he did save my mother's life," Neona insisted. "And he promised to kill Lord Liao for us."

Freddie shrugged. "If you can believe a promise from a vampire."

With a sigh, Neona resumed her task of combing her hair. "It's not just Lord Liao who's the problem. His soldiers were different. Stronger and faster than any mortal men I've ever seen."

Freddie nodded. "That's true. There was something bizarre about them."

Freya waved a hand in dismissal. "Let's not talk about the battle anymore. We should be celebrating! Neona's found a gorgeous man, and soon we'll have a new baby girl!"

How could she spend the night with a vampire? With trembling hands, Neona struggled to get the comb through a tangle in her hair.

Tashi gave her a worried look. "I hope you don't fall in love with him. You know what will happen once you're pregnant . . ."

The comb slipped from Neona's hand, dropping with a splash into the bathwater. She couldn't bear to see Zoltan die. Even if he did have fangs. But there was an easy way to avoid his execution. If she never bedded him, she couldn't get pregnant. The thought of bedding him was too frightening anyway. She'd seen how he reacted in a moment of intense pain. What if the same thing happened in a moment of intense pleasure? Would his fangs shoot out and rip into her neck?

"Let's not think about the future," Freya insisted. "It's Neona's first night with her mate. We need to make it perfect!"

Freddie returned to the trunk at the foot of her bed. "I think she should wear this." She pulled out a white gown embroidered with pink flowers.

Tashi gasped. "I remember that! It was Calliope's. She wore it to the ceremony she had with Frederic."

Freddie lay the white gown on her bed. "Mother told us about it. Father refused to bed her until they exchanged vows." She turned to Neona, her golden brown eyes bright with excitement. "We would be honored if you wore it."

"Oh, yes!" Freya clasped her hands together. "Say you will, Neona. Our mother was so fond of you."

Neona's eyes filled with tears. She'd loved Calliope, too. As the two healers, they'd learned a great deal from each other. "I will."

"Yes!" Freya jumped. "You'll look like a real bride!"

Freddie grinned. "You must be so excited!"

Neona's nerves tensed. Soon she would have to see Zoltan, and she didn't know what to do or say to him.

Tashi picked up the watch. "We have fifteen minutes left."

Panic ignited in Neona's chest. Human or monster? How could she spend the night with him? At some point, he would get hungry, and she'd be the only one there. "Do you have any wine?"

With a laugh, Freddie grabbed a pitcher of rice wine. "Let's have a drink!"

Freya found four earthenware cups and filled them all. "To Neona and her wedding night!"

Zoltan teleported to Neona's house with three minutes to spare. One of the chests was mostly empty, Minerva's he assumed. He stashed his duffel bag and small ice chest in there. Then he paced about the room, growing increasingly nervous. Would Neona accept him? He recalled the look of horror on her face when his fangs had popped out.

He needed to convince her he was safe. He glanced down at the new clothes he was wearing. In anticipation of proposing marriage, he'd dressed well, but now he realized the new clothes might frighten her. It would be better to look the same way he had when she'd last seen him. Shirtless with jeans.

With vampire speed, he pulled off his suit, tie, and dress shoes. He grabbed a pair of jeans from the duffel bag and put them on. Then he tossed the new clothes into the chest, making sure to retrieve the small black box from his coat pocket.

He opened the box to study the rings. Was he out of his mind to want to marry someone he'd met only five nights ago? No, he corrected that. They'd first met in 1241 when Neona had saved his life. He had no memory of it, but she remembered him. She'd dreamed of him. And it was her arrow in Russell's quiver that had led him here. It was his quest for the truth that had brought him here.

The truth was he loved her. He'd waited almost eight hundred years for her. Why should he wait another blasted night? He'd suspected from the beginning that their fates were connected. He knew it now for sure.

A clanging noise and laughter sounded outside. It sounded like metal pot lids being knocked together. He set the jewelry box on the bed, then walked in his stocking feet to the door. With his superhearing, he could detect voices outside.

"You're all drunk," Lydia fussed. "How will you guard this house through the night? We can't let the prisoner escape."

Someone scoffed. "I don't think he'll be wanting to escape tonight!"

The others laughed.

Lydia scoffed. "Don't let the queen see you like this. She's busy in the cave tonight."

The cave? Where the Living Water was? At some point, Zoltan needed to sneak in there for a taste test. He'd brought an empty bottle for the task.

The bar on the door scraped. "Go inside, Neona," Lydia ordered. "The rest of you, go sleep it off. You can guard during the day."

Zoltan stepped back between the beds so it wouldn't look like he'd been eavesdropping.

When Neona stumbled inside, his mouth dropped open. She was more beautiful than ever. She smelled of wildflowers and looked heavenly in white silk. The front part of her hair had been braided and wrapped across the top of her head like a crown. Wildflowers had been inserted in the braid, making her look like a fairy princess. The back section of her hair hung loose down her back like a shiny black curtain. More flowers blossomed in thread on her white silk gown and red silk slippers.

She looked at him and her eyes widened. When the door slammed shut behind her, she jumped and hiccoughed. Wincing, she lifted a hand to her mouth. The bell-shaped sleeve of her gown fell back toward her elbow, revealing the Hello Kitty watch fastened to her wrist.

He smiled. "You look beautiful."

She frowned. "So do you." Her gaze swept over his bare chest, and her frown deepened. "You took off the bandages."

"They were a little bloody, and I wanted to wash up." He took a step toward her.

She stepped back. "The wounds didn't bleed?"

He shook his head. "That ointment you put on

them worked well." He took another step toward her. "Thank you for saving me. Twice."

She moved over to the table. The bowl and pitcher were still there, untouched. She peered into the pitcher and grazed her fingertips across the dry bowl.

No doubt she was wondering how he was standing here squeaky clean with wet hair. She shot him a wary look, then eased behind the table.

"Careful." He stepped toward her, worried that her long gown was too close to the fire.

She grabbed the knife off the uneaten plate of food and pointed it at him. "Don't come any closer."

He sighed. So much for his wedding night. And that knife was clearly meant for spreading jam. "You should find a sharper knife if you want to kill me."

Her face crumbled. "I don't really want to kill you."

"That's a relief."

"I don't know what to do with you." She gazed sadly at the knife in her hand. "Maybe I should go cut the donkey." She hiccoughed. "Poor donkey."

Zoltan's mouth twitched. "I think you're drunk."

Her eyes narrowed. "I think you're smirking at me."

"Never." He wiped the smile off his face.

"I had a little wine. Four cups. No, five." She lifted her chin. "It's in my blood now, so I'm warning you. I won't taste good."

His mouth twitched again. She would still taste wonderful to him. "Is that why you drank?"

"Partly. But I also wanted the courage to—" She swayed to the side and caught herself on the back of a chair.

"To have sex with me?"

"No!" She pointed the knife at him. "I know your secret. You're a monster!"

"I know *your* secret. You're a two-thousand-year-old crone."

She gasped. "I'm not a crone!"

"I'm not a monster."

She huffed. "You have fangs!"

"You have a gray hair."

"I do?" With a stunned look, she lifted her hand to her hair, forgetting she still had the knife in it.

"Careful!" With vampire speed, he raced forward, yanked the knife from her hand, and pulled her away from the fireplace.

"Get back!" She shoved at his chest.

He released her but remained in front of her.

"Move!" She shoved again, but he didn't budge. She pushed again. "You're like a rock."

She paused, her hands splayed across his chest. Her eyes widened. "So . . . hard." Her fingertips pressed gently into him. "But soft."

He drew in a steadying breath as her fingers slid down his torso, caressing his bare skin. He needed to stay in control and keep his eyes from glowing and frightening her.

"You feel like a human," she whispered.

"I am human."

"No!" She fisted a hand and pounded it against his chest to accentuate each sentence. "You're a vampire. With fangs. You'll get hungry. And bite me."

"I won't."

"I don't trust you—"

"I won't bite you. Here, I'll prove it to you." He walked over to the wooden chest and pulled out the small ice chest. "I brought plenty of blood with me." He showed her a bottle, then opened it to drink a few gulps.

Her eyes widened with horror.

Damn. Instead of reassuring her, he was scaring her. He stuffed the bottle back into the ice chest.

She hiccoughed. "Where did you get all that blood?"

"It's synthetic blood. Manufactured."

"You didn't . . . drain it from someone?"

"No, it's made in a factory. All of us good Vamps drink synthetic blood. We don't attack people for food." He opened the wooden chest again to set the ice chest inside.

She stumbled closer for a quick look. "You brought clothes here? Where did you go?"

"I went home for a little while. I can teleport to another place in a second."

She blinked at him. "That's how you disappear? You tele—pork?"

His mouth twitched. "Teleport."

"Oh. So you . . . teleported home?" When he nodded, she gave him an incredulous look. "Then why did you come back?"

His heart sank. "You . . . don't want me here?"

"There are people here who would like to kill you. If you had any sense, you would stay away!"

"So you're worried about me?" He smiled. "You care about me?"

She crossed her arms. "I don't want to talk about it."

"You mean you don't want to admit that you care about me."

She scowled at him. "Why did you come back?"

"I can't leave you here alone to shoulder all the blame. Not when I want you to trust me." He turned to close the lid on the wooden chest.

With a grimace, she eyed the arrow wound in his shoulder. "If you can teleport whenever you like, why didn't you disappear when Lydia shot the arrow?"

"The arrow would have hit you." He frowned at

her. "Don't ever leap in front of me like that again."

"I-I wasn't thinking."

He arched an eyebrow at her. "One might get the idea that you cared about me."

She huffed. "I am a healer. It is my natural instinct to spare people from pain." She reached for his shoulder. "Should I heal it now?"

"No." He grabbed her hand. "It will heal during my death-sleep."

"*Death-sleep*?" With a shudder, she pulled her hand away. "If everything heals while you're . . . asleep, why do you still have the old scars on your back?"

"I was mortal then. Only fourteen."

She regarded him solemnly for a moment, then swayed on her feet.

He took hold of her shoulders to keep her steady. "Maybe you should lie down."

She shook her head, and one of the wildflowers slipped from her hair and fluttered to the floor. "I cannot believe it is really you. The boy. Do you know you're the only human male I have ever healed?"

"I didn't know."

She rested her hands upon his chest, then circled behind him, moving her hands across his chest and shoulder to keep herself steady. "I remember this so clearly." She touched the burn mark on his back. "Like it was yesterday."

He drew in a deep breath. "I'm still the same person. Just a little older."

She touched a few scars across his shoulder blades. "I healed these first." She moved her hand up the back of his neck to his head, then her fingers delved through his wet hair to stroke his scalp. "You had a nasty cut here. Swollen and bleeding. It was the blow that knocked you unconscious."

He closed his eyes, enjoying the feel of her fingers.

Her hand skimmed down his neck to the red scar that marred his back. "I was afraid to touch this. I knew it would hurt something fierce."

"But you did. You saved me."

"I have been dreaming about that day since the first night we met in the woods. Somehow, deep inside, I knew that it was you."

He turned slowly. "Then I am the man of your dreams."

She hiccoughed. "Or a nightmare."

He plucked a wildflower from her hair. "I would never harm you."

"You are hurting me. You're making my heart ache."

"Sweetheart." He dragged the flower down her cheek. "It doesn't need to hurt. If you'll accept me for what I am—"

"You're a vampire."

"Who loves you." He kissed her brow.

"You shouldn't say that."

"But it's true." He kissed her nose.

"Why are you kissing me?"

"Because I love you." He brushed his lips against hers. "We were meant for each other from the beginning."

She shook her head. "I'm afraid you'll bite me."

"I've kissed you before without biting you." He nuzzled her neck. "I've nibbled your neck without biting you." He palmed her breast. "I've kissed your breasts without biting you."

She moaned and gave him a sleepy-eyed look. Then she flinched and jumped back. "Your eyes are turning red!"

"It only means that I want you—"

"No!" She grabbed the knife off the floor where it had fallen earlier. "My mind is made up, and I will not be swayed." She pointed the knife at him. "I will not fornicate with you."

He raised his eyebrows. "That's good. Because I'd much rather make love."

"That's even worse!" She motioned with the knife. "Go to bed."

"Come with me."

"No! That is your bed. This one is mine." She scrambled onto the other bed, then settled against the wall with her legs drawn up and her knees bent. She hugged her knees with one hand and pointed the knife at him with the other.

With a sigh, he sat on the edge of the other bed. "You don't need the knife, Neona. I understand the word no."

She frowned, flexing her hand around the knife handle. "I've never had to spend the night alone with a vampire."

"I'm not going to hurt you." He moved the black box from the bed to the bedside table. It didn't look like he'd be proposing tonight.

"What is in the box?"

"I'll show you later."

She yawned.

"You're used to sleeping at night, aren't you? You can sleep if you want."

"I have to keep an eye on you."

He snorted. "You think I'm going to fly across the room and attack you?"

"Isn't that how you became a vampire? Didn't another one attack you?"

He sighed. "Sometimes that happens. In my case, I asked for it."

Her eyes widened with shock. "Why would you do that?"

"I lost my brother and parents within a week. I was fourteen, and suddenly I was a count, responsible for a destroyed castle and a burned village. The only friend I had left was an old vampire. Istvan. He gave me advice and money so I could rebuild the castle and village. He helped me defeat the Mongols when they invaded a second time. And he watched over my domain when I would go searching for answers."

"He was a good friend," Neona whispered.

Zoltan nodded. "My best friend. And a second father to me. I had the arrow that killed my real father, and I would spend every summer hunting for those who had murdered him and destroyed my village."

Neona winced. "I'm not sure who killed your father."

"I know." He smiled at her. "You were with me, healing me. But still, I wanted answers, and I wouldn't give up."

Her eyes softened. "You were always stubborn."

"Yes. When I turned twenty-nine, I became worried that I would grow too old or infirm to continue the search, so I asked Istvan to transform me. And he did. He said something about my mother having an ancient soul, and that he'd always known I was destined for the same fate. It didn't make any sense to me at the time, but it does now."

"What happened to Istvan?"

"He died in the Great Vampire War of 1710."

She blinked. "There was a vampire war?"

"Yes." His mouth curled up. "Don't worry, the good guys won."

"But you lost your best friend. It must have been lonely for you."

"Not anymore." He smiled. "Now I've found you."

She frowned. "Don't smile at me. It makes me feel strange."

His smile widened.

She bit her lip. "So there really are good vampires who fight the bad ones?"

He nodded. "We've been fighting them for centuries. Lately, we've been fighting Master Han and his vampire lords. You met Russell. He's more determined than anyone to kill Master Han."

"You know Russell?"

"Yes. He drops by my castle twice a month for a supply of blood and weapons. It was your arrow in his quiver that caused me to come looking for you that first night."

"Oh." She made a face. "I asked Russell to use it to kill Liao. He's the monster who killed my sister."

"We'll get him. We've already killed the other two lords. And we got rid of the demon Darafer."

She winced. "There was a demon?"

"Yes. Don't worry. We'll defeat Lord Liao and Master Han. You can trust us." Zoltan felt the pull of the upcoming sunrise. He stood and dropped his jeans.

She stiffened. "What are you doing?"

"The sun will rise soon." He tossed the jeans on top of the wooden chest. "I'm making myself comfortable." He stretched out on the bed and tugged the sheet up to his hips, even with the band of his black boxer briefs.

"You're going to fall asleep?"

"Death-sleep." He rolled onto his side to look at her. "I'll be completely vulnerable. I'm trusting you to keep me safe."

She studied him, searching his eyes. "Why do you trust me?"

"You've saved me twice. I don't figure you would let me die now."

"What do you mean by death-sleep?"

"I'll be dead. Then I wake up right after sunset."

"How can you wake from the dead?"

"I'm not sure. I'm just damned grateful that it keeps happening."

She frowned. "Does it hurt? When you die?"

"A little," he lied. Then he sat up with alarm. "If I look like I'm in pain going into my death-sleep, do not touch me. Do you understand? It's the pain of death, and if you take that upon yourself, you would probably die."

Her face paled and she nodded.

He lay back down as another tug pulled at his senses. "Why the no fornication rule?"

"Isn't it obvious? They'll kill you as soon as I'm pregnant. So the best way to keep you alive is to make sure that I never get pregnant."

"So you're rejecting me because you care about me."

"I don't want you to be killed because of me." She hugged her knees. "And I don't trust you. I saw how your fangs sprang out in a moment of intense pain. They might do it again if you feel . . . intense pleasure."

"You think I'll bite you while I'm climaxing?"

"Yes." Her cheeks turned pink as she gave him a wary look. "Does that usually happen?"

He yawned. "I can control it."

"It would be foolish for me to trust you."

"I understand. Trust has to be earned." He felt a stronger pull tugging him into the deep dark hole, but he fought to remain conscious. "We'll start with something small. Then if I don't bite you, we'll move on to something bigger. Do you agree?"

She nodded sleepily. "I guess."

"Fine. Then tomorrow, I'll give you one little climax and not bite you."

She blinked. "What?"

"I know." He yawned. "You wanted ten. When we get through all ten climaxes without me biting you, then you'll know you can trust me. And then we'll make love."

"What? I can't agree to that!"

"You already did." One final tug swept over him, seizing his heart with a burst of pain. With his last breath, he whispered, "Tomorrow."

Chapter Sixteen

$\mathcal{T}$*he boy was near death, his body bleeding and bruised, an angry red burn seared across his back. Neona moved her hands over the gashes and bruises, taking in as much of his pain as she could endure. In the distance, where the village and castle were located, smoke billowed into the sky. The stench of burning bodies made her choke. Gathering up her courage, she reached for the red burn on his back.*

Suddenly, he grabbed her, pulling her down and rolling on top of her. It was Zoltan, grown up and smiling at her in the way that always made her stomach quiver. "Neona," he whispered. "It's time to give you that first climax."

She woke with a jolt. Then a groan. Her head hurt. She was lying on top of her comforter with her knees hugged to her chest. She glanced at the other bed. Zoltan was there, still and quiet. With another groan, she slowly stretched out her legs. They were stiff and achy from sleeping hunched up in a ball.

She sat up. Her white silk gown was a wrinkled mess. She should have taken it off before sleeping, but she hadn't dared undress in front of Zoltan. He was lying on his side, facing her, barely visible in the dim light that filtered into the room around the door and windows.

It was daylight outside. She'd spent the night with a vampire. And she'd survived without a single bite mark.

She eased out of bed, her stiff legs protesting. He appeared to be sleeping. Death-sleep, he'd called it. She remembered how Russell had sizzled when sunlight had touched his body.

Alarmed, she lurched toward him to make sure he was all right. A sliver of light illuminated a narrow strip down his bed about a foot from his back. If he rolled over, he might get burned. She checked his back and exhaled with relief. No injuries.

The arrow wound was almost completely healed. Only a red mark remained where the puncture hole had been. She pressed her fingers to his neck. No pulse. She winced. Was he really dead? How could he be dead when his body was healing itself? For the change to occur, there had to be some part of him still alive. She'd heard stories of Buddhist monks who could slow their heartbeat to the point it was no longer discernible. Perhaps that was what happened to vampires.

She gave him a little shake, but there was no reaction. He was unresponsive. Defenseless and vulnerable. And he was trusting her to keep him safe. Her heart squeezed in her chest. He trusted her. And God help her, she wanted to trust him. The attraction was still there. The yearning. Her feelings had taken a shock when she'd realized he was a vampire, but they hadn't withered away.

His eyes were shut, with a line of thick eyelashes that were so pretty, her fingers itched to touch him. She brushed his shoulder-length hair back from his

brow. His hair was soft and silky. She ran a finger-
tip over his eyebrow, then down his whiskered jaw
to his square chin. A stubborn chin, she thought with
a smile. And a wide, sensual mouth. She touched his
lips. Too gorgeous.

Too dangerous. Her gaze drifted down his muscled
chest to the waistband of his underwear, low on his
hips. She could see the outline of his long legs underneath the sheet. So he thought he could earn her trust,
one climax at a time. She snorted. The rascal would
come up with a plan like that.

Her gaze shifted back to the arrow wound. Instead
of teleporting away, he'd taken the hit to protect her.
He'd tried to protect her from her pet leopard, too.
And even though he could have stayed in the safety
of his own home, he'd returned to be with her. No
matter how many times she tried to discourage him,
he refused to give up on her. With a sigh, she realized
he'd been earning her trust all along.

She removed the white silk gown and lay it over the
back of a chair. Then she wrapped a plain linen robe
over the white silk shift that Tashi had insisted she
wear, claiming it was easy to rip. With her legs still
stiff, she hobbled over to each window and pulled the
thick woolen curtains shut, making sure they blocked
out any light. The room grew darker. The fire in the
hearth had died out.

At the door, she slipped on her leather slippers,
then carefully opened the door, making sure no sunlight fell on Zoltan. She slipped outside, grimacing at
the bright light.

"You're up!" Someone called from the central fire pit.

Shielding her eyes from the sun's glare, Neona
spotted Tashi, Freddie, and Freya sitting around the
fire.

"We've been watching your house since sunrise." Tashi regarded her curiously. "There hasn't been a sound."

"It's already afternoon," Freddie said. "You missed breakfast and lunch."

"Are you all right?" Freya asked.

Neona nodded. "We were asleep."

"Worn out, huh?" Freya exchanged a grin with the other two.

Neona headed toward the outhouse, her stiff legs protesting.

"Good heavens," Freddie whispered loudly. "She can hardly walk."

"He must have been good," Tashi said, and they all laughed.

Neona groaned and kept walking.

"Should we take him a tray of food?" Freddie called after her.

"No!" Neona whirled to face them. Their surprised expressions made her realize she'd overreacted. "He's asleep now. I'll feed him later." Wincing, she resumed her walk to the outhouse.

"She seems a bit . . . possessive," Freya said.

"Doesn't even want us to look at him," Freddie added.

"He must have been damned good," Tashi muttered, and the others laughed again.

Neona hurried to the outhouse, then washed her hands and face in the stream before returning to the central fire pit, where Freya was stirring a pot near the fire.

"We've kept the soup hot for you and your man."

"His name is Zoltan." Neona glanced at her house before taking a seat.

"We figure it's best not to get too familiar with him," Tashi murmured.

Because they believed they would have to kill him, Neona thought. Luckily, if they tried to execute Zoltan, he could teleport away. But only at night. He was helpless now, and she was his only protection.

"Here." Freya ladled some hot soup into an earthenware bowl, then added a lump of sticky rice. "You must be hungry."

"Thanks." Neona looked around. "Where are the others?"

"My mother's asleep," Tashi said, referring to Lydia. "She guarded your house all night."

"The queen is busy in the cave," Freddie added.

Neona nodded, then spooned some soup broth into her mouth. Soon she would need to tell everyone that Zoltan was a vampire. But she'd better wait till nighttime, when he could defend himself or teleport away, in case the news didn't go over well.

"So how was it?" Freya whispered. "We've been dying to know."

"If you don't mind talking about it," Freddie added with a hopeful look.

Tashi snorted. "As if we don't know what they were doing. Did he rip your shift off?"

Neona used her wooden spoon to break up the lump of rice in her soup. "Nothing happened."

"What?" All three women gasped.

"He was . . . weak and running a fever. Because of the wound. He needs rest, so don't go in there. I'll nurse him back to health." Neona stood, careful not to spill any soup. "I'll give him some of this. Thanks." As she walked toward her house, the women talked in hushed voices.

"I can't believe it," Freya whispered.

"I know," Tashi agreed. "He couldn't even do it?"

Freddie huffed. "I thought he was stronger than that."

Neona winced. Thank God Zoltan's pride was as dead as he was at the moment. She slipped inside the house, quickly shutting the door behind her. He was still stretched out on Minerva's bed, barely visible in the dark.

She set the bowl of soup on the table next to the un-eaten dinner from last night. Then she took a candle from the mantelpiece and hurried back outside. The women hushed and exchanged glances when she approached. No doubt they had been discussing Zoltan's inability to perform. He would most proba-bly be annoyed by her current strategy, but it seemed like the best way to buy some time. They wouldn't kill him as long as they were waiting for her to get pregnant.

Freddie stood and brushed off her pants. "Freya and I are going to our father's cabin to bring back the presents. You want to come?"

"I should keep an eye on Zoltan." Neona lit her candle from the central fire pit. "I'll see you in a few hours."

She rushed back to her house and lit the fire in the hearth. Then she wedged the lit candle into the holder on her bedside table.

"There. Now I can see." She glanced at Zoltan. His eyes were still closed, and he hadn't budged.

Her gaze drifted to the black box sitting on the bed-side table. "Is this another gift for me?"

No response. He just lay there, looking gorgeous with the firelight glimmering over his muscled body and handsome face.

She opened the black box, and her breath caught. Two gold bands. A larger one for a man. A smaller one for a woman. She'd read about these in the books Frederic had left behind. A man and woman exchanged vows and rings at their wedding.

Her eyes misted with tears. Zoltan wanted to marry her. Didn't he realize that marriage never worked for the women of Beyul-La? Calliope's husband had deserted her. And Zoltan's mother, Dohna, had ended up dead.

Would Zoltan try to repeat his father's actions? Would he try to lure her away from the valley and her sacred duty?

Just last night Neona had urged Tashi to run away and live with the man she loved. But he was a villager. A mortal, who lived close by. She and any future daughters she had could still visit Beyul-La and help fulfill their sacred duty.

Marriage to Zoltan would mean marriage to a vampire. A husband with fangs? Would she have children with fangs?

She snapped the box shut and set it back on the table. There was no point in even imagining it. She couldn't leave Beyul-La. She was the only healer left. Everyone counted on her.

Her eyes filled with tears as she removed her sparkly watch and set it beside the black box. Then she sat on the edge of her bed and gazed at Zoltan.

"It's impossible," she whispered.

Neona woke to a loud squeaking noise. She lay in bed, disoriented for a few seconds. She hadn't intended to fall asleep again, but after eating all the food on the table, she'd stretched out on her bed with nothing to do other than stare at Zoltan.

She blinked. His bed was empty.

With a gasp, she sat up.

"Good evening." He smiled at her as he twisted the top off a bottle of blood.

While he drank, Neona looked him over. He was standing next to the wooden chest. The open box, containing ice and his bottles of blood, sat on top of the chest. He'd slipped his blue pants back on, but they were unfastened and rested low on his hips. A line of dark hair ran from his navel into his black underwear. She swallowed hard and lifted her gaze. The stab wound by his ribs was completely gone. No doubt his arrow wound was completely healed, too.

She ventured a quick glance at his face and stiffened when she realized he had been studying her, too. She looked away and busied herself, unbraiding her hair. The wildflowers had fallen from her hair onto her pillow while she'd slept. She gathered the wilted flowers up, then eased past Zoltan to the fireplace, where she tossed them in. Another log had been added to the fire.

She glanced at Zoltan. "Have you been up long?"

"Just a few minutes." He finished his bottle and grimaced. "Cold blood." He shoved the empty bottle back into the box. When he closed the lid, it made the same squeaking noise that had awakened her.

"Of course, I could have enjoyed some fresh, warm blood." He turned to her, his eyes darkening as he looked her over. "I woke up with a terrible hunger and there you were, lying so close, smelling so sweet. Tempting the hell out of me."

She stepped back. "You wanted to bite me?"

"I'm a vampire. Of course I did." He shrugged. "But I didn't. So do you trust me now?"

"No!"

His amber-colored eyes gleamed with humor. "Then we have no choice but to continue with the original plan to earn your trust. Ten climaxes, one at a time."

She had a feeling he'd set her up. "I didn't agree to that."

The corner of his mouth curled up. "One little climax. You're not afraid of that, are you?"

"I'm a warrior. I laugh at fear."

His eyes sparkled. "Good. Then we'll start tonight."

"Says who?" She lifted her chin. "Are you smirking at me?"

His smile widened. "Never." He opened the wooden chest and put his supply of blood back in. Then he removed a small bag from his duffel bag. "Is there a place to shower around here?"

"I usually go to Frederic's valley, where the stream from Beyul-La shoots out from the rock wall."

"I know where that is. Do you have any towels?"

"We cannot leave this valley."

"Of course we can. They'll never know we left the house. We'll teleport."

Her mouth dropped open. "I-I'd rather not."

"Afraid?"

"Of course not. But I'm supposed to keep you here."

"You're supposed to guard me. That's why you should come with me." He stepped closer. "What if I tried to escape?"

She snorted. "You could escape anytime you want."

"Towel?"

"Fine." She moved to the shelves in the corner next to the hearth. "Here. Go take your shower." She grabbed a linen towel from the stack.

When she turned, her breath caught. He was right next to her. With a very determined look on his face.

"What are you doing? You shouldn't sneak up—"

He grabbed her and everything went black. A few seconds later, her feet landed and she stumbled.

"Easy." He steadied her.

"You startled me!" She shoved at his chest.

With a smile, he released her and stepped back. "Just one of the many thrills in store for you tonight."

"I didn't agree!" She threw the towel at him.

He caught it and sauntered along the stream, headed for the rock wall.

She looked around. Good Lord, she'd actually teleported with him. They were in the next valley, not far from Frederic's cabin. In the distance, she could see where the water jetted through the rock wall. The grass felt cold and damp under her bare feet. She hadn't even had time to put on her shoes.

As she approached the waterfall, she watched Zoltan setting his towel and small bag on a flat rock.

He waved at her before heading toward a clump of trees and bushes. "I'm not running away. I'll be right back."

What was he doing? She ventured closer, then turned away when she realized he was relieving himself. She leaned over to peer at his small bag. It had the same sort of metal closure that his blue pants did. She tugged at the metal tab and smiled when it slid along the top of the bag, opening it.

"You like zippers?" He stopped beside her and dropped his pants to the ground. "I'll let you practice with my jeans next time."

"Jeans?"

"My pants." He folded them and set them on the rock next to the towel. "Would you like to shower with me?"

"No. I'm fine." She stepped back. When he hooked

his thumbs into the waistband of his underwear, she quickly looked away. Something grazed her toes, and she jumped back. The rascal had tossed his underwear at her as if he was daring her to take a peek.

Very well. She wasn't a coward. She did. He was leaning over his small bag, and he pulled out two of the smallest containers she'd ever seen. And they were clear. She could see some sort of liquid inside. When he straightened, she caught a glimpse of his manhood before turning away. Good Lord, he was huge.

She swallowed hard. "Those are interesting. What are they?"

"My balls."

She gritted her teeth and gave him a wry look, being careful to only look at his face. "In your hand."

"Ah." He smiled as he raised his hand to her. "Shampoo and conditioner. Travel size. Would you like to try it?"

"No, thanks." She lifted her chin. "Are you smirking at me?"

"Never." His smile widened. "Are you ogling me?"

"Never." Her gaze slid down as he turned. Good Lord, could a man's back and buttocks be that gorgeous?

He strode into the shallow pool at the base of the waterfall. The water only reached midcalf, for it rushed down a rocky path to join the main stream in the valley.

After setting the small containers on a rock, he leaned into the cascade of water, his back to her.

She took a deep breath to ease the quivers in her stomach. Even with the scars on his back, he was beautiful to behold. He lifted his arms to smooth his hands over his slick hair. The muscles in his arms and shoulders rippled. His buttocks flexed.

And her knees nearly gave out. With a muffled squeak, she steadied herself.

He glanced back as he squirted shampoo into his hand. "Are you all right?"

"Yes. I—I'll just rinse out your underwear." She grabbed it off the ground and hurried to the stream.

Crouching next to the water, she dunked his underwear in and swished it about. She glanced back. He was vigorously lathering up his hair. Trails of soap trickled down his back, meandering around his muscles, till they reached his rump.

She turned away, sucking in a deep breath. How could a man's rear end look so enticing? So touchable. She wanted to dig her fingers into those cheeks and feel the muscles flexing beneath her hands.

She squeezed his underwear in her hands, wringing out the water. Her thighs tensed as an odd sensation settled between her legs. An empty, aching need. It made her press her thighs together.

She glanced back and gasped softly. He'd turned to face her. His eyes were closed, and he was leaning back to rinse his hair. His hands glided over his hair, biceps bulging. Rivulets of water ran down his chest and stomach to the patch of dark hair that surrounded his manhood.

He was aroused. Jutting out. Her mouth went dry, and moisture pooled between her legs.

He stepped toward her, and with another gasp, she realized his eyes were now open. He'd caught her ogling him. She stumbled to her feet.

"Is that my underwear?" He pointed downstream.

"Oh!" In her shock, she must have dropped it. It was tumbling down the creek, halfway to Frederic's cabin. "I'll get it!" She ran along the bank of the stream, then plunged in to grab it where it had caught on a tree branch.

Suddenly, Zoltan appeared in the middle of the

creek, right in front of her. With a squeal, she fell back, landing on her rump. Cold water enveloped her to her chin.

With a laugh, he plucked his underwear off the branch, then pulled her to her feet. "Now that you're all wet, you might as well shower with me."

"I—" Everything went black again, then she stumbled in the pool by the waterfall. "Stop doing that!" She shoved at him, but he didn't budge.

He untied her sash, then pulled off her robe. She was still wearing the sheer white silk shift underneath.

Zoltan tossed her robe onto the grass, then squeezed some shampoo into the palm of his hand. "Is your hair wet?"

She leaned into the spray of water to dampen her hair, then he led her over to a rock.

"Sit." He stepped behind her. "Close your eyes."

She sat with a huff. "You shouldn't order me about." She swiveled on the rock to glare at him but found her nose inches away from his manhood. Her jaw dropped. The cold stream had doused his arousal a bit, but the shaft was still thick and heavy, swollen with desire.

"You should close your mouth," he said softly. "It's giving me ideas."

She snapped her mouth shut and glowered at him. "Are you smirking again?"

"Are you ogling again?"

She scoffed, then turned her back to him and squeezed her eyes shut. But even with her eyes closed, she kept seeing his manhood.

His hands moved over her scalp, his fingers massaging her temples and the back of her neck. It felt heavenly. Sensual. She gripped her knees.

"Come." He pulled her to her feet and led her back to the waterfall. Then he arched her back to rinse her hair.

When she straightened, her silk shift was soaked and plastered to body. And his eyes were red and glowing.

He palmed her breast, kneading it gently. "Neona."

She shuddered. "Why do your eyes turn red?"

"It's a sign of how much I want to make love to you." He nuzzled her neck as his fingers teased the hardened tip of her nipple.

Her thighs pressed together.

He kissed a path up her neck to her ear. "Are you ready?" he whispered. He gently tugged at the tip of her nipple, making her moan. "Ready for your little climax?"

She clutched his shoulders. "We mustn't have intercourse. I mustn't get pregnant." Even though she suddenly wanted it more than anything. She wanted to take him deep inside and feel his seed gushing out, filling her with heat. And giving her hope for a little girl with long dark hair and amber eyes. But would the child have fangs?

"I'm only going to touch you." His hands slipped under her shift and squeezed her buttocks.

She wouldn't let herself worry for now. She'd live for the moment and pretend that she had an eternity to spend with Zoltan. Even if it was impossible.

He nuzzled her ear. "Do you agree?"

Her heart felt like it was going to burst. She wrapped her arms around his neck. "Yes."

Chapter Seventeen

Zoltan's heart swelled. She'd said yes. He cradled her face in his hands and rested his forehead against hers, savoring the moment. This would be the first of many yesses, he vowed to himself. He would not give up on her, not allow their future to be sabotaged by an ancient lifestyle that had forced her to live alone and secluded for centuries. Whatever pact she'd made, whatever her sacred duty was, he would not lose her because of it. She would be his. Forever.

He kissed her thoroughly until she clung to him, breathless and trembling at his touch. As she gasped for air, he moved his hands slowly. The white silk was soaked through till it was practically transparent. He could see the color of her nipples, a dark, dusty pink. He could feel the pebbled skin and the tip that grew harder as he gently tugged.

"Wait," she whispered, stepping back.

For a second he feared she'd changed her mind, but she gave him a flirtatious smile. With one smooth move, she pulled her shift off and tossed it onto the grass.

His breath caught. The first time to see her totally nude. His groin reacted, growing hard.

Her eyes widened. "You don't seem to have trouble getting in the mood now."

"I never did." His red glowing eyes tinted her beautiful body in shades of pink. He gritted his teeth to stay in control. "I wanted you from the first night you clonked me on the head and demanded my seed."

She gave him a wry look. "I didn't realize I was seducing a vampire."

He stepped toward her till the tip of his erection was a mere inch from her. "Each time we meet, I want you even more."

Her blue eyes sparkled with passion. She lunged toward him just as he pulled her into his arms and claimed her mouth. She kissed him back, delving her hands into his hair. He moved down to her breasts, suckling on the hardened tips, tugging at her until she writhed in his arms. His erection pressed against her stomach, growing more strained as her lithe, supple body rubbed against him.

When he slid a hand between her legs, the amount of moisture there made him growl with satisfaction. His warrior woman was no shy maid. With a groan, she rocked against his hand. His fingers were drenched, making it so easy to slide between the folds. He stroked her, and she whimpered, her knees buckling.

He smiled. At this rate, she was going to melt into a puddle. He spotted the rock nearby with the towel on top. "Come." He sat on the towel and grasped her hips, pulling her down till she was straddling him, sitting on his thighs, facing him.

She held onto his shoulders, her eyes clouded with passion. "Zoltan."

He stroked her wet, swollen flesh and she whimpered, her fingers digging into his skin.

"You're so wet. So sweet." He quickened the pace, rubbing her harder.

She groaned, her hands slipping up to his head to grasp handfuls of hair.

He spread his legs forcing her to open wider. When he pressed on her clitoris, she shuddered. He fondled her faster and faster, applying vampire speed, till she stiffened and squealed. She fell against him, her swollen flesh throbbing against his fingertips.

He held her close with his free arm, keeping his right hand pressed against her drenched skin so he could coax more aftershocks from her. Each time she twitched, he smiled. She was so responsive, so highly charged that the slightest flex of his fingers sent a shudder through her entire body. Unfortunately, it also made him so painfully swollen that he was about to burst.

She moaned, her head buried in his shoulder.

"Are you all right?" he asked.

She sat back and frowned at him, her eyes bleary and unfocused. "You lied."

"I didn't bite you."

She pushed lightly at his shoulder. "You said it would be a *little* climax."

He grinned.

Her eyes softened. "You're smirking again."

"You're ogling again."

"I am not. I can hardly see straight." Her gaze lowered and she gasped. "Oh, my God."

There was no hiding the fact that he was engorged to the max.

"I proved that I can make love without biting you." He grasped her hips, moving her closer to the tip of his rigid penis.

"But I don't want to risk getting pregnant." She

splayed her hands on his chest to stop him. "Everyone would want to kill you, and you'd have to leave. I don't want to lose you."

Her declaration made his heart rejoice. It also made him more desperate to make love. Maybe it was time to tell her the truth. "Neona, you don't have to worry about getting pregnant."

She was still studying his erection. "It looks so uncomfortable. Are you in pain?"

"Yes. If you would let me inside—"

"Maybe my healing powers could help." She wrapped a hand around his shaft. When he flinched, she loosened her grip. "Did that hurt?"

"I-it's good." He moaned when her hand tightened around him. "So good."

"I'm not sure I'm helping. Look how your blood vessels are sticking out." She stroked a finger along a vein.

He shuddered. "Let me inside you before I explode."

"But—"

"You can't get pregnant! My seed is—" He gasped when she caressed the crown with her thumb. "Is coming!" With a loud groan, he climaxed and ejaculated on her stomach.

"Oh, my!" She released him, watching him with a stunned look as he kept pumping till he was spent.

"Oh, shit." He grimaced. He'd lost control like a young pup. He ventured a look at her face to see how horrified she was.

She was gazing at her sperm-covered stomach, her eyes wide with wonder.

"I'm so sorry . . ." he mumbled.

She looked up at him and grinned. "You have so much seed! It's amazing!"

"No, it's not."

She dragged her fingers through it, collected a glob, then rubbed her thumb against her gooey fingers. "I've never seen a man's seed before. To think this can cause life to form—it is truly astounding."

He drew in a shaky breath. It was strange, but the way she was fondling his semen was turning him on. "Neona, I have to tell you—"

"Your seed is wondrous."

"My seed is dead."

She blinked.

His heart sank. Would she reject him now, like all the other women he'd ever grown close to? God, no. Not Neona. She had to be the one for him. "I'm a vampire. My sperm is dead. I'm sorry."

She looked at the glob in her hand. "How can it be dead? You're alive right now. Your heart is working. Your brain is working. You're alive."

"I'm sorry. But the good news is we can make love all we want without worrying about you getting pregnant." He gave her a hopeful look, but it soon faded at the sight of her tear-filled eyes. "You want children."

She blinked away the tears. "I know it's selfish of me, but I wanted a daughter with your hair and eyes."

But Neona's eyes would be so much better. He imagined a little boy and girl with Neona's black hair and bright blue eyes, and for the first time, he understood the pain. Always before, he'd resented the women who had wanted a child more than they had wanted him. He'd wanted to come first in a woman's heart. "You could mate with a mortal—"

"No!" She looked aghast. "I want you! Only you."

His heart swelled and he gathered her close in his arms. She wanted him first. "Then what you said to the others about wanting me as a sperm donor—"

"I said that so my mother would accept you. It is the

only reason she thinks a man exists." Neona sat back, frowning. "I guess it is just as well we cannot have children. What if they had fangs and attacked people?"

"They wouldn't. The half-vampire children I know are all surprisingly normal. They're awake during the day and eat normal—"

"What? You just said it was impossible."

"I said my sperm is dead. But it is still possible."

Her eyes widened. "How?"

He gripped her shoulders. "You would seriously consider having a child with me? A vampire?"

She bit her lip, then nodded.

"We would have to teleport somewhere to have a procedure done." He could probably talk Roman into taking a vacation at the castle with his family, then Roman could do the work there.

Her shoulders slumped. "I cannot leave Beyul-La."

"It would be for only a short time. Nobody would even have to know. They don't know we're here now."

With a sigh, she glanced down at his manhood. "Maybe I can heal you."

"Sweetheart, my sperm has been dead for almost eight hundred—" He sucked in a breath when her hand curled around his shaft and squeezed. "But you could always try."

"I will try." She stroked him gently.

Damn, he ought to let her know it wasn't going to work, but her hand felt so good.

A clap of thunder sounded in the distance, and she stopped. "We should go back. Storms can happen very quickly here in the mountains."

"We'll teleport to your house." And start on climax number two. He still had nine to go, and he never quit till a job was done.

He gathered up their belongings while she washed

off his semen in the waterfall. As soon as they returned to her house, she stretched the wet clothes on the backs of the two chairs in front of the fire so they could dry.

"We should—" they both said at the same time, then laughed.

"You first." Zoltan hoped she wanted to jump in bed like him. She was still nude, and her lovely body was making it hard for him to think of anything else.

"We should join the others at the fire pit," she said. "So they'll know you're cooperating. It is the best way to earn their trust."

He sighed. She was right. He needed the whole group of women to trust him. "All right." He shuffled over to the wooden chest to retrieve some clean clothes.

She gave him a sympathetic look. "It won't be for long. I think it will rain soon."

After they dressed, she led him outside. The wind had picked up, whistling through the valley. The fire in the central pit provided the only light. Thick clouds were covering the stars and moon.

He spotted the five women seated around the fire. They exchanged looks, then eyed him with disdain. Great. They still wanted to kill him. He bowed. "Good evening."

The queen scoffed. "Don't speak unless you have permission." She motioned for them to sit.

Neona sat, then patted the ground beside her. He sat and crossed his legs, aware that his every move was being frowned upon.

"You were late for dinner," the queen announced. "We saved you some food."

"Thank you." Neona accepted two plates that were passed to her. She handed one to Zoltan with a wary look.

He glanced down at the plate in his lap. Some kind of meat. Rice. Flatbread. Neona tore off a piece of her bread, then used it to scoop up some meat and rice. He followed suit, tearing off a piece of bread. When he looked up, the other women were still scowling at him.

What had he done wrong? How could he ask if he wasn't allowed to speak? He spotted Neona's pet leopard lounging nearby on the grass, watching him with narrowed eyes.

The queen grumbled something in Tibetan, and Neona nearly choked on her food. Then the other women joined in, pointing at him and fussing.

Cat, what the hell is going on? He asked Zhan.

They're disappointed in you. The cat sneered. *They thought you were so manly, but it turns out you're just a weakling. Couldn't even get it up—*

What? Zoltan mentally shouted.

"What?" Tashi switched to English, staring at Zoltan. "What is he doing?"

Lydia pointed at him. "He was communicating with the cat! I heard him!"

"What?" Neona turned to him, her eyes wide with shock.

Gasps circled around the fire pit.

Lydia rose to her feet. "Explain yourself."

"Very well." Zoltan set the plate of food aside. "I'm not a weakling. And Neona can verify that I can indeed get it up—"

"That's not what I meant!" Lydia yelled. "You were talking to the cat!"

"You can talk to Zhan?" Neona leaned toward him, her eyes intense.

"Sure." Zoltan shrugged. "I've always been able to talk to animals. My mother could communicate with animals and birds, but I guess I only inherited the animal part."

Neona sat back with a gasp. More gasps echoed around the fire. Even the queen looked shocked.

The leopard gave him a sheepish look. *I guess I should have warned you. Tashi and Lydia can hear us.*

Zoltan nodded. *I understand.* Those two women had always been away whenever he'd communicated with Zhan before.

Neona stumbled to her feet, her plate falling over and spilling food on the ground. Her face had paled, and she was breathing shakily as she faced the queen. "You told us male children could never inherit our gifts."

The queen's face grew pale, but harsh. "I didn't believe they could."

Tears glittered in Neona's eyes as she pointed at Zoltan. "He inherited a gift from Dohna. What if Minerva's son is gifted? How would we know when we gave him *away*?" Her voice rose and cracked on the last word.

"Sit down, Neona," the queen hissed.

"No!" Tears flowed down her cheeks. "We should have kept him. What if he has Minerva's gift? What if he can talk to—"

"*Enough!*" the queen shouted. "What is done is done."

Neona shook her head. "If we had kept him, Minerva would still be alive!" With a sob, she turned and ran.

Thunder rumbled in the distance.

Zoltan jumped to his feet to follow her, but the queen held up a hand to stop him.

He gritted his teeth. "She shouldn't be alone."

The queen glanced toward the burial mounds,

where Neona was headed. "She won't be. You're our prisoner. You will remain here."

He'd had all he could take of this coldhearted queen. "You've lost one daughter, and the other is suffering."

Nima arched a brow at him. "Then do your part and give us another female."

More thunder rolled, sounding closer, and the wind grew stronger.

"It will rain soon." The queen stood and motioned toward Neona's house. "Go there and wait for her."

"I'll go wherever I please," Zoltan said softly. "And you can't stop me."

The women stiffened and gave the queen worried looks. Lydia pulled the knife from the sheath strapped to her leg.

The queen approached him. "Are you anxious to die, human? I have spared you so far only because you are the son of Dohna, whom I loved dearly." She whipped a sharp dagger from a sheath on her belt. "But she wronged us by letting you live so long. I should rectify that tonight."

"My mother never wronged you," Zoltan said. "She never spoke of this place, never revealed your damned secrets, and never gave me a drop of your Living Water."

More gasps echoed around the fire. The flames danced wildly in the strong wind.

Queen Nima studied him, her eyes narrowing. "Then how have you lived so long?"

Lightning cracked close by, illuminating with a flash the women's pale, shocked faces.

"It's simple." Zoltan stepped back so he could keep all the women and their weapons in view. "I'm a vampire."

Chapter Eighteen

"I knew it!" Queen Nima raised her dagger, ready to strike. "You're a spy for Lord Liao!"

The other women drew their knives.

He extended his hands to the side so they would see he was unarmed. "I'm not here to harm you. I want to help—"

"You've helped yourself to my daughter, you monster!" the queen shouted, her face turning red with rage. "I will not tolerate this insult—"

"Enough!" He took a deep breath to calm his own growing anger. "Do you think so highly of yourself that you're prepared to take on Master Han and his army? He has nine hundred soldiers!"

Nima glared at him, while the other women exchanged worried looks. "Pay no heed to his lies," she hissed.

"You want the truth?" Zoltan snorted. "If I was your enemy, you would all be dead by now." He teleported behind Freya, ripped the knife from her hand and tossed it aside, then zoomed back to where he'd been standing.

"What?" Freya blinked. "How did you—"

"Vampire speed," Zoltan explained. "I could disarm you all—" He dodged to the side and caught the knife Lydia had just thrown, plucking it out of the air with ease.

Another bolt of lightning flashed and lit up the shocked faces of the women.

"As I was saying—" He tested the tip of the knife with a finger. It was deadly sharp. And damn if it wasn't one of the hunting knives he'd left in Frederic's cabin as a gift. "I'm not here to harm you. I belong to a group of good Vamps, and we'd like to help you defeat Lord Liao and Master Han."

"Ridiculous," Nima muttered. "No vampires are good."

"Remember Russell? The guy who saved your life? He's a friend of mine. He joined in your battle, hoping to kill Lord Liao."

"He did attack him," Freddie muttered. "But Liao vanished."

Zoltan nodded. "Liao and Han have some special powers, so no matter how strong or fast you are, you can't compete with them. Since my friends and I are Vamps, we possess the same powers. We're your best bet at defeating them."

"That makes sense, actually," Freya murmured.

"Don't listen to this monster." Nima motioned to him with her dagger. "He will twist your thoughts, using his evil mind control. You saw what he's done to Neona. He's turning her against—"

A clap of thunder burst overhead, so deafeningly loud that everyone flinched. A drop of rain landed on Zoltan's head.

"Neona's mind works perfectly well without any help from me," he told the queen. "If she's questioning you, it's because you deserve it."

"You will destroy our way of life!" Nima shouted. A few more drops of rain plopped down around them, some landing with a hiss in the fire. "We cannot allow you to interfere with our sacred duty!"

"What is your sacred duty?" he asked.

"We will not discuss it with you. Leave!"

"If your sacred duty is that precious to you, you'll need our help to survive so you can keep doing it. Lord Liao is looking for you. He won't stop until he finds you."

"He'll never find us," Nima insisted. "We've been here for millennia. No one finds us!"

"I did! Liao will, too. You cannot hope to remain hidden. Modern technology will make it impossible. Satellites in outer space can pinpoint your location here. Times are changing, and you will have to change with it."

Freddie exchanged a look with her sister. "Our father warned us that the outside world was changing fast."

"Frederic was right," Zoltan said. "Master Han and his army will find you. Not only will they outnumber you but his soldiers have also been altered genetically, so they're super fast and strong. If you don't accept our help, they will annihilate you."

A crack of lightning lit the sky and the women's worried faces.

"The soldiers were extra strong and fast," Tashi shouted over the wind. "That was how they managed to kill five of us."

"But why would these vampires want to help us?" Nima glared at Zoltan. "They want something from us."

"We want what we have always wanted," Zoltan replied. "To protect mortals from the bad vampires."

The queen snorted. "You expect us to believe that?"

The wind whirled around them, blowing Zoltan's wet hair in his face. He shoved it back. "We have no interest in your Living Water. We're already immortal."

The queen's eyes narrowed. "Unless we kill you."

"Try it! See what happens." He was damned tired of arguing with this woman. The wind was causing the rain to pelt them hard now. "But you would be foolish to face Lord Liao or Master Han without our help."

The fire dwindled down to a few tiny flames, then hissed a final death, leaving them in darkness.

"I think we should consider—" Freddie started.

"Hush!" Nima interrupted. "We will wait out the rest of this storm in the cave. Go!" As the other women ran upstream, she held up a hand to stop Zoltan. "You are not allowed in the sacred cave. Wait for Neona in her house."

Zoltan watched the women scurry off so he could see the location of their precious cave. The entrance was at the base of the highest mountain, partially hidden behind some huge boulders. He would have to investigate it later.

He teleported to the burial mounds and found Neona beside her sister's grave, her clothes soaked through.

"Come." He extended a hand to her. "Let's get out of the rain."

She glanced up at him, her cheeks wet with tears. "A little water is the least of my problems right now."

He hunched down beside her. "I know it's difficult. You're questioning a life you've lived for over two thousand years."

She wiped her face. "I feel like I'm becoming a traitor. That should be wrong, but somehow it feels right."

"Let's talk about it in your house." He extended a hand again. "We can't have a healer who's sick with a cold, right?"

"Fine." She placed her hand in his. "But I don't feel like talking. I would like to be alone for a while."

"We can do that." He pulled her to her feet. "I'll leave you there while I go home to get more blood."

After teleporting her home, he retrieved his ice chest and duffel bag from the wooden chest. "Before I go, I should warn you that I let the other women know I'm a vampire."

She paused in the middle of removing her wet tunic, turning toward him with a shocked face. "How did they react? What did they say?"

He shrugged. "The queen wants me dead, but she always wanted me dead, so not much of a change there. I told them how the good Vamps want to help you defeat Lord Liao and Master Han. Since Han has an army of nine hundred supersoldiers, you're going to need our help."

Neona nodded, her face pale. "I understand."

"I'll be back in an hour or so. Try to get some rest. You've been through a lot."

She sighed. "I have a feeling there's a lot more to come. And nothing will ever be the same."

He stepped toward her. "Some things will remain constant. I will always love you."

Her eyes glittered with tears. "You're a good man, Zoltan."

He smiled. "Even though I'm dead half the time?"

She smiled back. "I'm adjusting to that."

"Good."

"I'll see you later then." She finished removing her wet tunic.

He swallowed hard. Her silk camisole was soaked

through and plastered to her breasts, clearly showing her nipples, which were pebbled, the tips hardened. "An hour is too long. I'll be back in thirty minutes."

"No need to hurry." She stretched the tunic out on the table in front of the fire.

"We still have nine climaxes to go." He grabbed the ice chest and duffel bag. "And I'm the type of guy who doesn't quit till a job is done." He grinned at the bemused look on her face.

She scoffed. "Are you smirking again?"

"Never." His gaze drifted down her body. "I'm too busy ogling." He winked at her, then teleported away.

When Zoltan arrived in the kitchen of his castle, he found Elsa slipping two frozen pizzas into the oven.

"Oh, there you are." Her smile quickly turned to a frown. "You're soaked through."

"It's raining in the Himalayas." He set his ice chest on the counter.

"Howard's with the others upstairs. They've collected a bunch of supplies in the Great Hall. But—" Elsa lowered her voice. "Howard is upset with you."

"What else is new?" Zoltan dumped the water from the ice chest into the sink. "What did I do now?"

"You left without taking a sat phone with you." Elsa leaned against the counter, eying him curiously. "I told him you probably had other things on your mind. You mentioned something about a wedding night?"

"Did I?" He removed six new bottles of synthetic blood from the refrigerator and loaded them into the ice chest.

"Domokos said he had to pay for some wedding rings you bought in town."

"Domokos talks too much." Zoltan started filling the ice chest with ice.

"Oh, come on." Elsa gave him an exasperated look. "We're all wondering if you really got married."

"Did he?" Emma asked as she entered the kitchen.

"Emma, can you come to Beyul-La tomorrow night?" Zoltan asked. "I just told the women that we want to help."

"I'll be ready. Be sure to take a sat phone with you so you can call. Howard's been a bit peeved—"

"More than a bit," Howard grumbled as he entered the kitchen. "You'd better take one tonight."

"Yes, I know." Zoltan finished filling the ice chest and shut it.

"So is it true?" Emma asked. "Did you get married?"

"We're preparing for battle, and that's what you want to know?" Zoltan asked. When they stared back without a word, he sighed. "Not yet. Neona needs some time to adjust to me being a vampire."

Elsa nodded. "I remember how frightened I was when I first found out about Howard being a werebear."

"Maybe we should introduce her to some of the other wives," Emma suggested.

A thought struck Zoltan so suddenly that he stepped back and bumped into the refrigerator. His married vampire friends were all dreading having to turn their wives someday. But they wouldn't have to if the warrior women of Beyul-La allowed the wives to drink some of the Living Water.

He quickly squelched the thought. The queen already thought he was using them for some nefarious purpose, when the truth was the good Vamps simply wanted to put an end to Master Han's evil empire. And

Zoltan wanted to make sure Neona and her friends would be able to continue their way of life, though hopefully they would make an exception and accept him and any children he and Neona might have.

"Are you all right?" Elsa gave him a curious look.

"Yes, of course." Zoltan tossed his empty bottles into the recycle bin, keeping one in his duffel bag so he could use it to collect some of the Living Water.

"You mentioned a cabin in a neighboring valley that we could use as headquarters?" Howard asked.

"Yes, Frederic's cabin." Zoltan put a bottle of blood into the microwave so he could enjoy a warm meal for a change. "No electricity or running water there."

Howard nodded. "I figured as much. I have a solar-powered generator we can take. It'll be quiet. We don't want to advertise our location."

"Tonight we're moving the supplies to Tiger Town," Emma said. "J.L., Mikhail, and Jack just left. Angus is teleporting westward tonight, so he can stop at the clinic in Japan and pick up a bunch of the tranquilizer darts. He wants to save as many of Master Han's soldiers as we can."

"The other guys, like Robby and Ian, are teleporting westward with Angus," Howard added. "And they're bringing the shifters with them. Everyone will gather at Tiger Town and wait for you to give the okay for us to move to Frederic's cabin."

"Sounds good." Zoltan removed his bottle from the microwave and poured the warm blood into a glass. "I'm going upstairs for a few minutes. Be right back." He grabbed his duffel bag and glass of blood and teleported to his bedroom.

He sipped warm blood as he shaved and packed more clothes. After a quick shower, he dressed and called Milan in Budapest.

"I've been trying to contact you, sir!" Milan responded with an excited voice. "The scientists—"

"How is the land deal going?" Zoltan interrupted.

"Oh, it's fine. Rajiv has the papers. He said he'd use Vamp delivery service to get them to you. But, sir, the scientists at the university are astounded! They think you've discovered a new species! They've been calling me nonstop, wanting to know where you found the scale."

"The scale?"

"Yes! The black thing you gave me," Milan explained. "The scientists have never seen anything like it before. They said it was a cross between a turtle shell and a reptile scale. Where did you find it?"

Zoltan remained quiet, trying to make sense of this. Turtle shell? Reptile? What the hell?

"But it's much bigger than the normal lizard scale," Milan continued. "The scientists want to announce it to the world, but they need more information. Where did you find it? Have you seen the creature?"

"Creature?"

"Yes! Judging from the size of the scale, it has to be really large. Like an enormous iguana. I don't know how you could miss it."

"I haven't seen anything." The image of the cave flitted through Zoltan's mind. Was there something strange living inside? Damn, but the last thing he needed was a bunch of scientists demanding access to Beyul-La. "I think the animal is dead. Long dead. Probably extinct."

"Oh." Milan sounded disappointed.

"I found the scale buried in the ground," Zoltan lied. "Like a fossil. There was nothing else around it. I didn't write down the exact location. It was somewhere in China."

"Oh, I see," Milan mumbled. "I'll let them know."

Zoltan hung up and dragged a hand through his damp hair. What the hell was going on at Beyul-La? He needed to go back and investigate.

He teleported with his duffel bag back to the kitchen.

"There you are." Howard and his wife were eating pizza at the kitchen table. He motioned to the counter. "I brought you down a sat phone. So you wouldn't forget."

"Thanks." Zoltan slipped it inside his jacket pocket. "What's this?" He opened a folder to look at the papers inside.

"J.L. brought that back from Tiger Town," Howard explained. "Rajiv said you wanted it."

"Excellent." It was the land deed for the valley of Beyul-La and surrounding territory. Zoltan stashed it inside his duffel bag.

"We have a visitor!" Emma called out as she entered the kitchen with a man behind her.

Howard sat back, his eyes narrowing. "Hello, Russell."

"He has news for us," Emma announced. "And I talked him into taking a sat phone with him."

"Amazing," Howard grumbled.

"What's the news?" Zoltan asked as he handed Russell a Bleer.

"I tracked down Lord Liao." Russell unscrewed the top off the bottle. "He went back to one of Master Han's major outposts in the Yunnan province. Apparently he convinced Han that there was something in Tibet worth fighting for, because he's headed back that way."

"We think we figured out what they're after," Zoltan said. "The women of Beyul-La have a fountain of youth. Living Water, they call it. Some of them are thousands of years old."

"Sheesh." Russell gulped down some Bleer. "Lord Liao is headed in their direction with a new group of soldiers. Two hundred of them."

Zoltan winced. Even with all the Vamps and shifters they could gather, they would be terribly outnumbered.

"Can you follow them?" Emma asked Russell. "Call as often as you can to give us an update of their location."

Russell nodded. "I will." He gave Zoltan a worried look. "They're moving fast. They'll be near Beyul-La in three or four days."

Zoltan gathered up his ice chest and duffel bag. "I'd better get back."

Chapter Nineteen

$\mathcal{N}$eona paced back and forth in her house, too agitated to sleep. It had been a huge shock to find out that Zoltan had inherited a gift from his mother. What if Minerva's son had inherited her gift?

"I'm so sorry." Neona touched her sister's pillow. "I shouldn't have let Mother take away your son. I should have rebelled then." Instead of waiting till now. Now, when Minerva was gone.

Tears burned Neona's eyes, and she angrily wiped them away. Why had it taken so long for her to see the truth? Was it because of Zoltan? She shook her head. No, she'd already suspected her mother of lying. And she'd hated the way Minerva had been forced to give up her son. The seed of rebellion had already taken root inside her. Zoltan's arrival had just caused it to burst into full bloom. Each time she tried to explain their way of life to him, she caught a glimpse of it through his eyes, and things she'd accepted before seemed suddenly strange. Wrong.

She paced toward the fireplace. How was Minerva's son faring? Was he happy? Or did he feel abandoned?

Unloved? God help her, she didn't even know what name he'd been given. She needed to find him, but he was thirty miles away at a Buddhist monastery.

Could Zoltan teleport her there? And if he did, would she have the courage to bring the boy back here to his rightful home? No doubt the queen would be livid. It was a severe breach of their laws to allow a human male to live in Beyul-La. The queen was only tolerating Zoltan until he impregnated her.

But who had come up with these laws? Had it been part of the original pact, like the queen said, or was it a decision she'd made afterward? Had she excluded men simply because she hated them? Or did she fear that someday a gifted male child would grow up and challenge her position as ruler?

There was no way to know. The pact had been made with the three original women—Nima, Dohna, and Anjali. Only Nima remained.

Neona paced faster as her anger grew, not just anger at her mother but anger at herself as well. For centuries, she'd considered herself a brave warrior, always fighting to protect the secrets of Beyul-La. But the truth was she'd been a coward.

It seemed pathetic that just a few days ago, she had panicked out of fear of having and losing a son. Now she was filled with a new, hardened determination. There was no way on earth she would allow a child of hers, boy or girl, to be given away. If she decided to have children with Zoltan, nothing would stop her!

Except his dead seed. Her pacing stopped with a jerk. Could she heal his dead seed? She looked at her hands. If she touched his male parts enough, could she heal him?

She inhaled sharply as a new idea sprang to mind. Could the Living Water bring his seed back to life?

It was against their law to give the water to a human male, but to hell with that. She was already considering bringing Minerva's son here to live. If she could break that law, why not break them all? Why not marry Zoltan and have all the sons and daughters she wanted?

She peeked outside. It was still raining, but with the mood she was in, a little rain was not about to stop her. A small army wouldn't stop her. She put her damp tunic back on, then dashed to the storeroom where they kept all their dishes, pottery, linens, food, firewood, and medical supplies. She'd spent enough time in the small building over the years to know her way around in the dark. She searched the shelf where empty bowls and jugs were kept and selected a small clay flask with a cork in the top.

The wind and rain buffeted her as she ran toward the cave. Her leather slippers splashed through puddles till they were soaked through. As she neared the entrance, she slowed down, easing around the boulders silently, listening for any voices.

It was quiet. She peeked inside. The throne room was well lit with torches, and it was empty, except for Zhan, who rested close to the entrance. He sat up and tilted his head, giving her a curious and concerned look that touched her heart.

"Good kitty," she whispered, patting him on the head. "Don't tell anyone I was here, okay?"

He butted her leg.

The other women had to be in the back cavern with the young ones. No doubt the storm had frightened the young ones, and with good reason. They had lost many an ancestor to the lightning and strong winds that accompanied a storm.

Neona kicked off her leather slippers so she

wouldn't leave a muddy trail straight to the pool. Her tunic was dripping, so she took it off, too, and left it by the entrance. Then she ran past the area where they held their meetings and past the throne, until she reached the dark, glistening pool. Hunching down beside the water, she uncorked the small flask and filled it. Then she corked it and scurried back to the entrance.

One glance back, and she groaned. She'd still left a few small puddles. Zhan trotted up to the biggest one and flopped down in it, rubbing his back against the stone till his fur had soaked up most of the water.

She smiled as she slipped her tunic and slippers back on. Her pet ran back to her and butted her leg.

"You're the best kitty in the world." She gave him a hug, then slipped back outside into the rain.

She ran home, then hid the flask in the wooden chest at the foot of her bed. During the day, when Zoltan was in his death-sleep, she would slip some of the Living Water into his bottles of blood.

After putting another log on the fire, she peeled off her wet clothes, then toweled herself dry. Just as she was leaning over her open wooden chest to retrieve some clean clothes, she heard a voice behind her.

"Now that's a beautiful sight. Hold that position."

She spun around, her clean clothes clutched to her chest. "You're back."

Zoltan smiled as he kicked off his shoes and dropped his belongings on top of his chest. "I was afraid you'd be asleep." His gaze drifted over her while he removed his jacket.

The intense way he looked at her made her stomach quiver. "I was getting ready for bed."

"Good." He pulled his T-shirt over his head and tossed it on his bed. "We have some unfinished business." He stepped toward her, his eyes darkening. "Nine more climaxes. Nine more positions."

Her eyes widened. "Surely you don't expect to do all that in one night?"

He unfastened his pants. "I've always prided myself on never quitting a task till it's done."

"I see." Her heart thudded loudly in her ears. "Well, I would certainly hate to damage your pride."

His mouth curled up. "How thoughtful of you. One might get the idea that you care about me."

Her heart squeezed in her chest. "Can we truly belong to each other, Zoltan? A vampire and a—?"

"An old crone?" His smile widened.

With a snort she tossed her clean clothes back into her wooden chest. "Do I look like an old crone to you?"

His smile faded as his gaze traveled down her body. By the time his eyes met hers once again, they were red and glowing.

Moisture gathered between her legs. Her skin tingled, just knowing she had such an immediate effect on him. He dropped his pants to the floor and kicked them aside. The bulge in his underwear was blatant. Maybe she should start trying to heal him tonight.

She reached for the waistband of his underwear, but he spun her around to face her wooden chest. He dropped the lid, then bent her over it, planting her hands on top.

"What are you doing?" She glanced over her shoulder. He was leaning over her, his chest against her back and his erection pressed against her rump.

"This is position number two," he whispered in her ear as he nudged her legs apart with a bare foot.

Her knees trembled, and more moisture seeped from her core. Whatever he was doing, she wanted it.

His hands trailed up her arms, then swept her hair over a shoulder so her back was bare. "Beautiful." He kissed the back of her neck, then nibbled a trail down her spine. His hands cupped her breasts, his fingers gently teasing her nipples.

She shivered, digging her fingers into the wooden chest.

He reached the small of her back and ran his tongue up the indentation of her spine. With a moan, she arched.

When would he touch her? She needed his touch. She rubbed her rump against his groin. "Please."

He grasped her hips, holding her steady. "I love this." His hands smoothed up to her narrow waist, then back down the flare of her hips. "You're so beautiful."

Her legs trembled, and she locked her knees to keep from falling. "Zoltan," she whispered. "Please."

"Yes." He leaned over to trail nibbling kisses over her rear end. She gasped when his hand slipped between her legs. Oh, God, yes. Finally.

"So wet."

She whimpered at the feel of his fingers. Insistent, bold, possessive.

"This time I want to be inside you." He inserted a finger.

She cried out. He plunged another finger inside her, stroking her, tickling her. She gasped for air, moaning and rocking against him. Tension spiraled inside her, climbing higher and higher till she shattered.

With another cry, her knees collapsed, and he held her up, supporting her with his free arm while she throbbed against his fingers.

She was still hazy when he tossed her on the bed and flipped her over.

"Position number three." He spread her legs, then settled between them, his face just inches away from her wet, swollen flesh.

"Wait!"

He propped himself up on his elbows, and a corner of his mouth curled up. "Do you need a break?"

"I-I think we need to reconsider the—"

"Ten climaxes with no biting, and then you would trust me. That was the deal."

"Yes." She took a deep breath to calm her racing heart. "But I think there is a flaw—"

"Looks perfect to me."

The rascal was studying her womanly parts. And with his face only inches away, he was certainly getting a good view. She'd never felt so exposed before. Nor this excited. Just knowing that he was watching made her skin tingle and her core ache to be touched. "What kind of position is this? Do you plan to stare at me till I climax?"

His smile widened. "Do you think that would work?"

"You're smirking again."

"And ogling." He inched closer. "You're so wet, you're glistening in the firelight."

She swallowed hard as more moisture seeped from her. Good Lord, it was working. She could feel the tension inside her coiling tighter and tighter.

"And your scent is driving me wild," he continued.

Her hands fisted in the sheet. "As I was saying, there is a flaw in your thinking. It's not my—" She gasped when his tongue swept over her wet, swollen skin.

"You were saying?"

Good Lord, she'd never imagined anything like this. "Yes, I—" She jerked when he licked an especially sensitive part.

"Something about a flaw? Should I stop?"

"No!"

"That's my girl." He grasped her hips to hold her steady, then drew her sensitive part into his mouth and suckled.

She screamed as another climax seized her, shaking her violently. By the time she could see straight, he was lying beside her on the bed.

"Are you all right?" He brushed her hair back from her face.

"Are you sure you're not trying to kill me?"

He kissed her brow. "Just trying to earn your trust. That's three climaxes without my fangs popping out."

She inhaled deeply to clear her mind. "As much as I'm enjoying your plan, I don't think it's going to work."

He stiffened. "What?"

"Giving me climaxes is not the right way to test your control. It's *your* climaxes I'm worried about. That's when you would lose control and bite me." She sat up. "That's the flaw I was talking about earlier."

He frowned. "I had a climax at the waterfall and didn't bite you."

"That is true." She glanced down at his underwear where his erection strained against the fabric. "But I think I should test you again. Just to make sure."

He scoffed. "You shouldn't play with a loaded dick. I'm about to explode."

"You're my prisoner. I can do whatever I like." She gave him a wry look. "Shall I tie you to the bedpost?"

"I'll manage not to strangle you."

"That's my guy."

He snorted. "This is payback, isn't it? You want to torture me."

With a smile, she pulled down his underwear, and

his penis sprang free. Her breath caught. He was huge. And gloriously erect. All his male parts were completely engaged, so this was the perfect time to attempt to heal his seed. After a few minutes of therapy, she would bring him to climax and test his control of his fangs.

She cupped his balls and gave them a squeeze. Then she wrapped her other hand around his rigid staff. He hissed in a breath. A bead of moisture seeped from the crown, and she rubbed it with her thumb. He did look like he was ready to explode. She'd have to hurry.

Closing her eyes, she concentrated on the healing ability deep inside her. It rushed down her arms, settling into her fingers with a familiar tingle.

He shuddered beneath her. No doubt he was feeling a slight vibration. She increased her power, then opened herself to take away any illness inside him.

With a rush, his sensations swept up her arms to her chest. She gasped, her eyes opening wide. This wasn't illness. Instantly she was shocked with a powerful, electric current of raw desire and desperation. It shot down to her core and ignited a series of spasms that rocked her so hard that she cried out and fell back onto the bed.

With a hoarse shout, Zoltan jolted beside her and climaxed.

Slowly her heart stopped thundering. Her core stopped throbbing. Her eyes focused, and she saw Zoltan sitting beside her. He'd taken her discarded towel and was wiping himself clean.

She sat up. "Are you all right?"

He glanced at her, and with a gasp, she scooted back. His fangs were out.

"I'm not going to bite you." He tossed the towel on

the floor. "I didn't expect to lose control. I never have before, but that was the biggest damned orgasm I've ever had. What did you do?"

"I was trying to heal you." She winced. "I thought I was taking in your pain, but I . . . I think I shared your climax."

He snorted. "You more than shared it. You amplified it."

"Oh. Sorry."

He laughed, and his fangs slid back into place. "Nothing to be sorry about. *Damn.* That was intense." He laughed again. "That's one hell of a gift you have. God, I'm starving." He hurried to the box that contained his bottles of blood and guzzled one down.

He set the empty bottle back into the box and opened a second one. "I know I should be cuddling you and reminding you how much I love you, but under the circumstances, I think I'd better make sure I'm not hungry."

She smiled, knowing he was doing his best to protect her.

He drank half the second bottle, then gave her a wry look. "If I can survive a mega-climax like that without biting you, then I think you can consider yourself safe. Do you trust me now?"

Her gaze drifted over him as he stood there gloriously naked, sipping blood from a bottle. "Yes."

He smiled, then drank some more.

She pulled the sheet up to her chest, then lounged back against the pillows, enjoying the view and the sleepy hum of satisfaction that still tingled along the length of her body. "Could you teleport me somewhere tomorrow?"

"Sure." He took another sip. "Where would you like to go? Paris? Venice? My castle in Transylvania?"

She shook her head. "A Buddhist monastery about thirty miles from here."

"Ah. You want to see your sister's son." He screwed the top back on the bottle. "Do you think he inherited a gift?"

"It doesn't matter if he did or didn't. He's still my nephew. And if he'll accept me, I hope to become his mother." She bit her lip, wondering how Zoltan would react to that.

His eyes softened. "You'll be an excellent mother."

Her heart squeezed. How could she not love this man? A wave of peaceful drowsiness swept over her. Life was good. "If Minerva's son has a gift, I'll know with one look at him. I should have known you were gifted with your amber eyes, but it never occurred to me that men could be gifted."

"What do you mean?" He approached the bed and sat down beside her.

"You have the same-colored eyes as Tashi and Lydia." Neona yawned and settled deeper into bed. "It's a sign that you can communicate with animals. Freya's eyes are green, which means she can make plants grow and flourish."

"Then your blue eyes mean you're a healer?"

Neona nodded. "Calliope had blue eyes like me."

"And your mother has golden eyes."

"Winifred, too." Neona yawned again and closed her eyes. "They can communicate with winged creatures."

"Go ahead and sleep." He kissed her brow. "I'll see you tomorrow."

Tomorrow, she thought as she drifted off. With Zoltan, she could have an eternity of tomorrows.

It was near dawn when Zoltan's superior hearing caught the sound of voices outside. He'd spent the last few hours cuddling Neona in bed, listening to her soft breathing while she slept. The rain had stopped, so apparently the women had left the cave. That meant he might have a chance to sneak inside the cave before the sun rose.

He quickly dressed and slipped an empty bottle into his jacket pocket. Then he teleported behind Neona's house and peered around the corner.

In the dim moonlight, he spotted the queen, Lydia, Tashi, and the pet snow leopard by the central fire pit, which was now a heap of wet ashes. Winifred and Freya emerged from the storeroom, their arms filled with dry firewood and kindling. They dropped their load onto the fire pit.

It seemed obvious they were going to start a new fire. And probably cook breakfast. Zoltan glanced over at the cave entrance. This was his best chance to go inside.

Just as he was about to teleport, a figure ran from the cave. Zoltan stiffened with surprise. It was a boy. In Beyul-La? Weren't males forbidden here?

The queen greeted the boy with a smile and a hug. What the hell? Why was this boy welcome here, when Minerva's son had been given away?

The women discussed something in Tibetan. Zoltan couldn't understand, but it was clear they were giving the boy encouraging words and smiles. He nodded, then closed his eyes as if he was concentrating. He took a few deep breaths, then opened his eyes and mouth. A streak of fire shot from his mouth, striking the firewood and setting it ablaze.

Zoltan gasped. Luckily, the sound wasn't heard.

The women were too busy clapping and congratulating the boy. The queen gave him another hug.

What the bloody hell? Zoltan pressed back against the stone wall, his mind racing. Who was this boy? Did he live in the cave? Didn't the leopard tell him that males weren't allowed in the cave?

Human males. *Shit!* Of course the boy wasn't human. What human could breathe fire?

The first tug of death-sleep pulled at Zoltan. That meant he had about seven minutes before sunrise. He could figure this mess out later. For now, he'd better take his chance at getting inside the cave.

He teleported to the entrance and peered inside. No one in sight. The giant room was lit with a few torches slid into brackets on the cave walls. Light flickered over the glistening pink- and cream-colored stalactites that extended from the high ceiling.

He eased inside. Far to the left, he spotted a stash of weapons and armor. The new swords and arrows he'd given them were there. In the center, a large throne chair sat. Toward the back, he noted the dark, glimmering pool. The Living Water trickled from a fissure in the rock wall, then fell into the pool below.

He squatted beside the pool and filled his bottle. As he screwed the top back on, he heard a voice outside. The queen. Was she bringing the mysterious boy back?

He looked around, wondering where the boy lived. There, on the far side of the pool, a narrow corridor led into the heart of the mountain.

With vampire speed, he rushed down the corridor. It grew darker, but with his superior night vision, he could see the sudden turn to his left, then another to the right.

He stopped, his mouth dropping open. The room

before him was dimly lit with a few torches. And it was huge. The size of several soccer fields. So many stalactites were growing across the wide expanse of the ceiling that it resembled a giant upside-down forest.

He eased inside. Was this where the boy lived? Zoltan circled to the right, staying close to the wall and hiding behind the stalagmites that lined the perimeter of the huge cavern. Apparently, any other stalagmites had been knocked down, for the vast expanse of the floor was smooth.

The queen's voice echoed in the narrow corridor. Zoltan looked around for the likeliest place to hide, then teleported to the stalactite forest overhead. As soon as he materialized, he levitated to keep himself hovering close to the ceiling. Most of the stalactites were twelve feet or more in length, so he was well hidden in the dark recesses between them.

The queen entered the giant room with the boy, who skipped happily over to the wall on the left. There, Zoltan spotted a row of pallets. The boy settled in one, drawing a blanket up to his chest.

The queen hunched down beside him, and with a smile, she tucked him in. Two more children sat up, and she glanced their way. No words were spoken, but Zoltan could sense there was a conversation going on.

Queen Nima hurried over to them and gave them reassuring hugs. The children clung to her as if she were their mother.

Zoltan frowned, not sure he could believe his eyes. This was the coldhearted bitch who was always threatening to kill him? The grandmother who had ruthlessly given away Minerva's son? Why was she here, mothering these children with such tenderness?

As far as he could tell, there were two boys and one girl. The boy who had breathed fire looked about twelve, while the other two appeared about half his age. There were more pallets in the row, but they were empty. The queen settled on the first and largest pallet, and they all went to sleep.

Another tug of death-sleep pulled at Zoltan and his levitation slipped, dropping him down a few inches. He shook himself. He'd have to teleport back to Neona's house soon. He pivoted, scanning the large cavern to make sure he hadn't missed anything.

There, behind some stalagmites, was another corridor with a light inside. He teleported to the corridor and eased quietly down the narrow path.

Another room lay before him. A much smaller room with only one torch. He passed by a heap of hay, hollowed out in the center like a giant nest. It was empty. A second one was also empty. He came to a stop. There were three more nests. And inside were eggs. Large eggs. Two in the third nest. Three in the next one, and two more in the final one.

Death-sleep tugged at him once more, but he shook it off and stepped closer to the eggs. No bird was this big. What the hell was going on?

He glanced at the two empty nests. Had the sleeping children come from those nests? No, that couldn't be right. Since when did children come out of eggs?

Confused, he teleported back to Neona's house. He only had a minute or so left, and he still needed to spike his blood supply with the Living Water. There were six bottles in the ice chest. One empty, and another half empty. He opened all six, then poured blood from the full ones into the other two. Soon he had six bottles about three-quarters full. He topped them off with the Living Water, then shook each bottle and put them back into the ice chest.

With that job done, his thoughts returned to the children in the cave. Clearly, they weren't normal. Or even human. The oldest one could breathe fire. And they all seemed to communicate silently with the queen. What was her gift? The special gift that allowed her to be queen and made Winifred the heir to the throne. An ability to communicate with . . . birds?

Death-sleep pulled at him harder, and he stumbled toward Neona's bed. What was the term she had used? Not birds.

Winged creatures.

He glanced at the fireplace that was lined with the odd black tiles. A scale, Milan had called it. A cross between a turtle shell and a reptile scale. But too large. Much too large for an iguana.

A winged creature. With scales. That could breathe fire?

He inhaled sharply. It couldn't be.

Death-sleep gripped him, and he collapsed onto Neona's bed. "Neona, wake up." He shook her shoulder.

She moaned. "Not another climax . . ."

"Not that." Death-sleep crept over him, making it difficult to talk. Or even think. "The big secret . . . the pact you made . . . are you protecting . . . dragons?"

With another moan, she rolled over.

An intense pain struck Zoltan in the chest. The pain of death. So close to Neona. He reeled away from her, falling off the bed and landing with a thud on the floor.

The pain subsided as he fell into a pit of darkness.

Chapter Twenty

*W*hen Neona woke, she stretched lazily in bed as memories of Zoltan's lovemaking meandered through her mind. She rolled over to look at him.

He wasn't in her bed. Or Minerva's. She sat up and gasped at the sight of him on the floor. What was he doing? She stiffened as another memory flitted through her mind.

Dragons! He'd asked her about dragons. She'd been half asleep when he'd asked her, but then the room had become quiet again and she'd fallen back asleep.

"How did you find out?" she whispered.

No answer.

"Why are you on the floor?"

No answer.

She tried lifting him, but he was like a rock. Giving up, she slipped a pillow under his head. He was fully dressed, so he must have gone out while she was sleeping.

"Did you sneak inside the cave?"

No answer.

With a sigh, she brushed his hair back from his brow. "Too smart for your own good. And too handsome." She smiled to herself, remembering how she'd once called him seemingly intelligent. "The queen will be upset that you know, but I think it's just as well. If you and your friends are going to protect our valley and our secrets, then you have the right to know what you're protecting."

After dressing, Neona removed the flask of Living Water from her chest. Then she opened Zoltan's box and removed his bottles of blood. Carefully, she cracked open a window, making sure no sunlight hit Zoltan's body. She peered outside. No one in sight.

She poured a little from each bottle out the window, then topped them off with Living Water. "There." She gave him a wry look. "You're not the only one sneaking around, breaking the rules."

She hurried to the outhouse, then washed up in the stream before joining the other women at the fire pit. They were all there, except Winifred. Freddie was probably in the cave. Since she could also communicate with winged creatures, she took turns with the queen, watching over the young ones.

The women were sitting on straw mats, since the ground was still damp from last night's rain. Their voices hushed as Neona approached and took a seat. She bowed her head in greeting, waiting for the queen to speak first. The women were all staring at her.

Finally, Queen Nima cleared her throat. "You're late. You missed breakfast and the midday meal."

"We saved you some food." Freya ladled soup into a bowl.

"Thank you." Neona accepted the bowl and a wooden spoon. She ate, aware that the women were still staring.

Nima's eyes narrowed. "I don't see any bite marks on her."

Tashi snorted. "I guess he bit her where the sun doesn't shine."

Neona choked on her food. "Excuse me?"

"Didn't that monster bite you?" Lydia asked.

Tashi leaned forward. "Did he finally get it up?"

"Of course," Neona started.

"He bit you?" the queen shouted. "I should kill him!"

"He didn't bite me!" Neona set her bowl aside. "He doesn't bite anyone. He drinks fake blood out of bottles."

"Fake blood?" Lydia asked.

"Yes, he brought some here from his castle in Transylvania."

"He has a castle?" Freya's eyes lit up. "How exciting!"

"Don't be so easily swayed," Nima grumbled at her.

"He and his friends want to help us," Neona insisted. "I don't see how we can defeat Liao without their help."

Lydia shuddered. "I hate the thought of working with those monsters."

Nima nodded. "I hate it, too, but sometimes it takes one monster to kill another. We will accept their help but watch them carefully for any sign of betrayal."

Lydia sighed. "Very well. I suppose desperate times call for desperate measures."

"True," Nima agreed. "It is always dangerous when we're at the beginning of a new cycle. The young ones and the remaining eggs are defenseless. We must do everything in our power to protect them until they reach maturity. It is our sacred duty."

Everyone murmured their agreement. Once the young ones were old enough to shift into dragon form, they would be able to protect themselves. But for now, they were entirely dependent on the warrior women of Beyul-La.

Neona picked up her bowl of soup and resumed eating. "When Zoltan wakes up, I'll tell him we have accepted his offer of assistance."

"As long as he understands our position," the queen added. "Once our valley is safe again, the monsters need to go away and leave us alone. Your affair with Dohna's son will be over."

Neona took a few more bites of soup, then set the bowl down again. Steeling her nerves, she faced her mother. "I'm not giving Zoltan up. And if I have a son with him, I'm not giving him up, either."

A series of gasps echoed around the fire.

The queen's golden eyes burned hot as she stared at Neona. "You would knowingly defy our laws?"

"I question the validity of our laws."

Nima stiffened, her face flushing with anger. "If you cannot abide by them, you must leave."

"I understand how important our sacred duty is," Neona said. "But I also believe we should be open to change. I see no reason why I cannot live with Zoltan and my children in the next valley. And since I'm the only healer, you should be willing—"

"You think to coerce me?" Nima cursed under her breath. "I knew we couldn't trust that vampire. He's been corrupting you—"

"I made this decision on my own," Neona insisted. "I haven't even discussed it with him."

Nima snorted. "You know the man for a week, and now you wish to reject a way of life that is over three thousand years old?"

Neona shook her head. "You cannot blame this on Zoltan. I've been coming to this conclusion for a long time."

Tashi cleared her throat. "I've been thinking about getting married, too."

"*What*?" her mother gasped.

"I'm in love with a farmer from the village—" Tashi started.

"A farmer?" Lydia looked aghast.

"We want to marry and have children," Tashi continued quickly. "And you could live with us, Mother. We could have normal lives."

"We are the immortal women of Beyul-La!" Nima shouted. "Why would you want a *normal* life with a lowly farmer?"

Tashi gritted her teeth. "You don't need me here. I can't communicate with the dragons like you. Or Winifred."

Nima huffed. "You ungrateful child. You've been blessed with a gift, and you will remain here, where it can be put to good use."

"*Child*?" Tashi yelled. "I'm almost five hundred years old! And as for my precious gift, all I do here is occasionally fuss at the donkey for being lazy or tell Neona what her pet cat wants for dinner! If I have to live like that for another hundred years, I'll go crazy!"

"Then leave!" Nima rose to her feet. "If you are so useless to us, go!"

Lydia leaned close to her daughter and whispered, "Apologize!"

Tashi remained silent, but tears glistened in her eyes. "I'm not abandoning our sacred duty. My sisters died to protect this valley, and I won't leave until it is safe. And when I do leave, I'll be only fifteen miles away. If you send your owl to me, I will know I am needed, and I will come."

Nima scoffed.

Freya reached over and touched Tashi's arm. "I never thought you were useless. You make beautiful pottery. You tell great stories, and you have such a pretty voice. The young ones love it when you sing. So do I."

"I'm grateful you told me about Zoltan being gifted," Neona said. She stood and faced her mother. "I'm going to the monastery tonight to find Minerva's son. And if I can, I'm bringing him back to his rightful home."

Another series of gasps went around the fire.

Nima's eyes narrowed. "You wish to defy me at every turn?"

"I wish to do what I know to be right."

"I decide what is right!"

Neona lifted her chin. "We should put aside our disagreements for now. Liao is coming, and our first priority must be to protect this valley."

"Now you're telling me my job?" Nima snorted. "I know we have to work with those monsters to save our valley and the young ones who depend on us. I also know those monsters will seek to destroy our way of life. And you seem content to help them." She stalked off toward the cave.

When Zoltan woke, he sat up, wondering why he was on the floor. Then it came back to him. *Dragons.* He'd been asking Neona about them when he'd fallen into his death-sleep.

He headed straight to the ice chest and grabbed a bottle of blood. It was a shade lighter than normal, probably from the Living Water he'd added.

"It can't kill you," he whispered to himself and drank the bottle down.

"You're awake!" Neona entered the house and smiled as he turned toward her. "I have good news.

The queen will accept you and your friends. That is, for the time it takes to defeat our common foe."

"That's a relief." He stuffed the empty bottle back into the ice chest. As far as he could tell, he wasn't having any sort of reaction to the Living Water. But he was still hungry. One bottle wasn't filling him up. He pulled out a second bottle.

"Are you all right?" She glanced warily at the ice chest.

"I guess I'm extra hungry tonight." Probably from all the sex. Just thinking about last night made his groin tighten. Made him want more. He guzzled down the second bottle, wondering how much time he would have before Emma called.

"Are we going to the monastery tonight?"

"Yes. After my friends arrive, we should be able to go while they get settled in."

"All right. I—" Neona shifted her weight. "I need to ask you something. I'm not sure if I dreamed it. I was so tired last night—"

"From all the sex?"

She nodded. "I think you—"

"I gave you three more climaxes."

"Yes, but then later, you came—"

"I came, yes. Biggest damned orgasm—"

"You came back to bed and asked me—"

"You want to have sex?"

She blinked. "That's not what you asked. You wanted to know if our secret pact was with—"

"Oh, the dragons. Right." He adjusted his jeans. They were already too confining against his groin.

"You don't find it shocking?"

"No. My pants are always too tight when I—"

"I meant the dragons!" She gave him an exasperated look. "Are you always thinking about sex?"

He shook his head. "Not until I met you. I . . . hunger for you all the time."

Her eyes softened. "Your mind is still working well enough to figure out we have dragons. You weren't shocked?"

"I was. A bit. So the kids are shifters? They'll turn into dragons?"

"Yes. About the time of puberty."

He nodded. "That figures. It's the same for the other shifters I know."

"Other . . . shifters?"

"Werewolves, were-panthers and tigers, were-bears—"

She gasped. "Such creatures exist?"

"You didn't know? You'll probably meet some tonight." He glanced at his watch. If he was going to give her climax number five, he'd better hurry. "Let's go to the waterfall to shower." He grabbed his toiletry kit from his duffel bag. "Bring some towels."

She selected two towels from her shelf. "Do we have time before your friends come?"

"We'll have to hurry." He grabbed Neona and teleported her to the waterfall that burst through the rock wall.

She looked around, then stared at him as he stripped with vampire speed. "Why are you moving so quickly?"

He untied her sash and pulled off her tunic. "Once my friends start moving into this valley, we won't have any privacy."

"Oh." She glanced at the waterfall. "It's our last chance to shower for a while."

"Among other things," he muttered as he removed the shampoo and bar of soap from his toiletry kit.

Using vampire speed, he was able to finish washing by the time she joined him, naked, in the spray. He shampooed her hair, enjoying her little moans as he caressed her scalp. With her hair rinsed, he lathered up his hands with soap and started on her body.

She laughed. "You seem to think my breasts are extra dirty."

"Extra beautiful." He wiped the soap off her hardened nipples and gave them a kiss.

"You're the beautiful one." She smoothed her hands down his chest to his stomach. "Do we have time for another healing session?"

He inhaled sharply when she cupped his balls with one hand and squeezed his dick with the other. "Neona." He grasped her hips. Within seconds, he could feel the tingling sensation, then the hum of vibration. His vision turned rosy pink as his eyes glowed red.

"You're getting so thick," she whispered. "And hard."

He groaned. "Are you ready for climax number five?"

"We don't have to count them anymore. The plan worked, and I trust you."

He splayed his hands on her rump. "What if I can't trust you?"

Her hands stilled. "What do you mean?"

"You agreed to ravish me in the woods, and you haven't delivered."

"Oh." Her mouth curled up. "Does it disturb you?"

"Yes! You shouldn't make promises you can't keep."

Her smile widened. "Do I need to knock you down and tie you up?"

"No. I surrender." He led her from the water and grabbed a towel. Then he teleported her to the clearing where they'd met and fought that first night.

"I think we were right about here." He lay the towel down, then stretched out on top. "Okay, I'm ready."

"I can see that." She gave his groin a wry look. "You seem to get in the mood much quicker these days."

"I was always in the mood. It's not every day that a beautiful woman tries to ravish me in the woods."

Her gaze drifted down his body. "It's not every day that I find such an excellent specimen. You are strong and fleet of foot. Fair of face—"

"And seemingly intelligent?" he added.

"Yes." With a smile, she kneeled at his feet. "If you are willing, I plan to take your seed."

He raised himself on his elbows so he could see her. "How were you going to do it?"

She smoothed her hands up his bare legs. "I was going to pull your pants off. And your underwear."

His dick grew harder. "And then?"

Straddling his legs, she crawled closer to his groin. "I was going to touch you and stroke you until you were ready." She glanced at his erection. "But you already are."

"I was hard that night."

Her eyes widened. "Really?"

He snorted. "I've been hard most of the week." He lay back and grabbed her hips. "What would you have done next?"

"I would have made sure I was ready." She straddled his hips and rubbed herself against the length of his erection.

He groaned. She was slick with moisture. "Neona."

"And then . . ." She took hold of him and eased him inside her slick entrance.

Grasping her hips, he pulled her down. She gasped and grew still.

"What's wrong? Did I hurt you?"

Her eyes glistened with tears. "You fill me up."

"Yes." He gritted his teeth. She felt gloriously tight.

"I was afraid that first night that I would fall for you. And I have."

His heart squeezed. "Is that bad?"

A tear rolled down her cheek. "Relationships never seem to work for us. It always ends with abandonment. Or death and destruction."

"We'll make it work." He pulled her down and rolled on top of her, making sure he remained deep inside her. "I love you, Neona. I'll never give you up."

She cradled his face in her hands. "I love you, too."

Her words sent him over the edge, and he moved inside her faster and faster, till he arched with a shout. She squealed beneath him, her inner muscles clutching him tight. With a long groan, he pumped his seed into her.

They held each other tight for a while. He listened to her breathing and the gentle breeze that stirred the trees around them. It was a shame they couldn't stay like this forever. But danger was approaching, and they would have to be ready.

He eased himself to his feet and helped her up. After grabbing the towel, he teleported them back to the waterfall. They rinsed off, clinging to each other under the spray of water.

A buzzing noise emanated from his jacket he'd left on a nearby rock, and he sighed. Their idyllic moment was over.

He pulled the sat phone out. "Yes?"

"Where have you been?" Emma asked. "I've been calling for ten minutes. We're ready to go."

"Give me five minutes, and I'll call back." He hung up.

"And so it begins." Neona gave him a worried look.

"We'll defeat Liao. We'll make it through. I promise."

Chapter Twenty-one

"*Y*ou brought us new clothes?" Neona asked as she studied the black vest she'd pulled from one of the tote bags.

"They're called Kevlar vests," Emma explained. "They're bulletproof and provide some protection against stabs."

"How wonderful." Lydia grabbed one to look at it. "Then this is a modern type of armor?"

"Yes." Emma nodded. "We are honored to be fighting by your side in our quest to defeat Lord Liao and Master Han. Please accept these vests as a token of our friendship."

Nima, who had at first ignored the tote bags, removed a vest and admired it. "We will accept your gift. Thank you."

"You're welcome." Emma exchanged a smile with Lady Pamela.

After Zoltan had teleported Neona back to her house, she'd gathered all the women around the central fire pit to tell them that a vampire warrior woman would be arriving soon. Then he had called Emma so she could use his voice to teleport. To everyone's surprise, she hadn't come alone. Mikhail's wife, Lady Pamela, had accompanied her, and they'd both been loaded down with tote bags.

Any feelings of suspicion or distrust had quickly evaporated when the women of Beyul-La had taken a look at their gifts. Luxurious bath products, cookware and dishes—it was like Christmas, Zoltan thought. But the most popular bags were the ones containing Kevlar vests.

Emma bowed her head to Nima. "If you are ready, your majesty, we can discuss business."

"I am ready." Nima sat in her usual place at the fire pit. Zoltan sat next to Neona and took her hand in his.

"Liao is coming this way with two hundred soldiers," Emma began, but she was interrupted by a series of gasps.

"How many warriors are you providing?" Nima demanded.

"Around fifty," Emma replied, then held up her hands when the women objected. "I know it sounds bad, but even though we're outnumbered, we've been making good progress in our battle against Master Han. With help from the God Warriors, we dispatched the demon, Darafer, back to hell, and we've successfully turned a hundred of their supersoldiers back to normal."

"Is it true what Zoltan said?" Freddie asked. "That Master Han has nine hundred soldiers?"

Emma nodded. "Yes. But with Darafer gone, Master Han can't make any more."

The queen huffed. "And how are we supposed to defeat Liao and his two hundred soldiers?"

"A war of attrition," Emma replied. "Liao doesn't know the exact location of this valley. In order to cover all of Tibet, he will have to divide his men into search parties. Our friend Russell is following them. Once we know the location of a search party, we'll teleport in to attack. By the time Liao finds this valley, his army will be whittled down to a much more manageable size."

The women nodded in approval.

"Your strategy is sound," Nima announced. "We will assist you in your attacks."

"Excellent." Emma smiled. "Then you will not object to our men moving into the neighboring valley?"

"They may come," Nima agreed. "But they must understand that they need to remain in the next valley. Men are not allowed here in Beyul-La." She cast a disparaging look at Zoltan. "We made an exception for Dohna's son."

"And I appreciate it." When he smiled at her, the queen's frown deepened. He groaned inwardly. As far as he could tell, his future mother-in-law still wanted to kill him. Maybe the land deed would change her mind.

"Excuse me." He hurried back to Neona's house and took the folder from his duffel bag. When he returned to the fire pit, Tashi was taking Pamela to the next valley so Pamela could call in the troops.

He sat next between Neona and her mother. "Your majesty, I have a gift for you." He handed her the folder. "This is the land deed for Beyul-La and the surrounding area. Legal proof that the land is yours."

The queen's eyes widened as she opened the folder.

"Thank you." Neona squeezed his arm and smiled at him.

"Who is this?" Nima pointed at Rajiv's name.

"He's a friend and a Chinese citizen. I had to buy the land through him."

The queen shut the folder, frowning. "How can we trust him? He might steal the valley from us."

"He won't," Zoltan assured her. "He's the Grand Tiger of Tiger Town. He's on our side."

"That's true," Emma added. "The were-tigers are our biggest ally against Master Han."

"Were-tigers?" Freya's eyes lit up. "You mean there are men who turn into tigers?"

Emma smiled. "Yes. We have a number of shifters on our side. Wolves, bears, tigers, and panthers. You needn't be concerned about your Living Water where they're concerned. They can all live five hundred years or more."

Zoltan noticed how the women exchanged glances. Were they expecting to keep their were-dragons a secret?

Nima shot him an angry look. "You told her about our Living Water?"

"They're going to risk their lives for you." Zoltan gave her a pointed look. "They have a right to know *all* the secrets they are protecting."

Her eyes narrowed.

"We understand why you keep the Living Water a secret," Emma said. "We can't let Liao or Han find it. They would use it to gain power over the entire planet."

Nima nodded stiffly. "That is true."

"I need to show you these." Emma unzipped her backpack and removed a pistol. "I brought one for each of you."

"We've never used guns before," Freddie said.

"Don't worry. We'll train you." Emma removed a box of darts from her backpack. "These are actually dart guns. And practice darts. When we attack a search party, we'll use the real darts and shoot as many of the soldiers as possible. The darts will knock them out."

The queen crossed her arms. "We are accustomed to bows and arrows. Or swords."

Emma nodded. "You will have your usual weapons with you in case you need them. But remember, Han's soldiers are super fast and strong. The minute you engage in close combat, you will be at a disadvantage."

"We know," Freddie muttered. "They killed five of us three weeks ago."

"We're determined not to lose any of you," Emma assured her. "The best way to deal with the supersoldiers is a surprise attack, knocking them unconscious with a dart before they even know we're there."

"And then we kill them?" the queen asked.

Emma shook her head. "Remember how I said that we've changed a hundred of the soldiers back to normal? That is our goal. We'll teleport the unconscious soldiers to our clinic in Japan or the new one we're setting up in Tiger Town, and there we'll be able to save them."

"Why are we bothering to save them?" Lydia asked.

"They're mortal," Emma explained. "And it has always been our mission as Vamps to protect mortals. The soldiers are under Master Han's mental control. And they've been changed by Darafer, the demon. Once we change them back and break Han's control over them, they're happy to be free."

"If they die in battle, their souls belong to Darafer," Zoltan added. "They'll go straight to hell."

The women winced.

"So we try to rescue as many as we can. It pays off in the end because the rescued soldiers usually agree to help us defeat Han. Since we're so outnumbered, we'll need them someday." Emma pulled a tablet from her backpack. "Before we head to the next valley, I have one more thing to share with you. Well, with Winifred and Freya, to be precise."

"Yes?" Freddie and Freya sat up.

"A few nights ago, Zoltan asked my husband, Angus, to search for your father," Emma explained. When the girls' faces lit up, she quickly added, "I'm afraid I have sad news for you. Frederic passed away about sixty years ago during a bombing raid in World War II."

"Oh," Freya whispered. "Poor Papa."

Freddie sighed. "I always wondered what happened. He said he would come back."

"I'm sorry." Emma turned on her tablet and touched some buttons. "Angus was able to locate your younger brother, Franklin—"

"Frankie?" Freya gasped. "He's alive?"

Freddie grinned. "How is he?"

"You can see for yourself." Emma handed Freya the tablet. "Angus recorded this for you."

Freddie and Freya squealed when a man's voice emanated from the tablet.

"Oh, my God!" Freya dropped the tablet.

Freddie poked at it with a finger. "What is this thing? Is that Frankie?"

"I want to see him!" Neona scurried around the fire pit, then hunched behind the two women, looking over their shoulders.

Freddie leaned closer. "He looks so old!"

Freya looked aghast. "If we didn't have the Living Water, we would look even older!"

Neona winced. "I helped deliver him. And I used to change his nappies."

"Did you?" Freya glanced back at her.

Neona snorted. "I changed your nappies, too."

"You probably remember him better than we do," Freddie murmured. "We were so young."

"I remember him." Lydia scooted closer so she could see.

"He's talking!" Freya picked up the tablet. "And we're missing it."

"I'll start it over for you." Emma reached over to touch some buttons.

The four women hunched over the tablet to watch the video. Zoltan smiled at the joy on their faces. Too bad the queen was still sitting there like a grumpy toad.

"Hi, Freddie! Hello, Freya!" Frankie's voice began.

"Hello?" Freya whispered hesitantly.

"It's recorded," Emma explained. "He can't hear you."

"Hush." Freddie nudged her sister.

"Angus assures me that you'll see this," Frankie continued. "What a thrill it was to hear that you're still alive and well in Beyul-La. I was very sorry to hear about Mum. I suppose you heard about Papa. He died during an air raid sixty years ago. I know he promised to come back to you, and he truly meant to, but when the war started, travel was impossible, and then he didn't survive the war."

"He never meant to abandon us," Freya whispered.

"I was only six when we left," Frankie said, "but Papa always talked about Beyul-La, so I have all of his memories. I know that Freddie used to suck two of her fingers and Freya was late learning how to walk because she loved making Papa carry her everywhere."

"That's true," Freddie muttered. "You were such a big baby."

"Hush." Freya nudged her sister.

"Papa and I talked about you all the time. It was our own secret." Frankie sighed. "I still miss him. I always wanted to come back to see you, but I didn't know where you are exactly. And I didn't want to hire anyone to find you when you're supposed to remain hidden. And then I was always busy. I'm the head gardener at a huge estate here in England. I've always been able to grow things."

Freya gasped. "He has the same gift that I do!"

Another son who had inherited a gift. Zoltan glanced over at the queen, who was scowling. Did she realize the world she'd controlled for centuries was changing? Hopefully, she'd learn to trust him someday. He intended to do all he could to safeguard the valley.

"And my family keeps me busy," Frankie continued. "I have a wife, three children, and five grandchildren."

Freddie grinned. "We have family there."

"Look!" Freya pointed. "He's showing pictures of them!"

"Angus says he could teleport me back to Papa's cabin if that's all right with you. Vampires, can you believe it?" Frankie laughed. "Now I have another secret to keep."

"Oh, yes!" Freya clasped her hands together.

"That would be wonderful!" Freddie gave Emma a beseeching look. "When can you bring him here?"

With a smile, Emma retrieved the tablet. "As soon as the situation is safe."

"Thank you! Thank you!" Freddie and Freya jumped to their feet. With a grin, Neona hugged them.

Zoltan noticed the queen's hands had clenched in

silent anger. No one had asked her permission for Frankie to visit.

Emma's phone buzzed and she answered it. "All right." She pocketed the phone and rose to her feet, swinging her backpack over a shoulder. "Angus says they're ready."

Nima stood stiffly. "I will show you the way." She frowned at Winifred. "Check on the cave before you come."

"Yes, your majesty." Freddie dashed toward the cave.

Emma watched her go, then gave Zoltan a questioning look. He nodded to let her know he'd explain it to her.

They followed the queen to the rock wall. When they reached the top, he noted the next valley was now bustling with people.

Freya surveyed the crowd. "Are the were-tigers here?"

Emma pointed to three men who were examining supply boxes. "The Grand Tiger and two of his companions."

"How interesting." Freya tossed the rope ladder over the wall.

Winifred ran to catch up with them. "Everything's fine," she whispered to the queen. "If they need you, they'll send the owl. Zhan is guarding the entrance. If anyone approaches, he'll let us know."

Nima nodded. "Good."

"Your majesty," Zoltan addressed her. "You and the other women will need to get used to being teleported, so I'll show you how easy it is." He grabbed Neona and materialized in the valley below.

Neona waved at the other women to let them know she was okay. They waved back, then started down the rope ladder one by one. Tashi, who was already in the valley, ran to the base of the wall to hold the ladder steady.

Emma materialized beside him. "Okay. What's in the bloody cave?"

"It's the reason they drink the Living Water," Zoltan whispered. "They're staying alive for millennia so they can protect what is probably the last remaining group of were-dragons on the planet."

Emma gasped. "Are you kidding me? Dragons?"

"Yes. Fire-breathing dragons." He turned to Neona. "I assume they're able to fly? Is that how you managed to get to Transylvania so quickly when my mother was in danger?"

"Yes." Neona stepped closer. "As soon as the villagers captured your mother, she sent the news to us by an eagle. Then we rode the dragons there."

"So it was the dragons who burned down the village?" Zoltan asked.

"Yes." Neona sighed. "They're extremely fast and fierce when fully mature, but now we're at the beginning of a cycle, so they're defenseless. We have three children and three remaining nests of eggs. We must keep them safe."

Emma's expression was still stunned. "You say they're fast and fierce?"

"They destroyed my village," Zoltan muttered.

"And they can fly incredibly fast," Neona added. "I suppose that's one of the reasons why we've always enjoyed being their guardians. You cannot imagine how exhilarating it is to soar through the sky on the back of a dragon."

"It does sound exciting." Emma nodded slowly. "Could it be the dragons that Liao is after? Are there rumors that he might have heard?"

Neona winced. "That is possible. The dragons are hunters by nature. We always urge them to hunt in the wild, but over the years, there have been a few occasions when they've stolen cows or sheep from farmers. Fortunately, they know to do that only if they're hundreds of miles away, so that it's hard to trace them back here."

Emma's eyes narrowed. "Imagine Master Han's supersoldiers attacking villages on fire-breathing dragons. I have to let Angus know about this." She ran off to find her husband.

Neona glanced at her mother, who was still at the top of the rock wall, waiting to climb down the rope ladder. "I'm going to have to tell her that the secret is out. She will not be happy."

Zoltan wrapped an arm around her shoulder. "Come on, let me introduce you to some of the guys."

He led her to the nearest group.

"Way to go, Zoltan!" Phineas waved at him. "When I heard you'd found some Amazon women, I wasn't expecting them to be hot."

Gregori gave Zoltan a thumbs-up. "J.L. was betting us that they would look like abominable snowwomen. Big, mean, and hairy."

"Aye." Dougal nudged J.L. "Ye owe me ten pounds."

J.L. Wang didn't respond. With his mouth dropped open, he focused on the women climbing down the rope ladder.

"J.L.?" Howard waved a hand in front of his face. "Wangster, are you still with us?"

Dougal snorted. "I think he's smitten."

"Oh, yeah," Phineas agreed. "Trapped in a tractor beam of hotness. Quick!" He spun J.L. around. "We've got to break the connection before he's a goner."

Dougal opened a flask of Blissky and waved it under J.L.'s nose. "Come back to us, lad."

J.L. blinked, then whispered, "She's a goddess."

Zoltan glanced back at the warrior women, wondering which one had affected J.L. "Let me introduce you to Neona, my future wife."

She gave him a wry look. "When did I agree to that?"

The guys laughed and shook hands with her.

Howard smirked at Zoltan. "No wonder you were letting her beat the crap out of you."

Zoltan laughed, then led Neona away so they could talk in private. "We'd better go to the monastery before practice begins."

She nodded. "As soon as it's safe, I want to bring Minerva's son back here so I can be his mother."

Zoltan took her in his arms. "Then he'll gain a father, too."

Her eyes gleamed with tears. "Have I told you that I love you?"

"Yes. Climax number five, I believe it was."

She snorted. "You're always thinking about sex."

"And you." He kissed her brow. "Let's go."

Chapter Twenty-two

$\mathcal{N}$eona peered inside the open gate of the monastery. The courtyard was empty. The soothing sound of chanting male voices drifted from the small temple in the center. A stone wall topped with clay shingles ran along all four sides of the square-shaped compound. A line of one-story buildings ran along the wall to the right. Private rooms, she figured, by the number of doors. To the left, there was a row of low tables with baskets containing rice and vegetables. A few chickens pecked at the ground.

Zoltan gave the chain by the gate a yank, and the bell overhead clanged. The chanting in the temple stopped.

Neona winced. The monks might think they were rude to interrupt.

Two monks, bald and dressed in dark red robes, emerged from the temple. They pressed their hands together and bowed.

Neona bowed back.

The eldest-looking monk descended the two steps and slid his feet into slides made of woven reeds. As he approached, his sharp gaze shifted between her and Zoltan. The chanting began once again in the temple.

"How may I help you?" he asked in Tibetan.

Neona bowed once again. "Venerable Father, I apologize for interrupting your meditations."

The monk smiled gently. "We are usually asleep by now, but one of our younger brothers is gifted with the sight and has had a vision." He glanced back, his smile fading. "A vision of evil approaching."

Neona wondered if the younger monk had sensed that Lord Liao was coming. She gave Zoltan a worried glance, then realized he had no idea what was being said in Tibetan. She'd have to fill him in later.

The elderly monk tilted his head, studying her, then Zoltan. "I do not sense any evil in you." His gaze returned to her. "But there is a great sadness in your heart."

Was it that easy to see? Neona steeled her nerves so she wouldn't cry. "Yes. I lost my twin sister three weeks ago. And she lost her son seven years ago. It was a terrible blow to her, and she never truly recovered. The boy was brought here . . ."

"Ah." The monk nodded. "You speak of Norjee."

His name was Norjee. In spite of her best effort, Neona's eyes still filled with tears. "Is he all right? May I see him?"

"Of course." The elderly monk gestured to the buildings on the right. "Come this way." Halfway to the buildings, he paused to speak to the second monk, who still stood on the temple steps. "Will you bring us tea and the child Norjee?"

The second monk bowed, then descended the steps.

The first monk led them to the first door of the buildings, left his slides on the first step, then ascended a second step to open the door.

Neona removed her slippers. Zoltan, who was watching everything, kicked off his shoes and followed her inside.

It was a small room with a pallet rolled up and stashed against the wall next to a bookcase holding old scrolls. In the center was a short table. The monk sat cross-legged behind the table and motioned for them to join him.

After they sat, the monk took a deep breath. "Am I to understand that the boy's mother did not wish to give him to our care?"

Neona shook her head. "It was our mother who brought the baby here."

The monk glanced at Zoltan. "Is this man the boy's father?"

"No." Neona took Zoltan's hand in hers. "He is my betrothed. When I told him I wanted to find my sister's son and raise him as my own, he agreed to help me."

The monk nodded approvingly.

The second monk entered with a tray containing a teapot and three small cups. He set the tray on the table. "I will bring the boy now." He bowed and left.

The elderly monk poured three cups of tea. "I will not lie to you. Raising Norjee has been . . . a bit of a challenge." He smiled. "There are only a dozen of us brothers here, and there are times when Norjee seems to have more energy than all of us put together."

Neona winced inwardly. "Has he been difficult?"

The monk gave her a sympathetic look. "Please do not misunderstand. We love the boy. And he loves us. But we are a group of old men. We spend our days working our small rice field or tending the animals. In our free time, we like to read, meditate, or pray.

These are not interesting pastimes for a boy like Norjee, who is so full of life."

"I see." Neona drank some tea.

The monk took a sip. "He has been both a challenge and a blessing. A challenge, for we have trouble convincing him to do his chores. But a blessing, for he sees the world as a wondrous place, as if every small event is a miracle to behold, and we have treasured those moments. He is a joy to us." The monk sighed. "A joy we do not know how to control. Indeed, it seemed wrong to even attempt it. For he is a child with a special gift."

Neona's heart stilled. "What kind of gift?"

"He can communicate with the birds of the air."

She inhaled sharply. He'd inherited Minerva's gift! He'd be able to communicate with the dragons.

"Even when he was a baby, birds would come to his windowsill and chirp," the monk continued. "It wasn't until he was older and could talk to us that we understood what was happening. He was only three years old the first time he tried to run away. He claimed the birds were free to fly away, and he should be like them. We had a terrible time convincing him to stay here. When it was time to do his chores, he'd run off to spend the afternoon talking to a family of eagles. The mother eagle would ask him about his parents, and then he would return to question us. Why was he not living with a mother and father like the baby eagles?"

The door opened, and the second monk announced, "He's not in his room. We cannot find him in the compound."

Neona jumped to her feet. "He's run away?"

"Do not worry." The first monk stood slowly. "Norjee does this at least once a week. He will come back when he's hungry."

"He's wandering the forest by himself?" Neona asked. "He's only seven years old!"

Zoltan stood and whispered, "What's wrong?"

"He's in the forest somewhere," she replied in English.

"He is never alone," the monk assured her. "Not when he can talk to the birds. Come. We will call him."

They hurried to the gate, and the monk rang the bell.

She looked around. Beyond the rice field, the woods appeared ominously dark. "I don't like this. There are wolves, bears, and wildcats."

"I'll see what I can do," Zoltan told her.

The clanging of the bell brought more monks to the gate. When they learned Norjee was missing, they returned to the temple to pray.

After a few agonizing minutes, Neona spotted movement at the edge of the forest.

"That's him." Zoltan pointed.

Soon she could see him in the moonlight. A family of foxes was leading him back, while several small birds circled overhead. Every now and then, a bird would dive down to peck at a fox's head, and the furry red creature would jump and hiss. The boy laughed as he skipped along beside them.

Neona turned to Zoltan. "Did you contact the foxes?"

He nodded, smiling.

The monk stepped forward. "Norjee, you left again without permission."

The boy bowed. "I am sorry, Venerable Father. The birds were calling to me." His gaze landed on Neona and Zoltan, and his eyes widened.

Neona blinked away tears. He looked so much like her sister. And he had her golden eyes.

The monk motioned to her. "She has come for you, Norjee."

The boy approached her slowly, a hopeful look on his face. "Are you . . . ?"

It made her heart ache to disappoint him. "I'm your aunt. Your mother was my twin sister."

His chin trembled. "Was?"

"She passed away." A tear rolled down Neona's cheek. "But she always loved you."

"I-I always wondered." Norjee sniffed. "The eagle mama told me I had to have a mother and father. She says I must have fallen out of the nest."

Neona smiled through her tears. "I'm afraid you did. But I'd like to take you back." She hunched down. "If you'll accept me, I would be honored to be your mother."

He ran toward her and threw his arms around her neck. She held him tight as more tears flowed. *I'll be a good mother to him, Minerva, I promise.*

Norjee glanced up at Zoltan. "Will he be my papa?"

"Yes." Neona brushed the boy's long hair back from his brow. "He doesn't know Tibetan, so it will be a while before you can talk to each other. But he can talk to animals. He's the one who sent the foxes after you."

Norjee's eyes lit up and he grinned. "That's great!"

Zoltan smiled and said in English, "I guess I've been accepted." He leaned over and tousled the boy's hair.

"We will have his belongings packed for you," the monk said.

Neona stood. "I'm afraid it's not safe for us to take

him tonight. Our valley may come under attack soon."

The monk nodded. "We know the evil ones are coming. We've been praying that the boy would be delivered from danger. You must take Norjee tonight."

"But—"

The monk held up a hand to stop her. "Our brother's visions are never wrong. The evil is coming here. I will try to convince my brothers to evacuate tomorrow."

The second monk arrived with a canvas bag. With a bow, he handed it to Neona.

"What's happening?" Zoltan asked.

"They want us to take Norjee tonight." She cast a worried look at the boy. "I guess he would be safe with the young ones in the cave."

"All right. I'll teleport him to Beyul-La, then come right back for you." Zoltan reached for Norjee, but the boy slipped past him and ran toward the monks.

With tears in their eyes, they held him tight, then nudged him toward Zoltan. "Peace be with you, Norjee."

"And you, Venerable Fathers," he whispered.

Zoltan took hold of the boy's shoulders and vanished.

The monks gasped.

"What manner of man is he?" The elderly monk shook his head in disbelief. "I could tell he was different, but I never sensed anything unholy about him."

"He's a vampire, but a good man," Neona explained. "He and some other good vampires are helping us. There's an evil vampire, Lord Liao, who is marching this way with an army of two hundred men."

The monks exchanged grim, resigned looks.

"Our Venerable Brother warned us there is great evil approaching," the elderly monk said. "We feared we would not be able to protect Norjee. You have answered our prayers by coming tonight."

Neona sighed. "I'm afraid I'm still taking him into danger."

The monk gave her a sad smile. "Your good vampire will protect him much better than we ever could."

Zoltan reappeared by her side. "Ready?"

"Almost." She bowed to the monks. "Thank you, Venerable Fathers, for raising Norjee and giving him love and kindness."

The monks pressed their hands together and bowed. "Peace be with you."

"When it is safe again, I'll bring him back every now and then to visit," she offered. The sadness in the monks' faces made her wonder just how bad the brother's vision had been.

Zoltan grabbed hold of her, and everything went black.

In Neona's house, Zoltan guzzled down a bottle of blood. He'd left Neona and Norjee by the central fire pit, where they were having a bowl of soup with Tashi and Lydia. He hadn't wanted to drink blood in front of the boy in case it frightened him.

A son. Zoltan finished the bottle and started on a second one. A week ago he'd set off to solve an old murder, and now he had a woman he intended to marry and a son. He'd protected hundreds of mortals over the centuries, so taking on this new responsibility didn't disturb him. Quite the contrary. Instead of countless faces, he finally had the chance to love and protect two people who would be special to him. He smiled to himself. If he could be half the father Istvan had been to him, then Norjee would do fine.

He eyed the second bottle, now empty. It must be because of the Living Water he'd added, for he'd had four bottles tonight and he still felt hungry. There were only two left in the ice chest. So far he hadn't noticed any effect other than hunger. It could be that it took time. Or perhaps his body undid any changes during his death-sleep.

He removed the bottles, then teleported to the kitchen in his castle with the ice chest. At vampire speed, he refilled the chest. Then, back in Neona's house, he poured a small portion of each new bottle into an empty one, then topped them all off with his supply of stolen Living Water.

He drank another bottle, then joined the others at the fire pit. Winifred and Freya had just arrived from target practice in the adjoining valley. The queen was with the dragon children in the cave.

Lydia was cooking flatbread over the fire and laughing at how fast Norjee could eat them. Freddie and Freya both hugged the boy and welcomed him home.

With a blush, he scooted up close to Zoltan and mumbled something.

Neona smiled. "He's not used to being around so many women."

Tashi passed Freddie and Freya each a bowl of soup. "You two were at target practice for a long time."

Freya exchanged a smile with her sister. "We've never seen so many fine warrior men before."

Freddie snorted. "Men? It was the tigers you wanted to meet."

Freya shrugged. "I thought the youngest were-tiger was very handsome. Rajiv is his name."

"I see you managed to get onto their team," Freddie said.

"And what about you?" Freya nudged her sister. "You're on the team with the man who calls you a goddess."

"We're being assigned to teams?" Neona asked.

"Don't worry," Zoltan told her. "We'll be on the same one."

Lydia passed Freya a hot loaf of bread. "I thought the dart gun was rather easy to use."

"It is." Freya tore the loaf in half and passed a piece to her sister. "But I insisted on practicing a lot."

Freddie snorted. "You didn't want to leave your pet tiger."

"Do not dare call him a pet." Freya grinned. "He claims to be ferocious."

Lydia shook her head. "We're preparing for battle, and all you can think about is men?"

Freya sighed. "I know. I'm blaming it on Zoltan."

"Excuse me?" he asked.

"You gave us those books to read," Freddie explained. "Now we have romance on our minds."

"Exactly." Freya stirred her soup as a dreamy look came over her face. "I've been reading *The Perils of a Passionate Pirate*. He has long, flowing black locks and sun-kissed bronze skin. Just like Rajiv. And the heroine—she stowed away on his ship, disguised as a cabin boy, but he saw right through that. He's very clever—"

"And passionate," Tashi muttered.

"I've been reading *Duke in Boots*," Freddie announced. "It's about a duke—"

"And his boots?" Neona asked, her mouth twitching.

Freddie nodded. "He doesn't dare leave his residence unless his fine Hessian boots are polished to a glossy finish. He's so incredibly handsome that the heroine took one look at him and stumbled, trampling all over his boots with her muddy shoes."

Freya gasped. "The horror!"

They both laughed.

Emma materialized close by and gave Zoltan an annoyed look. "You have yet to teach Neona how to fire her dart gun. She can't go on a mission tomorrow night unprepared."

"We'll do it soon." Zoltan motioned to the young boy, who was watching everyone curiously. "We brought Norjee back to live here."

The boy smiled when he heard his name.

Neona patted his back. "He inherited Minerva's gift. He can communicate with winged creatures."

"Like the dragons?" Emma asked. When some of the women gasped, she gave them a reassuring smile. "Don't worry. Your secret is safe with us."

Her smile faded as she took a seat by the fire. "Angus and I are worried that it may be the dragons that Lord Liao is after. He may have heard rumors of their existence."

Lydia nodded. "Our dragons have flown these skies for thousands of years. There will be peasants and farmers who have seen them or heard of them."

"That's what we figured." Emma frowned. "Master Han may want control of them. Imagine how easy it would be for him to take over new territory if his soldiers are flying about on fire-breathing dragons. Villagers will surrender to Master Han to keep from being burned."

Freddie grimaced. "We can't let Master Han get them."

Emma leaned forward, her elbows on her knees. "Tell me more about them. How many are there?"

"Three children," Neona replied. "Xiao Fang is the oldest. He hatched six years ago."

"Six?" Zoltan asked. "He looks about twelve."

"The dragon children age twice as fast," Lydia said. "Until they reach puberty and the time of their first shifting."

"Xiao Fang can already breathe fire." Freddie finished her bowl of soup. "He'll shift soon. Maybe two or three months from now."

"He had a sister," Freya added. "But a few minutes after she hatched, she turned blue and couldn't breathe."

Freddie sighed. "It was terrible. Our mother tried to save her, but they both ended up dying."

"That's how Calliope died?" Zoltan asked, and the two sisters nodded.

"I'm so sorry," Emma told them. "There are two more children?"

"A boy and girl." Neona ladled more soup into Norjee's bowl. "They hatched three years ago, so they look like six-year-olds."

"Wait a minute." Zoltan sat back. "The eggs are hatching every three years?"

"Yes." Neona gave him a worried look. "The next group could hatch any day now. Two eggs."

"I hope there will be more females." Lydia handed Norjee a fresh loaf of bread. "By the end of the last cycle, we had only five females left. That's why there are five nests."

Neona sighed. "The cycle before that, we had fifteen nests."

Zoltan winced. The dragons were dying out.

"What do you mean by cycle?" Emma asked.

"They live for about five hundred years," Neona explained. "Then the females lay their eggs and die. The males die soon after. If the last male doesn't manage to survive till all the eggs are hatched and the dragon children are able to take care of themselves, then the whole hive can perish."

"That's why they made a pact with us," Lydia added. "Three thousand years ago, when the original three women came here, there was one male dragon left, and he feared he would die before the eggs would hatch."

"The old dragon made a pact with the three women," Neona said. "They were given the Living Water and this valley to live in. In exchange, they were to become the mothers of the new hatchlings. It is our sacred duty to protect the young ones until they can shift and take care of themselves."

"Then they take care of us." Freya used her piece of bread to sop up the last of her soup. "They lift the heavy stones to help us build our homes. And they snatch up donkeys and goats and bring them here."

"And these are the only dragons left?" Emma asked.

"As far as we know," Neona said. "Thousands of years ago, they existed all over Europe and Asia. But some are hit by lightning and die. Or sometimes they have hunting accidents. When they dive down at great speeds to catch prey, they can crash into each other or into trees. Others are killed by slayers. There was a time when stragglers would fly here from Europe or eastern China, seeking refuge. The last one from Europe came over a thousand years ago."

Zoltan nodded. "They became extinct there. I don't recall ever seeing one."

Norjee sat up suddenly and looked toward the cave.

Emma inhaled sharply. "What was that?"

"Norjee heard the young ones," Freddie whispered. "I have the gift, so I can hear them, too. Norjee is answering them."

Norjee jumped to his feet and ran toward the cave just as the oldest dragon shifter dashed out.

The two boys stopped and looked at each other. Norjee reached a hand out to touch Xiao Fang's shoulder. The dragon boy grinned.

"What is going on?" The queen marched from the cave, frowning. She halted when she saw the two boys.

Neona jumped to her feet. "Your majesty, this is Minerva's son. Norjee. He has her gift."

Nima's face turned pale.

"Xiao Fang is inviting Norjee to sleep in the cave with him and the other children," Freddie whispered. "Norjee has agreed."

Norjee glanced back at Neona and grinned. He dashed toward her, gave her a hug, then ran back to Xiao Fang. The two boys went inside the cave.

Freddie smiled, her eyes glistening with tears. "Xiao Fang is calling Norjee his brother."

The queen stepped toward them, frowning at Emma. "They have told you all our secrets now?"

"We will do everything in our power to keep the dragon children safe," Emma promised her.

Nima nodded, then scowled at the other women. "Go to your homes to rest. I will watch over the young ones for now." She marched back into the cave.

"Good night, then." Tashi poured a bucket full of ashes on top of the fire to extinguish it.

"That reminds me." Emma watched the fire die. "From now on, no visible fires in this valley or the next. Liao will be looking for us, so the valleys must remain dark."

"We understand," Freddie told her. "Good night." She and Freya gathered up the dirty dishes and took them to the storeroom. Lydia and Tashi followed them with the cookware.

"Where will you do your death-sleep?" Zoltan asked Emma.

"Tiger Town. Most of the Vamps are teleporting there before sunrise." She tilted her head, gazing at the cave. "Do you hear them, Zoltan?"

"No. I only hear animals. The kind without wings."

"Maybe it's because I was a telepath before I was transformed." Emma turned to him and Neona. "I can hear them. Every word."

Chapter Twenty-three

*I*t was well after the noon hour when Neona woke up. She stretched in bed, marveling at how much her life had changed in the past week. Zoltan was in his death-sleep, sprawled naked on top of Minerva's bed. She smiled, remembering how they had made love again before sunrise; climax number six, he'd called it. When death-sleep had crept over him, he'd moved to Minerva's bed for fear that any contact between them during that time might cause her to die. She didn't know if that was true, but it was certainly too big a risk to find out.

She wondered how Norjee was doing and smiled again. He and Xiao Fang had become instant friends.

After dressing, she retrieved the flask of Living Water from her chest and added more to each of Zoltan's bottles of blood. Guilt nagged at her as she screwed the caps back on. It was wrong to deceive him like this. Tonight she would tell him the truth.

She brushed his hair back from his brow, then smoothed a hand over his broad shoulder to his arm, lingering on the bulge of his bicep. Her gorgeous vampire. Somehow they would have a future together.

After slipping out the door, she made a quick trip to the outhouse, then washed up in the stream. Hopefully, the others were already up and had cooked a midday meal in the cave. The children would be hungry.

The night before, when the others had gone to their homes to sleep, she'd returned to the next valley for target practice. Zoltan had introduced her to more of the vampires and shifters, but there had been so many she had trouble recalling their names. Howard she remembered. The giant were-bear was in charge of the operation during the day. Emma and her husband, Angus, were in charge at night. They had divided everyone up into six teams, each one comprised of three vampires, three shifters, and a woman warrior of Beyul-La.

Neona's team included Zoltan and two other vampires called Jack and Dougal. They both had odd accents, and one of them was wearing a skirt, but they seemed very friendly. The three shifters on the team were Howard and his twin nephews, Jesse and Jimmy. Howard admitted that the two younger werebears were still in training, but not to worry. If they messed up, he would clobber them.

Jimmy and Jesse had watched her practice, and each time she'd hit a target, they'd cheered and offered her something to eat from a white box. BEARs, they called them, which stood for Bearrific Energizing Attitudinal Restorative. Howard called them donuts. Apparently, the were-bears had brought a huge supply.

Before leaving for Tiger Town to do their deathsleep, the vampires had teleported a shifter from each team to where Russell was watching Lord Liao's progress. As a vampire, Russell planned to retreat to a safe place for his death-sleep. During the day, the six shifters would follow Liao's army, and when search parties went out, the shifters would divide up to track them.

From Neona's team, Jimmy had been selected to be their scout. After sunset, he would call his team and the three vampires would teleport Howard, Jesse, and Neona to where he was located so the attack could begin. Zoltan had cautioned her to get plenty of rest during the day, for they had a long night ahead of them.

Now, as she strode inside the cave, she found the other women relaxing around a small campfire. Freddie and Freya were reading their books. Nima and Tashi were napping on pallets. Lydia was spooning soup into four bowls for the children. Neona filled a fifth bowl for herself and helped Lydia carry the trays of food into the larger cavern.

At some point during the day, Norjee must have left the cavern to collect pinecones, for there were two dozen of them on the cavern floor, and he and Xiao Fang were running about kicking them and laughing.

Neona stopped to listen to Norjee's laughter. Even Lydia smiled at the sound of it. But it was Xiao Fang's laughter that surprised her. Because their throats were designed for breathing fire, the dragon children were incapable of speech. They were taught to comprehend Tibetan and Chinese, but they couldn't respond. The only way to hear their thoughts was through someone who had the gift, like Nima, Freddie, or Norjee.

The sound coming from Xiao Fang was an odd

cross between a bark and a wheeze. It was only the joy on his face that let her know it was a laugh. How sad that he'd been alive for six years, yet this was the first time she'd heard his laughter. She smiled at Norjee. The boy had a way of bringing joy into people's lives.

He ran up to her, grinning. "I was wondering when you would come. I missed you."

She set down the tray and hugged him. "I was up all night, so I slept late. How are you?"

"Great!" He wrapped an arm around Xiao Fang's shoulders. "I have a brother now who's a dragon!"

"I see that." Neona motioned to the tray. "Are you brothers hungry?"

Norjee and Xiao Fang sat, side by side, and ate. They kept glancing at each other, so Neona figured they must be communicating. The other two dragon children, Huo and Chu, ate their soup while casting forlorn looks at Xiao Fang. Neona suspected they were feeling left out.

"Can I take Xiao Fang outside to play?" Norjee asked.

Lydia shook her head. "The queen prefers for the dragon children to remain safe inside the cave."

"Why?" Norjee asked.

Lydia sighed. "Because we have to keep them safe. They are the only dragons left."

"But Xiao Fang wants to be free," Norjee argued.

"He can be free when he grows up," Lydia said. "Finish your meal."

Norjee frowned, then ate more soup.

As Neona ate, she became aware that Norjee and Xiao Fang were exchanging sly glances. The two were definitely planning something. "When was the last time you bathed, Norjee?"

He shrugged. "I don't know."

Neona gave him a sharp look. "Did you know that dragons have highly sensitive noses? They can smell prey from miles away. Or dirty little boys."

Norjee looked at Xiao Fang, who wrinkled his nose, then grinned. Norjee glanced at the other two dragon children and winced. "They say I'm stinky."

Neona nodded. "There's a place close by where we dammed up part of the stream to make a small pool. I'll take you there so you can bathe. And if Xiao Fang wants to come along, he's welcome."

Norjee sat up, grinning. "Really?"

"Your mother won't approve," Lydia mumbled.

"They'll be safe. I'll watch over them." Neona stood.

Norjee jumped up and hugged her. "Thank you, Mama!"

Her heart lurched, and she froze for a moment while the word *Mama* reverberated in her head. Tears sprang to her eyes.

Norjee linked arms with Xiao Fang. "Let's go!"

"Help me carry the dishes back to the storeroom." Neona leaned over to retrieve the bowls, but Norjee beat her to it, gathering all five bowls onto a tray, then picking it up.

With a smile, she motioned toward the narrow entrance. "This way. And be quiet so you don't wake up the queen."

When they dropped off the dirty dishes in the storeroom, Neona grabbed two towels, two clean sets of clothes, and some soap. The boys scampered ahead of her, following her instructions to find the pool a short way upstream. By the time she arrived, they'd already stripped and were bouncing around the pool, splashing each other.

She glanced at the burial mounds situated far up the hillside. "He's here, Minerva. Your son is home."

When the sun was lowering in the sky, she walked the two freshly scrubbed boys back to the cave. "You understand about tonight?"

Norjee nodded. "The queen explained it to us. You have to go fight the bad men."

"Yes, we'll be busy all night. Take turns watching over the eggs. The queen's owl will be with you. And my pet leopard, Zhan. If anything happens, send them to the next valley to alert us. We'll come immediately."

"Xiao Fang says not to worry. We'll be fine." Norjee gave her a worried look. "But you might be in danger."

She hugged him. "I'll be fine, too. I'll be with three vampires and three guys who shift into giant bears!"

Norjee's eyes lit up. "This place is a lot more fun than the monastery!"

"**I**s everyone ready?" Angus asked.

Neona checked her weapons once again. Her sword was sheathed, her quiver was full of arrows, her bow rested on her shoulder, and her knife was strapped to her calf. Wedged under her tight sword belt was her dart gun, and the pouch nearby was stuffed full of darts. She was dressed in plain brown linen, topped with a Kevlar vest, and her hair was pulled back into a tight braid.

Angus checked his watch. "The calls will start coming in soon. We need to take out as many as possible tonight. Once Lord Liao realizes his men are disappearing, he will retaliate. That's when the shit will hit the fan. Be prepared."

Neona gave Zoltan a worried glance, and he smiled and squeezed her hand. It was dark, since no fires were allowed, but in the moonlight, she managed to spot Winifred with her team. She was standing close to Jin Long Wang. Their team had three werewolves. Freya was on the team that had were-tigers.

A phone buzzed, and Emma answered it. "Got it." She hung up. "That was Russell. He's located Liao and the major part of the army. After you've neutralized your target, teleport your scout back to Russell so he can follow another search party. Then we'll start round two."

Everyone murmured their agreement, then waited.

Next to Neona, the were-bear Jesse shifted his weight back and forth. "Come on, Jimmy, call."

A phone buzzed, and everyone looked around.

"It's mine," Mikhail announced, and answered it. "Carlos? We're ready. Keep talking." He and another vampire grabbed hold of two shifters. Pamela took hold of Queen Nima, and the team of six teleported away.

Neona took a deep breath and sent out a silent prayer for her mother's safe return.

Howard's phone buzzed.

"Yes!" Jesse punched the air with his fist. "It's Jimmy!"

Howard gave his nephew a stern look. "Don't make a sound when we arrive." He answered the phone, then held it out.

Dougal stepped close so he could hear Jimmy's whispered voice. He grabbed Jesse and vanished. Zoltan held Neona tight, and everything went black.

She landed in the middle of a dark forest. Zoltan squeezed her shoulders, then let go. Dougal was close by. Jesse pretended he was going to slap hands with his twin, but they stopped with their hands an inch away and grinned at each other.

A twinge pricked at her heart. She'd had that sort of relationship with her twin.

Jack and Howard materialized beside them.

Jimmy lifted his hands, indicating with his fingers that there were eight in the search party. He pointed in their direction.

Howard motioned for Zoltan and Neona to follow him, and they veered off to the left. The rest of the team went right. Silently, they moved forward till they spotted the enemy.

The eight men were strolling along, talking with each other, totally oblivious that they were being followed. Howard took his dart gun from his belt and moved silently to the front of the search party. Zoltan positioned himself in the middle, and Neona took the rear. Hidden behind a tree, and with her heart pounding, she drew her pistol and selected a target.

On the far side, a twig snapped. The eight men stopped and looked to the right. Instantly, four of them were shot with darts. Two more jerked when Howard and Zoltan fired their guns.

Neona shot her target. He stumbled back, then shook his head and drew his sword. She quickly loaded another dart. Zoltan had warned her that some of the supersoldiers were so strong that it would take more than one dart to knock them out. The soldier lifted his sword and weaved toward her. She shot again. He swayed on his feet, dropped his sword, then fell on his face.

After all eight of the search party had fallen, the team moved in to tie up their arms and legs.

"Are you all right?" Zoltan asked Neona.

"Yes." She reloaded her gun. "It seemed fairly easy."

He smiled. "It'll get harder as the night goes on and we lose the element of surprise."

Jack and Dougal each picked up a soldier and teleported away.

Zoltan's smile faded. "This is the part of the plan that I don't like."

"I'll be fine," Neona assured him. "I have three bears with me. And I was able to beat you, remember?"

He kissed her brow. "I'll be back as quick as I can." He picked up the nearest soldier and vanished.

Neona helped Howard gather swords and weapons from the downed soldiers while the twins devoured some donuts. She wondered how the other women were doing. And how the children were faring in the cave. They'd promised to keep a close watch on the eggs. She glanced at her sparkly kitty watch. After five minutes, the vampires reappeared.

"Sorry it took so long," Zoltan told her. "We went to Tiger Town, but it was still dark in Japan, so they had us take the soldiers there. They want to fill up the lab there first."

Dougal bent down to pick up another soldier. "My wife is going to be verra busy tonight." He vanished.

Jack snorted. "He was in a hurry to get back to her." He disappeared with another soldier.

"His wife?" Neona asked.

"Dougal is married to Leah, the doctor who's changing the supersoldiers back to normal," Zoltan explained.

"Before you go," Howard said to Zoltan, "can you take our scout back to Russell? We need to line up our next target."

Jesse jumped to his feet. "I'll go. Jimmy's tired."

"Okay." Zoltan called Russell.

"Take it easy, bro." Jimmy slapped his twin on the back and handed him the donut box.

Zoltan vanished with Jesse, then reappeared a few seconds later so he could take another soldier.

After five more minutes, the last of the soldiers was delivered, and the Vamps teleported the team back to headquarters in Frederic's valley.

As the teams returned from their first round, they reported to Emma how many soldiers they'd taken.

"Fifty-two!" Emma announced when everyone had returned.

After they finished congratulating each other, Neona decided this was a good time to confess what she'd been doing to Zoltan's blood supply. She drew him aside. "I need to tell you something about your bottles of blood—"

"Oh, that reminds me," he said. "I should teleport home and drink some more. I'm hungry again."

She winced.

"Zoltan." The queen approached them. "Will you teleport me to the cave? I want to check on the children."

"Sure." He took hold of Nima's arm and smiled at Neona. "We'll be back soon."

She sighed, then wandered around the camp, checking on her friends. Lydia, Winifred, and Freya were eating some of the food that the were-tigers had cooked earlier in the day. Actually, Freddie and Freya appeared to be flirting more than eating. Tashi was sitting alone on a rock by the stream.

"Are you all right?" Neona asked as she sat next to her.

"Every now and then, I feel nauseated." Tashi glanced over at the were-tigers. "I tried some of their food. I guess it doesn't agree with me."

"If you don't feel like doing anything more tonight, I'm sure they can manage without you."

Tashi dipped a hand in the cold water and pressed it against her brow. "I'll be fine."

Neona leaned close and whispered, "Could you be pregnant?"

Tashi winced. "Perhaps. I'm not sure yet."

Neona patted her shoulder. "You'll be a wonderful mother."

"I hope so." Tashi looked about, frowning. "I'm not sure what the future holds for us all."

After a while, Zoltan reappeared with Nima, who reported that the children and eggs were fine. Neona approached Zoltan, planning to confess about the bottles, but Jesse called, and it was time to teleport.

Within a few minutes, they had nine soldiers unconscious. The Vamps teleported them to Tiger Town and took Jesse back to Russell.

"It seems too easy," Neona said when they returned to headquarters.

"This won't last much longer," Zoltan warned her. "By now, Lord Liao has to know that his search parties are not reporting in."

Emma announced that the count was now up to a hundred and three. They had managed to cut Lord Liao's army in half.

The camp grew quiet as the teams waited for their scouts to call and round three to begin.

Neona drew Zoltan off to the shelter of the nearby forest. "There's something I've been wanting to tell you."

"That you love me?"

She smiled. "I've already told you that."

"Not tonight." He pulled her behind a tree and whispered in her ear, "Are you thinking about climax number seven?"

"Are you still keeping count?"

"I promised you ten, and I always deliver."

She stepped back. "This is important."

"So it is about sex?"

She snorted. The man was insatiable. "I have a confession to make. About your bottles of blood." Wincing, she steeled her nerves. "I've been sneaking some of our Living Water into your bottles. I'm afraid that's why you're hungry—"

"What?" He gave her an incredulous look. "You've been spiking my blood supply?"

She nodded. "It was wrong of me. I should have told you. I'll understand if you're angry—"

He laughed.

She blinked. "You're not angry?"

"Sweetheart, I've been spiking my bottles, too. Good God, no wonder I've been so hungry."

"Y-you added Living Water? Where did you get it?"

"I stole it. Sneaked into the cave and took some." He gave her a sheepish grin. "I'll understand if you're angry."

"I-I'm stunned. We've both been doing it?"

He gave her a curious look. "Why did you do it?"

"Why did you?"

"I asked you first."

She sighed. "You said your seed was dead. I thought the Living Water might revive it."

"Ah." He reached for her. "You want to make babies."

"Not now." She gave him a playful shove. "What was your reason?"

"We wanted to know what happens to a vampire if he ingests the Living Water. In case Liao or Han get their hands on it, we wanted to know what to expect."

"I see." She tilted her head, studying him. "How do you feel?"

He shrugged. "About the same. I'm just hungry all the time."

She nodded. "It's only been two nights. It may take some time before the effects show up."

Howard whistled to get their attention. "Jesse called. It's time to move out."

They teleported to Jesse, who indicated a party of five ahead of them and ten behind them.

"Two groups?" Howard whispered.

Jesse nodded, a panicked look on his face. "They're armed with AK-47s."

Neona didn't know what that was, but from the looks on the men's faces, it was bad news.

"These men are no' searching for Beyul-La," Dougal muttered. "They're hunting us."

Howard nodded. "The first group is bait, and when we bite, the second group will move in for the kill."

Jesse gulped. "What do we do? Should we leave?"

Howard gave him an annoyed look.

"Oh, right." Jesse squared his shoulders. "Let's kick some ass."

Zoltan gave Neona a worried look, but before he could say anything, she shook her head. "I'm staying."

He grimaced. "We should pair up so the Vamps can teleport their partner away from the gunfire. I'll take Neona."

"Good plan," Howard said. "Jimmy, stick with Jack. Jesse, go with Dougal."

"What about you?" Jimmy asked.

"I'll manage." Howard patted his nephew on the back. "We should take the group of ten first."

Everyone agreed, and they moved quietly through the forest till they caught a glimpse of the group of ten.

Neona's breath caught. These supersoldiers were armed to the teeth. Not only swords and knives but they were also carrying the biggest rifles she'd ever seen.

"Those are automatic assault weapons," Zoltan whispered in her ear. "Stay close to me so I can teleport you."

She inched forward with him, keeping behind the cover of bushes and rocks. When Howard's birdcall whistled through the air, she was behind a bush with Zoltan. All six of their team shot their dart guns. Neona hit her target, and immediately Zoltan teleported her behind a huge boulder.

Rapid fire responded. Her hands shook as she reloaded her dart gun. She'd never heard such a terrible weapon before. Zoltan fired his dart gun again, then teleported her up into a tree. With a gasp, she grabbed onto the trunk. Down below, bullets were ricocheting off the boulder. The bush she and Zoltan had hidden behind was now ripped to shreds.

Only two soldiers remained standing, but they were shooting their assault weapons in a wide circle. Neona shot one with a dart just as four more on her team shot their guns. The soldiers stopped shooting to rip out the darts, but more darts came at them. Slowly, they slumped down to the ground.

"Hurry! Get their weapons," Howard shouted.

Zoltan teleported her down to the ground. The team rushed in to gather the weapons. As Neona approached a soldier, he grasped her ankle, yanked her off her feet, and raised his arm, his knife ready to strike. She grabbed his arm, but he was stronger than she was. Just as the knife sliced into her arm, Zoltan seized the man by the back of his neck and lifted him off the ground.

"Bastard!" Zoltan shook him.

"Take cover!" Howard shouted, and he and the were-bear twins ducked behind unconscious soldiers.

Rapid fire exploded from the nearby forest. The group of five had arrived. With vampire speed, Zoltan spun around, placing the soldier between him and the bullets. The soldier jerked and shuddered as bullets riddled his body.

Jack and Dougal teleported behind two of the soldiers, ripped the weapons from their hands, and manually stabbed them with a cluster of three darts. The men slumped to the ground.

Three were still shooting. Hidden behind Zoltan, Neona drew her knife and threw it at one, striking his arm so he dropped his weapon. Then she shot him with her dart gun. Meanwhile Jack and Dougal teleported behind the remaining two soldiers, disarmed them, and knocked them out.

The forest was silent for a moment before Jimmy jumped to his feet and yelled, "That was awesome!"

"I know, right?" Jesse slapped hands with his twin.

Zoltan dropped the dead soldier and helped Neona to her feet. "Are you all right?"

"You were awesome, warrior princess!" Jimmy lifted a hand, waiting for her to slap it.

She lifted her arm, and it was covered with blood.

"Shit," Zoltan whispered. "I'll take you to the doctor in Tiger Town."

"It's a small cut. I'll be fine if you take me to the storeroom where I keep my medical supplies."

"Are you sure?" he asked, then he glanced at the other guys. "We need to go."

"We'll be fine." Howard waved him on. "Go on."

He teleported her to the fire pit in Beyul-La, then

led her inside the storeroom where she kept her medical supplies. He opened a window so the moonlight would shine in.

She gave him instructions, and he washed her arm, applied the salve, and wrapped it tight with a strip of fresh linen.

"Are you sure about this?" He gave her arm a dubious look.

"The salve works," she assured him. "It stopped the bleeding on your wound, remember? And kept it clean."

"But I heal during my death-sleep. You don't." He escorted her from the storeroom. "We could go to the next valley. Mikhail has his medical kit there."

"I've been healing wounds here for close to two thousand years."

"At least take something for the pain." He pulled her close. "I can't bear to think of you hurting."

She turned when she heard a shouting noise. Norjee and Zhan were running from the cave. The owl flew out, headed for the next valley. Zhan raced after it.

"What's wrong?" she yelled in Tibetan.

Norjee came to a halt in front her, breathing hard. "The eggs . . . two eggs are hatching."

Chapter Twenty-four

"What's wrong?" Zoltan asked.

Neona told him in English, "Two eggs are hatching. Can you go to the next valley and bring back Nima or Winifred?"

"You can't take care of the eggs?"

She shook her head. "The hatchlings bond with the first person they see. It has to be someone who can communicate with them. Hurry! We'll be waiting for you." She grabbed Norjee's hand, and they ran toward the cave.

Zoltan teleported to Frederic's valley. It was mostly empty, since five of the teams were out working. Emma was there, coordinating all the missions. A few shifters had remained behind on guard duty. Tashi was sitting nearby, looking pale.

"Emma!" Zoltan ran up to her. "Where are Nima and Winifred?"

"Winifred just left," Emma said.

The owl landed on a rock next to Tashi, and she jumped up. "Is something wrong in the cave?"

"Two eggs are hatching," Zoltan told her.

"Oh no!" Tashi gasped. "We need Nima or Freddie."

Emma winced. "I tried my best to make sure one of them was always here. Nima's team is due back any second now. I wouldn't have let Freddie go otherwise."

"Nima has to come back now!" Tashi insisted.

"I'll call her team." Emma punched some numbers on her sat phone.

Tashi moaned. "This is all my fault. It was my turn to go, but I started throwing up, so Winifred went instead."

"You couldn't help that," Emma told her. "And if you're pregnant like we suspect, you shouldn't be out there fighting." She tilted her head toward the phone. "Mikhail? We need Nima back immediately. Okay. Thanks."

She hung up. "Mikhail and Pamela are in Tiger Town, delivering the last of their soldiers. They should have Nima here in a few minutes."

Tashi turned toward the rock wall. Neona's pet leopard was pacing along the edge. Zoltan heard the leopard's thoughts, too.

No time! The eggs are hatching now!

"We don't have a few minutes," Zoltan said. "The hatchlings bond with the first person they see, and it has to be someone they can communicate with."

"That's true!" Tashi grimaced as she rubbed her stomach. "They have to bond quickly, or they lose the ability. One time an egg hatched unexpectedly when my mother was there. The baby bonded with her, but when she couldn't communicate with him, his ability faded away. He couldn't hear Nima at all. Then all his senses shut down. The poor thing just lay there and died!"

Emma drew in a long breath. "All right. I'll do it."

"But you can't—" Tashi gasped when Emma vanished. "What is she doing? The babies will die if she—"

"She can communicate with them," Zoltan said.

Tashi's eyes widened. "She can?"

Zoltan glanced around and spotted Phil with some of the younger werewolf trainees. "Phil, take charge till Angus gets back."

Phil ran toward him. "What's going on?"

"Emma has to help two dragon babies hatch."

"What?" Phil looked stunned.

Zoltan imagined Emma's husband would look even more stunned when he learned the consequences. "Let's go." He grabbed Tashi and teleported her to the entrance of the cave.

"Go ahead." She rubbed her stomach. "I'll follow you soon. I need to be still for a moment."

He zoomed down the narrow corridor into the huge cavern where the dragon children lived. Norjee and the three dragon shifters sat on Nima's larger pallet, looking worried.

Norjee jumped to his feet. "Nima?"

"She'll be here soon," Zoltan replied, frustrated because he knew the boy couldn't understand him. He gave the children a reassuring smile, then hurried down the narrow tunnel to the cave room that housed the eggs.

Neona was hovering at the entrance, partially hidden behind a wall of stone. She glanced back at him.

"Nima will be here soon."

Neona winced. "She might be too late."

He peered into the room, dimly lit by a single torch. Emma was kneeling in front of a nest that contained two eggs. Both were covered with cracks and rocking slightly with movement.

He blinked when a foot suddenly burst through a shell. A tiny leg extended from the egg and kicked about.

Emma gasped. "It looks so human." She shot Neona a frantic look. "What do I do?"

"When the heads come out, make sure they see you," Neona said. "Look them in the eyes and communicate with them."

Another leg burst out, and the egg started to shake. Two arms broke free, the tiny hands fisted.

"Look at you." Emma took hold of one of the tiny hands. "You're doing great."

The little hand opened and curled around Emma's thumb.

"Oh, my God," she whispered.

The egg thrashed about, and pieces of shell fell away from the baby's head. With her free hand, Emma cleared shell away from its face.

Neona pulled Zoltan back behind the stone wall. "We can't risk the baby seeing us."

He waited, then heard a tearful whimper come from Emma.

"I can hear him crying." She sniffed. "He's a boy. A beautiful boy."

Neona exhaled with relief and smiled. "They're bonding. Thank God."

Zoltan peeked into the room. Emma was clearing away the last of the shell from a baby boy. His arms and legs were flailing about, but his eyes were entirely focused on her. She smiled at him, tears running down her cheeks.

A leg burst from the second shell.

"Your twin is coming," Emma whispered.

When a fisted hand broke free, she took hold of it. The egg shook violently, and the head appeared.

Zoltan stepped back behind the stone wall and waited.

Emma laughed. "I have a baby girl."

Neona's pet leopard ran up to her and Zoltan.

"Zhan." Neona patted his head. "Good kitty. Thank you for watching over the children."

He rubbed against her leg, then looked at Zoltan. *The queen has arrived. They're trying to call you.*

Thanks. "I'll be right back." He teleported to the cave entrance. His phone buzzed, and he answered it.

"I have Nima with me," Mikhail said. "I've been trying to convince her that she'll get home faster if I teleport her. Keep talking."

"Okay. I'm here at the cave entrance," Zoltan told Mikhail. "Waiting for you . . ."

Mikhail appeared with Nima, and she immediately ran into the cave. When Zoltan and Mikhail followed her, she turned around and glared at them. "Men are not allowed here. Go!"

Mikhail snorted, then vanished.

Zoltan followed her as she dashed down the narrow corridor into the larger cavern. Tashi was there, minding the children. Zhan was lounging on a pallet, letting Norjee and Xiao Fang pet him.

"The babies are fine," Zoltan told the queen.

She spun around to face him. "They hatched? With no one there to bond with them?"

"Emma did it."

"*What*? A vampire bonded with *my* dragons!" Nima drew her sword. "You let a monster steal my babies? I should kill you all. You are destroying our world!"

"Enough!" Neona ran into the large cavern. "Put

away the sword, Mother." She tilted her head toward the children, who had huddled together with frightened expressions. "Don't do this here."

Glaring at Zoltan, Nima sheathed her sword.

"Don't blame the vampires," Tashi said as she hugged the two younger children. "Freddie had to leave early because I was sick. There was only a short time when both you and Freddie were gone."

"Enough time for those monsters to steal our babies," Nima hissed.

"Emma saved the babies." Neona motioned toward the egg room. "Come and see."

Zoltan followed Nima and Neona down the narrow tunnel into the egg room.

Emma had transferred the babies to a clean nest. "Shouldn't I bathe them? And put nappies on them? What do you feed them?"

Nima scoffed. "Do you think we'll let you take our dragon babies away?"

Emma looked up at her. "I'll do whatever I have to do. I'm their mother now."

Nima huffed. "How can you possibly care for them? You're dead half the time."

"I'll help you," Neona offered. "The babies like goat milk. We have a few goats here in the valley. I'll go milk them."

"Thank you." Emma suddenly stiffened and looked back at her babies. "What's wrong? I can hear them crying!"

Everyone crowded around.

"They can't breathe!" Emma shouted. "Oh, God, they're turning blue."

Neona reached for one. "Maybe I can—"

"No!" Nima yanked her back. "This is what happened to Xiao Fang's sister. When Calliope tried to help her, they both died."

Neona grimaced. "We can't just let them die."

Emma gasped. "I have to save them."

"There is nothing we can do," Nima cried. "Oh, God, we're going to lose them both!"

"No!" Emma picked up one baby, then struggled to pick up the other. Zoltan leaned over to help her.

"I'll take them to a doctor." Emma stood. "Leah knows how to treat shifters."

"You cannot remove the dragons from their home!" Nima shouted.

"Watch me." Emma vanished, taking both babies with her.

Nima huffed. "She dares to steal them from us! Where is she taking them?"

"To Tiger Town," Zoltan explained. "That's where Leah is. She's a brilliant doctor and geneticist. She can figure out what's going wrong." He eyed the five nests. Only two remained with eggs. "I would guess it's a case of too much inbreeding."

Neona nodded. "We've been worried about that, but I don't know what can be done. These are the only dragons left in the world."

"Maybe Leah can come up with something. We have a number of excellent scientists on our side. They'll try their best to help."

Neona smiled and linked her arm with his. "Thank you."

"You're thanking him?" Nima scoffed. "These vampires are ruining everything." With a huff, she marched away. "I'm going to my house. I don't wish to be disturbed."

He watched the queen go, then muttered, "How

will we survive the rest of the night without her?"

Neona gave him a wry look.

"Alone at last." He wrapped his arms around her. "Thank you. Thank you for believing in me. And my friends."

She leaned her head against his shoulder. "Thank you for helping us."

He led her into the larger cavern. "I need to tell Angus what happened."

Neona nodded. "I'll stay here with Tashi and try to get the children to sleep." She yawned. "It has been a long night for all of us."

Zoltan teleported to the next valley. All the teams had returned. Lydia was climbing the rope ladder by the rock wall to return home. Freddie and Freya were walking slowly toward the rock wall, accompanied by J.L. and Rajiv.

"We're done for the night," Angus announced proudly. "A total of one hundred and fifty-three soldiers taken."

"Fantastic." Zoltan smiled. Lord Liao would have less than fifty soldiers left. "Liao must be livid."

"Aye." Angus grinned. "So how is Emma? I heard she went to the next valley. Something about eggs hatching."

Zoltan rested a hand on Angus's shoulder. "I have news for you."

Angus's smile faded. "Is Emma all right?"

"She's well. Did you know she can communicate with the dragon children?"

"Aye. What has happened, man? Tell me."

"The babies hatched and bonded with Emma. They believe she is their mother."

Angus blinked. "They . . . adopted Emma?"

"Yes. And she adopted them. A boy and a girl."

. Angus blinked again. "We have . . . bairns?"

Zoltan nodded. "But they took ill suddenly. They couldn't breathe. Emma teleported them to Tiger Town."

"Bloody hell," Angus whispered. "The bairns canna breathe?" He shook himself. "I have to go. Tell Robby he's in charge." He vanished.

Zoltan walked over to Robby MacKay to break the news that the MacKay family now included two dragon shifter babies. While everyone was drinking a toast to the new parents, Zoltan teleported back to Neona's house.

She was there, naked and washing herself from a bowl of water.

"Wow," he breathed as she gathered her hair up and wiped the back of her neck with a washcloth.

She spun around to face him. "You're back."

"Just in time." He grabbed a bottle of spiked blood and guzzled it down.

With a smile, she watched him drink. "I wonder if your seed is reviving itself."

"There's only one way to find out." His gaze drifted over her sweet body, then settled on the bandage on her arm. "How are you feeling? Are you in pain?"

"A little bit." She walked over to the bed and crooked a finger at him. "I expect climax number seven will take my mind off it."

She turned pink as his eyes glowed red. "I expect you're right."

Chapter Twenty-five

*I*t was late afternoon when Neona woke up. She glanced over at Zoltan. After climax number seven, she'd fallen fast asleep. He must have teleported home then, for his clothes were clean and his face shaven. She peeked into the box where he kept his blood bottles. Six new bottles and a half-full bottle of Living Water. While everyone was sleeping, he must have sneaked into the cave to get more Living Water to mix with his blood.

The women of Beyul-La drank only a small cup of it once a month in order to keep from aging. Zoltan was ingesting more than that every night. So far, he claimed there was no effect.

Neona looked him over. Gorgeous as always. It might take a week or more for any changes to be noticeable. Or it could be that his vampire healing abilities were erasing any changes during his death-sleep.

She dressed and hurried to the outhouse. While she was washing up in the stream, the alarm sounded. Someone was striking the old cowbell by the cave entrance.

The women rushed to the cave.

"They're gone!" Winifred announced. "Xiao Fang and Norjee are missing."

"What?" Nima shouted. "You were supposed to be watching them. How did you—"

"I'm sorry," Freddie cried. "I was so tired, I dozed off."

"Of course you were tired." Freya came to her defense. "We were up all night."

"They're probably in the valley somewhere," Neona said. "Maybe the pond where they bathed yesterday. They loved it there."

"I'll check." Lydia ran upstream.

"I'll see if the other children know anything." Nima rushed into the cave.

Freddie leaned close to Neona and lowered her voice. "Huo and Chu won't tell the queen anything. They're afraid of her temper. But they confessed to me."

Neona swallowed hard. "What did they do?"

"They were jealous that Xiao Fang and Norjee were getting so close. So they told Norjee that he wasn't wanted here. That his own grandmother had given him away because he was a nobody."

Neona winced.

"That was cruel," Freya whispered.

Tashi touched her stomach. "If I have a son, I'm not giving him away."

"They told Norjee that we keep only special children here, like the dragon shifters," Freddie continued. "They saw him slip out while I was sleeping. Then Xiao Fang got upset and followed him."

Lydia came back. "They're not at the pond."

"We'll have to check the entire valley," Tashi said.

Neona sighed. "I'm afraid Norjee will try to return to the only other home he knows."

"The monastery?" Freddie made a face. "That's thirty miles away!"

"I know. But he knows he was loved there." Neona blinked away tears. She should have let the boy know how much she loved him. "I should have spent more time with him."

"Don't blame yourself," Lydia said. "We're at war."

Tashi winced. "There are still fifty soldiers out there."

Neona nodded. "We have to find the boys. Lydia and Tashi, can you check the valley? Freddie and Freya, will you come with me? I'm going to head toward the monastery."

Freddie nodded. "There will be shifters in the next valley. We could ask for their help."

"Yes!" Freya's eyes lit up. "Rajiv and his friends will help us."

The three women went into the cave to grab their bows and arrows, swords, and knives.

"Where are you going?" Nima demanded.

"I think the boys may be headed toward the monastery," Neona explained. "We'll bring them back."

Nima's eyes narrowed. "This wouldn't have happened if you hadn't brought that boy back here."

"That *boy*?" Neona's hands clenched with a sudden surge of rage. "That boy is your grandson! This wouldn't have happened if we hadn't abandoned him! Or made him feel worthless!"

She strode from the cave with Freddie and Freya. At the top of the rock wall, they discovered that the rope ladder had been let down, a sure sign that the boys had left the valley.

The three women scrambled down the ladder. Neona spotted Howard in the distance and dashed toward him.

"Have you seen two boys?" she asked. "Norjee and the oldest dragon boy have run away."

Howard winced. "We haven't been watching the entrance to your valley. You guys are our allies. We've been guarding the perimeter of this valley in case any of Liao's men come along."

Neona sighed. No doubt Norjee was an expert at escaping. He'd done it regularly at the monastery. "Can you spare us a few shifters? We have to find the boys. I think they're headed west, toward the Buddhist monastery."

Howard waved some shifters over. "Rajiv, bring your men."

Freya smiled at Rajiv as he sauntered over with two were-tigers.

"How good are you at tracking?" Howard asked.

Rajiv glanced at Freya and lifted his chin. "We're the best."

"Grab some weapons," Howard told them. "And some hiking gear. You're going with these three women. Bring them back safely with the two missing boys."

"Two boys are missing?" Rajiv asked.

Howard nodded. "And one of them is a dragon shifter. We can't let the enemy find him."

An hour later, the path they had followed westward forked into two paths. The two older were-tigers divided up, one going north and the other south, while the rest waited for them to report back.

Rajiv opened his backpack and handed Freya a bottle of water. Since the other were-tigers knew only Chinese, they had all switched to that language.

"Rinzen and Tenzen will figure it out. They're the best trackers I know."

"I can't remember which one is which." Freya sipped some water, then passed the bottle to her sister. "They look so much alike."

Rajiv smiled. "They're twins. It's common for were-tigers."

Freddie drank some water, then passed the bottle on to Neona. "So which one of them is the Grand Tiger?"

Rajiv winced. "That . . . well, it's—"

"I don't think they went this way," Rinzen called out as he jogged back.

"Let's check the GPS." Rajiv pulled out his sat phone. "The southern path leads to the monastery. The boys must have gone that way."

Tenzen came back, shaking his head. "I can't see any sign of them."

"Would Norjee even know which way to go?" Freya asked. "He's never traveled from Beyul-La to the monastery before. Except when he was a baby."

"That's true." Freddie motioned toward the northern path. "He could have easily taken a wrong turn."

"You're right," Rajiv agreed. "He doesn't have a GPS."

"No, but he has something just as good." Neona looked up at the sky. "He could be asking the birds which way to go. And what would they tell him?" Her gaze lowered to the hillside in front of them.

"They would tell him the most direct route," Freddie said. "As the crow flies."

Neona nodded. "You can divide up and take the paths going north and south. I'm going straight west."

"I'll go with you," Tenzen said.

"I'll take the southern route," Freddie offered. "Rinzen can come with me."

"Then Freya and I will go north." Rajiv checked his watch. "If we see no sign of the boys in an hour, we'll return here."

After forty minutes of rocky and hilly terrain, Neona's legs were aching. This route might be fast for a bird, but it was tough for people.

"Are we going in the right direction?" she asked Tenzen once again.

He checked his GPS. "Yes. Do you need water?" He removed his backpack and handed her a bottle.

"Thank you." She took a sip, then screwed the cap back on. They had reached the rocky summit of a hill. Going down would be much easier.

As they scrambled downhill, she caught the sound of rushing water. There must be a stream in the valley.

They cleared the forest, and she stopped in dismay. It was more than a stream; it was a wide, rushing river.

Tenzen wiped sweat from his brow. "The path that went south probably has a bridge."

She approached the riverbank, weaving around stones and fallen trees. A month ago, when the snows had melted, the river must have plowed through here with enough force to move large boulders and rip trees from the ground. The river was lower now, but it was still moving fast. Her nerves tensed at the thought of the boys trying to cross.

"I found something," Tenzen called from downstream.

She rushed over. A fresh footprint by the muddy shore. A small foot. "They came this way?"

He nodded and pointed at another set of footprints.

She heaved a sigh of relief. "They're going downstream."

Tenzen motioned for her to follow. "They're probably looking for a safe place to cross."

After ten minutes, the narrow valley flattened out into a wide pasture. The river slowed down and widened till it was only a foot deep.

"There!" Tenzen pointed.

Her heart swelled. Farther downstream, Norjee and Xiao Fang were wading across the river. The water lapped against their legs.

Neona ran toward them. "Norjee! Xiao Fang!"

They stopped and looked back.

"Norjee!" She stepped into the river. "Please come with me. Come home."

He hung his head. "Nobody wants me there."

"I do! Lots of us want you there." Tears filled her eyes. "I love you! Would I have come all this way to find you if I didn't love you?"

Norjee's chin trembled. Xiao Fang rested a hand on his shoulder.

"Come back home." She waded toward him, then stopped with a gasp. On the far riverbank in the forest, something metallic had reflected the light from the lowering sun. Swords. There were soldiers in the forest.

Tenzen muttered a curse behind her.

"Hurry!" she shouted at the boys.

A troop of soldiers on horseback burst from the forest onto the far riverbank.

The boys ran toward her, splashing through the water. Her heart froze. How could she and the boys outrun mounted soldiers? When the boys reached her, she grabbed their hands and sprinted toward Tenzen.

"Keep running." Tenzen handed her his backpack and drew his sword. "I'll hold them off."

One man against a troop? Neona glanced back as she swung his backpack over her shoulder. A dozen horsemen were charging across the river.

She dashed with the boys to the forest. Maybe she could hide them in the trees while she led the horsemen away. She looked around frantically for a tree the boys could climb.

The sound of clashing swords came from the riverbank.

She spotted a good tree. "This way." She grabbed the boys.

Norjee's gasp made her glance at the river. Tenzen was down. Four soldiers lay dead next to him. With a bloodied hand, he pulled a knife from his chest, then his hand fell lifeless by his side.

She swallowed hard. The poor man hadn't had a chance. The eight remaining horsemen headed straight for the forest.

"Hurry." She tugged at the boys, leading them toward the tree she'd selected. "I want you to hide up here." She lifted Norjee so he could catch the lowest branch.

"I don't want to leave you," Norjee protested.

"I'll be fine." She gave Xiao Fang a boost, then dug through the backpack. The sat phone wasn't there. Tenzen must have kept it.

She handed the backpack to Norjee. "There's food and drink in there. Hide behind the leaves. Don't come out till it's safe."

The ground beneath her feet vibrated as the horsemen charged toward her. She ran eastward. An arrow whizzed past her head, lodging in a nearby tree. She ducked behind another tree, but within seconds, she was surrounded.

"Where are the others?" a soldier demanded. The

extra stripe on his sleeve made her suspect he was the leader.

"I was with one other." She glared at him. "And you killed him."

"He attacked us." The leader urged his horse closer to her.

She backed up as the tip of his sword came close to grazing her chest.

"Where are the others?" he repeated. "There were two boys in the river."

"Why are you attacking us?" she asked. "We're just local farmers."

He scoffed. "With swords?" He motioned to one of his men. "Take her weapons. Tie her up."

The soldier dismounted and approached her.

She jumped back and drew her sword. "Leave me be. Go on your way, and I will leave you alone."

The leader laughed. "Are you threatening us?" He motioned to his soldiers. "What are you waiting for?"

Six more men dismounted and stalked toward her.

She backed away, swinging her sword at them. If she could occupy all of the soldiers in her capture, they might forget about the boys. Three of the soldiers slipped around behind her. She whirled, slicing the air with her sword. They circled her, closing in.

"Very well." She stabbed her sword into the ground. "I surrender. Take me to your master."

One of the soldiers lunged toward her, his fist aimed for her face. She blocked the punch and kicked him in the balls. With a cry, he doubled over.

"I said I surrender," she hissed. "I will ride with you to your master."

Two soldiers grabbed her. They were definitely supersoldiers. She couldn't break their grip.

"Hold her still." The soldier she'd kicked in the

balls came at her again. "Bitch!" He slapped her hard.

She kicked at him, but he jumped back and sneered. "Maybe we should have some fun with her before we take her back."

She tensed. The sun was lowering in the sky, but it could still be an hour before sunset, when the vampires woke up.

The soldier unzipped his pants. "Hold her still."

She gritted her teeth. She would make it through this. She had to.

A blast of fire shot from the tree where the boys were hidden. The soldier screamed as he was engulfed in flames. He ran away, screeching, then fell to the ground, where he flailed. The stench of burning flesh filled the air. His cries died down to whimpers, then he was quiet.

Neona tugged hard, but the two soldiers held her fast.

The other soldiers cautiously surrounded the tree. The fire had burned away some of the leaves, and now the two boys were visible.

The leader nudged his horse forward. "Amazing. One of them must be a dragon. Or perhaps both." He waved his hand. "Come on down. We won't hurt you."

Norjee and Xiao Fang exchanged looks but didn't budge.

The leader sighed. "They need motivation. Now."

"Yes, sir." One of the soldiers holding Neona pressed a knife to her throat.

"All right, boys," the leader said. "Come down, or we slit her throat."

Norjee and Xiao Fang climbed down.

"Tie them up," the leader ordered. "I want to get them back before Lord Liao wakes up."

Neona and the boys were tied up and tossed onto horses like sacks of rice. They headed back toward the river. She caught a glimpse of Tenzen lying in a pool of blood, and her eyes burned with tears. He'd died for nothing.

After a long ride, the men pulled the horses to a stop and shoved her and the boys onto the ground. With a gasp, she realized where they were. The monastery. Lord Liao and his army of fifty had taken it over.

The soldiers hauled her and the boys to their feet and marched them through the gate into the courtyard. Her stomach twisted at the sight of the two elderly monks lying in pools of blood. Norjee cried out, and Xiao Fang trembled.

She pretended to stumble so she could lower her head to their level. "Don't say a word to them," she whispered. "Stay strong."

Norjee nodded with a whimper.

A soldier jerked her upright and shoved her toward the buildings on the right. Another soldier opened the first door, and they were all pushed into the small room.

It was the same room she'd visited only two nights before. She said a silent prayer for the monks. No wonder they had been so eager to send Norjee away. Hopefully, the other monks had safely evacuated before Liao's arrival.

The soldiers untied them and left, closing the door behind them. She huddled against the far wall and gathered the two boys close to her. Their trembling bodies made her heart ache.

The door opened, and the leader sauntered inside. As he looked them over, she lowered her gaze. "So you must be one of the legendary warrior women who guards the dragons." He scoffed. "Did you think it was a secret? How can you keep a bunch of flying dragons a secret? Did you think your meaningless threats would keep the peasants quiet?"

He hunched down in front of her so he could make eye contact. "The peasants are much more afraid of us. When we threaten death, we deliver."

She remained quiet and squeezed the boys' shoulders.

"Which one is the dragon?" the leader asked softly.

The boys buried their faces against her.

"There are no dragons," she replied. "It's a silly folktale that villagers tell to frighten their children into behaving."

The leader's mouth thinned as he straightened. "We saw the fire. One of those boys breathed fire."

"That soldier was going to rape me. The gods shot fire down at him to punish him."

The leader snorted. "Very funny." He turned away, then suddenly drew his sword and pointed it at her chest.

She pressed back against the wall. The boys clung to her, both breathing hard.

"Which one is the dragon?" the leader shouted.

She swallowed hard.

"Not afraid to die, are you?" He sheathed his sword. "Very well. Maybe you'll be more motivated if we put the boys in danger."

Her heart lurched.

The leader glanced at his watch. "Lord Liao will awaken in thirty minutes. At that time, both boys will be executed."

The boys stiffened, and she squeezed their shoulders hard.

The leader sighed. "But I'm feeling charitable tonight. I'll let you save one of them. It will be your choice. See you in thirty minutes." He strode from the room and shut the door.

She breathed deeply to calm her racing heart. The soldier must be assuming she would choose to save the dragon.

"Are we going to die?" Norjee whispered.

"No." She took each boy's hand. "We're going to make it through this. Do you understand?" She looked at one, then the other.

"They killed the Venerable Fathers." Norjee's eyes filled with tears. "They want to kill us."

"I will not let them harm you."

Norjee pulled his hand away and stumbled to the far corner. "You can only save one. You'll have to save Xiao Fang, because he's special." Norjee fell to the floor and burst into tears. "I have to die! I'm a nobody!"

"No!" Neona ran to him and pulled him to her in a tight embrace. "You are special to me, Norjee. You're my sweet, beautiful boy. You're the son of my beloved sister. You are the son my heart always wished for."

Norjee clung to her, sniffling.

"I love you, Norjee." She rubbed his back and kissed his head. "I will always love you."

Xiao Fang squatted beside them and hugged them both.

Norjee made a sound that was a cross between a laugh and a whimper. "Xiao Fang says he loves me, too."

"There, you see." Neona wiped the tears from Norjee's face. "Even the dragons know you're special."

Taking a deep breath, she looked around. They had thirty minutes to escape. There was one door, and no doubt it was being guarded. Her gaze landed on the window. It was covered with a decorative wooden grate.

She dashed over to it, curled her fingers through the grate, and pushed hard. It wouldn't give. There was a heavy bar across the outside. Even if she destroyed the grate, the bar would remain solid, and it divided the window into two tiny spaces, too small to escape through.

The sky was darkening as the sun lowered on the horizon. Lord Liao would wake soon, but so would all the good vampires.

Her breath caught with a sudden thought. "Norjee, come here."

He ran to her. "Yes, Mama?"

"You're so special, you're going to be the one who saves us."

"I am?"

"You know the birds who live around here, right?"

He nodded. "They're my friends. Especially the family of eagles."

"Call them." She moved the short table under the window and set Norjee on top so he was level with the windowsill. "Call the eagles. Call all your bird friends. Tell them to fly to the valley of the dragons and tell the people there that we are prisoners here at the monastery. We're in grave danger, and they must rescue us."

Norjee grinned. "I can do that!"

She smiled and patted his back. Xiao Fang stood next to the table and gave him an encouraging smile.

Neona watched the sky darken. Their fate would be decided now in less than thirty minutes.

Chapter Twenty-six

*N*eona paced across the floor as the small room grew darker. Norjee had assured her that the eagles were on their way to Beyul-La. He and Xiao Fang sat side by side against a wall, exchanging looks.

She squatted down in front of them. "Are you talking to each other?"

Norjee nodded. "I told him I was sorry I ran away and caused all this trouble. He said he's sorry the queen and the other children are mean to me. I told him he shouldn't have followed me, but he says he wants to be with me."

She smiled. "You've brought joy into his life. I never heard him laugh before you came."

Norjee's eyes filled with tears. "He says we're brothers because we're so much alike. He hates the way the queen makes him stay hidden in the cave. The same way I hated being stuck here in the monastery all the time. We both want to be free. I was trapped here with a bunch of old men, and he's trapped there with a bunch of old women."

"Excuse me?"

Norjee winced. "Well, you're . . . a little bit old."

With a snort, she tousled Norjee's hair, then tousled Xiao Fang's hair, too. "You two rascals."

A tear rolled down Norjee's cheek. "If anything happens to you or Xiao Fang because of me—"

"We're going to be fine." She wiped away his tear. "I won't let anything happen to you."

She stood and looked around the room for something that could be used as a weapon. Her gaze landed on the short table under the window. She turned it on its side, planted a foot on one of the table legs, and yanked hard at another leg. It ripped off with a jagged edge that ended with a point. With enough force, it could pierce a soldier. Or Lord Liao. She slid it into her tunic so that it rested against the sash tied around her waist.

The door opened, and a dozen soldiers marched in. Too many for her to attack. They tied her hands in front, then hauled her and the boys outside. Only a sliver of sunlight remained, so torches had been lit in the courtyard. The two dead monks had been stacked to the side like refuse. Flies buzzed around them and the pools of blood that stained the hard ground.

The soldiers pushed her and the boys up the stairs to the temple. It was dark inside except for the lit candles on the low altar in front of a dais where a four-foot brass statue of Buddha rested. The room was a large square, the high ceiling held up by round wooden pillars painted red.

They were shoved against the far right wall.

"Sit," the leader ordered.

She sat, and the boys settled on each side of her. The door to the temple was still open, and the air that wafted in became cooler as night fell.

A few whimpers emanated from across the room.

She narrowed her eyes and detected some people against the far wall. Other prisoners.

The dozen soldiers knelt in front of the altar. A gasp sounded behind the dais that held the Buddha statue, the sound similar to the gasp she heard at sunset when Zoltan woke from his death-sleep.

A red silk robe came into view as Lord Liao stepped around the Buddha. He was thin, his face sallow, his hair a long braid down his back. He faced the soldiers, and they bowed down till their foreheads touched the floor.

"We are hungry, Ding." He motioned with his hand to the leader.

Neona cringed at the sight of Liao's long yellow fingernails, which curled like vicious claws. *Zoltan is awake, too,* she reminded herself. The Vamps would be coming soon.

The leader, Ding, rose to his feet. "We have a special treat for your eminence tonight. One of the warrior women of Beyul-La."

Liao licked his lips. "Excellent. Her warrior blood will give us strength."

Neona's stomach roiled. As much as she hated the thought of that monster even touching her, it would be best to cooperate for now. Letting him bite her would delay any plans they had to execute the boys. And she needed to buy time for Zoltan and his friends to effect a rescue.

"We caught her with two boys," Ding added. "We believe one of them is a dragon."

Liao smiled, flashing his yellow teeth. "Finally. We have what Master Han covets. He will not dare eliminate us now." He flicked the air with his long fingernails. "Bring us the warrior woman so we may quench our thirst."

Two soldiers grabbed her and hauled her to her feet. The boys clung to her.

"It's all right," she whispered. "Stay here."

The boys let go, and the soldiers escorted her to the altar. She twisted her tied hands till she managed to slip one hand into her tunic. Her fingers curled around the stake. If Liao tried to kill her, she'd fight back.

A third soldier came up behind her, pulled her hair back, and tilted her head to expose her neck.

Liao looked her over, then reared his head back. Fangs sprang out, vicious and sharp. He moved toward her, then roared in disgust. "She reeks of another man! We want our food to be fresh!"

"I apologize, your eminence." Ding bowed. "We caught her just now." He gestured to the prisoners against the other wall. "Bring another."

Soldiers hauled a whimpering young woman to the altar. Without pausing to even look at her, Liao leaped at her neck and plunged in his fangs. The women screeched.

Neona attempted to break free so she could stake Liao, but the soldiers pulled her back and tossed her against the wall. The boys wrapped their arms around her and held tight.

She groaned inwardly as she watched the poor woman grow quiet and limp, supported only by the soldiers holding her.

Shouts sounded outside, and the air filled with the popping noise of automatic weapons.

Neona's heart lurched. Zoltan and his friends must have arrived, but they were being shot at.

"We're under attack!" Ding yelled. He and the soldiers ran outside. Liao grabbed a sword from behind the Buddha and followed them out, slamming the door behind him.

Neona ran to the door, but it wouldn't open. They must have barred it from the outside. She dashed behind the Buddha to see if Liao had left any other weapons. There was nothing there but a silk pallet on the floor. She rounded the Buddha and knelt where the woman had crumpled on the ground. She was still alive.

Neona took a deep breath and pressed her tied hands against the wound on the woman's neck. She closed her eyes, concentrating, then cried out when she felt a tearing pain as if teeth were ripping through her neck. She gritted her teeth, waiting for it to pass. Slowly, the pain subsided to a dull throb.

She opened her eyes. The wound was closing and the woman was awake, watching her with a shocked expression.

"You'll be all right now," Neona told her.

"Are you an angel?" the woman whispered.

"No."

"She's my mama!" Norjee ran up to hug her, and she patted his cheek.

She stood and stretched her tied hands over one of the candles on the altar till the fire burned through enough of the rope that she could pull her hands apart. She removed the primitive stake from her tunic and glanced toward the door. The battle was waging outside, and she was missing it.

She paced around the perimeter of the building, searching for another way out. As much as she wanted to fight, her first priority had to be the boys' safety. She had to help them escape.

Outside, the popping noise stopped, and the sound of clanging swords began. The door burst open, and Liao and his dozen retainers ran inside. Half of them closed the door and leaned against it, breathing heavily.

Neona eased along the dark perimeter till she was back beside the boys. The injured woman in front of the altar scrambled behind the Buddha.

"They've taken away all our AK-47s," Ding yelled. "Those bastards can teleport behind our men and knock them out."

"And there are tigers and bears out there, ripping the men to shreds!" another soldier cried.

Ding fell to his knees in front of Liao. "Save us, Master. Teleport us away."

"And go where?" Liao shouted. "We can't go back to Han. Not when we lost two hundred of his men! He'll kill us!"

"We could go to one of his camps—" Ding started.

"And hide?" Liao paced in front of the Buddha. "Cower in fear until Han finds us?" He came to a stop, his eyes narrowed. "We need someone stronger than Han. Someone who can protect us."

"The only one stronger than Han is the demon," Ding said.

"Exactly." Liao sneered. "Darafer gave me instructions on how to bring him back from hell. It takes a dozen men. That's why I always kept a dozen of you close to me."

The soldiers grew pale.

"B-but it is forbidden to bring the demon back," one of the soldiers cried.

"Han forbid it because he fears Darafer," Liao growled. "He cannot control a demon. But if we bring Darafer back, he will be beholden to us. Han wouldn't dare touch us!"

Neona swallowed hard.

"Demons are bad," Norjee whispered beside her. "The fathers were afraid of them."

She nodded. Somehow she had to stop this.

Liao waved at the men. "Quickly. Cut the palm of your right hand and use the blood to draw a pentagram on the floor."

When the men hesitated, Liao yelled at them. "Hurry! It won't work unless the blood of twelve men is used!"

The men sliced their hands and smeared blood on the wooden floor in the shape of a pentagram.

"Now gather around it. Press your hands together to seal the circle with blood." Liao smiled as the dozen men hurried into position. "Repeat these words together. *Oh, powerful Lucifer, hear our prayer. Grant our request, we beseech you.*"

The men repeated the words.

"Open the gates of hell and deliver unto us your unholy servant, the demon Darafer."

Neona's skin prickled with goose bumps as the men began to chant. How could she stop this? Maybe if she broke the circle of twelve.

"Stay here," she told the boys. She gripped her stake in her hand and eased toward the circle.

"Open the gates of hell and deliver unto us your unholy servant, the demon Darafer," the men chanted.

Outside, the clanging of swords and screams of the wounded continued.

In the middle of the circle, a black cloud appeared.

She lunged toward the nearest soldier, stabbing him in the back. With a cry, he fell to the floor. The black cloud grew thin and wispy.

"Bitch!" Liao tossed her back with vampire strength and quickly took the downed soldier's place.

She flew backward and crashed into the wall. Her head hit hard. Pain exploded across her skull like streaks of lightning, and she crumpled to the ground.

"Mama!" Norjee scrambled to her. Xiao Fang was right behind him. "Mama, we have to stop them."

She gritted her teeth against the pain and sat up. The room spun around her.

"Open the gates of hell and deliver unto us your unholy servant, the demon Darafer."

The black cloud was thick again, and now it started to swirl.

"Have to stop them." She stumbled to her feet.

The black cloud took on human shape. Oh God, was she too late?

Xiao Fang ran toward them and let loose a burst of fire. Liao screeched as flames enveloped him. The boy dashed around the circle, breathing fire till it was a giant burning ball, full of flailing, screaming bodies.

Xiao Fang stopped. His body trembled, and he looked horrified at what he'd done. Norjee ran up to him and pulled him gently back.

Suddenly, the fire was sucked to the center of the circle, leaving a dozen burned corpses on the floor. Liao's body turned to ash. The fire in the center took on human form, then extinguished with a swooshing noise.

A man stood there, dressed all in black, with long black hair and sharp green eyes. He brushed some ash off the sleeve of his long black coat and gave the dead bodies a wry look. "What took you so long?"

His gaze shifted to Xiao Fang, and his mouth curled up in a humorless smile.

The doors burst open, and Zoltan charged inside with a few of his vampire and shifter friends. They halted with a jerk.

"Darafer," Dougal growled.

"I'm back," the demon said with a singsongy voice. He waved a hand at them, and they were blown back out the door.

He stalked toward Xiao Fang.

"No!" Neona ran toward the dragon shifter, but with a flick of a hand, Darafer sent her flying back.

She crashed into a wall once again, her head hitting hard. As she crumpled to the floor, stars exploded in her vision, making it hard to see. But still she saw. And her heart sank.

Darafer grabbed Xiao Fang and vanished.

Chapter Twenty-seven

"*W*ill she be all right?" Zoltan asked for the fif-
tieth time. After finding Neona unconscious in the
temple, he'd teleported her straight to the clinic in
Tiger Town. Dougal had followed, bringing Norjee.

"She may have suffered a concussion," Leah said
as she gingerly probed Neona's head. "No external
bleeding. Her skull is intact."

Zoltan nodded. "She's very hardheaded." When the
doctor gave him a wry look, he added, "I meant that
in a good way. She's tough as a boot. A . . . . a good
boot." He winced. He was so tense with worry that he
was babbling like an idiot.

Leah smiled as she checked her pulse. "Her vital
signs are strong."

"She's very strong. Strong as an ox." He groaned
inwardly. Now he'd compared the love of his life to
an ox. "She's very brave. And beautiful."

Leah unwound the bandage on Neona's arm.

"How is the cut?" he asked. "I wanted to bring her
here, but she didn't think it was necessary. We used
some of her homemade medicine."

"Really?" Leah examined the wound. "I'd like to see her medicine. This is healing extremely well."

"That's because she's brilliant. And brave. And beautiful."

Leah's mouth twitched. "You mentioned that before."

He took Neona's hand in his. "She's a healer. She does something magical, but she can't do it to herself. So she may be in a lot of pain." He squeezed her hand. "Can you do something? I don't want her to be in pain."

"Then don't break her bones," Leah muttered. "You Vamps don't know your own strength."

"Oh." He dropped her hand, then patted it gently. "Will she be all right?"

When he'd awakened from his death-sleep to learn that she and the boys had been taken prisoner, he'd thought he would die. His heart had clenched hard in his chest, and he'd gasped for air. For centuries, he'd existed with a fear that a sunset would arrive when he wouldn't awaken. Now it was different. Now he feared he'd awaken and Neona would be gone. And then it would no longer matter if he ever woke up again.

There hadn't been any time to wallow in despair. Angus had demanded his help in putting together an attack plan. Zoltan and the other Vamps had spent several frantic minutes teleporting all the shifters and warrior women to the forest close to the monastery.

Finally, with their army ready, they had attacked. All his fear had been channeled into rage as he'd charged into battle. No one had worried about keeping the supersoldiers alive. They'd plowed through the enemy, intent on killing Lord Liao and saving Neona and the boys.

Unfortunately, they hadn't quite succeeded. The dragon boy was missing.

"She's coming to." Leah leaned over Neona. "Can you see me?"

Neona blinked and gazed up at the doctor.

"I'm Doctor Kincaid, but please call me Leah." She smiled. "I believe you know my husband, Dougal."

Neona licked her lips. "Zoltan?"

"I'm here," he whispered.

She turned toward him and smiled.

His heart squeezed in his chest. "I thought I was going to lose you."

"Never."

"Will you marry me?" He winced. "I didn't mean to blurt it out. Don't answer now. I'll take you somewhere romantic and give you flowers and make love to you—"

"Yes."

"Yes to making love?"

Her mouth twitched. "You still owe me three climaxes."

"Right. We'll do that as soon as the doctor says you're ready."

Leah snorted. "Eager, aren't we? I'll just check my other patients now." She wandered off.

Neona watched her go. "What is this place?"

"Tiger Town, Yunnan province, China," Zoltan replied. "This is the clinic where the doctor is changing supersoldiers back to normal." He motioned to the rows of stretchers where soldiers lay in stasis while the medication took effect.

Neona turned back to him. "Is Norjee all right?"

"He's fine. He's been waiting outside." Zoltan dashed to the clinic door and motioned for Norjee to come in.

"Mama!" The young boy ran up to her bed.

She struggled to sit up, and Zoltan helped her.

Norjee grinned as he said something in Tibetan, then he darted back outside and led in a were-tiger.

Neona gasped. "Tenzen?"

The were-tiger smiled as he explained in Chinese.

Her eyes widened, then she glanced at Zoltan. "The were-cats have nine lives! He's on his third life now."

Zoltan nodded. "When he woke up, he called us on his sat phone. We picked him up on the way to the battle."

Norjee held her hand and talked some more. His eyes filled with tears, and his chin trembled. Zoltan frowned. He was going to have to learn some Tibetan or Chinese.

Neona hugged the boy as she murmured soothing words. Then she turned to Zoltan. "Norjee blames himself for Xiao Fang getting captured. Do you know anything yet?"

He shook his head. "Most probably, Darafer has taken the boy to Master Han. Russell is searching for Han's camp now. We'll do whatever we can to save Xiao Fang."

Neona translated the response to Norjee. He replied, then hurried from the room with the were-tiger. She turned to Zoltan. "Norjee wants to help us fight Master Han. Tenzen offered to teach him how to shoot a bow and arrow."

"We're not going to let a seven-year-old fight."

"I know. But there's no harm in teaching him some self-defense. And he's so upset, I think it will be best to keep him busy."

Zoltan sat on the bed beside her. "There's more I need to tell you. Darafer will be able to read the dragon boy's mind. He'll know about the other children and the eggs. And he'll know exactly where to find them."

She gasped. "Then it is no longer safe in Beyul-La."

"I'm afraid we have to move the dragons."

"Oh, my God. My mother will throw a fit."

"What else is new?"

She winced. "No one will envy you for your new mother-in-law."

He shrugged. "I'll manage." He stiffened suddenly. "Does that mean you agree to marry me?"

"I said yes."

He blinked. "I thought you were talking about sex."

She gave him a wry look. "You always think we're talking about sex."

He grinned. "So you'll marry me?"

"Yes." Her mouth curled up. "You're smirking again."

He kissed her hand. "It's not every day that a vampire wins the heart of a warrior princess."

A half hour later, Zoltan was in the cave at Beyul-La, while Neona remained in Tiger Town, getting a blood test and an X-ray that Leah had insisted on. The queen sat stiffly on her throne while he explained the urgent need for evacuation. As expected, she exploded with anger.

"This is all your fault!" she screamed. "You and your friends are destroying our world! Why can't you leave us be?"

"If we could leave you here safely, we would," Zoltan replied. "But there is no doubt that Darafer and Master Han will come here for the dragons. The only way to save them is to move them."

"How can I expect you to save them?" Nima yelled. "You couldn't save Xiao Fang!"

"We'll find him," Zoltan insisted. "Russell is trying to locate Master Han's camp. Darafer probably took the boy there."

"What will they do to him?" Freya asked.

Nima clenched her fists. "If they're torturing my dragon—"

"They'll treat him well," Zoltan said, hoping that was the truth. "Most likely, they will be good to him in order to win him over to their side."

Nima snorted. "Xiao Fang is a good boy. He'll never side with them."

Zoltan took a deep breath. If Xiao Fang resisted, Master Han might resort to threats and even torture. The boy had to be rescued before that happened. "We'll save Xiao Fang. But right now, we have a chance to save the other children. And the eggs. We have to grab that chance before it's too late."

Winifred sighed. "He's right."

Lydia nodded. "We have to do whatever is necessary to keep them safe."

The queen tapped her fingers on the arm of her throne. "And where do you propose to take our dragons? If this demon is so powerful, what place on earth will be safe?"

"We have a place," Zoltan said. "It's called Dragon Nest Academy."

With a gasp, Nima jumped to her feet. "There are dragons there?"

He shook his head. "It's named after the founders, Roman and Shana Draganesti. It's a school for hybrid and shifter children, where they can be safe and free to be themselves. It seems quite fitting that Dragon Nest would become a safe haven for your dragons.

You are, of course, welcome to live there with the children and eggs."

Nima's eyes narrowed. "Then you will take me with you to this Dragon Nest? I must continue to be the dragons' guardian."

He nodded. "Of course. With your permission, we will start the evacuation tonight."

Nima heaved a sigh. "I don't suppose we have any choice."

"How are the babies doing that Emma took?" Tashi asked.

"Very well," Zoltan replied. "I saw them in Tiger Town before coming here. Emma was feeding one a bottle."

"What was wrong with them?" Nima asked.

"Apparently, after years of incubating inside the eggs with their lungs closed off, they needed some help getting their lungs to work. Leah inserted a tube down their throats and pumped some air inside. That was all it took."

Nima heaved a sigh of relief. "Thank God."

He stepped outside the cave and called Angus on his sat phone. A group of Vamps materialized by the entrance to the cave. It had been easy to find volunteers to teleport Nima, the two remaining dragon children, and the five eggs across Europe to the school located in the foothills of the Adirondack Mountains of New York. After leaving Dragon Nest, the Vamps would continue to teleport westward, following the moon, until they made it back to China.

Jack had volunteered, so they could stop in Venice, where he would visit his wife and new baby. Connor had volunteered, so they could stop in Scotland. Ian's wife and daughter lived at Dragon Nest, so he wanted to go. Robby and Jean-Luc had offered so they could stop in Texas to see their families. Phineas wanted to drop by Wyoming to see his wife and twins. J.L. was going so he could visit family in San Francisco.

Their first stop would be Zoltan's castle in Transylvania. As soon as the sun set there, they moved out.

The rest of the Vamps teleported back to the monastery to gather up all the weapons and any surviving supersoldiers. Later, they would return to Tiger Town to do their death-sleep. The shifters would remain in Frederic's valley and Beyul-La on the lookout for Darafer in case he made a surprise visit. With Nima gone, the men were free to guard both valleys.

Another hour passed by the time Zoltan had a chance to drop by Neona's house and drink two more bottles of spiked blood. He picked up the black jewelry box and teleported back to the clinic at Tiger Town.

Neona was resting with a sleeping Norjee curled up at the foot of the bed. "How did it go?" she whispered. "Did they take the dragons away?"

"Yes. How are you doing? How was your X-ray?"

"Good. I'm going to be fine."

"That's good." He perched on the edge of her bed and opened the jewelry box. "I brought these."

She smiled. "But we're not married yet."

"I don't care." He removed the lady's ring and slipped it on her finger. "This place is crawling with male were-tigers, and they're probably all in heat. And then there are about thirty soldiers in this room with you. I have to make sure they know you're taken."

She snorted. "They're unconscious."

"But they're dreaming of you."

Her eyes softened. "Is that so?"

"Yes. Every man dreams of the perfect woman, and that's you."

She sighed. "I love you, Zoltan. And I love this ring." She held her hand out to admire it. "It fits perfectly."

He tried putting on the man's ring, but it wouldn't go over his knuckle. "Damn."

She leaned close. "I just love a man with really big hands."

He glanced at her. "Are we talking about sex again?"

She gave him a coy look.

With a groan, he glanced around the room. "Dammit. We can't do anything tonight."

"We can tomorrow."

"It's a date then. Climax number eight. And nine." He leaned over to kiss her brow. "Till tomorrow."

He gave Norjee a pat on the shoulder, then teleported to his castle. The evacuation team had arrived safely with Nima, the children, and the eggs. The Vamps were drinking bottled blood in the kitchen. The eggs were nestled in soft blankets in laundry baskets. Domokos had ordered some pizza, which the children were enjoying. Nima was turning the kitchen faucet on and off, apparently mesmerized by the wonders of modern plumbing.

Zoltan teleported to the jewelry store, but to his surprise, he ended up in the village square. How the hell? This was the first time he'd ever missed a mark. He walked over to the jewelry store and strode inside. A second surprise. J.L. was there, attempting to talk to Janos.

"Oh, thank God you're here," J.L. told him. "I can't make this man understand what I want."

"Possibly because he doesn't speak English," Zoltan muttered.

"I pointed at the watches and said your name," J.L. explained. "Freddie has been bragging about a watch you gave Neona, so I thought I'd give her one just like it. And Rajiv wants to get one for Freya. But this guy keeps trying to sell me these Hello Kitty things. I told him there's no way you would give your girlfriend something that cheap."

Zoltan's jaw shifted. "It was all he had in the store at the time."

"You mean—you gave—"

"Yes. And Neona loves it."

J.L. snorted. "Could be worse. You could have gotten it as a free prize out of a cereal box." He turned to Janos and smiled. "Yes. Those two." He handed over a credit card.

"What can I do for you, my lord?" Janos asked in Romanian as he rang up J.L.'s sale.

Zoltan opened the jewelry box. "I need this ring resized."

Janos's face lit up. "Then you are getting married? We will have a countess at the castle?"

Zoltan nodded. "If everything goes well."

J.L.'s phone buzzed and he answered it. "I understand." He hung up and sighed. "That was Angus. Russell just reported in. Darafer took the dragon shifter to Master Han's camp in Myanmar. Three hundred soldiers are now marching toward Beyul-La."

Chapter Twenty-eight

*T*he next evening, Zoltan woke up in his bed at the castle. He quickly shaved and showered. Tonight the Vamps and shifters would need to decide how to handle Master Han's army of three hundred. And if all worked out well, he'd find time for the date he'd promised Neona.

In the kitchen, he drank a bottle of blood while he packed an ice chest with more blood. There were chocolate chip cookies left over from feeding the dragon children. Neona and Norjee might like them. Then he recalled Zhan, her pet leopard. He tossed some tuna into a plastic container. The ice chest was stuffed full when he teleported back to Beyul-La.

And missed. He looked around. He was in Frederic's valley, close to the rock wall.

Damn. Was the Living Water doing this to him? He couldn't afford a mistake like this in battle.

Hey! Zhan trotted up to him. *How is Neona? I miss her.*

Zoltan smiled at the leopard. *She's fine. I brought you some food.* He removed the plastic container from the ice chest and set the tuna in front of the cat.

I love this stuff! Zhan butted his head against Zoltan's leg, than proceeded to eat with gusto.

Zoltan rubbed the cat's head. *With Neona gone, I was worried you wouldn't have anything to eat.*

The cat looked up and licked his mouth. *The other women feed me. And the were-tigers give me food, too. They think I'm cute.* He went back to eating.

Zoltan snorted. The rascally cat was working both valleys, probably getting twice the food he was used to. *Keep this up, and you'll be too fat to hunt.*

"Zoltan!" Howard strode toward him. "We were wondering when you'd get back. Can you tell the warrior women to come over here? Angus wants a meeting in thirty minutes."

"All right." Zoltan teleported to Neona's house and set the ice chest down next to the old one that was now empty except for a half-full bottle of Living Water. He had intended to spike his new bottles of blood, but he decided against it. He couldn't afford to mess up his teleportation abilities. And Neona's wish to revive his sperm was probably hopeless.

He found the four remaining women in the cave and walked with them to the rock wall. He levitated down as they climbed down the rope ladder. Angus was gathering everyone in front of Frederic's cabin. The evacuation team had made it back from their trip around the world, but they looked exhausted.

"Have you found Xiao Fang yet?" Freddie asked as she took a seat on a rock by the stream.

"He could be traveling with Han's army," Angus replied. "Or he may be hidden at one of Master Han's military bases. I'll ask for some volunteers in a moment so we can check Han's compound in Myanmar, in case Xiao Fang was left there."

Angus waited for everyone to take a seat, then he

continued. "First off, I can report that Nima and the dragon children and eggs have been safely delivered to their new home. Master Han doesn't know that, so his army is still moving this way. Russell is following them now, and Carlos tracked them during the day. They estimate the army will be here in three nights. That gives us tonight and tomorrow to get ready."

Carlos's adopted son and young trainee, Emiliano, raised his hand. "If the dragons are safe, why don't we just leave? Wouldn't Master Han give up and go home if he doesn't find the dragons here?"

"There's still the Living Water," Angus replied. "Han may not know about it, but we can't risk him moving into Beyul-La and taking control of it."

"And we have to fight him sooner or later," Howard added. "If we can get rid of this group of three hundred, Han will have only four hundred left."

Lydia snorted. "How do we get rid of three hundred? There are only fifty of us."

"We got rid of two hundred," Freya reminded her.

Angus nodded. "We'll use a similar strategy. According to Russell, Han's army isn't sending out search parties. There's no need when they know exactly where they're going. They're moving quickly, so they're light on supplies. In order to feed three hundred, they're sending out raiding parties to loot the local villages as they pass by."

"Then we attack the raiding parties?" Howard asked.

Angus nodded. "That's what I'd like to do, but I have to warn you. Russell says the raiding parties number from twenty to twenty-five, and they're all armed with AK-47s."

"We confiscated a bunch of AK-47s from the monastery," Jesse said. "We could just shoot 'em down!"

"We may have to do that," Angus admitted. "But I still prefer to keep them alive and transform them back to normal. If we can capture four or five of these raiding parties, we can whittle the army down to two hundred."

"Then what?" Jimmy asked. "We're so outnumbered. And we can knock out only one at a time with those darts."

"Is there something that would knock them all out at once?" Zoltan asked.

Angus winced. "A gas that strong runs the risk of killing them. And us. 'Twould be hard to control outdoors."

"How about an enclosed place . . ." Zoltan's breath caught as an idea struck him. "What about the cavern? It's big enough to hold two hundred soldiers. We could trap them in there."

"Why would they go in there?" Jimmy asked.

"They're coming for the dragons, right?" Zoltan replied. "Darafer will know from Xiao Fang that the dragons are living in the cavern."

"So the army makes a beeline for the cave," Angus thought out loud. "How do we trap them inside?"

"I'll rig some kind of trapdoor," Howard offered.

"But what about the Living Water?" Lydia asked. "It's in the first cave room. They'll pass right by it."

"Can we drain it?" Angus asked.

Lydia shook her head. "It's fed by a spring. The water would come back."

"We need to drink a cup every month or we'll start to age," Freya said.

"We could hide it," Howard suggested. "We'll build a floor over it and cover it with sand and rocks."

"And we'll keep the area dark," Jesse added. "They'll run right past it without seeing it."

"Once we have the soldiers trapped, they'll start panicking," Angus warned. " 'Twill be too dangerous to teleport in."

J.L. raised a hand. "Stun grenades. The blast of light will blind them, and the bang will deafen them. We can use ones with multiple detonations and tear gas. They'll be so dizzy and disoriented that they'll be easy to shoot with darts."

Robby nodded. "A good idea, but we'll have to be verra careful. Our sight and hearing is even more sensitive than theirs."

"So we go back in to shoot them with darts and take them— Wait." Angus winced. "The clinics are almost full. Where will we put two hundred more soldiers?"

"We could leave them in the cavern," Zoltan suggested. "We teleport Leah and her team inside, put the soldiers into stasis, and start the treatment. In a few weeks, the soldiers can leave the cave, back to normal."

"All right. We'll work out the details later." Angus looked everyone over. "I want the women and shifters working on the cave. Vamps—ye're coming with me. Let's go!"

Over the next few hours, everyone was busy. Howard and the other shifters went over the rock wall to Beyul-La, and there they worked on disguising the Living Water and making a trapdoor that would fall down and close off the cavern.

Zoltan teleported with Angus and the other Vamps to Han's compound in Myanmar. Only a few soldiers were there, and they were easily knocked out and delivered to Tiger Town. Xiao Fang was nowhere in sight.

Russell called with the location of a raiding party, so the Vamps teleported there. After a few tense minutes of dodging bullets, they managed to capture twenty-three soldiers. An hour later, they repeated the mission and captured twenty-two more. Between missions, Zoltan teleported to Tiger Town to deliver the chocolate chip cookies to Neona and Norjee. They were staying in a guesthouse now, for every bed in the clinic was taken.

After a third mission, Angus called it quits for the night. Zoltan grabbed his ice chest and went back to Tiger Town. Thankfully, he'd experienced only one more problem with his teleporting. He'd teleported to a tree to escape a barrage of gunfire, and his feet had missed the branch. He'd managed to grab anther branch with his hands to keep from falling.

It was after three in the morning, and Norjee was sleeping on a pallet in the guesthouse. Most of Tiger Town was asleep. Quietly, Zoltan led Neona through a maze of buildings.

"Where are we going?" she whispered.

"The bathhouse. I made arrangements with Jia so we could have it to ourselves."

"Who is Jia?"

"She's the one in charge right now while the Grand Tiger is gone. She's his cousin." Zoltan escorted her up the steps to a small building and kicked his shoes off at the door.

"I haven't had a chance to meet her. It's been very hectic here with all the soldiers coming in." Neona stepped out of her shoes. "Which one is the Grand Tiger? Rinzen or Tenzen?"

"Neither. They're Rajiv's uncles. He's the Grand Tiger."

Neona gasped. "Rajiv? But he's so young." She winced. "I don't think Freya knows."

Zoltan shrugged. "I'm sure he'll tell her when he's

ready." He led her inside the bathhouse, then closed the door and slid the bar into place. "I promised you a date. I hope this will do."

She looked around. "It's lovely." The room was dominated by a large sunken tub. The surface of the water glimmered in the light from two candles.

She knelt down to touch the water. "It's warm."

With vampire speed, Zoltan threw off his clothes. She straightened slowly, watching him. Then she smiled as he approached her.

"I won't undress you that fast. I enjoy it too much." He untied the sash at her waist and peeled off her tunic.

She smoothed a hand down his chest. "I enjoyed watching you. If I were a vampire, my eyes would be glowing red."

"Like this?" He cupped her bare breasts, and his vision turned pink. His groin tightened at the thought of giving her climax number eight and nine. He teased her taut nipples, pinching gently at the hardened tips.

"I want you. Now." She wiggled out of her pants. "Actually, I've wanted you since last night. Ever since you came to rescue us at the monastery."

"Did I tell you how terrified I was? I thought I'd lost you." He climbed into the tub and pulled her in with him. "I've been desperate to hold you."

She wrapped her arms around his neck. "I didn't realize how much I loved you till I feared I would never see you again."

He kissed her hard, and she kissed him back. He couldn't get her close enough. Couldn't kiss her enough. Or touch her enough. He lifted her so he could suckle her breasts. Then lifted her more till she was perched on the edge of the pool and he could dive between her legs. Within seconds, she was crying out and her core was throbbing against his mouth.

With a satisfied growl, he plunged inside her. She wrapped her arms and legs around him. His pace was fast and hard, but she urged him to give her more. Desperation drove their desire. He pumped harder, faster, deeper, and she bucked against him, matching his every move.

With a shout, he grasped her hips and ground himself against her. She shattered with a scream just as he climaxed.

They slumped back into the pool, clinging to each other as their breathing returned to normal. And still they held each other, even as the water began to grow cold.

The first tug of death-sleep pulled at Zoltan. "The sun will be up soon."

She nodded. "When will the army arrive at Beyul-La?"

"The night after tomorrow. Can I talk you into staying here, where it's safe?"

"No." She kissed him. "I'm going to be with you."

The night arrived, and everyone was in their appointed place. Russell confirmed the army was crossing into Frederic's valley. Zoltan waited with Neona at the top of the rock wall. Lydia, Freya, and Freddie were there, along with Angus, Robby, and J.L. Tashi was in Tiger Town, helping Emma take care of the dragon babies.

Zoltan squeezed Neona's hand, then they readied their weapons. The Vamps were using dart guns. The women had bows and arrows, with the arrowheads treated with the same drug as the darts.

With his superior hearing, Zoltan could detect the soldiers coming down the hillside. "Just a few more seconds," he whispered.

Neona drew back her bow. He readied his pistol.

As soon as the soldiers cleared the forest, Zoltan and his companions let loose the first volley. Eight targets hit, and they reloaded to fire again. Eight more.

"Down!" Angus yelled just before a spray of bullets went over their heads.

"Let's go," Angus ordered, and each Vamp grabbed a warrior woman to teleport away. They'd done their job, luring the soldiers to the rock wall, which was the best way to access Beyul-La.

Zoltan materialized with Neona at the fire pit. *Damn.* They were supposed to have landed next to the cave entrance. He picked her up and zoomed to the cave at vampire speed.

"What the hell was that?" Angus asked. He and the others had arrived at the right place.

"Long story," Zoltan muttered.

A series of explosions sounded at the end of the valley. Han's army was acting just as expected. They'd used grenades to blast away the rock wall. Any second now, the soldiers would be streaming into the valley.

"You know what to do?" Angus asked the women.

"Yes," Lydia whispered. "We scream 'Save the dragons' and run into the cave."

"Start screaming as soon as they draw close to Nima's house," Zoltan said. "By the time they reach Neona's house, you've got to be in the cave."

They nodded. The night before, the Vamps had tested the range of the AK-47s to make sure the women would be out of range of the approaching army.

Zoltan squeezed Neona's shoulder. "Be careful." He and the other three Vamps slipped inside the cave.

Since they wanted to lure the soldiers quickly into the cave, it had seemed best to make them believe that only a few frightened women were guarding it. Then they would charge straight for it, thinking an easy victory was in their grasp.

Zoltan waited, his fists clenched as he imagined an army charging straight toward Neona. He and the other Vamps had captured more raiding parties the night before, so Han's army now numbered around one hundred and ninety.

He heard the women scream, then shout in Chinese. Then explosions burst so loud that he could no longer hear their voices. His heart lurched. Had the bastards shot some sort of rocket at the women? He lunged toward the cave entrance.

The women stood just outside, staring at the valley with stricken looks on their faces.

"Neona!" he shouted. "Hurry!"

She and the other women ran inside, and he grabbed her.

"What's wrong?" His heart clenched at the tears in her eyes.

"They blew up my house!" she cried.

"Let's go!" Angus shouted.

They teleported the women away before the soldiers could reach the cave. The designated landing spot was the forest above the burial mounds.

Zoltan landed with Neona behind Minerva's burial mound. Quickly he pushed her down so they were flat on the ground. Below, in the valley, soldiers were charging for the cave. Smoke rose from the ruins of the houses.

"What's wrong?" Neona whispered. "We're supposed to be in the forest."

He winced. "My teleportation is off. I think it's because of the Living Water."

He scooted to the edge of the mound and peered down into the valley. As expected, many of the soldiers ran straight into the cave, hoping to be the first ones to find the dragons so they could share in the glory of pleasing Master Han. To lure them into the second, larger cavern, the shifters had moved the empty nests there and hidden a tape recorder that played the sound of crying babies.

Some of the soldiers lingered outside the cave. It was the shifters' job to make them go inside. The shifters were hidden in the nearby woods and fired AK-47s at the ground in front of the soldiers. The soldiers retreated inside the cave but remained in the first cavern room. Tremendous roars shook the forest, then three grizzly bears, three tigers, and two panthers charged toward the cave. The men screamed and ran toward the second cavern.

A trapdoor had been tied in place along the ceiling in the corridor. Ian was levitated and hidden on the ceiling, and once all the soldiers entered the cavern, he would cut the rope, and the heavy door would swing down and block the only entrance. Then he would slide the steel bars into place, and the men would be trapped inside.

Zoltan stood and helped Neona to her feet. The valley was empty now, except for the shifters in animal form who prowled around the entrance of the cave.

Angus and the others emerged from the forest to join him by the burial mounds.

"Is something wrong with yer teleporting?" Angus asked.

Zoltan sighed. "I'll be fine. Don't worry about it."

"I do worry. Ye're no' going into the cave with the rest of us."

"Angus—"

"I mean it, lad." Angus scowled at him. "If ye're off a few feet, you could materialize into solid rock." He turned to look at the rest of the Vamps. "Jack, ye'll take his place."

With vampire speed, Robby carried a large duffel bag from the forest and handed out earplugs and gas masks with eye protection to Angus, J.L., Dougal, and Jack. He kept one set for himself, then passed out the stun grenades.

Zoltan cursed inwardly as the five men got ready to teleport without him.

Russell cursed out loud. "I didn't see Han with the army. Did anyone spot him? He always has that stupid gold mask on his face."

"I was looking for Xiao Fang." Freya sighed. "But I didn't see him."

Down below, the shifters returned to the forest to turn back into their human form. Dressed once again, they ran toward the burial mounds to join the others.

Ian materialized beside them. "The trapdoor is down! They're all inside."

The five Vamps vanished. Zoltan knew exactly what they were doing, since he was supposed to be with them. They would teleport close to the ceiling, levitate instantly to keep from falling, then drop the stun grenades and teleport out.

Neona gasped. "Someone's appearing!" She pointed toward the fire pit.

Zoltan whirled around to look. Master Han had

materialized in the valley, and he was holding Xiao Fang. Either they were escaping the cave, or they had just arrived.

"Han!" Russell teleported downhill and drew a pistol.

Zoltan zoomed down the hillside.

Han turned to face Russell, holding the boy in front of him as a shield.

Zoltan ran up behind him, cursing silently that the only weapons on him were a dart gun and a knife. He shot a dart at Han, then threw his knife.

Han stiffened as both struck his body, then he vanished, taking Xiao Fang with him.

"Dammit!" Russell shook clenched fists at the sky.

Angus and the other four Vamps materialized by the fire pit. As they removed their gas masks, a series of loud bangs sounded inside the mountain. The stun grenades were going off.

"Han was just here with Xiao Fang," Zoltan told them. "He's injured, but he escaped."

Angus sighed.

"Poor Xiao Fang," Freddie whispered. "He must be so afraid."

J.L. patted her shoulder. "We'll get him back."

The bangs inside the mountain stopped.

"Ready?" Angus asked the four other Vamps. "We shoot as many soldiers with darts as possible. If they look like they're recovering from the stun grenades, we toss in more tear gas. And shoot some more."

A loud explosion shook the ground. The mountain rumbled.

"What the hell?" Zoltan asked.

"The fools!" Angus shouted. "They're trying to blast their way out of the mountain."

More explosions sounded as the disoriented and

frantic soldiers detonated more grenades. The mountain shook. Rocks tumbled down.

"Run!" Zoltan picked up Neona and zoomed toward the burial mounds at vampire speed. Beside him, other Vamps were carrying women. The shifters were right behind them. The ground trembled under their feet.

Zoltan stopped close to the forest and set Neona down. They looked back at the rumbling mountain. With a huge creaking sound, the mountain imploded, the top part caving into the giant cavern, crushing the men inside. The impact was strong enough to shake the ground where they stood.

Zoltan grabbed Neona as she stumbled beside him. Smoke and debris rose into the air, clouding their vision, yet they all continued to stare, stunned by a mountain that was suddenly half the size it used to be.

"The devil take it," Angus whispered.

"The devil will take them," Robby said. "I doona think any of them survived."

"Bloody hell." Angus ripped off his gas mask and threw it down. "We were trying to save them."

"Our . . . our Living Water," Lydia whispered. "It's gone. We cannot get to it."

"Oh, my God!" Freya cried. "We'll grow old now!"

"The dragons can never come back," Freddie added. "Their home is gone. And our homes are gone."

Zoltan winced as he saw the tears on their faces.

"What will we do?" Freya sniffed.

Lydia heaved a forlorn sigh. "I suppose I'll have to live with Tashi and that farmer of hers."

"But we'll be separated," Freddie protested.

"It is the end of Beyul-La," Neona whispered.

Zoltan closed his eyes briefly. What had he done to these women?

"And we didn't even save Xiao Fang," Freddie mumbled.

"But he's still alive," J.L. told her. "We're all still alive. And we beat the bad guys."

"We creamed them!" Jimmy shouted.

"Yeah!" Jesse yelled.

"They creamed themselves, the puir bastards," Angus muttered, looking at the crumbled mountain.

"We've lost everything." Lydia collapsed on the ground by the burial mounds where her mother and two of her daughters were interred. "What did they die for? After three thousand years, it's over."

Neona sniffed as more tears rolled down her cheeks.

Zoltan's heart twisted in his chest. It had been his idea to trap the soldiers in the mountain. Now the dragons had lost their home. His beloved Neona had lost her home. All the women of Beyul-La had lost their homes and their Living Water.

Queen Nima had been right all along. He had destroyed their world.

Chapter Twenty-nine

Three days later

*N*eona woke with a jerk and sat up on her pallet in the guesthouse at Tiger Town. She'd fallen asleep again? Ever since the battle at Beyul-La, she couldn't seem to lie down without falling fast asleep. She suspected it was her mind's way of escaping a reality she was having a hard time accepting.

The life she'd lived for two thousand years was over. Jia, the were-tigress, had been very kind when Neona and the other women had arrived three days earlier. Jia had said they were welcome to stay in Tiger Town as long as they wished.

Neona stood and wandered over to the window. The sun would be setting soon. Where was Zoltan doing his death-sleep? At his castle? When night fell there and he woke up, would he teleport back here?

She hadn't seen him the last two nights. After dropping her off in Tiger Town, he'd gone back with the other Vamps to collect soldiers. There were some unconscious ones in Frederic's valley. Zoltan had returned to the guesthouse shortly before dawn with a grim look on his face.

"I love you," was all he'd said before falling into his death-sleep. She'd taken Norjee to breakfast, then to the school. She'd helped Emma with the dragon babies, then that afternoon, she'd fallen asleep. When she woke up, it was past sunset, and Zoltan was gone. He'd left a note.

I never quit a job till it's done to my satisfaction. I will fix things. Remember I love you.

What did he mean by fixing things? She'd read the note over and over, trying to decipher its meaning. Had he gone to his castle to fix things there? Was he planning for her and Norjee to live there with him? Or was he arranging things there so he could live here in Tiger Town? Why hadn't she heard from him?

She paced about the small room. She should have kept one of those sat phones so she could call him. Tashi had taken one with her when the Vamps had teleported her and her mother to the village, where her farmer lived.

Freddie and Freya were still in Tiger Town. They were helping Emma with the dragon babies, since Emma fell into her death-sleep during the day.

Neona leaned over to roll up Norjee's pallet. He seemed happy enough. He was going to the Tiger Town school with the other children and learning self-defense and archery. At night, he still cried, worrying about his friend Xiao Fang. She knew he wanted to stay here so he could be close to the action and the ongoing search for Xiao Fang.

It was interesting here in Tiger Town, but after centuries of taking care of herself, Neona grated at the thought of living off the were-tigers' charity. Jia assured her she would be earning her keep as a healer, but Neona still felt uneasy. She was used to mountains and valleys for as far as she could see. Rushing streams and crisp, cool mountain air. For days on end, she would roam the forests, hunting, with her pet leopard at her side.

Her heart twinged with worry for Zhan. When they'd teleported away from Beyul-La, she'd called and called for him. He hadn't come. Was he all right? Was he finding food to eat?

And where the hell was Zoltan? She could hear her mother's voice announcing with glee that she'd known all along he couldn't be trusted. He had abandoned her.

No! She shook that thought away and left the guesthouse.

As she approached the large courtyard, she spotted Norjee with two dozen other boys, learning martial arts from Rinzen and Tenzen. Norjee waved at her, grinning. She smiled back, then chuckled when Tenzen tapped the boy's head for not paying attention.

She wandered over to the top of the stairs that led downhill. Before her lay the Mekong River and the village of were-tiger houses built on stilts along the river's edge. The sky lit up with shades of pink and orange as the sun dipped below the horizon.

Her eyes filled with tears and she blinked them away, irritated by how emotional she'd been lately. She was homesick, that was all. She missed her sister, her valley, her pet leopard, her house, her way of life. How soon would she start aging now? Would she have to become a vampire like Zoltan in order to live with him forever? Would she have to lose the ability to be alive during the day? Would she lose the sun, too?

As if to twist the thorn in her side, the last of the sunlight disappeared, and she was left in darkness. A tear rolled down her cheek. How much would she have to lose? Hadn't she lost enough?

Were-tigers bustled around her, lighting torches. And she stood still, wondering if Zoltan had awakened somewhere. Where was he? Was she losing him, too?

"There you are!" Leah called to her.

Neona quickly wiped her face and turned toward the doctor.

Leah smiled as she approached. "I went to the guesthouse to look for you, but you were gone."

"Is something wrong?"

Leah shook her head. "We've been so busy lately with the clinic overflowing that it took me several days to get your blood work done." She took a deep breath. "I have news for you. You're pregnant."

Neona blinked. "What?"

"No mistake."

Neona inhaled sharply and pressed a hand to her stomach. "I'm with child?"

"Yes." Leah lowered her voice. "I wanted to tell you in private. I assume Zoltan isn't the father."

"But he is."

Leah's mouth dropped open. "How? His sperm is dead."

"He was drinking the Living Water." Neona grinned. "Oh, my God! It worked!"

Leah stepped closer. "Where is this Living Water? Can I get a sample of it?"

"It is gone. Buried beneath a mountain of rubble." Neona's breath caught. Was that what Zoltan was trying to fix? He could get himself killed! "Excuse me."

She ran to Emma's room. Pregnant! No wonder she

was falling asleep so much and getting emotional all the time. She was going to have a baby! She needed to find Zoltan fast.

She burst into Emma's room. "I need—"

"Guess what?" Freya pulled her into the room. "When Emma woke up, she invited Freddie and me to live with her and Angus at their townhouse in London!"

"And their castle in Scotland!" Freddie added.

Emma finished a bottle of synthetic blood. "I'm desperate. I need help. Angus does what he can, but we're both awake only at night."

Freya laughed. "You should have seen it, Neona. Last night, Angus was lifting the little boy in the air, and he threw up all over Angus's head. The look on his face was so funny!"

"Who?" Freddie asked, grinning. "Angus or the baby?"

"Both!" Freya turned back to Neona. "And while we're in England, we can see our brother, Frankie!"

"And our family there," Freddie nodded.

"That's wonderful," Neona said. "Emma, I—"

"Oh, dear." Emma turned toward the crib. "Aiden is crying again." She picked the male baby up. His mouth was open, but only a small wheezing sound came out.

"They named the babies Aiden and Amy," Freya told Neona.

"We'll pay you an excellent salary." Emma settled in a chair and stuck a baby bottle in Aiden's mouth. "And Angus will help you get identification papers."

"Emma," Neona tried again.

"And guess what?" Freya said. "Tashi called on her sat phone and invited us all to her wedding!"

"Zoltan is missing!" Neona shouted, and everyone hushed.

Emma frowned. "I thought he went to his castle."

"That was two nights ago! I haven't heard from him since."

"Here." Emma passed the baby and bottle to Freddie, then picked up her phone. "I'll call Howard. He's working security there." She punched some numbers and waited. "Howard, is Zoltan there?" She paused to listen, and Neona grabbed the phone.

"Howard, I haven't heard from Zoltan for two nights. Where is he?"

"I thought he was with you," Howard said. "He was here two nights ago. He picked up his wedding ring at the jewelry store and said something about getting the job done for you. I thought he was talking about marrying you."

"He never came back!" Neona cried.

"I'll check into it and get back to you." Howard hung up.

Neona's hand shook as she lowered the phone. "I-I'm afraid he's—"

"I'm calling Angus. It should still be dark in Japan." Emma took the phone and punched in a number. "Angus, we need you here right away. No, it's not about a stinky nappy. It's Zoltan. He's missing."

Angus appeared and pocketed his phone. "Where is Zoltan?"

"We don't know." Emma gave him an exasperated look.

"I'm afraid he may have gone back to the mountain," Neona said. "He left me a note that he would fix things. I think he's trying to get to the Living Water."

Angus winced. "That would be crazy."

Emma's phone rang and she answered it. "Yes,

Howard? He's not in Budapest or the castle," she repeated, then listened with a growing look of dismay. "I understand. As soon as the sun sets there, we'll pick you up."

She hung up. "Before Zoltan left, he visited the head gardener and borrowed some shovels and a pickax."

Neona's heart sank.

Freya's phone rang. "Tashi! What? All right, thank you." She hung up. "Tashi and her fiancé went to Beyul-La to get the donkey and the goats. They found your pet leopard."

Neona gasped. "How is he?"

"He's been digging at the mountain." Freya grimaced. "He told Tashi he heard Zoltan inside it last night. He's trapped!"

Angus ran from the room, shouting for the other Vamps.

Neona sank to the floor.

"We'll get a rescue party together fast," Emma assured her.

"I don't understand," Freddie said. "He's a vampire. Why doesn't he just teleport out?"

Neona's eyes burned with tears. "It must not be working for him. I'm afraid he's in trouble." She stood on shaky legs. "I have to go."

"I'll go with you." Freya followed her to the courtyard, where Angus had gathered a group of Vamps. Rinzen, Tenzen, and Rajiv joined them, their arms filled with shovels and axes.

Angus paced about.

"What are we waiting for?" Freya asked.

"Still daylight there," Rajiv told her.

Norjee ran up to Neona. "What's happening? Where are you going?"

"We have to find Zoltan." Neona knelt in front of

him. "Stay here and have supper with your friends. Maybe you can spend the night with one of them."

"I want to come!"

She tousled his hair and blinked away tears. "I need you to stay here. I'll be back with Zoltan as quick as I can."

Norjee's chin trembled. "You'll come back?"

"Yes!" She hugged him. "I love you."

"It's time," Angus announced.

Neona waved at Norjee as a Vamp teleported her away.

Neona's back ached as she passed another rock down the line. She hadn't told any of the rescue party that she was pregnant for fear they would insist she sit idly by while they labored. All night long, they had worked. Vamps had teleported in more shifters like Howard and his nephews, who had stayed at the castle with him.

As soon as she'd arrived, Zhan had run up to her. Tashi and her fiancé were still there in the valley, and Tashi had repeated to everyone what Zhan had told her. Zoltan had been talking to the leopard the night before. He'd managed to open a hole, where he'd discovered that even though the larger cavern room had collapsed, a small section of the cave by the Living Water was still intact. He'd teleported in and broken through the wooden covering over the Living Water. While he'd hacked away at the covering with a pickax, the vibrations had caused the mountain to shift. Rocks had fallen and plugged up the hole. He'd been unable to teleport out. Zhan had started digging, trying to save him. Tonight, Zhan had called out to Zoltan repeatedly, but Zoltan had been silent.

The Vamps tried calling him on his phone. Even if he didn't answer it, the noise could provide a beacon where a Vamp could teleport in. But there was no sound. They tried contacting him through vampire mind control, but no response. The worried looks they gave each other made Neona's heart clench. It was nighttime. Zoltan should be awake. He should be able to hear them.

She touched her stomach. Had she lost him? Was the baby all that was left of him?

She waited, her heart heavy, while the rescue party figured out the best place to open a hole. Then they formed a line, moving the rocks away carefully, making sure the ground didn't shift so that the ceiling over Zoltan didn't collapse on him.

As dawn approached Tiger Town, the Vamps reluctantly teleported away. Neona remained with the were-bears and were-tigers, and they continued to work. Just before sunrise reached Beyul-La, Freya, Tashi, and her fiancé caught some fish from the stream and found a skillet in the ruins of the storeroom. They lit the fire in the fire pit and cooked for everyone.

"We got it!" Howard yelled. Everyone stopped as he peered into a small hole with a flashlight. "I see him! Zoltan, can you hear me?"

No answer.

"Crap." Howard shoved more rocks aside to make the hole larger. "Jimmy, bring the rope. I'll climb down."

"You'll take the mountain with you," Jimmy grumbled. "You weigh a ton."

"I'll go." Neona scrambled toward them. "I'm lighter. And if he's injured, I can heal him."

Neona tied the end of the rope around her waist and wedged the flashlight under the rope with the light on, facing down. She stepped into the hole, and the were-bears lowered her into the cave.

In the small circle of light, she could see Zoltan's legs. He wasn't moving. Her heart clenched with fear.

She landed and looked up. "It's not far. About as high as one of the roofs on our houses." She untied the rope around her waist.

"In that case—" Howard jumped and landed with a thud beside her. Jimmy followed. Jesse and the were-tigers remained on top with the other end of the rope.

While Howard ran his flashlight around the small cave, Neona knelt beside Zoltan. He was lying next to the pool of Living Water. Boards and debris were piled close by where he'd uncovered the pool. She felt for a pulse at his neck. He was alive. Barely.

Tears stung her eyes. She hadn't lost him. "He's alive."

"God, that's a relief. He must have brought a supply of blood with him. Ah, there it is." Howard shone his flashlight on a plastic container of blood. It had been opened but discarded, and the blood had escaped to form a small pool. "That's weird. Why didn't he drink it?"

"I think he did," Jimmy said, beaming his flashlight on another puddle. "Looks like he barfed it up."

"Huh?" Howard looked closer. "This doesn't make any sense."

Neona ran her hands over Zoltan from head to toe. No broken bones. No injuries that she could see. Her vision blurred with tears. Her Zoltan was alive and safe.

The hole overhead lightened as the sun came up in the valley.

"Crap," Howard muttered. "Now he'll go into his

death-sleep. We won't be able to tell if he actually dies on us."

Neona quickly felt his neck again. "He's fine. He still has a pulse."

"What?" Howard pressed his fingers against the other side of his neck. "Holy crap! How is he alive?"

Neona looked at the pool close by. "The Living Water. He drank it so he could survive." She cupped some water in her palm and lifted Zoltan's head. The water dribbled on his mouth and down his chin.

"Wake up, Zoltan! You have a wedding to attend. A son to raise. And a dragon boy who still needs to be rescued!" She cupped some more water and tried again. This time his mouth opened.

Howard looked up at the opening. "Find us a cup. Or a bowl. Quick!"

A tin cup was dropped down, and Howard caught it. "Okay." He passed it to Neona.

She dipped it into the Living Water, then pressed it against Zoltan's mouth. He drank.

"Sheesh!" Jimmy jumped back. "He's alive during the day!"

Zoltan's eyes flickered open, and he looked at Neona. "You're here."

"Yes." She tilted the cup, and he drank more water. A tear ran down her cheek. "I don't know whether to hug you or scream at you. How could you risk your life like this? Don't you know how much I love you?"

"Your house, your valley was destroyed. I thought I could at least find a way to the Living Water for you."

She set the cup down and held him against her chest. "You silly man." Tears streamed down her face. "I thought I had lost you."

"I tried to teleport out," he whispered. "But I couldn't."

"I know." She stroked his hair.

"I'm hungry. The blood doesn't work for me any-more."

"Give us some of that fish!" Howard shouted.

After a few minutes, a package was dropped down, and Howard caught it. The fish was wrapped in a piece of cloth. He handed it to Neona, and she opened the cloth.

Zoltan sat up and stared at the light overhead. "It's daytime. I can see sunlight."

"Right, dude," Jimmy said. "And you're about to eat real food."

Zoltan gave the fish a wary look. "I haven't had food in almost eight hundred years."

"Here." With a smile, Neona pinched off a hunk of fish and placed it in his mouth.

As he chewed, his eyes widened with amazement. "It's good." He grabbed another piece of the fish and stuffed it in his mouth. "I'm not sure what has happened to me."

Howard knelt in front of him. "I think you're back to being human. Well, an immortal human like Neona."

"Shit, dude!" Jimmy punched the air. "You un-undeaded yourself."

Neona started crying again.

Zoltan gave her a bemused look. "Did you have your heart set on a vampire?"

"I'll take you however I can get you." She sniffled and touched her stomach. "And the baby will, too."

Zoltan blinked.

"You're pregnant?" Howard jumped to his feet. "What were you doing working all night?"

"I wanted to make sure this baby had a father," Neona cried. "I was so afraid I had lost you."

Zoltan wrapped an arm around her. "You can't lose me. I never quit until a job is done, remember?"

Jimmy snorted. "Looks to me like he got the job done. I mean, she's pregnant, right?"

Howard shoved his nephew on the shoulder. "Climb up the rope. Bring them more food. He's starving, and she's eating for two."

"Yes, sir!" Jimmy saluted and climbed up the rope.

With a sniffle, Neona wrapped her arms around Zoltan's neck.

Howard cleared his throat. "I'll give you some privacy." He climbed up the rope, and his nephews hauled him out.

"You're really pregnant?" Zoltan whispered.

She nodded, wiping the tears from her face. "I cry so easily now. It makes me feel silly and weak."

"You're the strongest woman I've ever known. You healed me, not only my body, but my heart. I love you, Neona."

"I love you, too." She cuddled up against him. "I thought I had lost you."

"You couldn't lose me." He kissed her brow. "I still owe you climax number ten."

She laughed. "Are you still thinking about sex?"

With a smile, he glanced up at the hole. "Your cat is glad we're all right. He wants to live with us. And Norjee. And the baby."

Neona sighed. "That will be wonderful."

His smile faded. "I'm so sorry you lost your house. I'll try to rebuild it for you."

"I don't need the house." She touched his cheek. "Wherever you are, that will be my home."

He gathered her close. "And my home is in your heart."

*G*ive in to your Impulses!

These unforgettable stories only take a second to buy and give you hours of reading pleasure!

Go to ***www.AvonImpulse.com*** and see what we have to offer.

Available wherever e-books are sold.

AVONIMPULSE

IMP 0811